CONTENTS

Rowan Thiesen

Eyes Open

First Edition

Dedication

Some people would think that the hardest part of writing a book is the act of writing the book—those people would be wrong. I have written and rewritten this dedication more times than I can count, but it never seems right. No combination of words here seems capable of expressing all the things I wish I knew how to say.

So, in the spirit of doing keeping it short, I think I'll give you the TLDR version: First and foremost, this is for Abba, as a thank you for all the ways that he never demanded anything of me I couldn't give or expected me to be anything that I wasn't. For all that I am exactly like him and for all that it has made this life more challenging, he's the only person in the world who saw me from the start and never lost sight—even when I did.

It's also for everyone else in the world who writes like they're running out of time. I hope you never do. I hope every word you carry inside of you finds its place on the page and every story you need to tell comes out exactly the way you want it to. The world may not deserve your story or your voice—it may never deserve it —but you deserve to tell it. That's all that matters.

Finally, though, I need to leave a space for the others like me: the mentally ill, the traumatized, and the broken. I need you to know that you have space here and that you're seen. I don't believe in romanticizing mental illness, but I also know that this would never have come to exist if I were someone else. If I weren't mentally ill and if I hadn't been traumatized—none of these characters would ever have taken their first breath.

And as much as the world would prefer otherwise—I would never want to change anything. The world can keep its judgement, it's shame, and it's fucked up idea of what normal looks like.

This is my normal. I wouldn't be me without the broken parts, and I would never sacrifice the gifts that my mental illness has given me for the sake of fitting in. And while I encourage you to do whatever you need to do to take care of yourself—I encourage you to do it because it's what you want and not because it's what the world demands of you.

Content Warnings

Eyes Open explores emotionally intense themes that may be triggering for some readers. Your mental health is more important than anything that this story contains, so please know that I will never fault you for putting it down and prioritizing your well-being.

This novel contains:

- ***Depictions of grief and loss***
- ***Sibling estrangement and rivalry***
- ***Emotional manipulation and gaslighting***
- ***Mild body horror and magical injury***
- ***Depictions of anxiety, panic attacks, and self-doubt***
- ***Violence, including magical combat and physical fights***
- ***Blood and injury detail***
- ***Institutional control and exile***
- ***Power imbalances in relationships***

PART ONE

1
Aliyah

I've never known anyone as good as Aviva at knocking and being halfway into a room before being acknowledged. This time is no exception. She's already in my bedroom by the time I look up from the book in my lap, and I barely have time to get out of the way before she vaults up into my bed and sprawls out beside me. She takes up more space than she has any right to, and I let her. I reach out and card my fingers through her hair as carefully as I can. They're soft, and they only barely catch in the tangled strands.

The windows are open, and the July breeze coming through is gentle, broken by the trees behind the building, even though I can hear it whipping through the square in front of Cobra House. Her curls blow in the wind, and the scent of her fills the room—blackberries and jasmine made richer by the sheen of sweat on her skin.

"Can I help you?" I ask, very aware of the annoyance in

my voice and not bothering to pretend it's not warranted. She'd be concerned if I acted happy to see her, I think. She grabs one of my pillows and props herself up, smiling brightly at me as though she isn't taking up two-thirds of my bed with her entire body. She has a dreamy sort of look on her face, and I don't think I've ever seen it before.

"They interviewed me for Alpha," she says. I don't mention my own interview because it doesn't matter. They'll never take me from Tamarak, and I'm almost certain interviewing me was a formality. I don't even have to make noise to keep her talking. She blazes on like a freight train and tells me how she answered every question they had for her.

When she's done, she takes a deep breath and closes her eyes. There's something dreamy in the way she relaxes—something loose and open in her face.

"It's mine—I can feel it."

Her voice sounds like victory, and I picture it for a second, her as Alpha of the new pack and me as Aiyanik Alpha. We'd be unstoppable. It would be the dawn of a new age in the Wolflands, and we would be at the forefront of it.

My stomach sinks unexpectedly.

It's the best-case scenario for both of us—the best way to make sure we both get what we want, in the end. The only way we don't spend the rest of our lives the way we've spent the first seventeen years. Somehow, it feels like a dream. Like nothing can ever be that perfect. It's what she wants, what she's wanted since the first time it occurred to her that she could want it—and she deserves to get it.

I turn my head to look out the window of the room we used to share and picture her as she used to be—barefoot and wild, climbing the trees and whistling at me until I put my book down to pay attention to her. It's not that different from the way she takes up space around me now, I suppose. Even though we have both changed, the way we exist together never does.

The wildness is still there, though. It still hides inside her, even as her eyes trace the shapes we painted on the ceiling and dart around the room. She hates the mess—always has—but she won't mention it. She knows it'll get her kicked out, and she doesn't seem interested in that. She's settled in like she plans to stay—I know I'll let her.

Aviva grew up as the second daughter. For some people, that wouldn't matter, but for us? Nothing else ever has. Not in Tamarak—not among the Aiyanik. We're twins, but she has always—will always—come last. Everything about us—right down to my status as heir—comes down to the order of our birth. All she will ever be is the spare. The extra. The "just in case."

No other pack is as stringent about its inheritance laws. In no other territory does birth order matter in naming an heir. The Aiyanik, though? Even the idea of breaking the tradition would be enough to incite a rebellion, and no one wants that. Least of all our mother, with her soft heart and idealist view of the world.

In every way she could, she pushed the limits of the law. But even she knew to toe the line—knew where it had been drawn in the sand. She did her best to give Aviva the life she deserved, and she never failed.

We grew up the same—met and exceeded the same expectations. And yet, we are fundamentally opposite under the law. We learned the same instruments, mastered similar languages, studied diplomacy, and even took the same dance lessons. None of that will matter after our birthday.

My mother wanted her to learn the same things I did—to see the world for what it was so that it could never take advantage of her. You never know when charm will get you what strength can't. You never know when being a woman is going to be a tool instead of a handicap. And so, we did it.

She did it.

I set the pace, and she kept up.

Right up until I decided to study medicine and she decided to study law instead, we were the same in every way. She'd tell you with no shame that there's less blood in law, and she wants to be where there's the least blood. Strange thought for a carnivore, if you ask me. I sometimes wonder if she has it all backwards, but I don't think she'd appreciate my pointing it out. Law—if you ask me—is the bloodiest field of all. And Aviva? Aviva is made for it.

That isn't the point, though. The point is much simpler than that.

Even now, sitting—lying—beside me in my bed, she's the second. They'd come for me if something triggered the wards. At the first sign of a threat, they'd sweep me away and leave her behind in the room. They'd get to her eventually, but I'd be first.

A memory flashes behind my eyes, and I shake my head to clear it away. I don't need help seeing—*her* face is as familiar as my own. I had been first that night.

I'm always first.

When they needed to interview Alpha candidates, they came to me first. I don't tell Aviva that, though. She doesn't need me to take away from her moment. Nothing about us will ever be fair to her. We will never be equals. So for a moment, I let her be the most important thing in the world—and I just listen.

"So it went well?" I ask her, setting my book aside to lean on my knees and watch her, her face so like mine, even though she's colored so much darker. Her eyes, her hair, even her voice remind me of rich earth and decadence. She looks just like our mother—except for her eyes. Those are all our father's. The rich color and the shark-like way she watches me. That's all him.

My mother's eyes are all mine—they stare back at me each morning and watch me in every surface I pass. Whatever it is she says next, I miss it completely. All I can think about is Noonchester Falls. About the kids who are about to have their worlds shredded in the name of tradition.

Building a new pack happens in two phases, really. The first phase is a marathon, and it's been happening for most of my life. While you run the marathon phase, you designate land, you build the reservation, you pay a warlock to build the wards that will protect it, and you write the rules that you expect the new pack will follow. Aviva could probably tell you every legal detail of the process, but that's what it boils down to. You build the foundation so that when the sprint starts, you can build the pack.

The sprint began in January of this year. Right at the moment when they published the updated list of Alpha candidates. Down to ten. But it doesn't get serious until the end of the week when they publish the finalists. They spent hours with me during my interview, and I imagine that they did the same for Aviva and the others. I know that whoever they select as finalists will have been thoroughly vetted and considered. I know that she will be on the list—there's no doubt in my mind about that. I won't be.

During the spring, you pick your pack. After that, you pick your Alpha and your Keeper. Some other things too. The Alpha and the Keeper are the big ones, though. The most important. Keeper selection is scheduled for later this month.

If you pick the wrong Keeper, at least, the land will tell you. The land will know. If you pick the wrong Alpha, you won't know until you're watching the world burn, and there will be nothing you can do to stop it. You just have to let the fire run its course and hope something is left behind in the ashes. None of the kids they'll send to the reservation deserves to experience that—the Elders have to get it right.

That's what they are, too—that's the thing. We're all just kids.

Aviva stops herself and takes a deep breath. Whatever came during my silence disappears, and what comes next is the part I need to hear. "I answered questions for them for two whole hours when it was over, and I just know they were impressed."

"I'm happy for you," I tell her, and I mean it.

"I saw that you were still in the pool when it came out, but I knew they wouldn't call you for an interview. You'd have to be like, extra crazy to take an heir off their reservation. Can you imagine if they took us both? That would be completely ridiculous. Mom would shit a chicken."

I don't mention Greyson—not to her. I don't mention that Mikael hasn't named an heir, and that everyone expects him to go anyway. The Blackwoods don't work like we do. Not like anyone actually thinks Mikael would choose him anyway.

That would mean he thought of him at all.

I laugh, and so does she, and the sound fills my room the way it has always been meant to. I look at her and she seems happy, something that becomes rarer every day closer we get to twenty-one and being eligible for succession.

This is the part of our lives where we're most likely to be kidnapped or killed, statistically speaking. The looming shadow of two Deltas outside my bedroom door is as good a reminder as any of that fact. I rotate sideways and lay my head in her lap so we're both staring at the mural on my ceiling. The one we painted together when this was our room—before they moved her to the general housing wing.

"I wonder what Dad would do. Nothing probably. I think it would be a big deal for them to do something like that. And to us? Aiyanik are the oldest pack in the realm, and Mom has done more for the Elders than anyone. They wouldn't do that, would they?" I feel her laughter in the movement of her stomach before I hear it.

"Probably not. I just really wanted to tell you about my interview. No one else would have been excited for me," she says. And she's right. My condition is the second-best-kept open secret in all of Tamarak, and no one is stupid enough to pretend that we don't need a spare. She can't be the backup if she's Alpha of another territory, another pack. She can't be the backup plan if she can't be trusted.

And she's done more than enough these past years to call her trustworthiness into question, all on her own.

Suddenly, I am reminded how fiercely I want her to get it, to be chosen, to be someone's first thought. She deserves it. I'll find another way—any other way. She doesn't deserve to be bound to me.

For all the years that we've spent competing to be the best on paper and fighting to know everything we need to know to do right by our people, moments like this are rare. Moments when we aren't the Heir and the Spare. Moments when we aren't adversaries.

Moments when we get to just be sisters, friends, even. I miss it so badly that it sends an ache down my spine and into my toes.

"I think they'd be crazy to choose anyone but you," I tell her. And then I immediately wonder if it's true. Aviva is a lot of things, but she's a good person. She's passionate and fiery, loving, and spirited, and loyal. She's wicked-smart and talented in so many ways that sometimes it makes my head spin. But she's other things too. She's temperamental and volatile, sometimes. Often prone to antisocial behavior. She's vivacious and warm as often as she's withdrawn and snide. She's a bitch and I love her for it—but that doesn't mean other people do.

I say the words because I want her to hear them, want her to know that she has my support—I don't actually consider that they're a lie until they're in the air between us.

Truth be told, I haven't been paying much attention to the selection process, even though I'm technically still a part of it. Blame it on wishful thinking or on the strength of my convictions, but I really do believe it won't matter. It won't happen.

They won't take me.

I repeat the words to myself for the rest of the night, wondering all the while what my life will look like when they split Aviva and me in two.

"Come in," she says—her warm voice carries through the crack in her office door, and I smile reflexively. I know exactly what to expect when I push the heavy door open—know that she'll be sitting at her desk with a half-empty pitcher of water beside her and her hair clipped back from her face with the same tortoise shell clip she has had my whole life.

The only variable at any given time is how many pencils will be sticking out of her head—today it's only two.

"Demetria said you wanted to see me?" I close the door and curl up in my favourite spot on her couch—the leather is worn soft from my continued presence over the years, and it gives under my weight. My mother hasn't changed a single thing in her office in my entire life. It's exactly as my grandmother left it when she handed Tamarak over to her—I wasn't even there, but I know it's true.

"Yes," she says, putting the pencil she's holding in her hair so she can close the file in front of her and look up at me—now there are three spikes sticking out from behind her head.

Like a porcupine.

"I heard from Theodora that you were gone today," she says neutrally. And I know she knows.

"They called me for an Alpha interview," I admit. It doesn't do me any good to keep quiet, and she won't say anything to anyone. If there's anyone in all of the Wolflands I would trust with the confession—it's her. And besides, she deserves to know.

"I assumed they would." She sits back and crosses her legs at the knee. "You've always been destined to lead—we just thought it would be here." I hear the hesitation in her voice.

She says it like they've already chosen me—but they haven't. They won't.

"Of course it will be here." *Our family has been leading in Tamarak for generations—since my great-great-grandmother won her challenge and shattered the world with her victory howl.* She raises a dark eyebrow at me and sighs.

"I know you understand the significance of what's happening—I won't waste either of our time reminding you how important expansion is for our continued growth and evolution." She sounds like she's preparing to say something more significant, but the door opens, and my father enters.

When he sees us, he comes up short and offers to come back. I use the opportunity to escape—grateful that it has fallen into my lap. I can't take another second of my mother acting like I'm about to be named Alpha of anything.

"It's okay, go. I'm not getting in the way of date night."

"Aliyah—"

"Mom, go. We can talk later."

My father follows her out of the office without hesitation, but he looks back at me for a brief moment before he crosses the threshold, and I wonder—very briefly—if he knows something I don't.

"I'll see you later, kiddo."

The rocks under my feet are smooth and slick, but each step along the river's edge is so familiar that I don't slip. Even in the worst period of the evening, when the loss of light makes it hard to see, I know where each step will be.

"Careful of the white water, Snowball," Shawn says, standing on the very precipice of the sheer cliff above my head. I'm smiling before I look up at him.

"I won't fall."

"I've heard that before." He drops, landing gracefully on the boulder ahead of me, his sneakers finding perfect purchase on the dry stone

"That was one time."

The corner of his mouth twitches up in that lopsided smile I love, and I can't wait anymore, I bound over the rocks between us and jump—I know he'll catch me.

He does.

"Just because only I saw it, doesn't mean it didn't happen," he teases, holding me against him so my feet don't touch the rock. We're eye to eye, and his heart is pounding under my hands.

"You know what they say about secrets?"

"You won't kill me, Snowball. Not even to protect your pride," he says. He kisses me then, and I understand what the stories say about fireworks. My entire nervous system sparks at the press of his lips and the warmth of his fingers where they barely touch the skin of my back.

"Sh," I say, pulling back and pressing my forehead to his mouth. "Let me pretend."

Pretend, what? I wonder. We both know I wouldn't hurt him—or anyone—not for my own protection.

"How did it go?" I blink at him—then it comes back. Every detail, every second, like I'm living it all over again.

"I've never seen anything so formal."

He sits down and takes me with him, situating me on his lap like I'm half my weight. I look toward Tamarak—toward the barrier that I can't see and the home beyond it. My home.

"That doesn't answer my question," he says. He tucks a strand of hair behind my ear.

"It—" The river is loud around us, the rapids churning whitewater into a perfect roar. Our voices won't carry—I look around for listening ears anyway. "Six hours."

"Six—they kept you for six hours?"

"Poor Theodora was alone all day. I felt so bad."

"Of course you did. How long did they keep Viv?"

I swallow.

"Two."

There's silence in the space between us. Nothing in his face gives him away, but the kick of his pulse at the base of his throat does.

"Did she tell you about hers?" I nod. He waits.

"Different." It's all I can make myself tell him. I replay every word of her account—the one I hardly remember hearing—and I swallow the lump in my throat. He nods, his hand moving up and down my spine in slow, easy strokes.

"What did Theodora say?"

"Nothing. She can't."

He raises an eyebrow, and I get the distinct feeling that he could guess how she reacted. To be fair, she really hadn't *said* anything. Not a word. She'd just raised an eyebrow and nodded.

She'd been *proud*.

"She loves you, you know." I hope she knows I love her too—deep in my soul. She's been the steadiest part of my life for as long as I can remember.

The urge to flee hits me, and I stand so fast that he can't stop me. He recovers in time to catch my hand before I can jump the river to the bank.

"Ali," he says, so softly that I can't look at him.

"They can't." He says my name again, but I can't bear it. I squeeze his fingers and step off the boulder. The water envelops me in an icy rush, and there's nothing but the cold.

Tamarak Valley is my home—if leaving my room is a bad dream, leaving Tamarak is a nightmare.

Sometimes nightmares have a way of coming to life.

Most families would be proud to have a child chosen as Alpha. My father would have been proud of Aviva—he had been, even, when he thought she was a sure choice.

I assumed that I would be safe, as heir to Tamarak, I never really believed they would choose me. The possibility had been the boogie man my whole life—always there, but never doing anything more than scaring me.

He's come for me now.

The land for the reservation was designated when I was

five, and the residence had been built by the time I turned twelve. A part of the marathon. I was sixteen when the list of one hundred potential Alphas came out, and I cried for hours when I saw my name. Even then, the odds didn't sit right with me.

No one thought they would do it, no matter how long I remained in the candidate pool. To take a Healer from her reservation? To take an Heir from her people? Not happening. And choosing me would mean doing both at the same time. Heirs, Keepers, and Healers—all sacred. Untouchable.

It was always supposed to be her. Aviva. I was never supposed to be Alpha. Not of Noonchester Falls.

They chose me.

Over her—me.

Tradition says I should have heard the selection results at the same time as the rest of the people did—on the broadcast and from the council's chambers. That's the way we do it in the Wolflands—but that isn't how it happened.

Chief Elder Vianbry—driven by pity or a sense of fairness—came to my holding room and told me I'd been chosen before I was called into the council's chambers. I didn't breathe from the time she left until the time I reached the platform—and then, it was only because I had to inhale so I wouldn't pass out and fall on my face on the cold stone.

She was kind, the Chief, and soft. She helped me tie my ceremonial robes while she watched me in the mirror—like she needed to see for herself the impact that the words had. I stood before the council twenty minutes later while the entire world—our entire world—watched. I still expected to hear her name when the Chief Elder spoke.

But she didn't say it.

Instead, she said *my* name, and I watched as Aviva fell

to her knees on the polished stone. She sobbed until one of the guards came to remove her.

I saw the collapse coming before they did, but I couldn't move. Maybe it was just me. Just the fact that she's my sister, but I saw the way her legs buckled once, then twice, before they gave out completely. I saw the way she fought the urge to be sick, and I did nothing but watch with the rest of them. The nameless guard had the decency to look sorry when he scooped her up. He barely got her through the heavy door before she let loose a violent sob, and I was grateful that the sound was cut off by the door swinging shut. She didn't deserve to be heard like that.

It was my fault. It's still my fault.

My mother followed me to my room that night and stayed with me as I prepared for bed. She was the one who told me what I'd be expected to give up. She was also the one who held me while I cried—big, ugly tears that left streaks down my face.

Before she closed my door that night, like a thousand times before, she reminded me to keep my eyes open. I stared for a long time after she was gone, the image of her pretty face bright and blurry through my tears.

"Through all of it, Ali, keep them open through every second."

I wondered why this time felt different, but I didn't ask. I closed my eyes and did my best to look like I was asleep, lest the walls report otherwise.

I think of Aviva until sleep claims me. The breaking sob hits me over and over again until my ears buzz with the sound.

I'm sweating when I sit up, throwing the blankets off with such force that they land in a tangle on the ground. The sudden rush of cool air against my skin makes me shiver, but I don't mind it, because my skin feels like it's on fire. I launch myself out of bed and run to the bathroom, where I throw up my dinner and every bit of acid in my stomach.

I look at the clock and curse.

Of course, it would be ten minutes before my alarm, I say to my reflection. I look like hell, and I know it's my own fault. I splash myself with water and rinse my mouth out before I strip out of my pajamas and open the window.

The cool night stings my sweat-dampened skin, and I gulp it down, willing my heartbeat to slow. I spend the remaining minutes before my alarm should blare standing naked in the middle of the room while the night air dries the sweat on my skin and chases away the remnants of my dreams.

No, not dreams. *Nightmares.* I see Aviva's face in each blink, feel the paralysis of failure and chaos lingering in my muscles.

I turn my alarm off just before the sound. Then I get dressed and go to meet Elder Vianbry. They chose their Alpha. Now the land has to choose her Keeper—and I have to watch.

2
Rose

"Those jeans are stunning on you, oh my G-d," I say without thinking. I've been staring at my phone the entire time I've been waiting in line for tacos, and *she's* the first thing I see when I look up. Her thighs strain against the denim—and so does her ass. Her hips are soft, and as she turns, my eyes drag over the plush softness of her belly and the swell of her breasts under her thin cotton shirt.

I recognize her as soon as I see her face, and my heart gives an unholy lurch in my chest. Of course, it's her. *Her.*

"Thank you! They're cashmere denim. Wanna feel?" she says, raising her thigh up so I can run my fingers over the soft material. They're like butter—smooth, expensive, and entirely distracting. I don't know if I'm even talking about her thighs or the jeans.

"Oh, that's nice," I admit. I'm trying hard not to stare, but I can't help it. She's beautiful, in a real, incredibly pleasant way. Her stomach has rolls, her skin is freckled, and there's frizz in her curls. Somehow, it makes her bright eyes and full mouth even more enticing. "I really like those. You look hot."

"Thanks. I'm loving what you have going on, too. I don't have the confidence to pull off things like that, but you look good," I can feel her eyes as they roam over my body, the exposed skin and delicate lace, the leather of my skirt, the heavy jewelry.

If she could whistle without drawing attention, I think she would. As it is, I can see her fighting to contain her appreciation in the rising fire of her cheeks. It makes me sad, in a way, even though I know why she does it. It can't be easy to carry a name like that, a legacy that heavy while you're still so young. I know I couldn't carry it. I definitely couldn't pretend I didn't care.

"I'm Rose," I tell her, offering up my hand so we look like two strangers to anyone curious enough to look. "Rose Westin."

"Hi Rose," she says. She holds my gaze with the kind of smile that meets her bright eyes. "I'm Ali. Aliyah. Aliyah Nathair. I'm visiting from Tamarak Valley for the weekend."

"I know who you are," I tell her. I immediately regret it, because her eyes shutter and her fingers grip mine for a moment so brief, I think I imagined it. My mind races for a second, and I try to think of something to say that will soothe her straightening posture. "You're dating my friend Shawn."

I don't know why it works, but it does, and she relaxes, moving with the line but not turning away from me.

"Is that what we're doing?" She says, laughing. The sound is bright and warm, and her face lights up with it.

"He's crazy about you," I tell her, and her cheeks settle into a soft, rosy shade of red. It looks nice on her. Less violent than the first one.

"Sometimes I wish it were that simple," she says. "Can I buy your lunch? I don't have to be back to the Apothecary for an hour or so, and the company would be kind of nice."

I should tell her no, for so many reasons, my name is chief among them. I should tell her no and pretend to be busy so that my reputation won't tarnish hers. Hers, so sterling that any touch of patina would detract from her shine. I don't know if she even knows what she's risking by talking to me. I don't know if she knows that I'm broken. I don't know if she sees the words they label me when she looks at me, but it's almost worse if she doesn't, because it means she doesn't know she should run.

I imagine her mother asking her why she was seen with the Tigress or why she's spending time with whores. I imagine her sister, who hates me for reasons I will never understand, and wonder if she'll ask too. Ask what business she has with the lesbian from Greenbriar.

I can hear the way she spits the word, even this far removed, and I wonder how Aliyah would say it. I wonder if she knows, then know immediately that she must.

I know I should tell her no, but I can't, because there's vulnerability in her eyes as she watches me. I realize a full heartbeat later that she's probably used to hearing no, and the whole tone of my thoughts changes. For just a moment, I imagine how heavy her crown must be. Perhaps heavier than anything I have ever carried. Definitely more delicate.

I imagine trying to make friends as royalty, as the heir to the oldest reservation and the richest pack in the Wolflands. I imagine how many of the friends she does make are actually there because they care about her, and how many are there for the reputation boost she gives them.

I imagine how hard she must work to keep that

reputation intact and how much she can't do publicly because of the way it would look. I wouldn't want that life, and I wonder if she does.

It's our turn to order, and I'm out of time.

"I'll buy and you'll provide the company," I tell her, bumping our shoulders together as I step up to order. She smiles, and as I watch her order, I mentally curse Shawn for getting to her before I could, and something in the way her blue eyes watch me under her lashes tells me that I would have had a chance.

We get our food and walk to the edge of the city center to sit on the curb while we eat. Her short nails are pristine, and her long fingers are covered in crema as she tries not to let her taco fall apart on its way to her mouth. She's the cutest thing I have ever seen.

"You're kind of amazing, do you know that?" There's food in her mouth, so it takes a second for her to answer me, but watching her try to chew faster so that she can speak makes me laugh.

"I don't think that's true," she says earnestly. "I'm just a normal person, like everyone else."

"That's bullshit and you know it," I tell her, but then I look more closely and realize that I'm completely wrong. Something opens up in my chest, and I wonder if I sound as stunned as I feel. "Unless you don't."

"It's hard to explain," she says, wiping a dollop of crema off of her bottom lip with her thumb and killing me softly as she sucks it clean.

"Try. I have time." I take a bite of my own taco and angle my body toward her so she knows she has my full attention. She eyes me suspiciously, but whatever she sees when she searches my face must be enough for her to believe me, because she starts talking and doesn't stop. Her words slam into one another in their rush to fall out of her mouth, and they land, each with intention, between us in the lukewarm daylight.

She tells me that everyone thinks she's lucky to be the firstborn, the heir, the eldest child, and the prodigal daughter. She tells me that everyone acts like she can do no wrong, can make no mistakes, and is always above reproach. My heart breaks a little when she tells me that she is none of those things and that hiding her flaws is what she spends the most time on every day.

She is the firstborn, she says, but only by a moment and only because it happened to work out that way. She is only the eldest because someone has to be first. Only the Heir because the law says she should be. And only the prodigal daughter everyone loves to rave about because she works her ass off to be the best at everything.

She does make mistakes, she says, constantly. But instead of being able to own up to them and correct them? Learn from them? Use them to be better? She is shamed for them, looked down on for them. A disappointment to anyone who sees her imperfection just because she makes mistakes like the rest of the world.

"There's no room for flaws when you live in a glass house. No room for mistakes, or anger, or tears. No room for weakness or strain," She's been talking for forty-five minutes by the time she slows and takes a bite of her taco. The spicy beef smells delicious, and looking down at my chicken makes me a little sad. When she speaks again, her mouth is full, and it's disgusting in a charming way. "I'm not amazing. I'm barely keeping it together, and the more pressure they put on me, the less I feel like I'm allowed to exist at all as a person."

"I think Alpha Apparent Aliyah Jade Nathair, heir to the Aiyanik people of Tamarak Valley, sounds like an absolutely awful weight to carry around," I tell her, offering her a napkin.

She nods, and I smile. "How about you just be Ali? That sounds like plenty to me."

"I... I'd like that a lot, actually. Just Ali?"

"Just Ali."

"And what exactly does Just Ali get to do?" she asks, blue eyes bright like shining crystal in the afternoon sun. It's hot enough now that we're both sweating, and the scent of her is rich in the air around us. My mouth is watering with the urge to taste her.

"Just Ali takes a long lunch instead of going back to the Apothecary, grabs her boyfriend and his friends, and goes skinny dipping in the river because she knows that the work will still be there after the sun goes down and that she deserves a little time to have fun," I tell her. I expect her to refuse or look hesitant, but she doesn't. All I see on her face is hope. Her eyes are wide when she answers.

"Let's do it."

"Rose?"

Her voice through the phone sounds tinny and harsh, but I can still hear the tears she's trying to swallow. I sit up immediately and look at the clock. They should be in the Elderlands awaiting the announcement.

"You're crying, are you okay? Did something happen?"

"They made their decision, Rose," she says, her voice breaking. "I'm not supposed to be calling you, but I didn't know what else to do."

I already know what she's going to say, I think, but through the sleepy haze and the shock, I can't make myself think straight.

"Baby, breathe. Tell me what happened?" I skip the light

on my nightstand and throw open the curtains to let the midday sun stream into my bedroom. Rachelle's bed is empty, but the bathroom light is on, so I know she hasn't gone far.

"Me," is all she says.

"You... what?"

"They chose me, Rose. Elder Vianbry just walked out of the room. She... she must have known it was going to be hard news to hear, because she told me early. I don't think Aviva knows yet," she says without breathing. She's crying openly, her voice thick with tears, and it breaks my heart.

"Ali, baby, that's a good thing. Why are you crying?"

"Because it isn't, Rose. It's not," she says, and it sounds like she slides down a wall and hits the floor. I know that's exactly what she does, and I want to be there. Beside her on the ground. "It should have been Viv. I shouldn't... They're sending Aviva anyway. She's going to be one of the new members. They're leaving Tamarak without both of us."

Fuck.

"Your parents don't have any other children," I say by accident. I can hear the surprise in my own voice, and I know it's not a helpful thing to point out right now, but I can't help thinking about what that could mean for Tamarak Valley.

"No, they don't. They stopped with us because they had an heir and a spare. And now they have nothing." Something hits the phone, and it sounds like she's wiping her tears, but I can say for sure.

"Whatever happens next, we're all going to figure it out together, okay? Shawn and I are going to the new reservation, and so are Rachelle and Marcus. You aren't going to be alone. Do you hear me? You aren't doing this alone."

I pull my phone away from my ear and mute myself just long enough to shout for my sister, who is out of the shower, but completely naked when she opens the door.

"Call Shawn. Get him over here, please," I say, throwing her phone at her with more force than I mean to.

"I need to go, Rose, it's time. Promise me we can talk again? I have to go to Keeper selection, and I can't do that alone."

"I promise, okay? I promise. You can do this. Just get through it."

Just get through it.

3
Aliyah

"Ms. Nathair?"

I bump my head on the bottom of the desk in the Apothecary as I straighten up, and I almost laugh—because it seems like such a stupid thing to do. The surface is smooth at least, so I don't end up with splinters.

Talk about a weird thing to need Theodora's help with. I smile as I picture the look on her face and raise my eyes, expecting to see a stranger's face amongst the bottles and rich colors of the apothecary.

When I see Chief Elder Cyan Vianbry standing in the doorway, holding an armful of files and smiling at me like she thinks I'm adorable, I freeze.

"Good morning, Chief Elder," I say, slowly straightening and putting my pen down on the desk.

"I did that very thing this morning," she tells me, "I have

a knot on the back of my head the size of a ping pong ball from it."

She comes all the way inside and puts the stack of files down on my desk with a gentle *thunk*. The stack looks bigger than I expected, each manila file straining to contain the information inside.

"What did you bring me?"

"Personnel files. I thought you might like to see who you're getting before relocation day, since they'll all already know you," she says. As she wanders around the Apothecary attached to medical, her heavy robes move with her, sweeping over the pristine concrete floor and sending her scent curling through the space toward me.

She smells exactly how I would expect her to—actually. I never noticed it, but it's true. She's the plain kind of pretty, and her scent is fresh in an earthy way. Her eyes are pale and almost colorless in the light of the Apothecary.

"That's… actually really kind of you," I say, scanning the names on each of the tabs out of curiosity and sighing with relief when I see the names I'm expecting tucked in amongst the rest. "Was there something you were looking for? I just finished refilling everything, so I should have whatever you need."

"I have a feral cat that I feed, and it has a penchant for getting skunked. Theodora told me you make a good de-skunking shampoo," she says, and she's smiling like she knows how absurd it sounds for her to try bathing a feral cat. I laugh and point at the shelf across from me.

"Blueberry, Peach, Vetiver, or Oatmeal? The big bottles are in the cabinet underneath if you want them."

"Thank you," she says, squatting down and opening the cabinet. "I also came to check on you. I thought you might be struggling with the decision that we've made."

"I'm grateful for the opportunity," I say, and it isn't a lie. I am grateful. Grateful to have even been considered. Grateful to have been chosen for something so incredible. But also terrified.

"You don't have to lie to me, dear," she says, standing up and bringing me the bottle. "I know you're angry."

"I'm... I'm a lot of things, but I don't know if angry is one of them."

"Talk to me. I can't help you if you don't," she says. She leans against the counter and fixes me with those piercing green eyes. I don't mean to start talking, but I do. I'm starting to think it might be something I need to work on at this point.

I tell her that I consider being chosen an honor and that I'm as grateful as I am uncertain. I tell her that I don't understand why they chose me or why they would leave Tamarak without an heir or a plan. I tell her about Theodora and about how she's going to have to find and train someone new now, before she can finally retire, and I tell her about myself. About how I've struggled my whole life thinking I was good or worthy enough to lead. I tell her about the years I've spent studying Tamarak just to feel like I know the people well enough to claim them when it's time.

And then I tell her how it feels to lose all of that. How I feel like I'm floating through the world with no foundation to stand on and nothing to tether myself to—because everything I've ever known has been taken so quickly that my head hasn't even had time to stop spinning. When I finally shut my mouth, I realize my fingernails have left dents in the wood on the desk and that tears are threatening to form in my eyes.

"Has it occurred to you, Aliyah, that those things are why we chose you?" she asks me, and I must look confused, because she laughs. "Your sister is confident. She's smart and charismatic. She's passionate and carries herself well. But she's also volatile. She's cocky and self-righteous. She's stubborn and inflexible. These are all words that were given to us repeatedly by people we interviewed as we tried to make a choice."

"Trust me, I know all of those things about her."

"You probably do. But you don't know very much about yourself, I think."

"What do you mean?"

"I mean that you've made it your life's mission and goal, even at this age with so many years left of your mother's leadership, to know the people of Tamarak Valley better than you've ever tried to know yourself," she says. There's a heavy gold cuff around her wrist, and it distracts me every time the sun hits it, but I force myself to stay focused. "That alone tells me that you're what they need. The Aiyanik will recover. They're an old people, with protocols and established families. There are other people who can lead them, and there is time before they must have answers."

Something shatters in Medical, and I hear Theodora's voice for a brief second as the front door opens and closes. I can't tell what she says by the time the wind carries her words through my open door, but it sounds soothing, like she's telling someone it's okay.

Maybe she's talking to me.

"Tamarak will be fine without me," I say. The words ring through me like a heavy bell's toll, and it feels like the world is shifting around under my feet. Whatever traces of humor might have remained die in my throat as I meet her gaze. "That's what you're saying."

"Yes, Ali, it is. Tamarak will be fine. The Aiyanik will be fine. But them?" She touches the stack of files with her left hand. "They need you."

"They would have been fine with Aviva."

"Probably, yes, but only fine. They would not have thrived under her leadership. They would not have been happy. With you, they get all the basics, the skills and talents you possess, and the training you've been through. And they get the rest of you, too. They get your patience and your kindness. They get your acceptance and your endless well of love. They get your sense of duty and justice, but they also get your flexibility. Those people need you in a way that Tamarak never will. In a way that they could never have needed her. I need you to trust us on this."

It's late by the time I've washed the oils off my fingers and scrubbed the herbs out from under my nails. The clock says it's only eleven, but that feels like a lie, right down to the soles of my feet.

I sit down at my desk and stare at the files Elder Vianbry gave me for a long time before I sort them. I set aside the files of the people I already know, watching as they form a stack of their own and smiling to myself. I pick up the first file in the pile of strangers and begin to read.

Sarah Elizabeth Parker of Archimedes Landing is the only child of Cora O'Malley and Johnathan Parker. She has two half-sisters, also chosen as part of the expansion project. She's in secondary school and has a noted interest in research relating to native and Aboriginal cultures, as well as various fields of mythology and folklore. She ballroom dances, runs, and lifts weights.

I put her file down and search the stack for her sisters. Piper Lillian and Sutton Victoria Crochan of Archimedes Landing are the daughters of Cora O'Malley and James Sutton Crochan. Piper enjoys efforts in sustainability, playing the violin, and studying photography, while her sister is a computer programmer interested in video games and soccer.

I'm already overwhelmed, so I change tactics and sort the files into reservations of origin. Archimedes Landing is sending me five women, a little girl, and three men. With Piper, Sarah, and Sutton, I am getting Hailey and Victoria. Leighann and I have met, and her file includes a notice of exception permitting her inclusion in selection despite her age. I know Greyson and Elijah, but I've never met Brandon. I study their faces for a moment and practice their names until I'm sure I'll get them right.

I repeat the process with the ten people joining us from Greenbriar. Shawn, Marcus, Rose, and Rachelle are familiar, so I set them aside. Jade, Matthew, Andie, Karlie, Samantha, and Adrian are all strangers. I quiz myself on their names and faces until I'm confident I know each one.

I do it again with Playa Del Rose. Kelly, Christina, Elena, Gianna, Jasmine, Jamie, Liam, Noah, Saoirse, and Tatiana.

When I've convinced myself I've got their names down, I go back to the beginning and cut out their photos so I can use them like flashcards, ignoring the way my fingers tremble. As I place their photos on the desk in front of me, something strange settles over me. They're like a yearbook that hasn't been printed yet. A future no one asked for. I shudder and force myself to breathe. Their eyes never leave my face, looking up at me from the desk in perfect rows. Hopeful, frozen. Something possessive rumbles down my spine, and I square my shoulders.

Mine.

This process is going to be hard enough on everyone as it is. I won't make it any harder by being unprepared. I start with just their names, then I add their reservations, then their parents and any siblings, and then their interests.

By the time I'm through for the night, I can tell you how tall they are, how old they are, and when their birthdays are, too.

They sleep on my nightstand, within reach, so that I can start my practice again tomorrow.

I will prove Cyan Vianbry right.

When I wake up in the middle of the night, I grab my tablet and let myself waste the rest of the night shopping for the clothes, shoes, and toiletries everyone will need when they arrive. I've always been good at spending other people's money, and by the time I've got sheets, towels, and everything else, I've racked up a total of over fifty thousand dollars.

I feel no shame when I charge it to the credit card we were given by the Council.

I know I'll do more damage as we grow closer to relocation day.

Spending their money isn't scary, even if it should be. At the thought, I feel something like pride and when I smile, it's real.

4
Aliyah

I have no words. None. But I have to find some. I have to write down what I saw tonight.

I…

I watched five people die, and I couldn't do anything to help them. I'm a Healer, and I couldn't even try.

It isn't the first time I've seen death, isn't even the first time I've seen suicide, but—never like that.

We arrived at Noonchester Falls at noon, the sun high overhead and beginning to warm the air. We went from the sanctuary to the Falls so quickly that I barely registered the construction. Not the Little People, the Souls, or the Wraiths.

I met the candidates one at a time, each wearing ceremonial robes and body paint depicting their life stories. We spoke at length about their lives, their motivations, and their dreams. One. Then two. Then four. Then all six. I'd read their dossiers beforehand, but hearing the words directly from them was different.

They assembled around the pool at the base of the falls as the sun went down, and I knew… I knew what was going to happen. But I wasn't ready.

As the sun sank below the horizon and the world went dark, they each withdrew their chosen method from their robes and ended their lives.

Alberto Foranza shot himself in the stomach.

Eloise Martens swallowed a tonic prepared by her Healer, and Jennifer Florence chewed a bundle of toxic herbs.

Tomas Evans and Samantha McKinney hung themselves in the trees around the pool.

Cristiana Kennedy slit her wrists with a ceremonial dagger.

I knew who my keeper was going to be before I realized that the stone set in the handle of the blade was a sapphire. The last of the day's heat slipped away, and I shivered standing in the clearing. Shivered, not from the still-warm breeze, but from the feeling of death lingering around me.

I didn't have to look to see that the Wraiths in the shadows felt it too.

Eloise died first. It took eight minutes and seventeen seconds for her heart to stop.

Samantha was next, the sounds of her struggling breath finally ceased after eight minutes and forty-two seconds. Tomas at nine minutes, three seconds.

Alberto panted on the ground for twenty-one minutes and sixteen seconds before his heart gave one last series of empty thuds and stopped.

Jennifer and Cristiana held on the longest, each fighting

for every breath. Jennifer stopped exhaling after ninety-one minutes, and I wanted to run to Cristiana. I wanted it to be over. But Elder Vianbry and Elder Lee both put their arms out to stop me with such speed that I'm sure I'll be bruised. I let myself be stopped only because I knew I had to. I could have gone to her. I could have made it stop. But I didn't. The Healer in me screamed as I watched her, begging me to save her like I knew I could. Begging me to move, to fight, to do something. And still, I remained.

I clasped my hands behind my back and swallowed, vowing to watch every second of it, no matter how badly it made me want to sob into the moss and scream at the sky.

Keep your eyes open.

Cristiana stared at the brilliant specks of light above us with wide, unblinking eyes as her blood seeped into the ground beneath her body, the mossy earth taking and taking all that she had to give. I got the feeling that it was waiting. The land, I mean. Eagerly pleading for more as her blood continued to spill around her, staining the surface a rusty, familiar red. Amongst the summer green, there's a dullness to the color of it.

The dagger was still clutched in her left hand, its gleaming blade slick with blood that didn't shine in the darkness of the new moon.

Two hours passed.

Three.

And then, we felt it.

The land under us began to vibrate. Cristiana was barely breathing, long past the point where she should have stopped altogether, and her lips were bloodless in her plain, pretty face.

The night air turned cold and then boiling hot, as the breeze became a wind that tore through the clearing. The blackest recesses of the sky reached for her as she lay there, nearly her entire blood volume staining her clothes and the moon-bleached ground. For all that the heat of summer had stolen, her blood seemed to give it back tenfold.

My heart stuttered. My brain struggled to make sense of what my eyes knew was real.

I watched as the land pulled her back, away from the tendrils of darkness and peace that had begun to gather. Away from the respite I knew she so desperately craved and the comfort that death would have offered her. The moss beneath her body cradled her as her wounds stitched themselves together and her skin gradually regained some of its color as she started blinking her eyes again.

I'm nearly certain that—even as I watched her eyelashes flutter—I did not blink.

At one hundred and ninety-six minutes, Cristiana sat up.

Cristiana Noonchester, Keeper of Noonchester Falls, was born in the wake of Cristiana Kennedy's death.

And through all of it, I never looked away.

Time of death, 11:54 PM.

5
Aliyah

When I return to Tamarak Valley, I do so as a new person. Broken apart and re-formed by what I've seen. I stumble into my bedroom, scald my skin with the hot water, trying to wash away the remnants of the night. I fall into bed without bothering to put on clothes.

For the first time in my life, I sleep through my alarm. When I do finally wake up enough to roll over and look at the clock, it's after ten and the sunlight is streaming through the open curtains.

"Fuck."

It's 10:12 AM.

I scramble out of bed and grab the first set of clean scrubs I can find in the basket of clean laundry I left by the door. I manage to dress myself and braid my hair before I shove my feet into my shoes and run through Cobra House to get to

Medical.

Theodora is waiting for me, and she doesn't seem to care that I'm four hours late. She welcomes me back to Medical with a warm smile and an even warmer hug, like I never left. Her embrace is glue, binding the sharpest edges of my soul.

Because no matter how she treats me, I did leave. I was gone, and what happened broke me in ways I don't have words to explain to anyone.

I came back a different person than I left, and I think she knows it, too. I can see the understanding in her eyes, but the familiarity of her touch is pleasant, so I let myself sink into it.

"Can you take inventory in the Apothecary while we're slow? I want to make sure we get everything filled before I lose you for good," she says, and I know she's doing it on purpose. It's kindness, maybe, or sympathy, but I don't care. The Apothecary is one of my favorite chores, and on a day like today, I would be a fool not to take it as the gift it is.

Theodora is old and, unlike the others who would have been younger and more unaware during Ramona's selection, she knows what the selection of a Keeper entails. She has children working all over the Wolflands as Healers, and her sister Evelin died alongside Ramona that day. If anyone can understand what I feel without having seen what I saw, it's her.

Sending me to the Apothecary is the only way for her to acknowledge the new scars on my heart, but it's enough.

I sink to the floor in the stockroom and hyperventilate for a few minutes before I can actually start the work. For the first time in my life, I don't scold myself. I stare at the toes of my waterproof shoes and the cracked tile beneath them, and I let myself cry until I feel like I have a better grip on the fractured pieces of my soul.

At 10:26 AM, I stand up and begin my inventory. By

eleven, I'm brewing birth control tonics for the non-royals. I fill little vials with anti-inflammatory tonic while ingredients simmer in the massive copper cauldron.

Theodora gives me four hours before she comes to check on me, and when she asks me how I'm holding up, it takes me a second to remember what she's talking about.

We're alone in the workroom, and the Apothecary is empty, but something tells me that if I tell her the truth, I'll be giving life to something that's better left hidden amongst the shards inside me. I want to tell her everything.

I breathe in the eucalyptus and mango scent of her, take a deep breath, and lie.

The best part?

She lets me.

For all that she is bound by her duty, Theodora Errapel gives me space to mourn. The space she wasn't given when her own sister fell to the Reaping. The land may need a Keeper, but sometimes the people that get left behind need them too.

I hear Rose and Shawn coming from a few hundred yards away, despite their desperate attempts to move carefully through the underbrush. I don't think about how they got here or how they found me, because I don't care. There are tears spilling openly down my cheeks, and the water lapping at my toes is still warm from the heat of the day. I don't want to be alone.

"Ali, I don't want to startle you," Rose says as she approaches, leading Shawn by a few feet because she's so much smaller.

"I hear you, you won't," I tell her. My voice sounds awful, and speaking hurts, but I know that both of those things are my fault.

"Why are you wet?" she asks as she clears the trees. She's on her knees in front of me, in the mud at the river's edge. A second later, her delicate hands are on my face, tilting my chin up so she can see my eyes.

"She screams underwater so no one hears her," Shawn says as he drops down next to me. I don't remember screaming. He takes my hand and presses it to his full mouth, kissing my knuckles. My hands are bruised and swollen from beating them against the rocks on the riverbed, but they'll heal soon.

I almost wish they wouldn't.

"You look awful," Rose tells me, fondness written all over her face. I expect her to sit beside me, like Shawn did, but she doesn't. She sits down between my feet and stretches her legs out so that they're on either side of my hips.

"Thank you for that," I say, laughing a little in spite of the raw, broken feeling that has taken up residence under my lungs.

"Don't get me wrong—you're still like, smokin' hot—but you look like crap. What happened?"

I don't want to answer her. I don't want to burden either of them with what I saw, but I can't carry it alone. I glance down at my watch, retrieved from my room when I changed out of my scrubs and into the jean shorts I have on.

"We need more time," I tell them, reaching for the hollowed-out place in my soul. Where my magic lives and breathes with me. It comes when I call for it, lured to the surface by the promise of use.

My watch stops ticking, and the river stops running, and the sounds of the forest around us fall silent. In the wake of my magic, there is nothing.

Nothing moves but us, on the bank of the river,

clinging to one another. The air is thicker somehow. Like we're underwater—but warmer. More forgiving. It moves like a slow tide without ever moving at all.

"Well that's cool," Rose says, and I laugh. It's not a quiet laugh, or a pretty one. It's a harsh laugh made of equal parts surprise and fondness for the look of absolute astonishment on her pretty face.

"I've never seen magic like this," Shawn says, reaching out to touch a lightning bug that's frozen in the air in front of him. It doesn't move, and he sort of pets it with one finger while he stares at it in amazement.

"You know what they say about keeping secrets," I say, hearing the bitterness in my own voice. The tumor in my brain pulses, like I need to be reminded that it's there, and I know I'll have a heinous headache in a few hours if I'm not careful. "This is what Aiyanik magic looks like. It'll hold as long as I do."

"As long as you do?"

"It'll start to wear her out eventually. When her energy is depleted, her magic will fail," Shawn tells Rose. She nods like she understands and then takes my free hand in both of hers.

"Now tell us, pretty baby, what happened yesterday?"

I lean into Shawn and hold both of them like they're lifelines and I tell them everything.

I tell them about Cyan's visit and about the files. I tell them about my sleepless night and waking early. I tell them about the clearing and the falls that roar like a lion in the night.

I tell them about Samantha.

About Tomas, and Eloise.

About Alberto and Jennifer.

About Cristiana.

I tell them about the land and the way it saved her. The way it brought Cici back from something even I couldn't have saved her from. Something no amount of venom, or magic, or healing could have saved her from.

I tell them everything I remember about the reservation at Noonchester Falls and the residence we saw on our way to the clearing.

I tell them everything I remember and by the time I stop talking, Rose is crying with me.

"I can't believe they made you be there for that," she says, and I don't know how to explain to her that I needed to see it.

"How can we help?" Shawn asks, switching my hand to his left so he can rub my back. There's heavy sadness in his eyes and I know it's because he can't take the burden from me. All he can do is share it, and I don't think he knows that's enough.

"Can you... can you stay? Just for a little while longer. I don't want to be alone the night before I leave. I don't know where Aviva and my mom are."

As though Aviva would see me. As though she would want any part of the storm raging inside of me right now after what I did to her. What I cost her.

"Of course we'll stay. We'll stay for as long as you need us, baby," Rose says, and she squeezes my hand so tightly that the bruises throb.

"She's right, Snowball. We're right here. Until you tell us to leave."

6
Aliyah

I wake before my alarm the night before the wards grant me access to my land, and I feel like I've been run over by Atlas' Earth. It's too late for last night and too early for today—no one else is awake in the residence, and the silence is endless. The sun won't think to stir or rise for nearly six hours, and there's something about leaving Tamarak in the dark that feels right. *Right* feels like a joke, but you get the idea.

My bedroom's walls are still purple, the same color Aviva and I painted them when we were ten, blasting pop music and singing into our hairbrushes while we danced and laughed. Our mother pretended to be mad about the mess when she found us, but she stayed up with us until we put everything back exactly how we wanted it. I remember the numbers, even now. It was 12:51 AM when she kissed us goodnight and closed the door.

She was exhausted the next day, but she never

complained once.

The walls haven't changed, and neither has the view out the window, but this room is not mine, and nothing is the same here. I've never slept on the third floor of Cobra House, and I've never heard the way the wind blows this high up. My bedroom isn't mine anymore, and the white walls around me are proof that this place isn't either.

I look at the clock.

Thirty-eight minutes until midnight.

The traditional ceremony associated with the formation of a new pack begins the moment the announcement is made. It requires that the new Alpha give up everything tying them to their previous pack. Everything they own is boxed up and burned. No funeral pyre, no honor—just gone in an instant as the incinerator roars.

I insisted that I be allowed to watch while they tossed my things in, and they only finished a few hours ago. It only took them an evening to incinerate a lifetime. Something about watching it made me feel very small and very fragile.

The whole thing is symbolic. It's the only way to ensure a fresh start. It leaves an Alpha with nothing that could tie them to their previous reservation, nothing that could stand between them and their people.

As if anything would stand a chance.

Aside from the pajamas I'm wearing and the small stack of clothes sitting on the floor by the door, I have nothing left —even these small scraps have been borrowed from others. They'll be incinerated in Noonchester Falls. I get up, and my whole body creaks like the springs in the old mattress. Even though it isn't mine. Not the mattress or the pillows—not even the blankets pooled at my hips. They're all sterile-smelling and unfamiliar. Even the hairbrush sitting on the counter in the bathroom belongs to my—I mean my mother's—pack.

I shut off the alarm clock before it has a chance to make a sound and note the time.

Thirty-one minutes until midnight.

I'm up. I'm not happy about it, but that's not important. I'm awake and out of bed, and the hairbrush they gave me feels like it's ripping my curls out of my head each time I drag it through. I wonder why my mother didn't give me a comb, and then I remember that it was my father's job to collect the things they gave me, not hers, and it makes more sense.

He would have had no reason to think that a hairbrush would be okay—it wouldn't have crossed his mind at all.

I braid my fluffy, frizzy curls into two braids on either side of my head and stare into my eyes in the mirror. My mother's clear, crystalline blue eyes. Every fleck of light and every line—replicated from her face to mine.

"We can do this," I tell the girl looking back at me. She stares at me blankly—then we both smile. In the mirror, my skin is smooth, and my eyes are gentle. They're framed by long lashes and smudged with the day-old mascara that I managed not to cry off sitting by the river. I stare at myself for a full minute before I push off the counter and strip out of my pajamas. The air is cool on my skin, and there are goosebumps all over me in a second.

There's a familiar scent on the night air, but I can't place it.

"Ali," someone says, and I look around for the person speaking. Someone laughs softly. It's Rose's laugh. I'd know it anywhere, but it takes me a second to realize that she's on the ground outside the window, standing next to Shawn.

They're still wearing the same clothes as they were the last time I saw them, and there's still mud caked to their skin.

"What are you doing here?" I say, climbing onto the bed and opening the window. I'm naked and the night air is cold, but I don't care.

"We made you something," she says. She's like a spider as she climbs the side of the building. Her feet are bare and silent against the concrete, and she finds handholds I wouldn't hope to see. But she makes it to my window and perches on the sill to offer me a bracelet made of string. Shawn, still on the ground, is watching me, drinking in every inch of the pale skin I've left exposed. He's seen it before, but it's always like this. Like the first time and the last. He never gets less stunned, and I never get more used to the way he looks at me.

"It's beautiful," I tell her, and it isn't a lie. It's a simple friendship bracelet, made of five colors, with little charms hanging from it.

"Purple for you, pink for me, light blue for Shawn, dark blue for Marcus, red for Rachelle. We'll be with you again soon. But until then, we wanted you to have something to take with you," she explains. Each charm has one of our initials on it.

"I love it, but I'm not allowed to take anything from the reservations with me," I explain. I'm already desperately attached to the bracelet, and the idea of giving it up makes my heart hurt.

"It isn't made with anything from the reservations. We went to the Neutral Lands to buy the materials. We ran the whole night to get back and just finished it when we saw your light come on," she says. I look down at Shawn, then back at her. Even a thread from Tamarak would be a risk. There can be no trace of this place.

"You're not messing with me?"

"Deadly serious. Let me put it on you," she says. Her fingers are quick and sure as she ties the length of intricately woven threads around my wrist. When she's done, she smiles at me. "You're my best friend. If you tell me to, I'll burn everything and come to you in a heartbeat. We all will."

"She's right," Shawn says from the ground. "If you need us, rules won't keep us away. All you have to do is call." Something rumbles in my chest, and I know instinctively that I won't even have to do that. They'd hear the howl from any corner of any world.

"I love you," I tell him. And then I meet her eyes, the slitted pupils dark against the vivid golden hue of her irises. They're almost orange in the light. Feline in every way. "I love you both so much."

"We know. And we absolutely have to leave before someone sees us and you get in trouble. Are you going to be okay?" She touches my face and kisses my forehead when I nod. "You've got this."

"I kind of have to, don't I?" I say, laughing softly at myself. "Go. I'll be okay."

She smiles and lets herself free-fall to the soft ground below. Shawn wraps an arm around her in a sort of half-hug, and I feel them both deep in my soul.

"By the way, nice tits, baby," she says as she hooks her arm through Shawns and tugs him away from Cobra House.

"Would you please stop hitting on my girlfriend? You're prettier than me, and I'll lose," he says. He turns his head and winks at me over her shoulder, but they're gone between the trees on their way back to Greenbriar sooner than I want them to be. They remain deep in the park of me that knows they're family.

Pack.

"Nice tits, baby," I echo, glancing down at my naked body and laughing at myself as I close the window. The delicate threads around my wrist feel like armor already.

Twenty minutes until midnight.

I dress so quickly that I nearly fall on my face wiggling into the jeans they gave me. They're almost a full size too small, but I manage to get them zipped. Bending over to shove my feet into the scuffed boots they left makes me feel like I'm going to throw up a kidney. There are definitely going to be marks on my skin by the end of the night. I'm out of breath by the time they're both tied. I look around my bedroom one last time, turn off the lights, and close the door behind me on my way out.

It sounds final.

It is.

I can hear my parents down the hall, and Aviva too. They're all asleep now, but Aviva will wake in a few hours to the same bare walls and empty space that was waiting for me. We'll each make the journey to our new home alone—but the others will come in groups—two, three, or even four at a time from their former homes.

It's the first time in my life that I haven't been able to cling to Aviva to get through something, and it'll be the first time she won't have me to stand between her and what's coming.

I look down at the little bracelet and force myself to take a deep, steady breath. Then, with every ounce of composure I have in my body, I force myself to walk down the hall and out the front door. Not another soul crosses my path, the entire way—but when I look to Medical, I see Theodora standing in the dark. Her long hair is loose, and all I can see of her is the way the dim lights from the machines turn the silvery streaks in her hair to glitter in the moonlight.

She shouldn't be awake. More than that, she shouldn't be anywhere near me. But she is. She is and she isn't leaving. Each step I take toward the boundary, I feel her eyes on my back. Rules be damned, I know that she will stay with me for as long as she can.

Eighteen minutes until midnight.

I start running as soon as the heavy metal door of Cobra House closes behind me, and I don't stop until the border of Tamarak Valley is within my sight. My steps slow of their own accord, and I stop for just a second before I cross through the wards, scared to find out what waits for me on the other side. I feel her gaze through the trees, and I wonder if she can still see me. She's with me, all the same.

Only briefly, I look back at Tamarak, sprawled out at the bottom of the valley, and my heart gives an almighty thump. I can see the river and Cobra House. I can pick out Medical and the school. I can even see the lake from my perch high above the city.

I glance up at the stars and sigh.

Ninety seconds until midnight.

I take one step forward, then another, all the while thinking about everything behind me and everything waiting for me in Noonchester Falls.

Never once have I considered refusing their selection or thought about trying to get out of it. Not even now.

Ten seconds until midnight.

All I think about as I step through the wards and into the unprotected air of the outer reservation is how badly I want to be a good Alpha for each of the people they're sending me.

I forget to brace for the pain of losing my marking—and it drives me to my knees in the damp earth. It burns like a blue flame, simultaneously more overwhelming and more bearable than I expect it to be, and the familiar pack marking on my collarbone flares once—a violent red—then unravels like burning parchment as it slowly disintegrates into my skin. When the heat fades, all that remains of the mark is a scar, thin as a whisper.

Before the tears welling up in my eyes can fall, I run. The freedom I feel without a mark makes me want to throw up.

Noonchester Falls is over a hundred miles away, and I'll run most of the day in the scorching sun to get there, because I have to pass through the wards to claim the land. I run and let myself dissociate for so long that my feet and legs are numb. I know that if I stop, I'll fall over, but I don't care. I push every thought that threatens to form out of my head and keep running as the sun rises and claims its place high in the sky.

I don't realize how quickly the distance is passing until Noonchester Falls smacks me right in the face.

I hit the wards full force and tumble headfirst through the underbrush. When I land, I can smell my own blood in the air, sweet and heavy. As I push myself up, I realize that I'm in an incredible amount of pain unrelated to the running. My blood is streaming down my fingers, falling in droplets to the leaves at my feet, soaking through my jeans, matting my hair. But none of those injuries explain the gnawing, fiery pain in my abdomen. From my diaphragm to my pelvis, everything burns.

"I tried to call out to you," Cici says, appearing between the trees like a shadow in her Keeper's robes. The old maples on either side of her seem to recognize her, and they bend to shade her from the burning sun. She's holding her hand out to me and waiting for me to take it—her fingers look like roots to me in the haze of disorientation.

"Why does it hurt?" I manage to ask her, grinding my teeth against the agonizing pain and pressing my fingers into my stomach as though I can make it stop. She doesn't blink. Doesn't flinch. Her voice is the wind in the leaves—gentle, but absolute—as she watches me.

"No name, no marking," she says, like I'm not being eviscerated right in front of her. I attempt to dust myself off and straighten up, but all I do is smear blood all over myself and make my head spin.

Five strands curl around my wrist, their strength immeasurable. It's the only thing that keeps me from collapsing.

"What do I need to do?" I ask. Cici gestures at the land around us, her chipped nail polish dull and dark at the tips of her short fingers.

"Give your people a name," she says. I listen to her, but I replay her words a few times to understand because I can't think around the pain. She takes a step back and waits for me, watching me with those incredibly patient blue-gray eyes. I can tell she knows I've already chosen.

The land must know too, because as soon as I think the word, the pain banks and fades away.

"Trevonaire," I say, straightening up and wiping the blood from my forehead to keep it out of my eyes.

I feel the fine lines of my Alpha marking spreading over the freckled skin of my forearm, and I don't mean to make any noise, but the relief that washes over me as the pain dims and the sense of belonging returns is like a cool shower and a fresh towel. For the first time since I crossed through the wards of Tamarak Valley, I feel like I have a place. Like I belong somewhere, to someone. And for the first time all day, I feel like I can breathe without feeling like every nerve in my lungs is on fire.

"To what principle will your people adhere?" Cici asks me, completely unaware of the near-transcendent experience I'm having in front of her. I close my eyes and breathe in the sticky air. Under the scent of the warming ground and the trees, the air is perfumed by the scent of apples and sunflowers, and lemon zest. The scent of Cici and of Noonchester.

"Above all else, protect and survive," I answer. I'm telling the words to the land and the trees and the Keeper beside me, and when they sink in, the marking on my arm blooms, etching itself into place with a delicate, slicing pain. The wings of the raven curl around my arm, and her talons keep her perched on the handle of the dagger she sits on. There's a matching mark on my thigh, hidden beneath the bloodstained denim. I can feel each feather and every line of the dagger's hilt. The stone set within that hilt looks up at me from my skin like it can see into my heart, and I can feel the marking on my soul as clearly as I can see it forming in front of my eyes.

When it's over and the magic has taken hold of me, the pain fades to a dull ache, and I slump forward, breath ragged, claws extended deep into the soil that is my new life.

Something has changed, fundamentally, and I don't yet know what it is.

Cici rests her hand on my shoulder, and when I turn to look at her, her eyes are rimmed with silver tears, full of something I can only describe as pride.

"This land belongs to you now, Ms. Nathair. The others should begin arriving tonight," she starts to turn around, like she's going to leave, but I seize her arm and hold on tight. The idea of being alone makes my heart stutter in my chest. The scars—those scars—are thick and smooth under the pads of my fingers. Cold to the touch and fizzy in the back of my mind.

"*Stay*?" I ask, too softly. I hate the way I sound, but Cici turns back toward me and nods like I'm crazy for thinking I even have to ask. "And it's Trevonaire. My name is Aliyah Trevonaire."

The last of my strength goes out of my body, and I collapse into the dirt. I only lose consciousness for a few seconds, but I fall for days into the darkness with only the land to catch me.

And it does.

When I open my eyes again, Cici is still standing there, watching me with the same look of pride on her face. I know she must be hot in her robes, but there's no indication of sweat of fatigue anywhere on her face.

I know, because I can see every pore—every line, and every place that her blood rushes under her skin. I can hear her heartbeat and the one that belongs to the mountain lion stalking through the trees.

Everything around us hits me like a wave. Every sound, every breath of the world around me. All at once—like the volume on the world has been left up way too high.

The leaves shine like uranium in the light—radioactive in the most basic way.

"It's okay," she says to me, hands open in front of her and voice low. Like she knows. "I know it's a lot."

A lot. I want to laugh. Or cry. Or howl. I feel the shift in my eyes, my vision sliding back and forth between human and wolfen. The change is just beneath my skin, and the control I've been praised for my whole life is slipping through my fingers.

She kneels in front of me and touches my face with both of her hands, holding me there with her. Present. Grounded.

"We go when you're ready, Alpha," she says. And below us, the land kneels, too.

Records will show Noonchester Falls, home of the Trevonaire, established August 5th, 2019.

We walk toward the center of the reservation at a lazy pace, and while she talks, I listen. She tells me about the Reaping—that's the name for the ceremony I watched—and about everything that happened to her after it was over. She tells me about her little house in the forest and the few days she has spent exploring the other buildings on the reservation.

Only later—after she's gone back to her little house and I've come to accept how empty the residence is around me—do I realize that the dagger in my marking is the one she used that night.

I fall asleep tracing the shape of the blade with the tips of my fingers. I can feel the scars on her wrists under my fingers in my dreams.

7
Aliyah

The reservation is quiet when I open my eyes, and the silence is so heavy I almost convince myself that I'm still alone. The steam of my coffee is warm on my face, and the nutty aroma is cashmere soft. I don't have to strain my ears to hear the others breathing, walking, or just existing in their rooms across the cavernous common space.

It's been about thirty hours since my arrival, by my guess, but I don't have a clock to check, and my phone had to be left at Tamarak, so I can't be sure. Last night, I had the opportunity to greet the newcomers and help them claim their rooms before our first family dinner, where the little people outdid themselves, covering the table with everyone's favorites and whisking the mess away before we even had to consider cleaning up.

I left them silver coins, marbles, and almonds as a thank you for their work. I hardly have the energy to deal with the big things, let alone the small things that feel menial. I've taken their presence and gentle footsteps for granted my entire life, and now that I'm here, in this unfamiliar place, their wispy scents and gentle hands feel like home.

My bedroom is in the far-right corner and takes up the first and second floors. I'm the only one with a two-level room, and that alone feels strange. I couldn't make it past the door of my bedroom until the dark hours of the night last night, and even then, I could only stay long enough to walk a lap around before I returned to the sublevels, where I played my violin until my body began to demand caffeine and sustenance.

"Are you up, or still up?" Shawn asks from the second floor, where I know he's leaning against the railing with his too-long hair hanging in his eyes. I smile into my coffee and set the mug down on the island. He's worried about me, and I don't need a pack bond to feel it. I can smell his concern in the air, wrapped up in the mandarin and patchouli scent I know so well. It's nestled beside the raspberry notes of his scent like it's been there a while.

At this distance, I should hardly smell him at all.

I turn to look at him, then turn back to the journal I've been writing in, discovered amongst the contents of the office I haven't accepted as my own.

"Still up. This is my second cup of coffee," I admit, writing as I speak and managing not to screw up either thing in the process.

"Snowball, you need to sleep," he says, and he's right, but it's too late. I turn around and look at the clock on the stove.

7:34 AM.

"Does all of this seem cruel to you?" I ask, gesturing vaguely to the house, the land, and the wards that hold us apart from the world. He laughs, and even though I know he's laughing at me, I enjoy the sound. It's warm and free, and it feels like it's been crafted just for me. I want to pinch myself for even thinking that, and I'm pretty sure my cheeks are turning pink, but there's nothing I can do about it now.

Before he answers, he vaults over the railing and lets himself fall to the first floor. I can't help myself; I roll my eyes.

Boys.

"What? You mean it doesn't seem totally normal to take a bunch of teenagers from rival packs, strip them of their affiliations, possessions, and families, and then shove them into a new house to serve a new Alpha that they've likely never met?" he says, the sarcasm dripping from his words as he walks through the sunken living room toward me, "Ali, it's insane. It's tradition, but it's insane. It's supposed to be."

He steps up behind me and slips his arms around my waist, his hands resting on the softest part of my belly. I don't really mean to lean into him, but I do, and he takes my weight with ease, holding me tightly and leaning down to rest his chin on my shoulder.

"What if they got it wrong?" I ask, and I immediately feel his confusion run through his body. I don't want to move, but I have to see his face, so I turn in his arms and look up at him.

If I fail—if I break them—it won't be the council who suffers. It'll be the people I'm supposed to protect. It will be them—him. His freckles, his sun-kissed skin—just the sight of him unwinds the knot of tension I haven't been able to loosen. I know Rose would be offended at even the suggestion that I'm not the right choice, but Shawn is different. He knows that I don't need blind support, and that isn't what he gives.

"They narrowed it down to you and Aviva for a reason. You were both qualified and they chose you. They made their choice, Ali, and they didn't make it lightly," he says, and I watch his full mouth as he speaks, occasionally flicking my eyes to his to search for evidence that he's lying. I never find any.

"What if they chose wrong?" I press, and he shakes his head, leaning down to kiss my forehead.

"They didn't, my love," he says confidently. I still can't shake the gnawing panic in the pit of my stomach. Alphas are supposed to be the pinnacle—the very point of the summit —but we aren't meant to stand alone. Every second I spend pretending not to miss Aviva's unsteady presence is a lie.

"How do you know?" I ask him. There are tears in my eyes and when he smiles at me, they nearly spill over. We stand there, in the middle of the kitchen, in complete silence before he says anything and each time a tear runs down my face. He doesn't rush me or hush me. Just lets me cry—quiet, honest tears I didn't realize I had left—and wipes each away with the swipe of his thumb.

The land beneath our feet gives a gentle pulse.

"Because there is nothing in this world—or any other— that you aren't capable of and there is no force strong enough to come between you and the people you love," he says. I open my mouth to argue with him, but he holds up a finger and silences me with a gentle tap on my mouth. "I can see it in your eyes, the way you love them—love us—already. You can do this. You're already doing it."

He's right. Not that that's unusual—another pulse.

"Ali, baby, are you okay?" Rose asks, standing at the railing with her bedroom door open behind her. She looks ready to tear Shawn apart if I tell her he's done something wrong, and that's all it takes. I trip over my anxiety and free-fall into blind panic.

Pulse.

"I'm going to go for a run. You should go back to bed," I say, taking a step back before I suck in a too-big lungful of air that isn't enough. The walls don't move, but I can feel them pressing in on me, the weight heavier and heavier by the heartbeat.

Pulse.

"Shawn?" I hear Rose say, and by the sound of it, she's said my name too and gotten no response. He holds up a hand to her, and I can feel him searching my face for any sign that he should be concerned. When he finds none, he backs off and lets me go.

Pulse.

"Stay inside the boundary line," he reminds me, and I'm already stripping as I head for the bay door. I drop my clothes in the bin with my name on it as I run through and I hit the grass beyond a short beat later. With no rain and no morning dew left by the already scorching sun, the grass is soft and dry against the pads of my paws. It's welcoming, like the land is inviting me into the out. I run without thinking or choosing a destination, because just moving is enough to keep the panic from continuing to rise in my chest.

Pulse.

It's harder to hyperventilate as a wolf, but not impossible.

Pulse.

The falls on the reservation are loud and can be heard for miles in every direction, churning and roaring as the water launches itself over the rocks and into the air. It cascades down the jagged cliff face in ribbons of white, melting into the near-black pool below.

I run until I can't hear anything over the building,

booming sound of the falls, weaving back and forth up the side of the mountain until I'm standing beside the mouth of the river that fuels them. Looking down at the water, rushing past a few inches in front of my paws, I begin to feel the panic rise again. I watch the water for a long moment, breathing in the blood-tinged air that lingers in the clearing, rising from my own lungs—a side effect of ruptured capillaries. The burning air of the morning sun combines with the bloody taste in my mouth to remind me that I am alive.

I shift my attention to the pool of water at the base of the falls and stare for so long that I see her face in the churning water. I can smell the blood on her skin and the death in the air around us. I watch until I can't anymore, until I see her blue eyes close, and then I push off, changing in midair so that I can follow the water over the falls and into the pool below.

The flash of cold that meets my bare, exposed skin sends the ever-rising panic running in the opposite direction, and if I could cry out in relief without drowning myself, I would.

If I were human, my jump from the top of the falls would be suicidal, but we all know that I've never been either of those things.

I sink to the bottom of the pool, hook my foot in a root, and stay there until my lungs are burning for air. Anchored, I let the current rage around me until the silence begins to stitch me back together.

My ears ring, and I can't help but think it sounds like a Banshee's scream.

8
Aliyah

I wake, drenched in sweat and shaking. I'm in an impersonal room, in a bed I didn't choose, under sheets that reek of detergent. The walls are beige, the furniture is all the same rich brown, and the floors are light enough that they draw in the light from the pointed wall of windows in the room.

It's mine, but none of it is really mine. None of it feels like it's mine.

Somewhere in the fog, I hear Shawn pounding on my door, but my ears are ringing too loudly for it to feel real. The dream is already foggy, and after a few seconds of forcing myself to breathe, the panic subsides just enough that I can feel my limbs again. I drag myself out of bed and dress as quickly as I can, pulling on clothing at random from the generic-looking pile. I ordered the same things for everyone.

I'm grateful that I got a say in it, but that doesn't mean

the generic styles and colors aren't still horrible.

When I look in the mirror, I get my first glimpse of what I've chosen. The leggings are black with a 'v' shaped waistline, and the oversized long-sleeved shirt is made of a waffle material I like more than I expected I would. The bra and underwear are the ones I slept in, and I already know I'll be mad at myself for wearing a bra this long. I don't have time to think about it. I skip shoes, throw open the door to my bedroom, and step out into the hallway.

They're all waiting for me downstairs, but he's in the hallway, searching my face for any sign that he should be worried. As I pass, I squeeze his calloused hand twice, and when I face them, I take a deep breath that fills my lungs until they hurt.

When I open my mouth to speak, my voice does not waver.

"Good morning, everyone," I say, and my voice grows steadier by the word. They all look at me, suddenly and completely silent. "This is the part where our parents and the elders would expect me to make a speech about how great the opportunity is and how lucky we are to be the ones representing the new era of peace for our kind."

I come down the stairs and stand in front of them, on even ground with them, and I meet each pair of eyes as the silence stretches between us. Even my mother—fearless as she is—never did this. We always remained above. Apart. I want them to see—to understand that I'm not above them. I'm beside them. I want them to know that we're all the same. I want them to know that there is nothing separating us but a title. This close to so many bodies, their scent drenches me. Their emotions—their heartbeats—everything about their proximity feels like it's trying to smother me.

"But that's not the speech I'm going to give—because

none of that matters. If you're anything like me, you're scared, unsure, and a little angry. Some of you may have asked for this, may have even been proud to be chosen to be a part of it, but I'm not foolish enough to believe that is the case for all or even most of you," they shift, eyes and bodies moving to distract from the truth in my words. I can tell my words are landing, but I need to push a little farther, need to reach them in the way I've been afraid I wouldn't be able to.

"I'm not asking any of you to be excited, or to trust me. I'm asking you to give me a chance and let me show you that I deserve the trust you have to give. I want you to know that you can come to me with anything and that I won't just send you away. No matter what it is that you need, we'll face it together," Aviva shifts this time, but she's the only one. She turns just slightly away from me, tucking herself behind Greyson's broad body like he might shield her. I'm not sure what she thinks she needs shielded from, and I'm even less sure what to make of the look in her eyes. The way they seem to burn with whatever it is makes me uneasy. Shawn nods encouragingly, and Rose winks at me. They're clustered together with their respective siblings, and the sight of their familiar faces brings about the distinct urge to cry. Talk about a first impression.

"I don't know how to do this on my own, and I won't pretend that I do. That's why I've spent so much time trying to decide what to do about my Beta selection and why, instead of choosing one Beta, I have chosen three. Betas are meant to help, to lead alongside their Alphas, and to be sources of information. Instead of choosing one, as would be customary for a pack this size, I've chosen three. One representative from each unrepresented pack to ensure that there will always be someone around to tell me the things I don't want to hear," I say. I take a deep breath and hold out my hand.

"To represent Playa Del Rose and the Rosendes members we have with us, Kelly Rosendes," He flashes me a cock-sure grin and pushes his way gently through the group until he's standing in front of me. He takes my hand, kneels before me, and lets my hand go once he's settled. The land stirs beneath us. Waiting.

"To represent Archimedes Landing and our Blackwoods', Greyson Marquis," I know Greyson, but only so well. He's Aviva's... not really boyfriend? Where Kelly is long and lean, Greyson is broad, and watching him try to slide through the crowd is almost comical. The poor man is all shoulders, and every time he takes a step, he's bumping into someone. He's rigid and quiet, and Aviva is glaring at me over his shoulder as he approaches and joins Kelly on the ground. She shrinks back as he takes his place before me. Not with fear, but with fury. Her glare does not shake me. Greyson presses a polite kiss to my hand, and I feel more than hear Shawn's answering growl. I don't try to prevent myself from laughing as I wave him off.

Boys.

"And finally," I say, straightening my shoulders, "to represent Greenbriar Hill and our Ravenswell members, Shawn Marksberry."

Shawn bumps fists with his brother, winks at Rose, and wiggles his fingers at Rachelle before he steps out of their little group to approach me. He's only a few steps away, and in a second he's in front of me, taking both of my hands as he kneels. He kisses each one and then squeezes before he lets them go, his dark eyes never leaving my face. Rose whistles playfully and there are laughs throughout the group.

As the laughter fades, the room stills. One by one—and then all at once—their Beta markings bloom—dark lines curling like smoke across their skin, echoing the pattern burned into my own. Not twins, but too close to only be siblings. I'm still staring at their markings when I realize that there are waves of anger rolling off Aviva and toward me. She's in the back of the crowd, staring me down like she's already sharpening her claws, daring me to falter. I wonder, briefly, if she'll challenge me on the spot. I don't flinch. But I don't blink either.

I almost dare her to try.

The land under us coils—like it also thinks she should give it a go. I wonder briefly how it would end. Whether the land would accept her victory—whether she'd win at all.

Movement at the bay door snags everyone's attention before anything too crazy can happen.

"Cici, you can come in. You're welcome here," I say. I don't need to see her to know it's her standing there. I can smell her, feel her warmth, hear the too-slow beat of her heart. She stands apart from everyone else, no matter how close she gets, and it's as familiar as it is sad. Every Keeper I have known has been that way. Touched by death but starved of it. Never really among the living, but not allowed among the dead.

It lingers, even in her scent—the mossy night air and the hint of blood-soaked dirt.

"I'm sorry, I didn't want to intrude," she says as she comes around the corner. She has her long hair twisted back from her face and is dressed casually in jeans and a t-shirt. She lowers her head when she greets us, but not because she's weary. Her blue-gray eyes dart around the room, taking in each face before she turns to me.

"Who's she?" one of the girls asks. It takes me a second to call up her name. Tatiana's short, almost hidden amongst the crowd. She's Rosendes and had originally been expected to arrive with her sister, but had come alone after her sister turned up pregnant and was required to stay in Playa Del Rose. The anger that Tatiana has carried since I met her is still there in her voice when she speaks, and I try not to bristle at it. Rose does. She takes a small step and places herself just so—between

Tatiana and me. I don't even know if she realizes that she does it.

"This is Cristiana Noonchester, the Keeper of Noonchester Falls," I say, motioning for Cici to step forward. "Cici is here to protect us and serve as a sort of ambassador. She's also very nice and would be more than willing to help you in any way she can, I'm sure."

Cici nods, but I can feel the tension in her body, like she doesn't like having their attention on her. We're the same in that way, I think, so I squeeze her hand in what I hope is a reassuring way.

"Does that mean she's part of the pack?" Leighann asks. She's in the back near Aviva, standing on a chair that she has put on the stone fireplace so she can see. Where Greyson had been hovering protectively around her, trying to make sure she didn't fall and aiming to be prepared in case she did, Aviva is keeping her distance. The way my sister looks at the little girl makes me uncomfortable, and I can't decide why.

Her question makes me realize how little some of them know about our culture, and it breaks my heart. I've never given much thought to my privilege before that moment, never realized that I've been taught more, shown more, and given more than all the others. As the Alpha's daughters, Aviva and I had the best of everything. We were raised to see and understand, to lead and to follow, and when we spoke, people listened. I've never thought much about my privilege. Not until now. Not until I see the questions in their eyes—until I realize how many answers they were never offered.

There are others like us in the group, of course.

Greyson, for example. As the eldest son of the Alpha male who has run Archimedes Landing for the last sixty years, Greyson has had every opportunity to be the best version of himself. As a result, he's brilliant, poised, and well educated,

Like every other Prince or Princess is.

I finally understand the derogatory term now, hearing it in my thoughts as they stand before me. *Princess.* Like I'm above them. Alpha? Even worse.

Greyson, Aviva, and I are lucky. The others, by and large, have only ever learned what they needed to know to be functional members of their respective packs. Some, like Tatiana, learned even less than that. Her ignorance makes her kind of unpleasant, but I want so badly to find out what's underneath all the anger, frustration, and insecurity. I have plenty of time, but still. I wonder how long she's spent having to raise her voice just to be heard.

"No, I'm not," Cici says—apparently, I've forgotten how to answer a question when it's asked. I look over at her, grateful, and she nods in acknowledgement. "Keepers are their own kind of pack, in a way. We don't answer to an Alpha, just to the land that we represent."

Cici pulls her shirt up to expose the markings on her abdomen, and the first thing I see are the stretch marks on her stomach. I didn't know she had children, and I've never met them or smelled them on her, but I recognize the silvery scars for what they are.

Over the stretch marks, spanning her entire torso, is her Keeper's mark. The intricate tree is purple; its roots wrapped tightly around the moon. The branches fan over her breasts and chest like wings, each delicate and strong. It pulses faintly to the too-slow beat of her heavy heart—alive, like she is, and *haunted by it.*

"I'm here to help you," she says, then to me, "I'm here right now to help you receive the gift that your land is ready to give you."

I nod, and she turns to continue addressing them.

"The Blackwood's have the ability to manipulate the weather, the Rosendes' can understand every language that they hear, and the Ravenswell's have their eidetic memories. Now we have to find out what your gift is going to be," she says. I can tell from the little bounce in her step that she already knows. My own anticipation spikes.

"What about the others? Don't the people of the Elizabethan Mountains and the people of Tamarak Valley have gifts?" Leighann's looking at me like she'll be able to read my gift in my eyes, but I know she won't. Next to her, Aviva is radiating pride that feels out of place.

"Natalia Nathair and Anya Kivleneiks have both chosen to maintain the secrecy around the gifts that their people receive, and we have to respect that," Cici says simply. "Are you ready to find out what your land is going to give you?"

"Will we lose the gifts we already have?" Rose asks, her hand raised uselessly and out of habit. She doesn't need permission here, and she's never asked for it anywhere else either.

"No, you'll keep the gifts you already have, but you won't have the ability to pass them on to your children anymore after today," I explain, grateful that someone asked so everyone is on the same page. When I look at Aviva, her face is pale. I don't have the chance to ask her if she's okay, because Cici is looking at me.

"We should make our way outside," she says. She's dropped her voice and angled her body toward me so that I can be the one to give the instructions. I'm grateful for her and the way she's trying to make it clear that I'm in charge, even though she doesn't have to.

"Outside—all of you. Line up against the house," I say, surprised when they obey without hesitation. It isn't an order, not really, and it shouldn't surprise me—but it does. I let them follow after Cici, and I fall into step behind them, next to Aviva. She looks pale, distant—but not really weak. Still, I ask.

"Are you okay? You don't look so good. I can check you out in Medical after we're done, if you think you're getting sick," I whisper, voice as low as it goes so that no one will realize there's anything worth listening to being said. I'm aware, however distantly, that the land under my feet has started to hum. It feels… impatient. I wonder if it's excited—like we are.

I don't know this land like I know Tamarak, but I want to. The hum flares brightly, and I smile. I think maybe the land wants that too.

"I'm fine, my G-d, why do you always have to stick your nose into other people's business? You didn't care about me half an hour ago, and you don't need to pretend you do now."

I stop walking and stare after her. The rest of them continue walking—either oblivious or respectful—but I remain rooted where I am.

It feels strange. How someone I've loved so long and so unconditionally can hate me so easily.

"I don't feel any different," Shawn says. I can't see him, but I know his voice. I can hear him even over the roaring in my ears, and as his words register, I realize he must be crazy to say them and mean it. There's no way he can be serious. I feel like there's fire licking at my eyes, and my heart is racing in my chest. It hurts so badly that I don't even have the capacity to think about Aviva's harshness.

"Of course you don't, you wear your heart pinned to your sleeve," Cici says, smiling. "Your Alpha can feel the difference."

Every pair of eyes turns to me, and I can smell their

curiosity like incense in the air. There's no avoiding their gazes, so I square my shoulders.

"So, how about a demonstration?"

The strange feeling in my eyes is fading, or settling, but it's still there. It clings to me, a fog that refuses to lift. Cici pulls me forward, and I let her. I stand beside her and try to look normal, hopeful that it works.

"Take a deep breath. Ground yourself into your land. It'll settle the magic," she tells me, her voice low and her mouth right at my ear so no one will hear. I meet her eyes and she nods encouragingly. I dig my toes into the soft ground beneath my feet and breathe deep. The strange feeling flares and then settles, lingering at the base of my spine and collapsing in on itself until I can almost not tell that it's there. Almost.

"Mr. Weatherly, would you mind?" Cici says. Ever the gentleman, he lets himself be summoned and comes to stand patiently beside me. He brushes our knuckles together and looks down at me, winking conspiratorially. His dark eyes flicker with... something—and then it's gone. So fast, I almost believe I imagined it. His fingers twitch like he wants to take my hand, and I feel my chest tighten. The feeling at the base of my spine pulses, and my eyes burn briefly. Not unpleasant, but warm.

"Did anyone see that?" Cici asks, watching me, but talking to them. Most everyone is looking around in confusion. Aviva is the only one who speaks up.

"Her eyes changed," she says—and when I look up, it startles me to see that she's looking right at me for the first time in days. Her eyes are almost red in the sunlight. One look at Cici tells me that her answer was correct, but I still don't understand it.

The red in Aviva's eyes doesn't fade when the wispy

clouds cast a brief shadow over her face.

"How did they change?" Cici asks. She's rocking her weight back and forth from one foot to the other and has her arms folded across her chest. There's a sort of smug smile on her face that I don't understand.

"They're blue, her eyes, I mean, but when he walked up next to her, they flickered and looked almost pink." Cici nods and then walks across the small clearing to whisper in Aviva's ear. For a second, we all wait, and I watch Aviva, whose dark eyes widen slightly in amusement, just before Cici pulls away from her.

She turns to face us, and Aviva struts forward through the path Cici left, heading straight for Shawn. I know Aviva, and I know the look in her eye. I realize what's about to happen half a second before it does—and I grab her. My eyes burn painfully for a split second as I drag her backward and when I sweep her legs and take her gently to her ass on the ground, everyone gasps. Everyone but Rose, Shawn, and Greyson, that is. She lets out a low 'oof' when she bounces off the grass, but I don't look down at her.

"What colors were her eyes then?" Cici asks, visibly pleased. If she'd been anyone else, I might have dropped her, too, just to make myself feel better.

Leighann calls down to us from the open window of my bedroom, her sandals flashing like signal flares in the bright morning light. "Blue, then green, then red—then blue again."

Aviva drags herself up from the ground and stands next to Shawn, careful to leave a considerable distance between them and folding her arms over her chest.

At the edge of my awareness, I feel Rose's barely contained snarl. Her face is placid when I look at her, but her slitted pupils are thin and swimming in red. I follow her eyes back to Aviva and realize there's nothing left in her familiar face. She's looking at me, but I've never seen her face look like this. In her eyes, I'm a rival. In mine, she's my sister.

"His changed, too," Marcus says, nodding toward Shawn. He's leaning lazily against the wall of the house with his arms folded over his chest, and Rachelle at his side. Always inseparable, those two. His tone is casual, but I don't miss the way his jaw tightens. "I thought it was the light when he first walked up, but it wasn't. His eyes are brown. Dark brown, even, and when he looked at her, they were bright pink. And then when Aviva was coming toward him, they were gray. When Ali pulled her backward, I saw purple. His are brighter than hers, though, so it was easier to see the changes."

Like mirrors. No—like windows. Every flicker burns, and I know what they're seeing. My every thought in screaming color.

"Why do you think that is?" Cici asks. I suddenly hate everything about this master class she's hosting. She's smiling as she asks her questions, radiating the same energy as every elementary school teacher I have ever known. Her voice is syrup-sweet, each question tilted like she's sure we won't know the answers. I never noticed the slyness in her before, and the glint of something secret shines bright before my eyes.

"Because Shawn wears his heart on his sleeve," I suggest. Before I can finish my thought, Aviva speaks up.

"And Ali is heartless," she says. No one laughs or says a word. It surprises me, and a glance at her face tells me that it surprises her too. More than one growl of warning answers her barb, and not even one comes from me.

"Aliyah does control her emotions very tightly. She tries not to let them cloud her judgment. And Shawn is very much the opposite. He follows his heart, letting it tell him where he should go. That's what makes the colors different. Brighter for him, more subtle for her. If Aliyah were to relax, they'd seem just as bright," she says, still doing her best impersonation of a teacher. She's good at it. I wonder if she might have been one once.

"This gift sucks. What are we supposed to do with color-changing eyes?" I'm too busy thinking about Cici to identify the speaker, but that's why I get to see her take the complaint in stride, a smile painted across her plain face.

"This isn't your gift," Cici says. "This is the shadow it casts."

Something sharpens in her eyes as she turns her attention to Aviva again. She looks every bit the predator I know she is and just for a moment, I'm left wondering what her exact instructions to Aviva were.

"Ms. Nathair, if you would, close your eyes for me," Aviva narrows them instead and starts to argue, but Cici manages a 'humor me' look that shuts her up. Aviva's dark eyes, so like our mother's, close. "I want you to reach for the place inside you where your magic lives, and I want you to touch it. Not your Nathair magic, the new magic that shares that space. I want you to touch it, and I want you to think about how you would look if you could control every aspect of your appearance."

The change starts with the subtle narrowing of her face, then the lightening of the ends of her curls. By the time it's over, her hair is blonde, and the freckles have faded from the bridge of her nose. She opens her eyes, and they meet mine, a clear, glassy shade of blue just like the one that I see every time I look in the mirror. There's no mirror in the clearing behind the house, and I'm still staring at my own reflection. Too many pairs of our mother's eyes exist in the clearing.

I'll have to ask Shawn later about the way the others reacted, because I don't have the ability to look for myself. All I can see is Aviva. Aviva as she would be if we were identical twins instead. Aviva, if she had control of her appearance. Aviva, if she were me.

She wears my face like a costume. Looks at me like she's always wanted it.

She has it now—even if only for a second. And suddenly, I think I understand exactly what it is that she wants. Cici makes a satisfied noise in the back of her throat and turns her attention to the rest of them, apparently done getting her lick back. I don't know if she's helping—or testing how much power she really has.

"Leighann, do you want to help with the next part? It'll be fun," Cici says. Leighann nods and jumps down out of the window. Cici squats down by the time she reaches her and takes both of her hands and leans in to whisper something long and careful into her ear.

I look at Greyson, who's watching Leighann with a protective sharpness to his gaze, and I'm grateful to the Elders for letting her come with us.

"Do you think you can do that, sweetie?" Cici asks, bringing my attention back to Leighann. I catch sight of Aviva's jealous glare, but don't actually acknowledge it.

"Yes, ma'am," Leighann says. She sits down on the ground, and Cici sits behind her, hands on her delicate shoulders. She's so small, but the way she stands tall under Cici's hands makes her look older. Braver.

"Go ahead," she whispers. I wonder again about her children, but any question I would ask dies quickly when Cici tells us all to watch closely. We watch, and at first, nothing happens. Then, there is laughter coming from behind us, high up. We all whirl at once and find Leighann sitting on the roof of the residence with her little legs dangling over the edge. The jewels on her sandals are still shining brightly as she swings her feet and her dress. Her dress blows gently around her legs in the breeze.

I turn back to Cici, expecting to find her arms empty—but they aren't. Leighann is still there, her body limp, cradled gently against Cici's chest. Her eyes stare blankly at the blue sky, completely unresponsive. Two versions of the same little girl.

"How is that possible?" Greyson asks. He's looking between the two versions of his little girl like he's trying to make sure that neither is hurt and fighting valiantly against the panic we can all see in his eyes.

"It's your gift," Cici says simply, "Yes, you now have this inability to hide your emotions from one another, but you have also been freed from the confines of your bodies altogether. You can change what others see—even what you see in the mirror—or you can separate yourself entirely, but you never escape your emotions, no matter what form you take."

9
Aliyah

"It's our first full moon," Shawn says, sitting on the edge of my bed. I can smell the patchouli and orange burning in the main hall, and as the scent wafts through my open door, it brings with it the smell of him. Even if I couldn't smell, hear, or taste the preparations in the air, I'd still know it was a full moon. I can feel it in my spine—I could feel it before last night's hunt. The urge to run, to howl, to dance... to... I stop myself before I finish that thought, because he's right there—in my room, in my bed, in my space. Right there.

"They're building the bonfire now, I think," I tell him, digging through the assortment of plain clothes I still hadn't put away. I've already picked out a pair of paper bag shorts, but I can't find a shirt I want to wear. I keep digging. It feels like something new might appear if I just look long enough.

"Marcus was alarmingly happy to do physical labor," he says, and I laugh. For all the muscle he carries around, Marcus

Weatherly is not known for wanting to lift heavy things. "There's a crop top bra thing right there to the left that would be cute. It's green."

I grab the scrap of fabric and blindly pull it over my head, looking at myself in the mirror as I smooth it down. The ribbed material feels nice under my hands. I glance down at the generic pile of clothes and remind myself that I chose them, because the alternative would have been whatever the Elders gave us. That doesn't make the muted colors and plain styles feel any less suffocating, though. In the laundry basket, there are a few pairs of shorts, some leggings, a couple of sweatshirts, a jacket, and some other miscellaneous things. The shoes I picked out are still in a pile beside their boxes—almost brand new, still untouched. My entire sorry wardrobe is in a pile on the hardwood floor, because it doesn't deserve a place in the beautiful closet. I fully intend to live out of the chaotic pile of fabrics until I can order my own clothes.

"Do I need to wear a bra too, or do you think it's okay that everyone can tell my nipples are pierced?" I ask him, meeting his eyes in the mirror. He doesn't bother to pretend that he hasn't been staring.

"I think you look incredible," is all he says.

I take a deep breath, dragging in the mossy, earthy, wood-heavy smell of the world beyond my own window deep into my lungs, and I hold it there until I hear the delighted laughter and unique *whoosh* that accompany the lighting of the fire.

When I turn around and look at Shawn, he's still looking at me, his eyes a complicated mix of dark purples and pinks.

"The fire is ready," I tell him, taking a few steps to stand between his thighs. The way he's sprawled out leaves plenty of room between his thighs.

"How could you possibly know that?" he asks, and I don't say that I heard it.

"The same way I know you need to take five before you go anywhere near anyone else," I tell him, pointedly dropping my eyes and then bringing them back up to meet his. He lets out a low, wicked laugh and pulls me into his lap.

"Five minutes isn't nearly enough time to get you out of my head," he says, sliding his hands over my thighs and settling them on my hips. He squeezes gently at the softness, and the scent of his arousal surrounds me, thickening the air and making my legs feel like they might give out and send us both toppling onto the bed.

Not such a bad thing, overall, but definitely not ideal. If I miss our first full moon, I'll never forgive myself.

I grab his hand and drag him with me out of the open window. We land on the soft ground and run around the house laughing in the way only lovers do. We both stop short when we see the massive pillar of rippling fire that Marcus, Elijah, Rose, and Rachelle have built. It's crackling happily amongst the infinite greenery of the reservation, and it sends a warm glow over all of us. In the glow of the night, his eyes flash like the roaring fire—warm, shifting, and completely impossible to look away from.

"You have to dance with me," he says, and I can't imagine saying anything but yes. In the firelight, with his hand in mine, I don't even consider saying no.

Not even Aviva's glowering face could ruin the night.

10
Aliyah

"She can't keep ignoring you forever," Shawn says, appearing in the doorway of my bedroom and talking far louder than he should be. I tense and widen my eyes at him.

"This feels like a closed-door kind of conversation," I mutter, setting down the book I've been pretending to read all morning.

"I'm not talking that—okay, okay. Closing the door," he says, then locks it for good measure. He lingers near it for a few seconds before finally letting himself relax and crossing to sit on the floor in front of me. He mirrors my posture, folding his long legs and leaning forward onto his knees. I laugh, because I can't help myself, then sigh.

"Viv isn't capable of doing anything forever. Not even this," I say, watching him shake the hair out of his eyes. "She'll give it up. Or realize she needs something."

"That seems like a strange way to talk about your sister."

"You never think of Marcus that way?" I ask. He shakes his head, and I sigh, leaning back against the bed. "Don't get me wrong—I love her. She's brilliant, kind, beautiful, all of that. But she's also petty and spiteful, selfish and entitled. This is just a tantrum over the fact that I got Alpha and she didn't."

"That's... All of this, over that?" he asks, genuinely stunned. I laugh because all his confusion proves is that he's never spent much time with my sister.

"She wanted it, and I didn't. More than that, she wanted it so desperately that she convinced herself it was hers. And then I didn't name her as a Beta. The Aiyanik were supposed to be mine, and you all were supposed to be hers. Now, she's pissed off and making it everyone else's problem because she doesn't know how to be a big girl about it and she doesn't want to talk it through with me yet," I explain. I know I sound exasperated, and I don't try to hide it. Aviva has hardly said a word to me since she arrived at Noonchester Falls, and everything she has said to me has been hateful. She's had plenty to say about me, though, and I know her well enough to know that it wouldn't matter to her to find out that I could hear any of it.

I don't think she's even realized that the pack bond has started to form, and if she has, she has no idea that she's broadcasting her every hateful thought down it.

"You were the right choice for the pack, and you made the right choice for the pack, that should be all that matters," he says, and that drags a real laugh out of me. The belly deep kind that fills a space and shakes your body. Shawn's relationship with Marcus isn't perfect and never has been, but it's good. They're both good people, even as opposite as they are. Where Marcus is loud, charming, and magnetic, Shawn is sweet, quiet, and warm. It works for them.

I see the similarities in them when they get going, barking at each other or roughhousing the way brothers so often do, but other times, the differences are all I see when I look at them.

Aviva and I are, at all times, too similar and too different to develop that kind of synergy.

"She won't see it that way. She's my baby sister, and she's used to getting everything she wants," I tell him. My eyes snap toward a sudden *thud* in the other room, but I relax when the sound is followed by peals of joyous laughter. I remind myself that they deserve the right to be as rowdy as they want and that they need it. We all do, I think. I look at Shawn and shut my thoughts down.

"I thought you were twins," he says. He didn't even flinch at the sound, and his eyes remained focused solely on me, tinged pink around the edges.

"Twins or not, someone has to come out first."

"Do you think she'll challenge you? She never did over the Aiyanik, so I want to say no, but she seems so angry," he says. I consider it briefly, just to make sure my thoughts on it haven't changed, and then I shrug. She has the right, technically, but I'm not sure she's ever been angry or will ever be angry enough to actually do it.

"Aviva is a lot of things," I say, tucking my knees to my chest and dragging the hem of my sweatshirt over them. "But she's not a killer."

"You'd accept it," he says, in awe and surprise. He's searching my face for any evidence that he's wrong, but he doesn't find it. "You'd accept her challenge."

I've taken to staring out the window, and I continue to do so as I answer him, watching the leaves shake as the breeze flows through them and feeling a little like I belong on the branch beside them. I can tell that there's more to his emotions than the concern etched into his face or the surprise widening his eyes. In there amongst the other feelings, there's a firm thread of pride.

"Of course, I would." My gaze drifts to the trees beyond the window. "No one takes what's mine without a fight. If she wants you all, she's going to have to kill me to get you."

I think about how the fight would end—about whether I could kill my sister, if it came to that. I think she would, if pushed far enough, but I don't think I can say the same of myself. I've spent too many years fighting to save lives—I don't think I'd have it in me. Living through a failed challenge could be seen as a mercy—or a punishment. But maybe it's just proof that I have a weakness worth exploiting. I decide not to think too much about it and hope it never comes to that. His heartbeat catches and stutters for a split second, and I feel it in the air between us as much as I hear it.

"I should've known you'd find a way to punish me. I always knew you were a good liar—but even I bought it this time." I'm mid-sip, a book in one hand, when Aviva finally decides she's ready to speak. She's been lurking just out of sight, frustration rising in waves until it boils over.

"Excuse me?"

"No. You don't get to do that. Don't act like you don't know exactly what I'm talking about," she says. She walks around the island and plants her hands on the marble directly across from me.

"It's not an act. What are you even talking about? I didn't lie to you, and I'm not punishing you."

"Bullshit, Ali. You know that's crap," she snaps, voice rising. I set my coffee mug down and pressed my fingers into my eyes.

"Viv, it's nine in the morning. What the hell are you even talking about? I can't argue with you if I don't know what I'm arguing about." My anger is written in my eyes, and I can feel each burning fleck of red, but I can't pull it back. Can't respond to her with the same infinite patience I usually show. I have no idea why, but this fight feels different.

"Alpha, you complete moron. I'm talking about how you secretly interviewed for Alpha and then lied to my face about not wanting it. I'm talking about how you had the option to make it up to me by making me your Beta, and you decided not to do that. I'm talking," she takes a deep breath. "I'm talking about how you had everything and then still decided to take everything from me too."

Something in me snaps.

"You think I wanted this? You think I wanted to lose Tamarak? To lose my people? Or to have to leave Theodora? My life has been laid out for me since the day we were born, and it never mattered how I felt about it because it was going to happen either way," I tell her, my voice cold. "I didn't ask to have twenty years of acceptance thrown away. I didn't ask to even be considered. I didn't ask for any of this the way you did. And I'm still here. Still taking it with grace and trying my damn best to be what they need me to be."

Doors open, and I spare a look to see who's listening. Rose is first to the railing, then Greyson. Rachelle is next and runs quietly to my room to rouse Shawn. I try not to think too much about how she knew where he was.

"You're failing," she says. The words sing through me like fire—I wasn't ready for that. "You're failing all of us by pretending that you haven't been angling for this for years."

"Aviva, that's enough," Rose says, dropping over the railing to enforce her warning.

"No, it isn't. It isn't enough. You took everything from

me, and now you expect me to just accept it? No way."

"I don't expect anything from you anymore, Viv. Because I'm always disappointed when I make that mistake," I take a deep breath and pull back on my anger, determined not to meet her where she is. "Your behavior's been embarrassing for months—and I let it slide because I love you. Because I wanted you to get what you deserve out of life. But it stops now."

"And what are you gonna do about it?" she demands, arms crossed, hip cocked like she's daring me. I can taste her resolve so acutely that it hurts—burning like acid on my tongue.

"I'm asking you, as your sister, not to make me show you what the consequences of defying an order and failing to meet behavior expectations will be," I say. There is no emotion in the words or in my eyes. Just ice.

Shawn stumbles out of my room, asking Rachelle what's going on. She's still mid-explanation when Aviva steps forward, pinning me back against the counter.

"I asked you a question," Aviva says. Rose growls in response.

"Aviva Nathair, you've been demoted to Omega. Your voting rights in pack matters are suspended until you can conduct yourself with grace and dignity. Any questions about this decision must be brought directly to me. Are we clear?"

Her hand comes up, claws out, and Rose catches it in midair.

"That's my Alpha, bitch," Rose growls, twisting Aviva's arm behind her and shoving her face-first into the fridge. I hear the bones grind and give way, but Aviva doesn't cry out. The same bitter taste burns my tongue again.

"I said," I repeat, cold and quiet, "are we clear?"

Silence. "While you're simmering in your new status, consider this: this exact behavior might be why the Elders chose me over you in the first place. Consider it your homework."

"You're a condescending, cold-hearted bitch," she spits. I smile.

I smile.

"Condescending, cold-hearted *Alpha* bitch," I correct her. "If you're going to insult me, at least be accurate."

The land pulses joyfully under my feet, and the potent rush of power sings up my spine. I feel it in my eyes, and I know they sense it. Rose's nails turn to claws for a heartbeat, then return to their perfectly manicured state. Aviva's spine ripples. She sags in Rose's hold, and I know it's the only evidence I will get of her surrender.

11
Aliyah

Humans have their suspicions about Friday the 13th. They say it's bad luck, just like they swear that each appearance of the full moon brings forth the craziest, most unstable members of society. Maybe it does, in their eyes, but I don't believe a word of any of their superstitious bullshit until I see it for myself.

I'm running in human form--relevant only because it's how I end up flat on my back, legs straddling a tree trunk. The sky above me is the most awful shade of red I've ever seen. Blood is less vicious than the wards above me, been covered in it. Panic seizes me in an instant.

The sun's still an hour from rising, and the crescent moon is still hanging proudly in the sky when I leave the residence. Music blares so loudly in my ears that I miss the warning blasts entirely. Not hearing the warning makes the sudden pulse of red light more terrifying and sends me tumbling through the underbrush, my earbuds ripped violently from my ears as I crash to the ground and slide.

I stare at the wards for a long time, even though I know I need to move. Normally transparent and virtually undetectable—the wards around Noonchester Falls have turned thick, and the pulsing in the air is violent. I rip off my sweatshirt, kick free of my sneakers, and launch into a full sprint. My phone and everything else I was carrying stay behind, in a pile on the forest floor for the little people to collect and return. I hope they won't wait too long.

I make it to the residence in under two minutes—inside is chaos. Frantic voices, shuffling bodies, and wide eyes greet me in every direction. Cici sees me coming from a hundred feet out and grabs my robe from just inside the doorway so I can cover myself. I scan the room as I tie the sash on my robe, looking for Rose, or Shawn, or even Aviva.

In my entire life, I've only seen the wards go off twice. The first time, I was five, too young to understand and too old not to be told. We were in the middle of a full moon celebration, and a pack of nomads slammed full force into the wards along the southern border. There were enough of them that the wards interpreted it as an invasion. They were black then, stealing away the moon's light and leeching away the warm light of the fire.

I remember being terrified, searching for my mother and only finding Aviva. She had been a comfort then—I doubt she would be now.

The second time the wards went off, I was nine, and a young girl killed herself in the woods. They were blue that time, but she was dead before we got there. Theodora held me as I cried and told me it was best to learn early that we wouldn't be able to save everyone.

I can't hear anything in the cacophony, and my sensitive

ears ring as I try to tease the voices around me apart.

"All of you, shut up!" I roar, and the effect of the Command is immediate. They all freeze and fall silent, staring at me like they're seeing me for the first time.

"One Beta needs to tell me what's happening," I say, my voice a little rough from yelling over their noise. Three mouths open and shut before they figure themselves out.

"There's an envoy," Greyson says, his voice clipped. "Waiting for you in the sanctuary." He and Shawn are standing with rigid spines on either side of the sanctuary door, watching me.

"Who is it?" I ask. They both shrug, and before I can ask another question, Aviva speaks, the discomfort of breaking through my orders clear on her face.

"It smells like Demetria," she says. The scent hits me like a punch, then—sharp, familiar, and very out of place. I leash the panic that swells in my chest and shut my eyes tightly to slow the cycling colors. Shawn's eyes are the first thing I find when I open mine again, and in them, I find a brief heartbeat of peace.

"Open the doors, let her in," I say. It isn't customary, and she won't be able to come more than a few steps through the Sanctuary door, but it's the only way for all of us to hear what she has to say. Shawn and Greyson both nod, then open the double doors to reveal Demetria McAllistair and her guards—standing in the doorway. They look like they've been dragged from Tamarak to Noonchester by their ankles.

Sanctuaries exist to allow visitors to enter the reservation without passing through the wards—so the envoy should not have triggered ours when they arrived. The bubble of unwarded space extends to just beyond the sanctuary door, and as they emerge into the Residence, I realize it's the fiery red stone at Demetria's throat that triggered the wards. If not for its presence, she would have been able to run all the way to the Sanctuary undetected.

The hairs at the base of my skull rise, and I feel the same feeling again—the long-traveled echo of the Banshee's scream.

I glance at Cici. A shake of her head is all it takes for me to understand—Tamarak's wards that are going off, not ours. Ramona's face flashes in my mind for a second. The Keeper of Tamarak Valley isn't among the envoy—for obvious reasons—but I catch myself hoping that she's alright.

Cici silences the wards, but Demetria's necklace continues to pulse as she stares at me. There's something in her crimson eyes that makes me shift my weight and look beyond the tangled mats in her long hair. She's as beautiful as I remember—but there's blood in the mud that's caked to her hairline, and it isn't hers. My mother's Beta continues to watch me for a long time before she finds her voice. She touches her forearm and raises her chin.

I know what she's going to say before she speaks—I need to hear her say the words. The Banshee's scream echoes somewhere in the distance, like it's bouncing off the mountains and coming back to me.

"Ali…" she starts, and her voice breaks. My heart lurches unsteadily in my chest, and I grab onto Cici for support.

"Demetria, what is it?" Aviva demands. She and a few others are watching Demetria, but everyone else has their attention fixed completely on me. When she speaks, she speaks only to my sister and me.

"Natalia Nathair is dead," she says, and Aviva sags against the wall, a wrecked sob breaking free of her chest as she slides to the floor.

The marking on her arm.

Alpha, it says.

Because my mother is dead. It's me that screams then, and it might as well be the Banshee for all the weight that it carries. Everyone in the room recoils from the sound.

Under us, the land lets out an unholy, howling pulse of energy, and it's all it takes to make me start moving again.

I shed the robe I'm wearing and run full speed for the boundary line. The change happens so quickly that I don't even feel the flare of pain that usually accompanies it, and the first falls of my feet against the soft ground send flashes of light through me. Someone shouts—probably Cici—but I don't slow or look back. She and Shawn follow me through the open bay door, their clothes falling haphazardly as they try to chase me. I can hear every soft fall of their paws in the damp underbrush—and still, I do not slow.

They're trying, but they aren't fast enough. Not now and maybe not ever. To catch an Alpha would take an Alpha, and the only other Alpha in Noonchester Falls can't follow me. And so, I run. I dart among the trees with precision, and I don't slow down, even when I scare a troop of Little People and send them skittering into the underbrush.

My mother is a beautiful woman. Was a beautiful woman. Soft eyes. Strong jaw. Brave heart. She was also kind and strong—intelligent and loyal. Fierce in every way. She and my father have been married—were married—for thirty years. Our Alpha. My Alpha. Their Alpha, now.

She can't be dead.

As the boundary line approaches, I hear Shawn's voice clearly in my head. He's been calling out to me the entire time, but the sound has been getting lost amongst the other voices and my own thoughts.

You have to stop; you can't cross the boundary line. Ali, it could kill you.

I close my eyes and focus on where I want to go. My magic coils in anticipation—still a snake where it curls deep inside the hollow spot. The place where the wolf lives—where my magic lives.

The land coils and propels me forward—its magic all I need to turn my nerves to steel. I feel myself smile a very human, very dangerous smile from where my human mind lives alongside the mind of the wolf.

Watch me, I say sharply through the bond.

I let my body hit the ground and continue through the wards unharmed. I feel my bones snap and pop as my body returns to its human form, but every bit of it feels far away.

12
Shawn

"Will the wards let her through when she gets back to Tamarak?" I ask, looking down at her familiar shape among the moss and mud. The change has finished, and her hair is spread out around her, leaves sticking to the curls and twisting them through the damp dirt under her pale skin. I can't stop staring—but I manage to look away long enough to find Cici, standing in the shadow of a weeping willow, ten yards from the boundary line.

She's looking at the wards like they might bite her.

I've seen Cici run—I know she's faster than me by a mile. She should have reached the boundary line before me, but she didn't. Once, she would have been faster than Ali, too. But not tonight. The way Ali ran—it was unlike anything I'd ever seen. I wonder for a second why Cici would want to hold herself back, but then I think about it again. About the way Ali moved. Like an Alpha, and I realize that she didn't. Cici has been chasing—Ali was just that fast.

I was just that slow. That *normal.*

The thought train is derailed when Cici processes that I've spoken to her and turns to look at me.

"You don't know, do you?" She asks me, stepping out of the shadows of the tree and kneeling to pick leaves and sticks from the twisting mass of Ali's curls. I kneel beside her and lift Ali's body into my arms. As I stand, her fingers brush the shimmering wall of the wards—like her body is reaching for her soul beyond.

"Know what?" I ask her, standing and shifting Aliyah's weight into my chest to make it easier to carry her. If I could, I would push the mass of curls away from her face and close her eyes. Cici must notice me looking, because she reaches out and fixes both problems. Now, instead of looking dead, Ali just looks like she's sleeping.

"They'd let her in," she says, walking back in the direction of the residence and shifting like she doesn't know what to do with her hands. "Even if she waltzed through the wards in her physical body, they would let her in. They won't even detect her like this."

If Cici were anyone else, I would ask a follow-up question, but she isn't. In the short time I've known her, I've learned to be patient and let her deliver her lessons in her own time. I waited and walked beside her in silence for a few feet before she spoke.

"Aliyah Nathair was royalty, and Aliyah Trevonaire is too, but I don't mean either in the way you think. She can walk through the wards of every reservation, enter every building, and forgo every Sanctuary in the Wolflands because of the reputation she has built for herself and the number of lives she has saved," she says. "Not the Elizabethian Mountains, obviously. Anya Kivleneiks doesn't do visitors, but you know what I mean."

I think for a second of the first time I met her, the stitches she gave me, and the way Jedediah laughed with her, her whole face lighting up even as her hands remained steady on the sutures.

"How is that possible?" I ask—out of curiosity, not doubt. There are no laws against visiting other reservations, and it isn't uncommon for students or family members to be granted special access to study or visit residents. I've never heard of someone having that kind of unilateral welcome. Not ever. That kind of mingling between packs—and pack royalty, no less—just doesn't happen.

"She's special," Cici says. She climbs over a fallen log and stops walking to wait for me to do the same. The bark scrapes my hip and thigh, but it doesn't touch Ali—and that's a success in my book. "She's a gifted Healer, but she has also been Tamarak's unofficial ambassador since she was twelve. She knows every Alpha, every Beta, and every Healer by name and has built a relationship with each of them. Aliyah—there's no one else like her in all of the Wolflands. There hasn't been for a long time."

We walk in silence for a long time after that, stepping over fallen trees and puddles of cloud-filled water turned brilliant by the rising sun. I can see the residence when I think of Demetria again. She and her Envoy had been in the Sanctuary, and I wondered distantly if they still are. I kind of hope not.

I let my mind go blank as we finish our walk, Ali's limp body against my chest is the only thing that matters.

"You have something to say," I tell Cici as we descend the final hill. I don't look at her.

"I was just thinking about how you love her," she says. If I were holding anything but Aliyah, I would have dropped it onto the ground and looked at her like she was losing her mind. She doesn't shy away from her statement when I do turn to look at her, and it feels insane to think that there's any way that's something she just knows. She gestures at the open window of Ali's bedroom and takes two long strides to vault herself up onto the second floor. When she lands lightly on the windowsill, she turns and gestures for me to toss Ali up to her. I immediately refuse, shaking my head and shifting my weight so I can drape her over one shoulder and have a free hand to catch myself when I jump.

When I'm sure Ali's weight is stable, I climb up the side of the building and through the open window of her bedroom. I pretend Cici isn't watching me when I get there, but I know she is.

"I've loved her since the day I met her," I admit. "She sewed up my face and told me not to be an idiot, and it was over for me."

"We ought to dress her. Even I'm not totally sure if anyone will be able to see her, and it seems like she would prefer to be decent," Cici says. She's heading for the bathroom, where she wets a washcloth, and when she comes back, she sets her attention on scrubbing the dirt from Ali's porcelain skin. Together, we pick the remaining pieces of vegetation out of her hair, and I lay her down on the bed to dig through the crate of clothes she still hasn't put away. They're all soft—shades of green, tan, black, and gray—which somehow makes it harder to choose. I settle for a soft sweater and a pair of black sweatpants, then Cici and I work together to dress her and tuck her under the heavy blankets on her bed.

Cici retreats to the windowsill as soon as she can and sits with her legs pulled up to her chest while she talks to me. With her head on her knees, she looks younger than her four decades, and her face is almost soft.

"Did she tell you that Chief Elder Vianbry told her she'd

been chosen before they announced it?" Cici asks me. And I lie, because I don't know her like that.

"Isn't that against the law?" I ask, knowing that she called Rose the second Elder Vianbry was out of the room, and Rose called me as soon as they hung up.

"Very much so," Cici says, letting out a little half laugh and dropping her head back against the window so she can stare at the wooden ceiling. "I wasn't even your Keeper yet, but I was so invested in making sure you all got the Alpha you deserved that I sent Viviana Errapel to testify before the Elder Council in a last-ditch effort that they knew everything they needed to know to make the right choice."

"Viviana," I echo, chewing on the name for a second. "She's the Healer of Archimedes, isn't she?"

"She's Theodora's eldest daughter, and she's been the Primary Healer there for a long time. She was there the day Greyson and Leighann came in. The day Ali saved her," she says. I immediately picture Leighann's scars, hidden by high collars and long sleeves. Never an inch of skin visible except her hands and feet.

"I didn't know she was there that day," I admit. "She thinks the Council made a mistake when they made their choice."

"Aviva would have been a mistake," Cici says firmly, looking at me with furious, stone eyes. She takes a deep breath and glances at Aliyah before she speaks, reining in her temper so easily that I'm almost jealous.

"What do you mean?"

"Aviva Nathair will do great things in her life. She's smart and strong, but she's also selfish, overconfident, and heavy-handed. Aliyah is none of those things. Her cleverness, selflessness, flexibility, and kindness make her a unique candidate, and when you add in the fairness, the sternness, the honesty, and the ruthlessness, she's the only right choice. The only thing that made them hesitant was how little they knew about her. She was Tamarak's heir, so she never tried to campaign for anything. Never gave anyone else the chance to know her. Aviva was the one they knew because Aviva wants to know everyone," Cici says. I try to imagine her ever fading into the background—but I can't.

I don't know if it's because she so quickly became the center of my universe or if it's because I noticed her from the very beginning—I don't think the why matters. I couldn't imagine her ever fading into the background or going unnoticed in any room. I don't know if it's because she so quickly became the center of my universe or if it's because I noticed her from the very beginning. I don't think the why matters.

"They asked Chief Elder Vianbry to vote and break their tie, but after Viviana's testimony, they voted again. It was unanimous. For the first time in almost a thousand years, everyone voted the same way on an issue," Cici says. She looks at Ali and sighs. "I never told her that part, and I doubt Cyan did either."

"You son of a—"

"Careful, Shrimpy, we're twins," Marcus says, retrieving his fallen staff and swatting my hand aside so he can see the source of the bright blood running down my cheek. My hand is covered, and so is the front of my shirt, but it hurts less than I expect it to. That seems like it should be a red flag or something.

"You should go to Medical, that's—gnarly."

"You're an asshole," I tell him, shoving past him just hard enough that he takes an involuntary step backwards. He shrugs and lets me pass, stopping to retrieve the staff I left abandoned on

the ground and returning it to the weapons rack.

The path to Medical is familiar, and I let myself follow the winding road on autopilot; my sweaty shirt pulled up to slow the flow of blood. It smells of baked goods and autumnal fruit in the square as I walk.

I barely acknowledge anyone until after the automatic doors open, their awful whooshing *noise worsening my rapidly forming headache—and suddenly, there are feet in my line of sight.*

"Hello, do you need me to take a look at that?" she asks, and it takes me a second to meet her eyes. My eyes lift from her feet with involuntary slowness, taking in the lines of her thighs, her soft hips, and the full swell of her breasts—then, finally, her face.

Her face.

She's the most beautiful woman I've ever seen, and the fact that I don't say so out loud is proof that I'm struck stupid by the sight of her. Her eyes are a shade of blue I've never seen before, and her cheeks are rosy, rounded, and speckled with freckles that spread over the bridge of her nose and her forehead. Her curls are wild, barely contained by a messy topknot that looks one sneeze away from a total structural collapse.

Maybe she'll blame it on the six-inch gash on my face. Or the head injury that probably came with it.

She lets me stare for what feels like a long time, then arches a perfect eyebrow and reaches up, pausing just before her hand touches mine to ask again. "Let me take a look at that?"

I nod stupidly and move my hand so she can see the deep, angry gash that runs from the corner of my eye, over my cheekbone, to just above my mouth. I can already feel the bruising and I know that I've probably got a fracture or two under the wound, but I don't care, because she's there and she's touching me, and those blue eyes are sparkling with strange curiosity.

"Sit down right there and quit staring at me," she says, pushing gently at my shoulder to get me started and then crossing the room to collect a small tray of supplies.

"It's just... where's Aline?" I ask when she returns. I look around for the Healer I'm used to seeing, and her curly head pops out from behind a shelf in the far corner of the room. She waves and smiles.

"I'm here!" she says, then steps out and dusts herself off. She sends a cloud out around herself as she does, and the look on her face says "oops!" but she doesn't apologize, not even to the intern who starts coughing. I laugh by accident, and it sends violent pain through my face.

"You look like a dust bunny," I tell our Junior Healer as she approaches. She scowls, narrowing her brown eyes. She smells like dust, and dirt, and gooseberries.

The word gooseberries is funny.

"Thank you very much for that. Such a gentleman, Mr. Weatherly," she gestures at the girl standing in front of me, organizing her supplies and preparing to irrigate the wound on my face. "This is Aliyah Nathair, she's visiting us this week from Tamarak Valley, and she's going to take good care of you. I bet you won't even have a scar."

I recognize the name as soon as she says it, but the girl doesn't look how I expect her to. I've met Aviva, the other Nathair twin, and the similarities in their faces are hard to find, even up close. They're both soft, all curves and no edges. They have the same sharp, discerning eyes, but even the colors are wildly different. Where Aviva is all dark hair, dark eyes, and tanned skin, Aliyah is bright, and light, and pale.

Jedediah Errapel's laugh rolls like thunder through the room, and even though I can't tell where it's coming from, I smile at the sound of it. It's involuntary—his laugh has always been contagious. Deep and warm and crackling like embers in every space it fills.

"He didn't ask my name before he checked me out," Aliyah tells Aline, eyes full of laughter and shining bright in the afternoon sun that's streaming through the windows. They share a look that's distinctly female, and then Aline winks instead of scolding me, which takes me by surprise.

"You'll have to forgive him, he's stupider than he looks, especially when he spends too much time with his brother," Aline says, pulling on gloves and picking up the little tray so she can hold it where Aliyah wants it. She's still talking when Aliyah begins spraying me with extremely cold saline. "I have no doubt that his brother is responsible for the insanely attractive cut."

"You're a twin too, aren't you, Mr. Weatherly?" Aliyah asks. The way her voice sounds saying my name makes me feel like my tongue is a giant head of cauliflower. I can't even begin to find the words to answer her for a solid five seconds, and she laughs. "Don't be an idiot."

She injects me with a mercifully large dose of whatever it is they use as a numbing agent, and the relief is nearly immediate. She picks up a curved needle and begins to stitch.

"I can be your idiot, if you want," I say, the relief making me bold. She smiles as she stitches, and for the first time since I walked through the doors, the scent of her hits me. Hits me, runs me over, and drowns me. She smells like neroli, raspberry, and vanilla—rich and bright and beautiful. I would let the scent of her suffocate me if that's what it took to bring those eyes back to my face.

"Down boy," she says, and even though her voice is pitched low, she's smiling, bright like the moon.

Something inside of me lets out a howl, mine.

I snap myself out of the daydream just as Marcus strolls past my open door—he grins as he flips me off. It's the smile that really does it. The faint scar on my cheek twinges, and I roll my eyes, turning back to face Ali—still resting peacefully among the blankets on my bed.

She hasn't moved since I brought her here, but I keep hoping I'll look over and find her eyes open. We took her to her own bedroom at first, but once the house was quiet, I carried her to mine so she could rest without the constant knocks on the door.

She started on her back, but I moved her to her side in case she vomited or something. I remembered she said that it was important, once.

None of us knows how the… projection thing works yet. I think it's better to be safe, and I promised Cici I would stay by her side. I haven't let her out of my sight since Cici returned to her little house for a few hours of sleep.

I haven't slept a wink.

I turn and stretch out beside her, content to stare at her until she comes back to me. However long it takes.

"So this is where you're keeping her," Aviva says from the doorway, her voice low and clipped. It's early, only a few minutes before four, and I don't hear her nudge the door open.

"Shouldn't you be asleep?" I ask her, choosing to ignore the snide tone—and the implication that I'm doing anything other than keeping an eye on her sister.

"Shouldn't you be brooding alone somewhere?"

"Why do you insist on being so unpleasant?" I ask, setting down the book I borrowed from Ali's nightstand. "I've done nothing to you. None of us has."

"Sure," she scoffs.

That's enough.

I swing my legs over the side of the bed and turn to face her.

"I'm so serious. What the hell is your problem?" She looks past me—at Ali—and I feel the sudden urge to shield her.

"She is. All of you are pretending everything is fine, and it's not." She looks like Ali—same cheekbones, same mouth—but I feel no warmth when I look at her. Not even appreciation for her appearance. Nothing.

"Everything *is* fine, Aviva. Or it would be—if you weren't acting like a perturbed toddler," I say, my voice rising in spite of myself. She brightens—like she *wants* the fight.

"Wow. 'Perturbed?' Big word for such a little guy. Did you rehearse that?" Her mocking tone is revolting.

"I'm not letting you bait me." I take a breath. "Your behavior is embarrassing, uncalled for, and completely inappropriate. You should be ashamed of yourself. And I know I'm not the only one that's disappointed in you,"

I don't have to look at Ali for her to know that she's one of the people I'm talking about.

"Your disappointment doesn't matter to me."

"I believe that, actually. But this isn't just about you. You're not the only one who had their life turned upside down. You're not the only one who just lost your mother. But you *are* the one making sure you both have to go through it alone." She flinched. For a second, I think maybe she hears what I'm saying. But she just huffs and walks away.

I hear her voice a beat later, just as she reaches her bedroom.

"She's due for an injection. I left a vial in Medical for her when she wakes up."

13
Aliyah

My arrival back to Noonchester Falls is wildly different from my departure.

I ran all the way to Tamarak, but only because I didn't know any better. I've reached my former home and sit in the warm light of my mother's funeral pyre before it hits me—I could have projected directly to the reservation and saved myself the run. Not that my body will pay the price, I guess.

When I was a little girl, first learning how to use my original gift, my mother sent me to my room with a needle and instructed me to close my eyes, reach down into the hollow part of my soul, and touch the spark of light that lived there each time I pricked my finger. I'd done it, too. For the remainder of the evening—even if only for a few seconds at a time—I stopped the world. When I came down for dinner that night, I'd practically mastered flipping the on/off switch, and I could feel the lingering soreness in every one of my fingertips.

That night was foremost in my mind as I sat on the cold cobblestones and watched the fire steal away the last ghosts of my mother. It was that memory of her that had me reaching down, and down, until I felt that new spark—the unfamiliar one. I touched it and felt my body calling to me—the distance yawning between us. My body is somewhere soft and warm, so I know I'm no longer lying on the hard ground where I fell. That's all the information I can glean.

I look at the dying flames one last time and grip the warm spark of light that lives there in that hollow place with my full strength. All at once, it drags me back to Noonchester Falls—back to my home—and drops me squarely back into my body.

I expect to be in Medical—or in my own bed. I don't have to open my eyes to know that I'm wrong. Someone dressed me, and as I wake, I become more and more aware of the weight of heavy blankets pressing down on me.

Somewhere beyond me, ice hits a glass—the sound is sharp in my still-ringing ears. There's nothing human in the way they twitch as I come back into myself. The sound physically *hurts.*

I blink. First once, and then twice. The haze in my vision lingers, and I'm curled up on my side. There's an intense heat blazing against my back, from my shoulders to my knees. I blink again and look around the room, hoping that everything will start to make more sense.

My vision is only just sharpening when I try to sit up, and I feel Shawn's arm tighten around my waist. The scent of him—earthy, warm—has saturated the space, and as he stirs, I realize he's the source of heat against my back. When I move away, he grunts and rubs his face. The clock says it's almost seven, and I feel a little guilty for waking him so early. He blinks sleepily against the first hints of light streaming through the windows, and it seems to take him a second too, to remember where he is. His sharp eyes find my face and fix, widening slightly in surprise.

They listed her time of death as 2:41 AM. My mother's life ended at 2:41 AM on Friday, September 13th.

The overwhelming feeling of panic that has been rooted in my bones since Demetria arrived at Noonchester Falls has long since faded into the background, and I refuse to let it take hold of me again. When he exhales, I force a soft smile—he sees right through it.

"Hey Snowball," he says, voice rough with sleep. His grogginess is gone, and he's pushing himself up onto his elbows so that we're face to face. "You're back."

I nod dumbly—he sounds so surprised and so relieved that I'm pretty sure my voice won't work if I try to speak. There's a soft ring of yellow glowing around his pupils. Subtle. Steady. It makes my heart lurch to know that he's happy to see me, even this early in the morning when he has clearly been so deeply asleep.

"Thank you for taking care of me," I say when the weight of his eyes on mine is too much, and I need an excuse to look away. I sit all the way up and face him, looking down at the sheets tangled around us instead of at him. He must have been expecting me to get up and leave, or to scold him, because he looks at me for a second with a dumbfounded expression on his face.

"I'll always take care of you," he says like it's the most obvious thing in the world. I pull the heavy comforter up from where it's nearly on the floor and shift so that I can use his chest as a pillow. Even with the blanket tucked right up under my chin, I'm shivering against the loss of the fire's warmth.

I realize later that it's my grief making me cold. But that isn't until many hours after he kisses my head, smooths my curls away from my face, and tells me to close my eyes.

I'm asleep before he has finished the words.

I woke this morning wrapped in his warmth, tucked away in the quiet retreat of his bedroom, his heartbeat steady against my back and his thumb drifting lazily across my lower belly as he slept. Through the bedroom windows, the trees sway in a gentle breeze, kissed by warm afternoon light and long free of the morning's dew.

He, like always, sleeps soundly as I blink against the light of the day. Staring out at the line of the trees beyond the windows, I lay there in his arms until my body is willing to accept that I'm awake.

Even then, I linger—warm and at peace.

But when I remember how I ended up in his bedroom—in his bed, in his arms—the panic returns, and I can't stay still any longer. It spreads faster than I can breathe, and I know I'll wake him if I stay. So, I slip from his arms, borrow a sweatshirt from his closet, and disappear through the open window into the sunlight. It must have rained overnight—the grass under my feet is wet and cold when I land. The bitter sting of it barely registers. I lean against the side of the residence to let myself feel the panic instead of running from it. The tears that fall aren't even salty. I've cried so many. Something about that makes me want to laugh.

I stay in the shadow of the residence until my breathing slows enough to see straight. Then I run—legs heavy—toward the sound of the falls.

When I reach the clearing, I skid to a stop and stare at the water as it tumbles over the rocks and into the pond below.

My mother's voice is there, in the sound of the water. In the way it rushes and rolls. I can see her face in the sunlight that streams through the ancient trees and smell the rich, vibrant scent of her among the flowers and the trees.

It's a lot. Too much. Too much and too fast, and I can tell that I'm not breathing, but only distantly.

I take one long step forward, then another, and I hit the water still fully dressed.

I hold on to a root to keep myself from returning to the surface, and even though the pressure on my ears is unbearable, I keep myself there anyway.

I count to thirty first.

Then sixty.

Ninety.

Then one hundred and twenty.

Two hundred and forty.

Then I don't count anymore because I can't think of anything but the cold water and the tears that I can't be sure are actually leaving my eyes.

I return to the surface only when my lungs are screaming for air and there are black spots forming in my vision. The water steals the last dregs of the pyre's warmth from my body. She's there when I emerge, sitting on the boulders piled just beyond the wards. I wipe the water from my eyes and blink at her, expecting her to disappear, but she doesn't.

She startles me. I don't like it. But she's alone, and so I swim closer.

She's a nomad. I can tell from the way she's dressed, the way she holds herself. There's a wildness to them, and she's no exception. Her layered clothing and untamed curls frame a plain face and shocking blue eyes. But beyond all that, there's something… off about her. Not feral, not uncivilized like some nomads I've met—but definitely odd.

"Most people take their clothes off before swimming," she says, voice weirdly trans-Atlantic and rusty from disuse. She isn't smiling, but her eyes are bright with laughter.

"I wasn't planning to get in. It just sort of happened," I admit, watching her slide down the side of the large rock she's been sitting on. When she lands, I realize she's tall. Not just tall—surprisingly so. She eyes the barrier like Cici does. Like it might bite. She reaches out to touch it, and I flinch, unsure how the wards between us will react to her. A ripple of energy spills out from her palm, and she watches with childlike wonder until it fades.

"May I come in? The water looks nice," she says. Her voice is grating—not loud, just... wrong. But I nod.

"You can't pass through the wards. They haven't opened yet."

She nods.

"My name is Saya Luddington," she says, picking her tattered bag up off the ground where it fell when she slid down. She shuffles awkwardly for a moment and then sits down with her back against the large stone. Even with a few feet between her and the wards, I can feel them singing.

Someone's here. Someone's close. Pay attention.

Eyes Open.

I look closely at the girl, curious more than anything. She has at least a hundred pounds on me, but it doesn't feel important. Important are the scars that curl around her throat and mark the right side of her face.

Those seem to scream, *pay attention*, just like the wards. Something about them makes my eyes linger.

"I'm Ali," I tell her. She cocks her head at me in a

distinctly dog-like way and scrunches up her button nose.

"Just Ali?" she asks. "I've never met an Alpha that doesn't give a rank, a surname, or a bloodline when they introduce themselves."

I want to tell her that she shouldn't spend so much time around arrogant Alphas, but I don't. She watches me with those unnerving blue eyes, and I wonder how she knows that I'm the Alpha of Noonchester Falls. As discreetly as I can, I push myself back toward the shore and away from her. I still can't stop coming back to the scars.

"I've never been that kind of person. I'd call myself a Healer before I'd say Alpha," I tell her. "My name is Aliyah Trevonaire—I am both the Healer and the Alpha of the Trevonaire pack at Noonchester Falls."

I've never said it out loud before, and it sounds like a lot of words that don't mean anything.

"None of that tells you anything about me, though," I say, kicking until I'm close enough to the shore to stand and climb out of the water.

"So tell me something about you then," she says. "If none of that's important."

"There's nothing to tell," I say, too quick. Defensive. She makes a noise in the back of her throat and I get the distinct feeling that it hurts her to make it. Like her throat is raw.

"Not only do I believe that's a lie, honey, I actually believe you think it's true," she says. She drags those eyes over me and smiles with only one side of her mouth. "So tell me something about the boy. Is he why you're in the water in your clothes?"

My brain spins, and while it does, she cards her thick fingers through her hair, teasing out tangles and leaves. She waits while I search for an answer, and the unease in my stomach grows.

"No," I admit, finally. She looks up at me. "No, he's not the reason. He's... Actually, he's the reason I'm not in a far worse situation right now."

"You love him," she says, her voice strangely flat. She works at a particularly nasty snarl in her hair, giving me a break from the weight of her eyes on my face. I don't tell her that she's right or that the idea of loving him scares me nearly as much as the knowledge that he loves me. He hasn't said it yet, and I know he's waiting until he thinks I'm ready to hear it —but I'm not sure I ever will be.

I know, either way, because I can see it in his eyes and feel it in the way his hands rest on my hips.

I've never admitted to loving him, not to anyone but my mother as her body turned to ash in that pyre, and I don't plan on starting now.

This nomad has no right to that information, and the unease in my stomach keeps growing the longer she stays close.

I tell Shawn about the nomad girl as soon as I get back to the Residence, because I need to tell someone. He listens as I describe her, but when I try to explain how she made me feel, he looks completely lost.

"This girl got under your skin, didn't she?" he asks, and I nod immediately.

"She feels important. But also dangerous. She doesn't expect me to be... well, anything. I've never experienced that before." He starts to protest, and I hold up my hand. "When we met, you weren't expecting me to be anything other than the girl sewing your face together. You didn't know me, but you'd heard things and made plenty of your own observations. You had opinions. This girl doesn't have any of that. She doesn't care and she's not afraid to be exactly who she is. Even if she makes me uncomfortable, I have to respect her for that."

"What is it about her that bothers you?" he asks, and it's infuriating, because I don't know. I picture her, and every detail is perfect in my mind's eye—right down to the scars. But nothing stands out.

"She's..."

But what is *she?*

"Disconcerting," says a small voice from the doorway. "The word you're looking for is disconcerting."

I turn and face Leighann, waving her in and pushing a strand of her long hair away from her face. From beneath dark lashes, her lavender eyes find mine and she cocks her head. Like she knows something I don't.

"That *is* the word I was looking for, little bird. Thank you. Do you need something?"

"Daddy dislocated his shoulder again, and he doesn't want you to know, so he's going to have Uncle M put it back. I think that's dumb, so I came to tell you to fix him and then smack him," she says. I can't help but laugh.

"Marcus should not be trusted to put a book back in its place, much less a shoulder," Shawn says, looking very alarmed. He's right.

"I guess we should stop them before it's too late. You want a ride?"

Leighann nods, and when I kneel down, she climbs onto my back with ease. Her legs wrap around my waist, and she clasps her sleeve-covered hands under my chin. I can feel her scars through the material.

"Let's go," I say, giving her legs a gentle squeeze as I start walking. Shawn follows close behind us into the sublevels, and as we descend, I reach for him through the pack bond.

This conversation isn't over. There's something not right about that girl, I tell him. He looks at me for a long time before he nods, like he's trying to find answers in my eyes.

I wonder if he sees anything else while he's there.

"Do you have a second?" Aviva asks, almost whispering and looking distinctly like she would rather not be asking in the first place. Shawn and I share a look, and then I slip away from the group I've been talking to. I lead her to the practice room where I've played violin all day and close the door behind us.

"What's up?" I ask. She looks like she might be sick.

"I owe you an apology," she says, and I nearly drop dead then and there. I can count on one hand the number of real apologies I've gotten from her over the years, and I wasn't expecting another for a long time.

"For what, exactly?"

"A lot of things, I think," she admits. She takes a deep breath and looks out through the window in the door at Shawn and Rose, who are talking and still managing to watch us. "My behavior has been horrible, and I left you to deal with losing Mom alone. It doesn't matter how angry I am with you, I shouldn't have done that."

"No, you shouldn't have, but I also know that you're going through your own shit. I don't have to like your behavior to understand it," I tell her. She looks surprised by my lack of anger, and I hope that it's a good thing. I hope I'm doing the right thing, showing her the grace I know she wouldn't show me.

"Did you get to see her funeral pyre?" She asks. I nod.

"It was beautiful. Demetria and our father did right by her. You would have loved it."

"Did they tell you what happened? Any cause of death?" I wish I had answers for her questions and my own, but I don't.

"No. Theodora says they brought in a neutral examiner to do the autopsy, but the report hasn't been finalized yet. She doesn't know what's taking so long, and no one she's asked seems to know either," I explain. She scowls.

"So what, we just have to wait and wonder? She was an Alpha, damnit." *She was our Alpha.* "They should refuse to stop searching for answers until they have them."

She was our mother.

2:41 AM.

I don't know how to tell her that all we can do is wait, so I don't. Instead, I tell her about the funeral pyre and about how Demetria, Theodora, our father, and the other Betas remained in the cool night air almost as long as I did. I tell her about the music they played and the rich smells of the wood they burned, and then I tell her stories about our mother until the others have returned to the main floors of the residence, and it's only us left behind.

Only she is there to witness my tears, and only I witness hers.

It's just the two of us and our grief in that little room, as I pick up my violin and begin to play the requiem that brought our mother to her pyre.

The final note rings like a Banshee's scream in the silence around us. I know I'm the only one who hears it.

My mother is dead.

14
Aliyah

I let them drag me into playing soccer today. It was the most fun I've had in a while—also easily the most nerve-wrecking thing I've done all year.

Greyson's the first person to go down with an injury—and it's only seven minutes into the game. He comes out of the goal to catch a ball that's coming in high, at the same time Jacob goes up to bring the ball down. Greyson gets the ball, and since Jacob can't get out of the way, he also gets a very powerful knee to the groin.

Greyson releases the ball, grabs hold of himself, and hits the ground completely unprotected.

The whole thing seems very dramatic, but since I've never been hit in the balls, I can't say for sure that it isn't exactly as bad as it looks.

"Son of a bitch, are you okay?" Jacob asks, already on his

knees beside Greyson's prone form. He waves me over, and the others take a knee so I can get there without having to work too hard for it. The field goes completely silent, and I have to swallow a laugh as I kneel down to tend to Greyson.

Greyson Marquis is one of the toughest people I know, and to see him curled in on himself and cursing colorfully is up there on the list of things I've seen in my life that feel absurd.

"Grey, use your words," I say, reaching out to touch his shoulder. There's a thin layer of sweat on his skin, and bruises still lingering from forcing his shoulder back into place less than twenty-four hours ago. The bruises are evidence that he's an idiot, but his healing has taken care of the worst of the pain. It's probably worth mentioning that the incident twenty-four hours ago was the second time in the last thirty-six hours that I've had to relocate the exact same shoulder.

"Just give me a second—I'll be fine," he says, half growling from the pain. I back off and sit on my feet, waiting patiently for his breathing to even out. He uncurls slowly until he's lying flat on his back, and when his eyes meet mine, he speaks through the pack bond, his voice so close it nearly startles me.

I need your help, he says. *Can we talk after the game? Privately?*

I nod my head once and stand, pulling him to his feet and giving him one last opportunity to check himself over before I'm willing to believe he's actually alright.

"Let's try not to castrate anyone or break any bones for the rest of the game, yeah?" I ask, loud enough that everyone can hear me trying to keep my voice light, but I can tell by the way Aviva's eyes narrow that she knows something's off. I force myself to smile and laugh as the others whoop and cheer.

I pick up the ball and throw it to midfield. The game is on as soon as it lands.

The next injury comes when Elijah punches Kelly in the nose and gets blood all over both of them. Elijah waves me off when I try to check on him, and there's a disgusting snap of cartilage before the game continues like nothing happened at all.

Neither of those things are what make me think I'll remember this game for the rest of my life. No, that came much, much later. I'm sprinting flat-out toward Jade, who's in the goal opposite Greyson, when I catch a strange scent on the air. I fire the ball and skid to a halt as it sails past her and hits the back of the net.

I'm too distracted to even celebrate, but only Rose seems to notice. She shifts into position at my flank, watching at a distance to see what I'll do.

The smell is strange—not because I don't recognize it, but because it doesn't belong here. Not with these people, not in this place. I close my eyes and draw a long, deep breath through my nose to make sure I'm not making it up. I tag myself out of the game and walk off the field toward my sister, who's sitting on a blanket near the sidelines. Rose tries to follow—she only remains when I push. Her watchful eyes linger on my back.

"Viv, a word?" I say. We haven't spoken since we sat together in that practice room, and things are still tense between us, but I need to know if she smells what I smell. She stands, and we move away, into the small lobby where the elevator and the stairwell are, so no one can hear us while we talk.

"What's so important that we need to talk about it right now?" she asks, turning to face me with her arms folded over her chest. She seems to realize how she sounds a beat too late and softens her expression a second later.

I take another breath, and the scent is stronger.

Stronger since we entered a smaller space. Stronger standing in front of her. I look at her closely—at the way her arms press her boobs up to her chin, and the way she's looking at me.

Like she's known this conversation had to happen eventually.

She looks like my sister, standing there in front of me. Like the little girl who used to run into my room when the dark got too loud, crawling into my bed without waking me. Like the same girl who used to reach for my hands and play with my fingernails when she was nervous.

But there's a tension in her shoulders and a defensiveness in her eyes that I don't recognize. In that moment, she's as much my Aviva as she's a stranger.

I take another deep breath, and the heavy scent floods my senses.

"It's you," I breathe, not bothering to hide my surprise—or the dismay that comes along with it.

"What's me?" she asks, looking at me like I'm crazy as I step close and press my nose against the side of her neck. I expect her to fight back, tell me that I'm wrong, or to get away from her, but she doesn't. She deflates like an old balloon, gaze drifting to Greyson through the glass that separates us from the field.

"I should have known you'd notice," she says softly.

The older sister in me wants to comfort her first and scold her later, but the Alpha in me is torn between her anger and her fear. Both are winning out over every sisterly and every motherly instinct that I have. The fear clogs my throat and steals away the oxygen I'm breathing in before it has a chance to reach my lungs.

She must see it, because she grabs my hand and squeezes until my fingers crack, willing me to breathe.

"You know the rules. Viv, that we're not allowed to have babies or weddings for two years. You're an unmated royal, you could—Viv, they could try to reclaim you or kill you and the baby if they wanted. No one would be able to stop them," I say, forcing my fear and panic down in favor of trying to understand. "Damnit, look at me."

She does, and there are tears burning in her brown eyes. It turns my stomach to see her that way, and my heart thuds heavily against my chest when I realize she looks as scared as I feel. I wonder if she's afraid of me—or just of what comes next. I hope it's the latter. That would mean we're still in sync.

"Ali, I…" she starts. She falls silent, like the words slipped right out of her reach. She wraps her arms protectively around her stomach, and the sight of it breaks whatever control I have left. I gather her in my arms and hold on tight as a broken, desperate sob slips free.

"It's going to be alright. I won't let them hurt you," I tell her, rubbing her back with one hand. I held her without expecting anything, so when her arms wrap around my waist, I break too.

Game's over, Snowball, they're coming your way, Shawn says down the bond. I look over and meet his eyes briefly, grateful not to have just been swarmed.

"You have to go. They're coming, and they'll know you've been crying," I tell her. She slips into the elevator just as it opens, the doors closing behind her just in time for the sweaty mass of soccer players to flood the lobby, erasing every lingering trace of her very pregnant scent. I wait until they've all passed me by—ever the insipid wallflower—and then I take the stairs out of the sublevels. Greyson is waiting for me when I reach Medical.

"You said you needed my help?" I ask, leaving the lights off until we reach the exam room. I keep my face turned away for as long as I can, hoping the tear tracks will dry before I look at him. He abandons his bag and shirt in one of the chairs and climbs obediently onto the table. He pulls his knees to his chest and wraps his arms around them like he might actually try to disappear, but all it does is highlight the angry bruising along his shoulder blade and the broad expanse of his back.

He should be healing faster than this, I think to myself as I pull on gloves.

"You'll work while I talk, right? I don't know why it hurts so bad," he says. I nod.

"You've definitely done more damage these past few days. Try to hold still," I tell him. He uncurls and then realizes that he's moving and goes still, staring at a fixed point on the wall ahead of him. "I really need to operate, sooner rather than later, before any of the damage becomes permanent."

I press my fingers into the bruising and feel around the joint as carefully as I can, expecting that he'll start talking. He doesn't.

"Something tells me that you've got a lot to say—and this isn't won't take me long," I say, hoping that it'll prompt him to start talking. The door is closed and Medical is soundproof, so there's no need to whisper or risk being overheard.

Greyson takes a terribly deep breath that makes my lungs burn, and then he starts talking.

He doesn't stop for nearly fifteen minutes.

He tells me about his father, the Blackwood Alpha, and about the treaty that Mikael has been negotiating since he was a child. He tells me about how he accepted his fate before his selection and about how he didn't mean to fall in love with Aviva.

He tells me about Elisabeth Kivleneiks and how she's

nothing like her mother.

Then, when I think it can't get any more complicated, he tells me about the letter his father sent him and the expectation he has that the treaty will move forward as planned. He tells me that now that he has Aviva, he can't let that happen. That he doesn't want to be the kind of man who runs away when a baby is involved.

It's the first confirmation I've gotten that he's the baby's father, and I'm sure Aviva would be furious to know that I had any doubts at all.

"You just found out, didn't you?" I ask. "About the baby?"

"I suspected. Things have been... tense, since we've been here, but you notice things. I confronted her about it earlier today, and she told me it was true," he admits.

The thing is, I know Greyson Marquis. Asking me for help is probably the hardest thing he's ever done—and I know he'd do it again if he had to. I continue working on his shoulder and waiting for him to speak, but he doesn't. When I declare him finished, he grabs his shirt and squares his shoulders.

"I have to marry her. She doesn't deserve to live her life branded like that—an unmarried mother. That's a shame she'd never escape." He doesn't even breathe. "I can't fix this until you fix the mess my father made for me. I don't want to be that kind of man."

Something in my stomach tightens. I can't tell him I don't know how to help. So, I don't. I take off my gloves, smile, and promise to do everything I can.

15
Aliyah

After I leave Greyson, I wander aimlessly until I end up at the falls. It's becoming a trend, I fear. I'm looking for peace, hoping that if I think about the situation long enough, I'll be able to find a path through the chaos. Instead, I find my Keeper sitting on a rock, talking to the nomad girl I met a few days ago. Saya, I remember.

Saya's sitting cross-legged just beyond the boundary line, and Cici mirrors her a few feet inside the wards—where she always seems to stay.

"You two seem to be hitting it off," I say, mostly just to announce myself so I don't startle them. Exceptional hearing is only so good when you're dealing with forest creatures who move with little to no sound in the first place.

"She's quite the character, your Keeper. She reminds me a bit of my mother," Saya says as Cici jumps to her feet and comes to guide me over.

"We were just talking about you," she says. I sit beside her, leaning forward onto my knees. I don't like being the subject of conversations I'm not part of, so I let it pass. Instead, I think about the wards. I don't realize I've zoned out until Saya cocks her head and Cici clears her throat.

"Something is bothering you," Cici says. Saya is looking back and forth between us, and she arches an overplucked eyebrow at me as she watches us. I say nothing. The same unsettling feeling settles over me, and I push it away.

"We won't push you to talk, but we'll listen if you want to," Saya says, and I don't know what it is about the statement that makes my stomach twist.

"Have you ever felt the weight of the world pressing down on you so hard your knees are about to give out?" I know Cici has, and the nomad girl nods immediately. I turn my head and stare at the falling water, like the answers to all of my questions are hidden there among the rocks.

"We might be able to help, if you want to try to talk it out," Cici says. They're both watching me watch the water, and I know that if I turn my head, there will be concern and pity in their eyes. The longer I sit, the more I can smell them. The familiar sunflower and apple scent of Cici combines with the spicy floral scent of Saya and the warm green scent of the trees to make the air I breathe feel alive. There's crisp mountain air in the scent of them—I swear I can taste the cold.

"I have to write a letter that might start a war, and as soon as I do, my pack could be disbanded," I admit, closing my eyes and taking a deep breath before I look at them.

"Someone's broken a rule, haven't they?" Saya asks, her eyes searching my face in that oddly inquisitive way that seems to tell her my secrets. Each word lifts, giving the question a hauntingly musical quality.

"Yeah. Yeah, they have," I say, sounding completely

defeated. "We have a strict set of behavioral rules we have to follow during the first year and a slightly less intense set for the second year. They're non-negotiable."

"What kind of rules are we talking about?" Saya asks. Cici answers for me, and I should be grateful, but I just feel numb.

"They're under lockdown for the first five months —they can't leave the reservation, and only official representatives can enter. For the first nine, their Alpha can be replaced without cause. No mating, no mating ceremonies, no treaty talks, no extended time away for a year. No voting either. They can't negotiate or have children until they're officially independent at the end of year two." It's a good summary, even if it is just the highlights.

"We can't declare loyalties, speak in diplomatic settings, or accumulate wealth during the first two years. At the end of year two, we petition the Council of Elders for our rights—and they have to accept it before we're granted independence. It's supposed to be like training wheels. A support system. Now it feels like a noose," I tell Saya. I drag my hands through my hair and pull through the snags. Anything would be better than this—this vast, awful nothingness I can't seem to shake. The hollowness in my chest is rapidly filling with something heavy —sorrow, maybe. Helplessness, even.

"Which rule was it?"

The first thing that returns when the dam breaks is dread—cold and heavy in the pit of my stomach. The words won't come. I reach and reach, but I can't control my mouth. When I don't answer, Cici turns to look at me.

"Ali, which—" she stops. Looks closer. At the tear tracks I know are still visible. I imagine that the dim light is making them even more obvious. "Someone's pregnant."

Devastation crashes over me, tangled with the feeling of utter failure. I sob into my knees so the sound doesn't carry through the trees. Cici crawls through the dirt to me and takes my hands. She says my name—I can't hear it. There's nothing but the roaring of the falls in my ears.

"I can help," Neither of us looks when Saya speaks. "Cristiana, bring her here. If I can touch her, I can help."

Cici glances at her, then at me—like she doesn't know what to do with the unraveling she's watching. It's worse than that—my body shakes, completely beyond my control.

"If you hurt her, I'll kill you myself," Cici warns. She slides her arms under my body and stands up to take me to the wards. I watch each step she takes from beyond my body—literally coming and going as my magic flares and sputters.

I'm still sobbing when Saya grits her teeth and reaches through the wards. Her scream comes immediately, but she doesn't jerk back. She closes her hand around my wrist and holds on, the pain sending beads of sweat running down her face.

She doesn't yield to the vicious burning—I know she feels it. At first, nothing changes.

Then, something shifts. Like rivulets of water, my hysteria flows down her arm. Her magic is the same unreal shade of blue as her eyes.

I watch. She does not let the pain take hold of her. Those blue eyes stay fixed on me, and she holds on, body shaking as she continues to subject herself to the ward magic.

The weight on my chest lifts. The burning in my lungs eases. The rush of cool air that fills my chest is ecstasy

She's panting, squeezing harder—pulling and pulling until the drain opens wide and every ounce of devastation, shame, and fear spirals down through the hole at the base of my soul.

When she lets go, I can tell it isn't voluntary. She falls back into the dirt, clutching her arm to her chest as her body spasms. Her skin is blistered and swollen from her fingers to her ear—the entire right side of her body looks like it's melting. The blood that flows from her arm stains her faded shirt—she'll need stitches, and it will still scar.

"I can fix that," I say, choking on the scratchiness of my voice. Saya eyes me skeptically, and I understand why. "You'll have to reach through again so I can heal it. If you don't, it'll take days—and it could get infected. I can fix it."

She looks at Cici, who nods—quiet but firm. I wonder if Cici knows, but nothing in her face tells me anything.

"I'll be fast, I promise," I tell her. She nods and braces herself like she's going to reach the burned arm back through. I panic. "The other one. Use the other arm."

The look of relief on her face is nearly comical. I hold out my hand, and when she reaches through, I grip her arm firmly and sink my fangs into the freckled skin. I hold the bite for a few seconds, and when I'm sure enough venom has passed through, I release it and let her withdraw her arm again. The four punctures heal over before she's fully retreated, and we all watch as the redness fades.

The wound lightens and the blood stops—then, her skin begins to stitch itself together. Pure astonishment is written on every line of her face. The look is mirrored on Cici's, and it makes me smile. I like knowing that they'll get to see the good I can do before I have to tell them about Aviva and the damage I'm going to do on her behalf.

As if there were ever a chance that I would choose any other path.

I start slowly, working past the hoarseness that clings to

my voice and wishing desperately for a long drink of the water that's just out of reach.

I tell them about the baby first—how Aviva could be forced to terminate, and how she'd never forgive herself. I tell them about the sanctions we would face if the Elders found out and about the possibility that the mother and baby could be forced to return to their former pack, if conception happened before we got to Noonchester Falls.

I save the political ramifications for last and take my time to explain the alliance that's being thrown away, the first that the Buria have ever willingly negotiated.

"What does the father have to say about it?" Cici asks, and I know that she's smart enough to have figured out it's Aviva and Greyson, even though I've been careful not to say so. I don't know this nomad well enough to trust that she won't run off and tell the world our secrets. I'm only trusting her with this much because I need to tell someone, and they're the first people I found that have no direct involvement in any of it.

"He loves her, I think. Or I think he thinks he does. I'm not really sure about how their relationship developed or how they feel. I think he cares about her more than she'll ever be able to care about him, and that breaks my heart," I tell them. I've moved back away from the wards again, and so has Cici, but only she keeps looking at them, and I'm starting to understand why. There's nothing but a faint trace left of the wound on Saya's arm, but I won't soon forget the screams she let out.

"You say he may not love her, but he's willing to throw away this alliance and this other girl for her, even knowing the risks. Would he do that if he didn't love her?" Saya asks. I still hate the sound of her voice, but it grates on me less the more I hear it.

"Yes. I think he would. For the baby—he would," I say,

because I know it's true.

"What about the other girl? The betrothed? You said they were supposed to marry at the new year, right? How does he feel about her?" Cici asks, and I realize I don't actually have an answer. I've only ever met Elisabeth Kivleneiks a few times, always in settings that require evening gowns and heirloom jewelry, and I've never talked to Greyson about her. Not at length anyway. So I tell her that.

"I don't know much about the other girl or their relationship. I assume it was a completely arranged marriage, but I don't know that either," I say. Cici is fiddling with the tattered edge of the sleeve on her waffle knit shirt and looking into the middle distance.

"Under Heritage Law, the moment a new pack is established, its Alpha becomes the ultimate authority. Any former rules, decrees, or obligations? Voided." She explains automatically—like she's reading. Her magic is thick in the air around her, and all I can smell is the scent of apple and moss that's radiating off her. I think it's her shampoo, because it's different from her usual scent. "Technically, the moment he became Trevonaire, the arrangement was terminated. You don't have to honor it. You don't even have to acknowledge it."

"He wants me to acknowledge it. Asked me to write a letter formally releasing him from the obligation—so he can be a father to the baby and a partner to the mother."

"It's the polite thing to do, but your Keeper is right, you don't have to," Saya says. "Really, as far as the pregnant girl goes, you only have two options."

"And those are?" I ask, already regretting the question—but needing the answer more.

"You either hide it or you own up to it. If the boy marries and mates with the mother, it'll make it easier for them to forgive, but they're still going to be upset," she says. I know she's right, but it doesn't help. I think back on the sight of Greyson and Aviva together and wonder if they would be happy as a mated pair.

They both deserve to be happy.

"If you hide it, you might protect them in the short term —but you're gambling with a much bigger fallout later. If you own up to it and claim the child outright, they'll punish you immediately and ultimately respect the transparency. They'll give you points for acknowledging your mistakes, but they'll still punish you for them to save face with the others. And there could be consequences beyond the Council of Elders that you have to consider," Cici says. Whatever has her focused on that middle distance releases her, and her magic settles as she turns to look at me again.

"So now the question of a lifetime is, do I dare? Do I dare to tell them what we did and take the risk?"

I don't know if I'm that brave, but it's what they deserve.

Of course I dare.

For them, I'll set the world on fire and call it a full moon. As though there was ever any chance of anything less.

16
Aliyah

Anya Kivleneiks:

My name is Aliyah Trevonaire. You may be familiar with me by name or title, or you may not. Either way, I am writing to you now not out of obligation, but out of respect—both for your station and for the weight of the decision I've had to make.

As of yesterday, I became aware of an intended alliance between your house and the Blackwoods, to be enacted through the marriage of Elisabeth Kivleneiks and Greyson Marquis. My understanding is that the union was scheduled for the coming New Year. However, as Mr. Marquis is now a member of the Trevonaire Pack. He is under my protection, governed by my law, and subject to my judgment. I alone determine what alliances are made by, for, and with my people.

With that in mind, I have taken some time to consider the situation as it has been presented. As a result of my time spent in contemplation, I have decided that I will not be honoring the arrangement made prior to our transition to this territory. That decision rests with me now, and I've made it. The marriage will not move forward. Should Mr. Marquis choose a different path for himself in the future, that will be his choice to make—but he will not be forced into an obligation that no longer serves his reality.

If your house still intends to pursue an alliance with the Blackwoods, I suggest you reach out to Mikael Marquis directly. I speak only for my pack, and I make no claims over his.

I regret any strain or inconvenience this decision may cause, but I believe in facing difficult truths head-on. If you wish to discuss the matter further, you are welcome to bring your concerns to my Sanctuary, where we can speak plainly as equals.

Best,

Aliyah Trevonaire, Alpha – Noonchester Falls

Aliyah Nathair:

I have received your correspondence and taken the time to review it in full. When a letter arrived—from Noonchester Falls of all places—sealed with your compass rose, I confess I was unsure what to expect. I did not anticipate disappointment, but alas, that is what you've given me.

Still, I am not without grace.

As a courtesy, and in the interest of preventing you from stepping blindly into a mistake of consequence, I am extending to you something I have never offered before: the opportunity to reconsider.

You are newly positioned, young, and no doubt eager to

prove yourself. I understand that. Your current course places your people at a distinct disadvantage—one I doubt you have been able to truly understand or consider during your "contemplation." You are not yet in a position to spurn longstanding agreements without incurring real cost.

Should you choose instead to honor the original arrangement and allow the union between Greyson Marquis and Elisabeth Kivleneiks to proceed as intended, you will gain far more than a marriage. You will receive my daughter, as tradition dictates, and in doing so, you will earn the formal alliance of the Kivleneiks—along with every privilege such an alliance affords.

If your decision changes before the next full moon, I believe we can move forward as though this little misunderstanding never occurred at all—an offer I believe will underline the seriousness of these circumstances and my desire for us to come to a mutually beneficial understanding.

To assist you in seeing matters more clearly, I will be sending Elisabeth to Noonchester Falls. She will arrive in your Sanctuary as our official envoy in three days' time and will remain there until the full moon rises. She will celebrate the moon with you, and you may send your revised decision back with her upon her departure.

I trust that you will treat her with all the respect due to her by name and position. She is, as you know, my only child and heir. Rest assured that I will respond to any transgression executed against her with swift and proportional force.

Choose wisely,

Anya Kivleneiks – Alpha

I've barely finished reading the letter when the door to my office whips open. All three of my Betas—looking unhinged and nearly frantic—try to cram themselves into the doorway at the same time. I know I stare at them for at least ten full seconds before anyone actually says anything.

To his own surprise, it's Greyson who speaks.

"We're *very* sorry to have disturbed you," he says, formal to conceal his panic. "But Mikael Marquis is waiting for you in the Sanctuary and growing very restless."

I look up—sure enough, the blue light above the door is lit.

"How long has he been here?" I ask. Greyson winces.

"Not very long. He's not a very patient man," he says. He looks like he might throw up on my rug at any second, but I'm impressed by the way he's holding himself together. I can barely see the fear in his eyes, even though I can smell it coming off him in waves. I leave the letter and make my way to the Sanctuary, letting them follow me as far as the door and then turning around to face them. Long before I reach the door, I can hear them—their hearts are steady, except for one.

"All of you, go read the letter on my desk. Wait in my office for me and I'll come back as soon as I'm finished," I tell them. Immediately, Kelly shakes his head.

"One of us should be in there with you," he says, and technically, I know he's right.

"Rose," I shout, knowing that there's no way she's far away. I hear her light footsteps immediately—she's in my doorway a second later. "I need you to come to a meeting with me. You're being given the rank Delta, effective immediately. Inform Elijah and Rachelle that they've also been given Delta rank and send them to guard the nomad girl who has been staying just outside the border."

There's a feeling building in my gut, and a storm on the horizon, I know I don't understand. I have to let my instincts lead.

Shawn drags Greyson and Kelly out of the room with him when he leaves. When I look at Rose, there's pride etched into every like of her feline face.

"Who is it?" She asks, jerking her chin at the sanctuary door and the blue light above.

"Mikael Marquis," a moment of silence. "Greyson's father."

She winces, but the trace of insecurity I see in her slight shoulders comes and goes in the span of a heartbeat. Everything about her reads as calm—except the harsh slash of her slitted pupils. *Predator,* they scream.

"Are you ready?"

"Are you?"

"Not at all," I admit. She gives me a slow once over and smiles.

"You look hot, so you'll be fine," she says. She winks and I laugh without really meaning to. I take her hand and squeeze, then open the door and step forward into the sanctuary, my face blank.

If I nearly break the handle off the door, well, no one has to know.

I don't have a lot of expectations when I open the door, but an official delegation was very, very low on my list of possibilities.

I actually think I'm hallucinating when I see them.

Mikael Marquis, Alpha of the Blackwoods and Archimedes Landing, looks like he has been pacing for hours—when he sees me, every member of the delegation straightens. They look like they've been watching his trainwreck since they got here. The most interesting person in the delegation isn't Mikael, though. No, that award goes to the woman standing just left of center in the ranks. Shoulder-length blonde hair is held away from her face with a bone clip that looks out of place with her official attire. Her eyes are soft. Her lightly lined face shows no signs of tension—her long body is loose and open.

I know her immediately—Greyson's mother. I can't remember her name.

Delilah. Greyson offers helpfully, lingering in the open connection between us in hopes that he'll hear something. I close the mental door on him as gently as I can —his indignant squawk nearly gets a laugh out of me. At his wife's gentle prompting, Mikael notices me and comes to an abrupt stop—a meaty finger pointed directly at my face.

"What have you done?"

"I'm afraid you'll have to be more specific, Sir," I tell him, clasping my hands loosely behind my back and taking a slow breath to give off the illusion of calm. It's an exercise my mother taught me, a way to look steady in a situation you can't control or predict.

"Aliyah, this isn't a game," he says, and his familiarity grates. Rose steps between us and holds up a hand, halting him mid-stride as he tries to approach. Her claws are not extended, but her long nails have the same effect.

He shrinks away from her—recognition flashing.

"You will speak to my Alpha with respect. I will only remind you once," she says. He looks like he's going to dismiss her altogether until he meets her eyes. There's bloodshed in them. I know, because I see it in the way her hackles raise.

"Ms. Trevonaire," Delilah's long fingers curl around Mikael's arm—guiding him back away from us. "I assure you, my husband didn't mean any insult."

There is it. Now, power is speaking.

"I believe that, Delilah. He would do well, however, to

remember that I am no longer just the Healer's apprentice. We're equals now, he and I," Mikael's fury disappears behind her elegant shoulder—everything about her radiates class and poise.

Too bad she married an oaf, Rose chirps—there's no trace of the smile I hear on her face.

To my surprise, there is laughter in Delilah's blue eyes. Mikael looks like I've slapped him, and she seems to enjoy it. I've never seen Mikael so incensed. I instinctively know that this is the most dangerous he has ever been—the primal part of me fights to bare its teeth.

"The situation is delicate, as I'm sure you can understand, and we're hoping to reach a peaceful resolution that works for everyone." She still has her hand on Mikael's arm. Her wedding band winks in the light—I make a mental note to ask Greyson about them when I can.

Now more grounded, Mikael squares his shoulders and blows out a long breath.

I wonder what she said to him. So do I.

"I received a letter this morning indicating that you have no intention of honoring the peace treaty I've spent decades building. The letter implies that your first official decision as Alpha is going to be to dissolve my years of hard work without so much as justifying your course of action." He looks like he wants to keep talking, but a squeeze of Delilah's hand brings him up short. The corner of her mouth tightens briefly.

"Forgive me if this comes across differently than I intend for it to, but what business is it of yours what decision I have made?" I ask. I look at him—but I'm asking her. The entire delegation looks at me with wide, scared eyes. Mikael sucks in an angry breath—Delilah simply blinks.

"You foolish little..." he starts. A beat of silence stretches out between us, thick and heavy. Even Delilah doesn't try to diffuse the tension.

The entire delegation remains perfectly still.

"Ms. Trevonaire, this treaty isn't some frivolous diplomatic affair. This is a chance at true peace," he says. "Anya Kivleneiks is a cruel, violent leader, and she won't take kindly to this dismissal. This could be considered a declaration of war."

"Aliyah," she purrs my name in a way that pricks my skin. "We already have reason to believe Anya Kivleneiks is responsible for your mother's death. Do you really want to risk drawing her attention if it's true?"

I see it then—the slithering thing inside her bares its fangs, and when I begin to recoil, Rose is there.

You will not back down from this woman, do you hear me? You will keep it together until you've dismissed them and fall apart when they're gone. Don't let her think she's winning. Whisper close inside my mind, Rose's voice wraps me in armor. I can feel her steel through the bond, and I lean into it, drawing her strength into me until I can raise my chin and smile. The snake in me coils.

"I sincerely apologize that you've all had to waste your day traveling here, but my decision on this matter is final. If your treaty is more important to you than your son, I'm sorry, but I cannot and will not help you. You are dismissed."

We turn and—with Rose at my back—I walk out of the Sanctuary.

The door is only barely closed when I fall to my knees and *scream*.

17
Aliyah

"You should have told me who you were going to piss off." Saya crashes through the brush, beating her fist against the wards. I hear her flesh sizzle, but she doesn't seem to notice. My mouth starts moving before I have the chance to stop it.

"You don't get to tell me what I should do or what information I should feel inclined to share with you." Then confusion gets the best of me. "Now, what? Who did I piss off and why should I have told you?"

Elijah and Rachelle come stumbling through the trees like Saya outran them. They flank me—sharing looks of confusion and dismay. I don't acknowledge them. When I try to focus on the nomad girl, my vision blurs.

"Anya Kivleneiks is *dangerous,*" she says, her blue eyes wide with fear. There's blood staining her jeans, like she ran toward me blindly and shredded her legs in the brush. I don't offer to heal her this time. "You are playing with something far worse than fire, and you don't even know it."

It's a whisper—let loose into the world completely involuntarily. Still standing before me, she's lost somewhere deep inside her own mind—hands trembling at her sides.

"Is that a threat?" Rachelle growls. I shake my head, and she backs down.

"No, it's a fact," she snaps. She's with us again—present. "You've never met her, never seen what happens when you make her angry, but I have. Leighann has."

She shuts her mouth so fast that her teeth clash. She can't take the words back—she has my full attention now. The fog in my vision clears, and my eyes lock on her face. On the scars that linger.

Something in me screams to pay attention, but I can't find what I'm looking for, and no answers come when I try to think about it.

"You're one of the nomads from her troop," I breathe—tears well in her eyes. Whatever this woman, this Alpha, has done to her has left scars deep in her soul. I can see them now, silver and shining as the tears roll down her face.

We wait.

"Anya is a collector. She finds people that she wants, and then she finds ways to get them. Pack members, nomads, free people, it doesn't matter. She's..." She exhales and turns away from us to try and get a grip on herself. There are still tears in her eyes when she looks at me again. "I know you've noticed the scent of the boy that lingers on me."

I think about it for a second, taking a discrete breath through my nose, and I realize she's right. Under the scent of her, there's another one. This one is spices and cigarettes and cold air, but it's drenched in blood and fear.

A death stench.

My stomach twists like it has every time she has been too close, and I realize that he's why. It's his fear bleeding over, the scent of him screams wrongness—his final warning.

"She's the reason that he's gone—and he's not the first. She wasn't even after *him*. Your little girl was in her grasp. She got lucky that day when the Blackwoods found her," she says. Elijah tenses behind me.

"Explain yourself," he demands, and she does.

"Nomads are either born nomads or they become nomadic by leaving their packs and refusing to settle anywhere new. Leighann and her sister were born nomads—to nomadic parents who might have even had nomadic parents. But they were special." She takes a painful, shuddering breath. "Rumors of their gifts spread, and it didn't take long before they reached Anya."

The mention of her sends goosebumps over what little of her skin I can see. "Within months, she pulled them into her orbit. As long as the girls remained on the reservation, their parents were allowed to come and go. Until one day when they just didn't come back."

Until one day they just didn't come back, I repeat to myself. And then the important part kicks in.

This girl knows about the Verdigris girls.

This girl knows about Maeve.

Fuck.

"We need to decide how we're handling the baby," I say as I enter my office. The door swings shut behind me, and I take a seat at my desk. Greyson sags in his chair.

"By my guess, we have about forty-six days until we

won't have a say anymore," he says, closing his eyes and pressing his fingers into them like he's developing a headache. I write the number forty-six down on a sticky.

"How did this happen, exactly?" Shawn asks. I don't look at Kelly, but I can feel him winding up for a birds-and-bees joke. I shut him down before he opens his mouth.

"What's the worst that happens if we come clean?" Greyson asks me, looking like he might already have figured out the answer on his own.

"That depends. Does this mean the baby was conceived before we arrived here?" I ask, holding up the sticky for him to see. Aviva hasn't let me examine her, so it's the first hint I've gotten about a timeline. Greyson nods. "Well, then Aviva was Nathair at the time of conception and my father could demand that she return to the reservation. You aren't married and we're underage. He could use the baby as a bargaining chip to try and put Aviva in charge of the Aiyanik."

"He might even use them as a bargaining chip to try and get you back to Tamarak. Why settle for the spare if you can have the heir?" Kelly says. I hadn't thought about it that way.

"He could. And he would likely have enough support to do it without Demetria being able to stop it," I say. "He's the least of our worries though. The Elders are going to be furious."

"And if we hide it?" Greyson asks, pressing his full lips into a thin line.

"We'd risk heavier penalties and complete dissolution if it ever came out. If we could hide it until our two years are up, dissolution would come off the table, but our rights would be up for suspension," I sit back in my chair for a second, but it feels wrong to pretend I'm relaxed.

"The baby is royal. Nathair by blood, just like you and Aviva. It will be born with a claim to Tamarak that wasn't negotiated in the expansion," Kelly says, examining something in the middle distance and looking less engaged than a goldfish.

"I'd lose my rights," Greyson gasps, eyes flashing. I hate that he's right. I want to argue that no one would actually put an infant in charge, but I know I have no ground to stand on.

This had been a year of unprecedented choices, after all. And it isn't unheard of for a regent to lead until an Alpha comes of age. A regent like the former King—my father.

"What if there's a third option?"

I can't explain the feeling that seizes me as the other path opens in my mind. Something golden shimmers at the edge of my awareness and I wonder how I didn't think of it before.

"Third option?" Greyson repeats.

"We're only restricted by the Council of Elders and their rules because we're on track to *join* the Council of Elders," I say, each word clearing the image in my mind.

"If we declared out intention to remain independent—"

Kelly's with us again, following the thread as clearly as I am.

"The admissions restrictions would no longer apply," I hesitate. "But we'd be stripped of their protections."

"We'd lose our wards—our Keeper," Shawn adds. He's making a valiant effort not to look terrified, but it isn't working.

"Why are we even considering any other option? If that's the price to keep you, Aviva, Greyson, and a baby, I'm willing to pay it," Kelly says. He must feel passionate about it, because he's nearly out of his seat and talking so loudly that it almost hurts. At least my office is soundproof.

"Because it would leave us vulnerable. We'd have no real connection to our land, and without Cici, we'd have nothing to anchor new wards to, even if we could find someone to build them for us," Greyson says. He looks like he wants desperately to believe there's a way to make it work, but I can see his confidence fading by the second.

I think back to that night at the falls and of the two hours that turned to three as we waited for the land to rally her magic.

I think of Cici, all but dead on the cold ground. That sapphire winking in the moonlight as the lang fought for her. Fought for her like we will.

"I'll find a way to make it work, okay? I will."

"You look like hell."

Greyson raises his head and smiles at me, but it doesn't reach his eyes. I can't tell if his skin is actually tinged grey or if it's charcoal, but I don't think either one is a good sign. I sit down on the floor of the little soundproof room he has commandeered and fold my legs under me to keep them out of his way.

"I talked to Saya today," he says, and I know he's trying to distract me from what's actually got him all worked up. His shoulders are practically at his ears, and it looks like it hurts.

"Nice try. What's up?" I ask, leaning back against the wall so I can watch him and also remain relaxed. He doesn't need my stress on top of his own.

"What do you mean?"

"I mean, I need you to be honest with me about what has you looking like you're going to your own funeral," I tell him. He laughs, and a fraction of the tension in the room dissipates.

"Close that," he tells me, jerking his chin in the direction of the door. I lean awkwardly until I can reach the handle, then swing it closed without getting up off of the ground. He laughs and as the door closes and makes the room soundproof, the sound bounces around and around the small space like music.

"I need more of that and less of whatever else you've got going on, so tell me how I can help," I tell him, resituating myself so I'm comfortable enough to focus only on him.

"I don't think I've actually come to terms with any of it," he admits, putting down the length of charcoal he's holding and wiping his stained fingers on his jeans.

"The baby, Elisabeth, Aviva, or all of the above?"

"The first two, mostly. But kind of all three."

"Okay, so talk me through it. What are you stuck on?" I ask. He looks at me and then at the clock on the wall and shakes his head. I flex the muscles that control my magic, and the hands of the clock stop moving. "Don't worry about time, we have plenty of it."

"Where do I start?" he asks, and he sounds so miserable that it makes my heart hurt.

"How about you start with whatever part hurts the worst? Let's get that out of the way first," I suggest. He opens his mouth and where I expect to hear him say Aviva's name, he says Elisabeth's.

He tells me about their childhood and how they were friends while they attended school in the Neutral Lands. Best friends, even if what I hear in his voice is real. He tells me about the years they spent chasing each other around and around on the playground, telling each other secrets and stories while they drank their apple juice and sandwiches at lunchtime. He tells me about the jokes that they endured during those years, about being Royalty, and about how Elisabeth never once hesitated to stand up for them both, planting herself between him and anyone who dared to tease him. He tells me that he was content to take the abuse and that all she ever did was tell him how he didn't deserve it.

There seems to be some irony in that, but I don't say so.

He tells me about Anya finding out about their friendship, even though Elisabeth tried for years to keep it a secret, and about how finding out that she wanted to hide it in the first place really hurt his feelings, until he understood why.

They were ten when Elisabeth was pulled out of school and taken back to her reservation to continue her education, he says. They weren't even eleven when the first whispers of news about an alliance started to spread and when he saw her again, everything about her had changed.

At her mother's request, Elisabeth began pursuing him. She would walk in on him in the bathroom or jump into the shower with him as an excuse for him to see her naked. He tells me about the look in her eyes every time she did something that made her feel disgusted with herself, and how he never could reach her after that. How she shut herself away behind glass so thick that no words would break through.

He tells me about drawing her for her sixteenth birthday, and about her showing up in Archimedes the next day, sobbing into his shoulder as she tells him that they're going to be forced to marry. And then, as though my heart can break into any smaller pieces, he tells me that he would have been happy to marry her.

Not because he was in love with her, even though he could have easily learned to love her, but because it would have gotten her out of the Elizabethan Mountains, away from her mother.

Because marrying her would have protected her from her mother. Because he could have protected her from her mother.

"And then I met Aviva," he says. He's been talking for so long that he has to stop and take a drink to keep his voice from cracking.

"When was that?" I ask, curious to see if he'll tell me, since she never did.

"Less than a year ago. Last summer, at a full moon party in the Neutral Lands. I had no idea who she was, but she knew me. I was looking for Elisabeth among the crowd of faces, hoping that I would find her so I would know she was okay, but I couldn't. Aviva intercepted me while I was looking and handed me a bottle of wine," he says, and I know he's hiding something.

"Why wouldn't she have been okay?" I ask him. He shakes his head.

"I can't," he says, and there's panic in his eyes.

"Okay. You don't have to. Keep going."

He tells me about Aviva and how she insisted he drink with her. Dance with her. Focus on her. He tells me about losing track of time by the third bottle of wine and falling into bed with her for the night, so drunk that he didn't even realize he needed to be careful until the next morning.

Everything he tells me about the way their relationship formed feels like it lines up with what I know about my sister. He tells me that after that night, they woke up together and he asked her name, only to nearly drop dead when she told him. He tells me that she showed up in Archimedes demanding that they go on a picnic a few days later, and how she texted him daily until he was so in love with her that her name didn't matter anymore. Until what he did didn't matter anymore.

"For what it's worth," I tell him, hoping to ease the crinkle between his eyebrows. "Our mother gave us the freedom to make our own matches. She introduces us to potential suitors sometimes, but the decision was always ours. As long as we were happy and we didn't bring home anyone dangerous, she would have been happy for us."

"Would she have been happy to hear that Aviva was pregnant and unmated?" he asks bitterly. I shake my head and shrug.

"Probably not. Not for personal reasons, though. It would have been all about the line of succession to her, about Aviva taking that kind of risk. She wouldn't have wanted there to be any chance that Mikael could have claimed the child. It would have been her nightmare because it would have made Aviva and me vulnerable, especially if the child were male. Not everyone is as open to the idea of a female Alpha as the people of Tamarak are," I explain. He seems to understand it, but I can tell something is still eating at him. I don't push.

As I listen, he tells me about their summer and about being so in love that they hardly noticed the time passing. And then he tells me about the night the selections were finalized, and it was made public who would be going to Noonchester Falls—still unnamed at the time. He tells me about her showing up in his room in the middle of the night with a bottle of champagne and a vibrant smile on her face.

"She was so convinced that it was a sign. That she was going to be Alpha and we were going to be together on the new reservation, where no one could tell us anything, and we could be happy. She believed it so much that I think I did too, and I let myself think it could be that easy," he says. He takes a deep breath. "I didn't think of Elisabeth or the treaty until after I'd snuck her back across the border and Leighann asked me why I smelled like you. It took her a few tries to notice enough of the differences in your scents to realize it was Aviva."

"So she knew?"

"I think she always knew. She likes Elisabeth, they get along really well, but she also likes things that make me happy. I think she intentionally didn't say anything until that day, and I think it's her asking that really made me stop and think about what I was doing," he says. He looks at the clock and laughs at himself when he remembers that it isn't moving.

"The treaty was common knowledge in Archimedes?" I ask. He shakes his head.

"No, not at all. But enough people knew to make it the worst-kept secret of its time," he tells me. "I think that's the night she got pregnant."

I want to tell him that he's wrong, but I can't. I want to tell him that it was an accident, or perfect timing, or anything other than a strategic and perfectly calculated risk, but I can't. So instead, I change the subject.

"Did you ever see Elisabeth again, after that?" I ask. He shakes his head immediately.

"No. She was in the hospital with a fractured skull and under constant guard. She might still be. I haven't heard anything since one of our mutual friends slipped me a note telling me she was alive," he sounds worried, and I don't blame him.

"You think you're the reason she was in the hospital?" I ask him. His face darkens, and he sighs.

"I know I am."

"That seems like a heavy thing to carry around all the time," I tell him. He nods and wipes his eyes.

"She's a good person, Ali. She didn't deserve any of this. If I had stayed on the path and not... not fallen in love with Aviva while I was already supposed to marry someone else, she wouldn't be in this situation. She never would have ended up in that hospital bed and we wouldn't have to figure out how to handle unexpected babies or the breaking of a treaty we didn't write," he drops his head until his hands and leans forward, his body shaking like the panic he's been trying to keep buried might finally be breaking free.

"I need you to tell me what you want me to do, Greyson," I say, giving him plenty of time to get control of himself.

"What do you mean?"

"I mean, I will do whatever you ask me to. If you want me to find a way to bring Elisabeth here, treaty or no treaty, I'll do it. If you want me to find a way for you to marry Aviva, I'll do that too. But you are the only one that can make that decision," the silence stretches out between us.

"What if I don't know what I want?"

"Then that's okay too, because you can focus on being a good dad until you figure it out. That part is going to stay the same, no matter what choice you make," he nods and stares down at his sneakers for a long time before he meets my eyes.

"Thank you," he says softly. "For not judging me."

"Oh, please, I do not have room for that in here," I tell him, tapping my head with my finger and smiling. I wink at him and release my hold on my magic so the clock can resume its slow ticking. You'd think that fifty-nine hours would be enough for a day, but I often find myself desperate for a few more. "We're going to get through this, one way or another."

"I believe you," he says, and I think he really does.

I leave him to his charcoals and return to my office several floors above, where I sit down in my chair and let myself have a few minutes to process everything he said.

When I'm able, I begin to plan for both possibilities.

18
Greyson

"Sarah!" I yell. The girl doesn't turn.

Saya, you moron. Her name is Saya. Ali says, her laughter mocking as it fills the inside of my head. I raise my voice and try again.

"Saya!" She tenses immediately and turns slowly toward the sound of my voice. She's beyond the border, almost invisible amongst the trunks of the trees and the shadows in the underbrush. Her eyes are like a flash of light amongst the darkness, centering my gaze on the shadowy place that is her face.

"Can I help you?" She says, her voice just as strange as Ali claimed it was, and tinged with uncertainty. Her dark form remains still as she watches me watch her, neither of us sure we should be having this conversation. Neither willing to walk away without finding out what the other will say, too. Her pale hands swing around and clasp at her waist, the pale skin of her fingers adding to what I can see in the dark. But it's her face that stands out.

The scars are too perfect.

"I wanted to ask you something about Leighann," I tell her, suddenly not sure where I should begin. I know I'm right. I have to be. I just don't know how to ask the right questions for this, how to draw out the right answers.

Aviva would know, but I don't think she has a place here. I don't think Saya would tell me anything if she were here. I get the feeling that she isn't fond of people, and Aviva has a way of putting everyone on edge.

Even me.

"Leighann," she says, and I can't tell if there's any recognition there. I hear nothing in her voice, and she's too far away for me to see anything in her eyes.

"You know her, don't you? Or, you used to?" I sound desperate, but I suppose that's because I am. It can't hurt to let her hear it, let her see how much love I have for that little girl. I hope it may make her want to help me more.

I want it to. I want her to tell me everything I don't already know. I want her to help me understand.

"I do—did. I was the one who reported them missing the morning you went out into the mountains. Her mother was my best friend. Her father was my brother. She and her sister were two of the most incredible people I have ever met," she says. Something shifts, but I can't tell what. "I shouldn't talk about her sister like she's dead. If she was, the magic would have defaulted to her."

"Her sister," I say, echoing the words back at her and trying to wrap my head around the idea that she wouldn't have told me after all these years.

"Twin sister. We called them the Verdigris girls," she

begins to walk, taking slow steps through the underbrush until she's close enough that I can see more than the vague shape of her.

"I didn't know," I admit.

"That surprises me," she says, letting her hands fall to her sides and drawing her shoulders back as she searches my face. It feels like she's looking for evidence that I can't be trusted, trying to find a reason Leighann would have kept something like that from me.

I am confident that she will find none.

"She told me," Ali says from behind me, stepping off the path we've worn into the dirt and coming to stand beside me. "Hello, Saya. I was coming to check on you. I hope I'm not interrupting."

"Leighann has a sister," I say, because it's all that I can think of. Ali laughs.

"We never pushed her to tell us anything that happened before the fire," she tells Saya. She sounds casual, like they've spoken enough that she can relax. "We never wanted her to have to relive what she went through."

"I always assumed her life before the fire wasn't pleasant, because of how it ended. I wanted her to know that she is safe with me and that I wouldn't ever force her to tell me anything she didn't want to," I tell Saya, feeling the acute urge to defend myself and the choices I've made. Wondering all the while whether they were the right ones.

"It wasn't all bad," she says, coming closer still. The moonlight cuts harsh lines over her face as she passes through patches of it, but when she settles in front of us, just beyond the wards, there's a softness about her I wasn't expecting. "She and Mini—that's what we called her sister—were all but attached at the hip before their parents started working with

Anya Kivleneiks."

"What do you mean, before? Did something happen?" I ask, grateful that Ali seems content to linger and let me look for the answers that brought me here. A part of me thinks that's the real reason she came all the way out here in the middle of the night.

"I don't know. I wasn't there. But it was like someone flipped a switch. Mini changed. She was distant and cold most of the time, cruel the rest. None of us knew what to do with her, and then Leighann disappeared the first time," Saya says. "She came back different, too."

I watch as the woman fiddles absently with the ring on her right hand. It's carved, worn on her middle finger where the nomads often wear their wedding rings, and I wonder if she has a mate nearby. I don't hear anyone. If the stripe of pale skin beneath the band is any indication, she never takes it off.

"They all disappeared a few months later, and if Cecily hadn't been recovering from a miscarriage, I might been willing to assume they ran. I wanted to believe that's all it was, that they tried to escape, but I knew that wasn't it," her voice begins to shake and she takes deep breaths, like remembering alone is enough to bring back the fear. "I was afraid they would kill Leighann. Mini was always easier to control and after what they did to her, she was obviously the better choice to turn. She's the cold one, the more calculating of the two of them, and they knew that those traits would only continue to develop as she grew."

"Turn? What do you mean, turn?" I ask, drinking down every detail she gives me and trying my best to place it in the bigger picture.

"Turn. Convert. Take advantage of. Leighann was never going to be a weapon for them. But Mini? Mini had all the right characteristics, and with Leighann dead, their magic would revert back to her. She'd be able to use it alone," Ali stiffens, and I can't tell if it's the mention of killing Leighann or if it's the gift I've never heard of. Based on the way she twists her fingers, I'm assuming this isn't the first she's heard of it. Saya looks at her, and I swear I see an almost imperceptible shake of her head.

It screams, *Don't tell him.* As plainly as if she'd said the words herself.

"The Verdigris girls are incredible. If you ever get the chance to see their gift work, you'll know that the outcome is worth the heavy price they pay. That's where they get the name, actually. The Verdigris that their magic leaves on their skin when they use it. Cecily always joked that it was their magic trying to protect their shine, but I don't know if I ever believed that," Saya says. Her blue eyes keep darting back to Ali, and if I didn't know better, I'd swear they were speaking down a pack bond.

"What do you know about the sister?" I ask, dragging her attention back to me. I know it won't do me any good to keep asking about their gift, but I know there has to be more she can tell me. I can feel it.

She tells me that Leighann looks like their father—her brother Damien. She says that they had the same light brown waves, perpetually sun-kissed skin, and purple eyes. Damien, she says, carries the same chromosomal defect that makes the girls so small. She tells her about his sense of humor and how he loved to dance. It's information I don't need, but it seems to be important to her that we know him, so I listen and try not to feel the sorrow that her fond, wistful tone brings on. I do anyway. She pauses to wipe her eyes and goes on to tell us about their mother, Cecily. She tells us that Mini looks just like her. She tells us about their porcelain skin, rich black hair, and red eyes with so much detail that I can picture them by the time she's done.

It isn't until she tells us about how they would sing that

she begins to cry.

"Maeve—that's the sister's name—she was always so serious, but her laugh was so like her mother's. When she or Cecily would laugh, it would hit you right in your chest, like music," she says. She sighs and gathers herself. We wait. "Mini cared for her sister more than her own life. She never let anyone touch her, not once. And I believe that's why she let herself be taken by Anya Kivleneiks that first time. I believe that's why she still lives. Because she has convinced Anya that she can bring Leighann in, that neither of them has to die for her to get what she wants."

"Which is... a weapon?"

"Which is power, at any cost," Ali says, speaking aloud for the first time since she appeared. She's tapping her fingers and has her arms wrapped tightly around herself, like she needs comfort.

"The fire that killed their parents wasn't an accident. You think it was Anya?" I ask, looking from Ali to Saya and back. Ali winces.

"Fire?" Saya repeats. She looks from me to Ali and back again, searching for answers in every line of our faces. "They died in a fire?"

I nod and hold my arms out, openly displaying the deep burn scars I still carry and bracing myself for the possibility that she might touch them. If not for the wards, I think she would. She's looking at them like they might bite her.

"Whoever took them when they disappeared, or found them after they tried to run... they," Ali swallows, eyes closed against the images I know must be playing behind her eyes. All she saw was the aftermath. I remember the rest well enough for all of us. "They tied the parents up. I don't know what they did to the girl before I got to them, but there was no trace of the sister when the search party arrived. The entire place was soaked in kerosene, Leighann included."

I shudder violently at the thought, grateful for the limits of olfactory memory and the fact that I can't remember the smell or the way the scent burned all the way to my lungs.

I remember the heat being the first thing I noticed, the way the air seared its way down into my lungs, and my body screamed desperately for me to run.

I remember the little scream that drew me in, called me toward the blaze. I remember finding her there, bound and burning.

"We were in the area where Blackwood territory becomes the Kivleneiks buffer zone when they disappeared. I waited a few hours to see if we could find them, but when we couldn't even pick up a trail, I ran straight for the Blackwood boundary. Delilah Blackwood took the report herself, but we couldn't stay. My husband—he's, he was high priority for them, and we were afraid that they'd come after him next," she says. She goes back to playing with the ring on her finger, and I think I know why.

"They killed him," I say, filling in the rest of the story as I watch her nod. "Kivleneiks soldiers found him waiting for you on the border and lured him out. When he wouldn't comply, they strung him up in the streets and left him for you to find."

"Oh my G-d," Ali breathes, "Saya, was that him?"

"Yes, it was."

"I didn't know. I was there when they found him. They wouldn't let me help prepare his body, but I was there. I'm so sorry," Ali says. I hear the part she doesn't say, and I know Saya does too. They wouldn't let her help prepare the body because of what had been done to him. What Saya had seen when she found him. What sent her running in the opposite direction, when she wanted to wait and find out what we found?

"They found the soldier who killed him, for whatever that's worth. He confessed to it all. I might even be able to get you a copy of the recording. Sometimes knowing that someone has paid the price for what has been done is enough," Ali says, looking like she would lope to reach through the wards and take Saya's hand.

"Anya Kivleneiks killed my husband. Only she can pay the price for what was done to him. To Cecily and Damien. To Leighann and Maeve. To me."

"I know, Saya. I know."

"Where the hell have you been?" is the greeting I get when I open the door to my bedroom. It's the middle of the night, and I want nothing more than to burn the last traces of my conversation with Saya off my skin under the scalding spray of a shower.

Instead, I find Aviva waiting for me in my bedroom with my phone in her hand, like she's been going through it again. She probably has, but she won't find anything. She never finds anything.

"Talking to that nomad girl who's been staying nearby. You can ask Ali if you don't believe me," I say. I'm so tired that I don't even hear my mistake until the words are already out of my mouth.

"So you were with my sister," she says, throwing my phone onto the bed. I half expect it to whiz past my head, but it doesn't. I'm too tired for that to feel like a victory.

"I was with our Alpha, Viv. Can we not do this right now, please?"

"Do what? Talk about you being out with my sister until the wee hours of the morning doing G-d knows what while I'm stuck in the Residence? No, we definitely have to do this right now," she says.

Normally, I would give in and fight back. Normally, I would let her yell and scream until she got it out of her system. But tonight is not normal, and I have nothing left to give her. I walk into the bathroom, close the door, and throw the lock.

Aviva Nathair is a problem for future me, even if putting it off is guaranteed to make it worse.

She beats on the door for a long time before she gives up, and when the sound of the door slamming shakes the walls, I sink to the ground and stare into the spray.

19
Aliyah

Elisabeth Kivleneiks arrived at Noonchester Falls at approximately five o'clock this morning. She will be here for twenty-five days.

I don't know what I expect to feel when I see her, but relief is far down the list. It's the first thing I can name, though, because when she steps through the Sanctuary doors and leaves her guards behind, she's in one piece. I reach down the bond for Greyson and find a bottomless well of relief hidden behind the calm mask of indifference I see on his face.

Whatever happened between them, he's glad she's alive, and so am I.

"Welcome, Ms. Kivleneiks. I'm Ali, we've met a few times," I say, offering her my hand. Instead of taking it, she throws her arms around me and hides her face in my neck.

"The guards are watching, don't say anything you

wouldn't want her to hear," she says, her voice so low I have to strain to pick up the words. I wrap my arms around her and smile, like I'm seeing an old friend.

"I'm really glad that you're here," I tell her as I let her go. When she straightens, she locks eyes with Greyson, and there is nothing but fear written there. He draws his shoulders back and locks down his urge to protect her.

I hate her hand and squeeze her fingers, hopeful that she'll see my promise to protect her in my eyes.

"You may go now," I tell the guards, still stuck on the other side of the wards.

"We're to stay with the Heir," the taller one says. I do my best to look apologetic over the smug satisfaction rising inside of me.

"Only Elders and Royalty are allowed to be guests while the wards are still closed. Assure Alpha Kivleneiks that we will take excellent care of her daughter," I say. Rose is there a second later, swinging the door closed on their protests without an ounce of regret.

Elisabeth tears her hand free of mine and throws herself at Greyson, who catches her weight and takes them both to the floor. She's sobbing, her whole body shaking with it, and I can tell that we're the only thing keeping him from doing the same, but I can't leave them in here together. We all know what Aviva will do if we give her any ammunition.

"Greyson," I say. He nods his head, like he knows, and holds her tighter.

"All of you, out. Rose, stay outside the door and tell anyone that asks that Elisabeth, Greyson, and I are in the middle of a debrief.

Rose nods and ushers the others out of the room.

Say nothing about this to anyone, I tell Shawn, Elijah,

and Kelly. I don't insult Rose by telling her to keep it a secret, because she will. She always does. Those wicked eyes flare brightly as she winks at me—only visible in the second before the door closes.

When I look back at Greyson, there's gratitude written all over his face just before he buries it in Elisabeth's hair and lets himself cry.

20
Aliyah

Elisabeth Kivleneiks showed up in my sanctuary at five o'clock yesterday morning, and I feel that I may have overreacted just a little bit to her arrival. I have since slept, showered, eaten an absurd amount of cereal, and come to my senses.

I feel much better.

Seeing her and Greyson together feels more like a fever dream than anything else, right now, but I know it's something I'll have to address with him eventually. Only the three of us know what happened behind the closed doors of my office, and I plan to keep it that way.

I would be lying if I tried to pretend it didn't change some things, though. Starting with the way I look at him.

Now, every time I look at Greyson, all I see is the way they fit together, like pieces of a puzzle, cut and sewn until they match up just so. It isn't natural, not by a long shot. No one would accuse them of having been born to be together in the way that some people seem to be. No, their compatibility is a combination of growing up friends, spending years expecting to be together, committing to make it work, and shared trauma that they may never fully recover from.

That doesn't mean that they aren't a handsome couple, or that I don't think they could have been happy together. Both of those things are true.

Elisabeth comes looking for me while I'm drinking my second glass of hot tea.

"Do you have a sweater I could borrow? Or do you think one of them would let me have one? I'm so cold," she says, rubbing color back into her hands as she talks. I look her up and down, taking in just how much of her pale skin I can see, and raise an eyebrow.

"You live in the mountains, why did you pack like you were going to the beach?" I ask her. I know the answer before she gives it, and I feel bad immediately for not seeing it sooner.

"My mother had my bags packed for me. She wanted me to take this as another opportunity to pursue Greyson," she says, looking down at her feet. Her toes are painted blue, and there are sparkles on them. It feels like a little rebellion, the most they can manage under her circumstances, I imagine.

"We're going to go raid Rose's closet and find you some things to wear while you're here. I won't stand for... this," I say, gesturing at her barely clothed body. We share a look of playful dismay, and I hook my arm in hers to lead her to Rose's bedroom. The door is open, and Rose waves at me from the floor as I enter, Elisabeth in tow.

"Oh, poor baby, is that all you brought to wear?!" she says immediately, turning herself right side up to look at us. Elisabeth nods, less embarrassed this time. Rose has that effect on people, me included, so I get it.

"My clothes are going to be too big on her, but I was hoping you might have some things she could borrow while she's here," I tell Rose. Rachelle slides past me on her way into the room and grabs a collection of seemingly random objects off her desk.

"She can have whatever she needs of my stuff, too. Mine'll fit her better in the, uh," she gestures at Elisabeth's ass and tosses a playful look at Rose, who glares and throws a pillow in our collective direction. It hits the wall and falls harmlessly to the ground.

"Close the door on your way out, you bitch," Rose says. We watch Rachelle go and laugh when she sticks her tongue out at us before she closes the door. I realize that I've never really looked at Elisabeth, so I take a moment to do it then.

She smells like mountain air and looks like her mother —if her mother weren't made of shards. Her heart-shaped face is soft, and her blue-gray eyes are warm. There's an alertness to her that I see in myself—the kind I see in everyone that was raised like we were. She's long and lean, muscled without being hard. Beautiful in a "barefoot in the sunshine" kind of way.

She's exactly what I would have thought Greyson would like—before Aviva.

"Now, please tell me this isn't your mother's idea of how to get Greyson Marquis' attention?" Rose says. She's on her feet in a heartbeat and giving Elisabeth a slow, appraising once-over. She sees what I see in the gentle curve of the young woman's waist—the elegant curve of her neck.

We're standing in the presence of the future Mrs. Greyson Marquis—and it will have nothing to do with the way she's dressed.

"It is," she says, nodding and rubbing her hands

together, "she never really bothered to get to know him."

"Obviously," Rose says, a bitter laugh slipping through her teeth. She throws a pair of leggings at Elisabeth and then follows it up with a sweater that hits her in the face and wraps around her head. "Put those on and let me see."

"It's better just to go with it," I tell Elisabeth with a conspiratorial giggle. The sweater leaves her hair a mess, but she doesn't seem to notice it.

There's a long silence in the room after that. No words are necessary as Rose appraises Elisabeth and tosses her different random pieces of clothing. She's acquired a near armful and tried every piece on by the time Rose decides she's had enough and folds her arms.

"Was the baby your idea, or your mother's?" she asks Elisabeth. To her credit, the girl looks just as startled and confused as I feel.

"What baby?" I ask Rose, but she's looking only at Elisabeth, who is staring at the clothes in her arms.

"My mother's," she says. She takes a soft, shuddering breath and presses her lips together while she decides what she should tell us. We wait, Rose staring her down, and I am still stuck somewhere in the middle, confused but not lost. "I hadn't even begun menstruating when she decided I would marry Greyson. He was my best friend, so I didn't care that much. I went along with it, just like I was supposed to. I didn't start fighting back until she started pushing me to seduce him. I didn't want to. I wanted him to be free to choose what kind of life we would have, since we'd had so much else taken from us."

"She wanted you to trap him," Rose says, and just like that, the image snaps into place in my mind. Elisabeth nods, then looks out the window, trying to hide the tears shining in her eyes.

"It was her backup plan. She told me that it was the only way to make the treaty bulletproof. If I were pregnant before the wedding, they wouldn't be able to back out," she tells us. She leans back against Rachelle's dresser and wipes her tears. "Every time I came home and told her that we hadn't slept together, she'd beat me. And then the one time—the one time we did, we were drunk, and it happened by accident. It never should have happened at all, but it did, and my mother had me locked in a room in Medical for weeks to see if I would bleed."

"And you did," I say, crossing the room to stand beside her and rubbing her arm just to remind her that I'm there.

"I did. She put me in the hospital after that. I… I tried for days to slip a note to Greyson after I woke up, but I never knew if he got it until I arrived here," she says. The tears are rolling down her face now, and she's given up trying to stop them. Rose and I share a stunned glance, and I know then that I'm not the only one way out of my depth.

You see, if this conversation taught me anything, it's that my problem isn't with Elisabeth. It's with everyone else involved in this whole stupid thing.

My problem is the treaty and the way that it tastes like a lie every time Aviva calls Greyson her mate. My problem is that we're all barely more than children, fighting for our lives in situations we can't control.

My problem is that I don't know how to fix it.

None of those are the problem that has me pacing the floor of my bedroom so intently, I'm afraid I'll wear a path in the hardwood ten hours later.

No, this problem is host unto itself.

My bedroom door is locked, and Shawn is who knows where. The idea of seeing anyone right now makes me feel like I might cry, vomit, and pass out. Likely all at the same time.

That seems like the definition of a really bad day. So, in hopes of avoiding it, I continue to pace, checking every now and then to ensure that the door is, in fact, still locked.

You see, when the question begins with, "do I dare?" the answer is always a resounding "yes."

And Anya Kivleneiks asked the question.

Do I dare defy the order of things? Do I dare risk a diplomatic incident? Do I dare risk everything to protect my people? Do I dare...?

I do.

I just hope that it's the right choice.

I stop pacing and walk to the windows to look out at the nearly full moon hanging low in the sky above the ancient rowan trees.

21
Greyson

It feels wrong to disturb her, so I linger in the hall for as long as I can.

Elisabeth leans against the frame of the open window and rubs her own arms—something I've seen her do before to soothe herself. She's watching Leighann and Elijah in the grass below. I know, because I saw them on my way up. She's tumbling through the too-tall grass, running the same routine over and over again because she isn't happy with it. Elijah—always the most patient among us—has been beside her since she started, sketching as he watches and giving the needed encouragement at the required intervals.

The sun is starting to set, and the Residence is quiet. No one has a clue that we're up here—Elisabeth hasn't noticed me yet.

Aviva is in Medical, so I don't have to look over my shoulder. I knock on the door frame, and Elisabeth smiles as she turns toward me, still hugging herself as she steps away from the window.

"You didn't have to defend me back there," she says softly. There's a kiss of sun on her cheeks because they get so little of it in the mountains. It makes her look healthier—more alive. My hands are shoved so deep in my pockets that I'm beginning to think they may rip.

"I know I didn't," I know I shouldn't have, but Aviva was so angry and she'd been so content to take it. She'd looked so used to being spoken to that way that I couldn't stand it.

"Your father is right," she says, that knowing, cheeky smile of hers playing with the corner of her mouth, "you *would* make a terrible politician."

It's a joke no one else could make.

"I know," I say. And then, together, we add, "because people are what really matter."

She rolls her eyes at me and rubs her neck with both hands, forcing her shoulders down and back as she works the tension out. I'm in no rush to speak, and there's nothing about the silence that makes me feel like I have to.

"I hate that you're never wrong." Her eyes are closed, and her long lashes are dark against her soft cheekbones as she rolls her neck and tilts her head back.

"I hate that you always have to answer for being right." Her eyes find mine, and goosebumps rise on her arms. Her eyes drift back to the window, and I wonder what she sees—I can't see anything other than the gradually reddening sky.

We stay like that for a long time—her watching the sun and me watching her. Longer than we should.

I turn to leave when I hear Aviva coming through the front door. Elisabeth doesn't move when she says my name, but she doesn't have to. I stop cold and wait.

"Thank you."

I have no idea what time it is or how long I've been walking. It's the kind of dark that only reaches us in the earliest hours of the morning, but that's the most I can say. I'm not even sure where I am—somewhere deep in the forest past the falls—but her scent finds me through the rain-dampened air.

"Elisabeth?" I call, my voice soft in the relative hush of the forest. There's no trace of her in the darkness, so I follow the scent of her deeper into the trees.

I don't know how she found the cave—I've spent months wandering through the forests and I've never seen it before. And it looks deep—cavernous, even. She's sitting in the open mouth of it wit a blanket over her legs and a book in her lap.

A single tealight rests on a small ledge above her, providing the only light in the deep shadows. Her hair is braided into pigtails, and the sweater she's wearing is definitely not hers, but she looks cozy.

She doesn't have a fire lit. The rain has introduced a mild chill, but the summer air is still warm. She's so intently focused on whatever she's reading that she doesn't notice me, so I clear my throat to get her attention.

"I just didn't want to scare you," I clarify, approaching slowly until I'm in the little pool of orange light that the candle has created around her. She just smiles and closes the book around her fingers.

"You're up late," she says softly, drawing her knees up to her chest and resting her chin on them.

"You're up early," I counter. Her smile is so warm in the dim light that I let myself be drawn in—the stone is cold when I sit down.

"I didn't expect it to feel so suffocating to be left alone—I always have guards at home, so it's never *really* quiet."

"How did you find it?" I ask, looking around at the cave. The candlelight doesn't reach the back wall, and it barely touches the ceiling. The space is massive. She looks around and shrugs.

"I don't know. It was a while ago. Like my second or third night? I was exhausted, but I couldn't sleep. I tripped and fell from up there around sunrise. I guess it kind of found me," she says. The ledge she gestures to is twenty feet in the air—the fall had to have been brutal.

"Ouch."

"Yeah, Ali wasn't amused. I didn't hurt myself too badly, and I've come back every night. I usually get a few hours of sleep around lunchtime."

We fall into another comfortable silence, and the rain picks up beyond the mouth of the cave. Her breathing is slow, and our hearts are steady. This far from the Residence, there's no trace of anyone else. Like no one else has found this place—like we're in a bubble.

She falls asleep a few minutes later, and I stay even though I shouldn't. The rain slows to a drizzle just before sunrise, and I can't bring myself to leave her there, so I carry her quietly back to the Residence. Several miles of hiking and three flights of stairs later, I lay her down on her borrowed bed and pushed a strand of hair back off of her damp forehead.

"Goodnight, Bette."

As I'm closing the door, she exhales.

"Goodnight, Rey."

22
Aliyah

The full moon is coming, and preparations are underway. There are logs and piles of firewood along the path to Medical, and the entire Residence smells like rich wine and slowly roasting meats.

The little people have started to relax, so I can see them darting amongst the buildings and climbing in the trees. Sometimes they chirp or wave as I pass, but mostly they just exist. It feels like a privilege to have been considered worthy and safe—I never saw them in Tamarak.

Somewhere in the distance, someone laughs, and the sound carries through the open bay door, tickling my ears. I smile to myself and continue working.

I've been here most of the day, and the herb mixture for the bonfire is almost finished. My fingers hurt, and the tips are stained.

It's worth it for the silence it brings me—the peace that comes with the routine work is unmatched, and right now, I need it.

Elisabeth has two more days, and then she'll carry my letter, already written and sealed in the top drawer of my desk, back to her mother.

Two more days of pretending that I don't see the way that she looks at Greyson—of pretending he isn't looking at her exactly the same way.

Two more days of keeping Aviva from tearing her apart, even if it means she turns her ire on me.

Two more days until she leaves, and I have to trust her to do her part. If she can't tell her story well enough to keep herself alive, I won't be able to save her.

She will leave, and it will be up to her to keep it together as she delivers my answer to her mother.

Greyson will never forgive me if we lose her.

PART TWO

1
Aliyah

The minute the wards open, we feel it.

The sun is still climbing its way into the sky, and the air is cold—I am still eating my breakfast when I feel the change. It comes out of nowhere and blooms like a flower in my belly. I'm looking at cereal when my pack markings flare, a brilliant white light flowing along the lines and bringing with it the strangest sensation I've ever felt. First, it's icy cold like the Falls in the morning, then molten hot only a heartbeat later. It settles into a buzzing like butterfly wings as the light fades, and I don't have to look around to know that they all feel it too.

Some of them are eating breakfast with me, staring at me over their eggs, toast, and cereal. Some of them are dragged from sleep and stumble out of their bedrooms in surprise. And some of them—by which I mean my sister—emerge from the sublevels in alarm, looking very disheveled.

Greyson is the only one that appears without me seeing

where he comes from, and he's also the one who looks like he's planning to speak when Cici comes sliding through the doorway in the midst of a shift, smiling like it's the greatest day of her life. She retrieves her black robe from the hook by the door and shrugs it on, tying the sash diligently before she moves out of the hallway and into the living space we're all occupying.

She catches my eye and nods, just once, and every single member of my pack erupts into loud, joyful cheers.

"You can go," I tell them, putting my spoon down and straightening my spine. "All of you, or anyone who wants to. You can go anywhere you want to go as long as you're careful. If you go back to your reservations, use the Sanctuaries, and remember that you're guests. If you decide to play human, be convincing. Remember your manners and don't end up naked anywhere you're going to get caught. If I get calls from the human police asking me to come get you, I will be angry and you will be... well, grounded."

Shawn laughs behind me and dutifully schools his features when I turn to look at him. When I turn back to them, I expect most of them to be gone, but they haven't moved an inch, and I realize it's because they, like all wayward children, need money.

"Ah, hold on."

Their credit cards are in Alphabetical order, bound with the hair tie I was wearing when they came in, and waiting on my desk to be handed out. When I retrieve them, I allow myself a beat to breathe and feel the same happiness that they feel, even if I don't have the freedoms that they will now enjoy.

Remarkably, they each wait patiently for the little piece of metal to be handed over and thank me before they take off running, vaulting the railings and bouncing up the stairs as they head for their rooms, their clothes, and their first days of freedom.

It only takes a few minutes for me to be standing in the kitchen, holding Shawn's credit card out to him.

"I know you aren't pretending you're staying here," he says as he takes it. He's already dressed for the day, so he slips it into his pocket and crosses his arms. I feel his eyes follow me as I pick up my coffee mug and take a long, slow drink. I don't think I made it to drink, I think I made it to keep my hands warm, and I remember that clearly when I realize I didn't sweeten it. He laughs at me while I swallow the bitter mouthful and lets me tap my fingers against the ceramic for a few seconds before I answer him.

"Everywhere I would go is off limits to me now," I tell him. I can still feel the joy radiating off of everyone, hear voices floating through open doors, and taste the feeling of freedom lingering in the air where they sat. It might be coming from the markings, actually, the crisp scent I keep smelling. Either way, the room is burning with it. Cici's long gone, and it's just Shawn and I standing in the kitchen, so when he closes the distance between us and presses himself against my back, I let him. His hands find my skin under the hem of my sweater and slide around until they're resting on the softest part of my stomach, and I let him do that too. He holds me for a long moment, his chin hooked over my shoulder, like he just wants to feel my warmth or knows that I need his.

I lean my head back and turn just enough to kiss his cheek, suddenly very grateful that he's there. His stomach rumbles loudly against my back, and the laugh it startles out of me is kind of scary sounding because my neck is cranked back, but it snaps the tension, and we both dissolve into fits of laughter, still wrapped up together.

"What if you come with me instead?" he says, the breathlessness of laughter still clear in his rich voice. "If we pretend to be madly in love, no one will even realize we're also pretending to be human."

I'm pretty sure he winks at me, even though I can't see it. Even if he didn't, he might as well have for the way the charm and laughter drip from each and every word. I don't need to see his face to know it's a confession, and I don't have to respond to know it isn't an unrequited one.

"You know," I say, turning in his arms to wrap mine around his neck. He lets me, and his hands immediately come to rest on the small of my back, sending a warm rush of blood down my spine. "I have a shiny new credit card burning a hole in my pocket."

"You do. So do I. What do you think we should do with them?" he's smiling again, the boyish, lopsided smile I like so much, and he's looking at me like I personally hung the moon for him. It gives me all the confidence I need for what I'm about to say.

"How do you feel about turning my room into ours today?"

The little people have already started to appear. Coming through to clean up the mess from breakfast and finishing by the time we're done trading lazy kisses, and dragging ourselves to our respective bedrooms to get ready.

The fact that I saw them at all is proof that I've earned their trust. I smile at that, catching a glimpse of my own joy in the mirror before it's gone and almost sinking into it. Almost. Instead, I stare at the miscellaneous pile of clothes I didn't pick and tell myself that I'm going to buy new ones while we're out.

"Here, wear this," Shawn says, swinging dramatically into my doorway and throwing me a sweatshirt that looks and feels a lot like the one he just had on. It's soft and warm, and when I press the fabric to my nose, it smells of him. Jasmine and Mandarin. Patchouli and vanilla. Warm and bubbly and sweet.

"Do you want mine?" I ask him, tossing the sweatshirt onto my bed and pulling my sweater over my head with a little wiggle. His eyes darken as they follow the line of newly exposed skin, and I can feel the growl that rumbles through his chest when it's gone and I'm standing there in the lace bralette I slept in.

"I want you, if that's what you're asking," he says as he enters my room and then his long legs eat up the distance until my back is pressed against the frame of one of the windows lining the far wall of my room. The glass is open, and only his grip on me keeps me from falling out of it. He kisses me when I open my mouth to speak and manages to somehow pull me against his chest and press me back against the cool metal all at once.

The kiss is warm and claiming, the growl low in his stomach the same, and that's when I realize, really realize for the first time that I'm allowed to have this. That I don't have to marry anyone specific or be careful of my reputation on the reservation. I don't have to do anything I don't want to do because it's my house. My land. Mine.

Like he is mine.

I wrap my arms around his neck and raise one of my legs up onto the windowsill, giving him room to come in closer. He takes it, his hands burning hot against my hips, my ribs, my breasts.

And then he pulls away and brings me with him, placing me gently on the edge of my bed and kissing my forehead.

"We have shopping to do, Snowball. Get dressed."

I watch him leave and realize that my heart is racing. My spine is tingling, and there's a pleasant heat in my belly, all of which I have to get rid of before I'm going to be able to be seen in public. I wonder if he's similarly affected, but realize a heartbeat later that I can smell it, and still feel the ghost of it pressed against me.

I close my eyes and think of cold things.

Like powdery snow and wolves racing downhill toward a pond, frozen solid in the coldest months of the year. I think of the feeling of the burr stuck in my paw pad and the way it felt to tumble through that snow, my white fur blending with the crystals that stuck to it as I tumbled all the way to the bottom and landed on my stomach at the side of the lake.

I think, just for a second, of the amused yip it earned me from Shawn before he shifted and knelt in the snow to help me.

I think of the first time he called me Snowball, there in a foot of powder, and smile.

Even the icy January air can't chase the warmth from my cheeks.

"Rose?" I say, tapping gently on the door that's half-open and waiting to see her shove her headphones off in the full-length mirror hanging on the wall. It's a new addition, like most everything else in the room, and it looks good.

"Come in," she says, looking up from the video game console she's holding to watch me step into the space she shares with her sister. She's lying on her bed with her feet in the air, and I can hear the heavy bass of her music even at a distance. "What's up?"

"I..." It suddenly feels stupid, but I force myself to pull the pin I bought out of the pocket of my jeans. "I bought you something today, and I wanted to give it to you."

She sits up, gracefully swinging her legs around and

holding out her sharp-tipped hand with an excited smile.

"Let me see?"

"Shawn and I found a little craft market while we were out, and um," I put the pin in her hand. It's enameled; a gold rose with petals the color of the lesbian pride flag. "It made me think of you. I know you like to put pins on your bags because it was always fascinating to me to see which ones you picked each day. I thought that since you lost your collection, I'd give you one to start a new collection with."

"Ali, it's beautiful," she says, her endlessly golden eyes filling with tears. She wipes them away with one long, sharp finger, and I am momentarily amazed by the fact that she doesn't stab herself in the eye. They're painted a vicious red this week, and there are little gems set at the base of each nail.

"Did you get them done while you were out today?" Rachelle comes in the door behind me and flashes her freshly manicured nails at me.

"We both did, aren't they pretty?" Hers are blue, shaped a little more squarely than Rose's, and shorter.

"I think they're beautiful. I could never have mine this long without hurting myself every five minutes, but I always envy people who can," I tell her, holding one of her hands in mine so I can look at it more closely. Rose offers up one of her hands, too, and I realize they both smell incredible, like rich cocoa butter and warmth.

"Look what she got me!" Rose says suddenly, tossing the pin through the air to Rachelle.

"Oh, nice. Lesbian pride flag, yeah?"

"Wait, is it? Let me see?" The pin flies back through the air, and I feel my cheeks turning pink.

"That's so cool! Did you pick this one on purpose?"

"Yeah, I did. I thought you would like to be able to wear your pride flag without it being like, really in your face. I like that kind of thing," Rose pushes herself to her feet and throws her arms around me, the pin clenched tight in her fist as she hugs me.

"Thank you," she says in my ear. "Thank you so much."

2
Aliyah

Finding a bladesmith in the human world that can make what I want takes me hours of searching and researching.

I find Aura Greenfeld after I've spent a week looking in every way I know how, and I know immediately that she's perfect. I send her a message, set a meeting, and sit down to go over the sketches I've done—again.

I know it would be easier to include Greyson or Shawn. Really, anybody with artistic talent. But I want this to be all me. I want to give the Deltas something that came from deep in my soul, and involving anyone else in the design process would taint the vision.

So, I don't call anyone. I don't ask for help, and I don't share my plans.

I sit at my computer and draw the same wicked shape

over and over again. The same words, in the blade, the same shape to the grip. But different in every other way. Unique to the person who will wield it.

It has to be perfect.

When Aura sends me back her digital renderings, I know I've done it.

It's the best ten thousand dollars I've ever spent.

They take six weeks, and when she calls me to come pick them up, I take Rose. She deserves to be the first to see them, after all that she's done for me.

Besides, I know she won't judge me when I cry.

3
Aliyah

Sometimes I find the sound of people knocking on my office door to be very ominous. This is one of those times.

The feeling begins long before Elijah and Kelly finally knock, though, because they stand outside and argue for a full five minutes about who should knock and who should speak first. I know this because the door is just barely unlatched, and I can hear every word.

They only find out when Elijah sighs, knocks on the door, and accidentally sends it swinging open. It takes five full seconds for them to look at each other and then turn their attention to me. It takes another five for them to realize I've heard them, go through the stages of grief about it, and walk into my office.

I choose not to acknowledge that they try to do so at the same time and briefly find themselves stuck in the doorway, because that feels like kicking them when they're already down.

"Do you have a minute?" Elijah asks, backtracking a step to close—and latch—the door before he follows Kelley in and stands behind one of the chairs opposite me.

"Several, probably. What's up?" I put my pencil down and sit up, looking them over carefully to make sure no one is injured, dead, or dying.

Kelly looks... nervous, which is almost concerning enough for me to be nervous, but Elijah is beside him, calm and steady, so I let myself relax a bit. Elijah also looks kind of hopeful, like he's excited about what he has to say and wants me to want it as bad as he does.

"Can we sit?" Kelly asks, gesturing at the seats and waiting for me to nod to round the chair and fold himself into it. They both look like giants in the chairs, and I make a mental note to try and find something more comfortable, since so many of the guys are so tall. A few of the girls, too. I've never noticed before, because I've only ever had a few guests in my office and of the small number who have been allowed to sit, not a single one has positioned themselves in the chairs properly while speaking to me.

There's probably a gay joke in there somewhere, but there are so few people in the world that know about me that I doubt it would land without pissing people off. Instead of thinking too long on that or its implications, I fold my hands in my lap, sit back, and wait to see who will speak first.

They speak at exactly the same time, and what I hear—which is a tangled mush of words and sounds—is so beyond what I expected them to say that my mouth literally drops wide open.

"Ali?" Elijah leans forward like he's concerned, and I hold my hand up to stop him from talking.

"One of you just said you wanted to be given permission to go to a human high school and college. Whichever one it was, say it again and then tell me why you've come to sit in my office and ask me something so outlandish on this fine Tuesday afternoon," I say, firmly closing my mouth when I'm finished, even though the astonishment hasn't faded at all.

"I said that, Alpha," Kelly says, looking like there's a live bird in his throat. "We... Elijah and I have been talking about it for weeks, and it's something that we think could be really beneficial for everyone, even if we only did it as a trial."

"How long is 'weeks'?"

"Since the wards opened," Elijah says, speaking up and immediately draining some of the tension from his best friend's face. "We ended up at a shopping mall somewhere in the human territory of Ohio, and there was this school field trip happening. We got to talk to some of the students, and the teachers tried twice to make us get on the busses with them before they realized we weren't students."

"That's not all, though," Kelly says. He pulls out a flash drive and puts it on my desk. "We've been researching the kinds of things that they teach in these human schools compared to the schools we have on the reservations, and we realized that we're basically being set up to be stuck here our entire lives because so much gets left out."

"What is it that you want to learn that the school in the Elderlands can't teach you? Or that we can't sign you up to learn remotely?" I ask. I could plug the flash drive in and give it a skim, but something about making them plead their cases seems important, so I do.

"How to be human, ma'am," Elijah says, looking down at his massive hands and picking at a piece of dead skin before he looks back up at me. "I'd only ever seen humans on television until that day, and I'm lucky that I'm not a total idiot, because if I were, I would have said and done so many things that drew attention to myself that you would have had worse than the human police to deal with."

"What he means is that we're stronger and faster than them, and it shows because we don't know how to hide it. Most of us speak several languages. And not one of us is familiar enough with human law not to get arrested or killed. We need help, and the best way for us to learn these things is to do them. And if it doesn't work, we kill it, but I think we could make a real difference here." Kelly takes a deep breath, and I can feel his heart racing well enough to know that he's passionate about the idea. "On top of that, earning degrees from human schools means we could work in the human world and bring in good money for the pack."

"He won't tell you himself, but he wants to work with Rose and Liam to develop a curriculum that we can sell to the other reservations. They've been talking about it a lot, and they have a lot of good ideas," Elijah sounds defensive, so I take a second to try and make sure I'm not doing anything to cause it. "They all have the basic skills to make it happen but would benefit from a formal education. They're all interested in earning degrees from human colleges."

My heart rate is slow, my breathing is even, and as far as I know, I don't have a wicked look on my face. All I can gather is that they're terrified I'll say no.

"Okay. Hypothetically, if I allow it, what's the end goal?"

"To blend in. And to be able to contribute to the pack financially. The ability for the people that life in the Wolflands to pass as human so that they can go beyond the sanctuaries and into human cities when they want to and the ability for the pack not to rely on internal trade and alliances for financial stability," Kelly says it like he's been thinking about it for a long time and I have to admit it's a solid answer.

"And then, hypothetically, if I allow it, how does it look?"

"Like school," Elijah says, and Kelly punches him in the arm before he can put his hands up in surrender. "I just mean that it looks like going to school. We'd get up in the morning, drive to school, and come home. Everyone young enough to attend a high school and get a high school diploma can, and everyone who's too old for that will need falsified documents."

"There are electronic versions of most of the coursework we have missed that we could read and retain well enough to look like we aren't too out of place." Watching them go back and forth is entertaining and distracting, but I manage to focus on what Kelly says enough to hear the ending. "And we could make friends, Ali. Real friends. In band or in choir, as athletes or in a chess club. Most of the people interested in being a part of this have never had that luxury before."

I know he's talking about Greyson. And himself. Kelly. Rose. Even Sutton, Sarah, and Piper.

Me.

I know he's referencing the weight of a name and a title and a role to play, and how you never know who is there for you versus who is there for a place at the table you'll set for them. I know he knows that what he's saying will land and I know he sees the moment it does, because he sits back in his chair and his usual cocky, smooth smile returns.

All that bickering outside my door.

All the back and forth.

All for school?

I wonder, kind of absently, if they even need my permission now that the wards are open, and realize that I don't think they do. But they want it. They want me to want them to partake in the opportunity, turn it into something bigger than them. They want me to pay for it.

And I want to see what they can do.

"First of all, Ohio is a state, not a territory. Humans in North America don't really do territories most of the time. Second of all, the next time one of your two boneheads spends weeks on something *before* involving me, I'm beating you with your own limbs and then reattaching them."

"And third?" Elijah pushes. He knows they've won, but he wants me to say it. I hum and sigh. Then close my eyes and drop my face into my hands, where it remains while I speak.

"I'm in," I say. They're high fiving when I look up. "But only for a term. If that goes well, we can consider doing an entire semester or year. And anyone that wants to be involved in this is going to have to consume whatever course information you have found so that they're caught up."

"We know it isn't going to be easy," Kelly says, shrugging. "But it's going to end up being worth it."

"Just don't make me regret it. At this point, that's the threshold."

When they leave my office, I sit in silence and think about exactly what I've just agreed to for a long time. I think about all the things that they could study, all the incredible work they could do. And then I let myself be selfish for just a second, and I think about what it could mean for me.

Pre-med? Medical school, maybe? The ability to practice medicine in the human world? A place at the table and the ability to engage with new research and developments?

A cure?

Maybe. Just, maybe.

4
Elijah

The fact that we make it to the shopping mall alive is impressive, and I give full credit to Kelly for that. If the keys had been in my hands, we'd have stopped and started, flown and crawled the whole way here. The car says we only drove five miles, and it took us twenty-five minutes.

I did an internet search—which was temporarily interrupted by Kelly screaming and nearly killing us as he raced through an intersection at twice the recommended speed—in the car, and learned that shopping malls are big buildings full of stores. It seemed like a good place to start our day of shopping, so that's where we went.

This one is apparently not very big, but from the outside, it looks insane. It's easily the biggest above-ground structure I've ever seen, and Kelly's telling me how he thought that malls were only in movies as we get out of the little Honda Civic neither of us fit very well in.

"There are like eight shoe stores here," I say as I scroll through the directory. I only recognize about a third of the names I'm seeing, but I expected worse. "There's also a place to make a stuffed animal. I bet Leighann would like to do that."

"I could use new shoes. What about clothes?" he asks. He comes around the car and presses right up into my space in that way of his. If he were anyone else, I would hate it, but I don't. He's harmless, and he's wearing cologne today, which tickles my nose in a non-unpleasant but still strange way.

"There are a few. And there are these big stores on the ends," I say, pointing at the giant cubes bracketing the parking lot we're in. There are three other cars, and I don't know whether that's a good sign or not. "The website says they should have like, home stuff. I'm so tired of only having one set of sheets."

"I haven't seen Marcus wash his hands even one time since we've been in Noonchester Falls, isn't that disgusting? I wash mine once a week, and then I end up waiting for them to finish so I can go to bed. She picked out nice ones though, I'll give her credit for that," Kelly is the one watching where we're going as we walk, and I'm following his shoulders with my peripheral vision while I scroll through the mall's website trying to figure out where things are. When we step inside, my ears are immediately overwhelmed by the noise, and the assault on my nostrils makes Kelly's cologne seem mild.

"Put that away," Kelly says, ears literally twitching as he tries to adjust to the sound. There's music coming from both sides of us, and it isn't the same style or volume. Something smells like sage, and nearby, one of the little stores smells like it has been doused in heavy cologne.

"Are we really doing this?"

"Yep. And that's not going to help you," he says, pushing my hand to get me to put my phone in my pocket. I do, but only because he spends more time with humans than I do. I take a deep breath, and all I can smell for a split second is pizza. My stomach growls enthusiastically, and Kelly laughs at me.

"I think there are restaurants here. Do you want to eat first, or later?" he asks. I look at the directory that's a dozen feet ahead of us and find something called a "food court" on the map. A quick internet search tells us that it's what we're looking for, and we follow the raucous laughter and almost indistinguishable roar of conversation through the massive building toward the intensely generic scent of *food*, so convoluted that I can only barely pick up on any one type. Except for the pizza, I can smell that at a distance, and my stomach refuses to let me forget it.

We find the moving stairs a few minutes later. We can see the food court from where we're standing, and the humans are using the thing—the internet says it's an escalator?—like it's easy, so we think it will be.

The first time we attempt it, Kelly falls off one of the treads and we tumble back to the bottom, landing on me and managing to dig his elbow into my sternum in the process. Three old ladies come to ask us if we're okay, and the security man nearby looks at us like we might be trying to create chaos on purpose. My shoving Kelly and telling him he's a fucking moron must be enough to prove to him that is was an accident, because he goes back to his lazy rounds without saying anything to us.

The second attempt at the escalator goes much more smoothly and results in no one doing the splits or falling backwards. The old ladies talk about our asses as we ascend and I listen with a smile on my face until their delicate voices are lost in the cacophony of the food court, which appears to have been overrun by people aged 15-20.

"That's so many people," I say. Kelly looks like he's living for it, but I can see the uncertainty in the corners of his eyes.

"You ready?" he asks. I look at the packed space and nod. One intricate handshake later, we enter the press of bodies. We don't gag at the stench of them, but only barely. Human males aren't known for their cleanliness, especially before and around puberty. The whole massive dome smells like food, body odor, and sticky perfume. The latter might just be from the group of girls near us. They've claimed a large patch of the ground, and someone has passed out coloring books.

They appear to be having a wonderful time, and they look like they're older than the others. I'm wondering why that is when Kelly tells me that he heard someone say there's a field trip going on. He runs a search of the phrase and shows it to me. That's when I see the buses and the much larger, much fuller parking lot beyond the sliding doors.

"Field trip. So these are... high school students?" I ask. He shrugs and nods at the same time.

I don't even see the girl approach, because I'm so busy looking at my phone, trying to understand what academic value a shopping mall would have.

"Hey, so, my friend is too afraid to come over here and wanted me to give you her num—oh, you're like, really cute," she says. The first part is directed at Kelly, and she has a coloring page held out to him, folded up small enough that I can't tell what it is. I can see two digits of a phone number, but that's it. The last part is directed at me, and I'm not proud of how long it takes me to realize that.

My eyes move from the numbers, written in crayon on the off-colored paper, to the vivid green polish on her thumb, the nails short. There are freckles on her arm, and I follow them up to her shoulder before my eyes find her face.

She's beautiful. Kelly is looking past her at the girl who sent her over, and I can't help finding her plain next to the girl standing in front of us. The girl flirting with Kelly is long and I can tell that even though she's sitting down. She's got dark hair and thick eyebrows, but there's something boring about her kind of pretty. This girl? The one looking at me like she wants to see what's under my clothes? She's stunning.

A bolt of lightning cracks the sky above us open, white against the clear blue sky, and Kelly's attention snaps to me so fast I don't even have time to pretend it isn't my fault.

The entire food court full of people gasps and jumps as the world shakes, and I thank every God I know that I didn't blow out a window.

The girl's still looking at me when I look back, like the crack of thunder didn't faze her.

Her green eyes are bright and sharp on my face, framed by delicate lashes and surrounded by freckles that I imagine cover her entire body. Her hair is long and thick, orange and soft-looking. Everything about her is soft-looking, from her hair to her full breasts and down to her soft stomach and thick thighs.

My stomach rumbles to remind me that I'm hungry, and my brain helpfully suggests that maybe she would make a good dessert.

"I'm Elijah," I say, suddenly very aware that the silence is going on too long. I remind myself to smile and offer her my hand. She takes it once Kelly takes the paper and tucks it into his jacket pocket, and I can feel her pulse in the palm of her hand. She doesn't let go.

"Trinity," she says. It takes me a second to realize it's her name.

"It's nice to meet you, Trinity," I say back. It's kind of awkward, but she doesn't seem to notice. Kelly takes my phone out of my hand and offers it to her.

"He's trying to figure out how to ask you for yours and

I'm starving, so here you go," he says. His grin is charming and sort of lopsided, but only because he's aiming for relatable and grounded. I can see in his eyes that he's decided that's what will help him fit into this particular group of humans.

The plain girl behind Trinity practically swoons when he turns that grin on her, and when he winks, I feel her heartbeat radiating from her, louder than anything else for a second.

"Here, you can just text me, yeah? Or like, you could call me?" Trinity says, handing my phone back to me. I nod.

"Here, I'll text you now so you have mine," I say, and she sags in relief, like she thought I was going to stand her up or something. I wonder if that's really how men behave, and decide it's a stupid question in the same heartbeat.

"Well, I have to go. We have to get everyone back on the bus, and it's going to be like herding cats. I'll talk to you soon though?" she says. She fishes her phone out of her back pocket and smiles at the message I've sent. She taps away for a second and then puts her phone away again. "Goodbye, Elijah."

"Nice to meet you, I'm Kelly. Does your friend have a name?" Kelly says as she returns to her group. We laugh and turn to order, the man behind the counter thoroughly unamused by how long we've been standing in the way. Only the butterflies in my stomach and the memory of Trinity's scent stops me from ordering an entire pizza for myself.

Have you thought about where you're going to go to college? You're a senior, right?

I look at the text message, then at my computer, then start the process all over again. A senior in high school, she means—according to the internet. It's what I should be, I think, or maybe a freshman in college. The internet is giving me too wide a range for everything, so I go with my gut.

I would be a freshman, but I took a year off. I have no idea where I want to go. I tell her. The little indicator pops up immediately to tell me she's typing, and I leave my phone unlocked on my desk as I read through as much information as I can about college.

I'm pretty set on NYU. They have a really good music program. Do you know what you want to study?

I don't need the internet to tell me the answer to that one. I've been considering studying in the human world for a long time, so I know what I would study. I do my best not to get too excited.

Statistics and Electrical Engineering, I think. I've wanted to study math for a long time. BYU is in New York City, isn't it?

I can almost feel her laughing at me before the emoji comes through.

Yes, BYU is in the city. It's the only strike against it on my list of pros and cons. She says. I search for New York City in my browser and read over the statistics. It sounds overwhelming even on paper.

But the program you want is worth it to you?

Her response isn't immediate.

I want to play music for as long as I can, and I want to teach it when I can't play anymore. NYU gives me that and gets me out of here, so it's worth it.

Here, she says. Here, like I know where she's from. I probably should, because that's probably the place I met her, but Kelly and I just sort of ended up there. Neither of us could even tell you what state we were in. It's probably on a receipt somewhere.

What do you play? I ask her, at a loss for what else to say, and not wanting the conversation to end.

While I wait for her answer, I look up NYU's Mathematics Department. I read about the professors and the kind of teaching they use. I do the same for the Engineering Department when I'm done, and I'm so absorbed in my research that I don't hear my phone go off. It's a message, then a picture, then three more messages.

I was researching NYU. But this is much better. My brain needs to reboot, give it a second and I'll have something charming to say.

I don't even put my phone down before I add another message.

You look incredible.

I stare at the photo for a long time after that.

5
Aliyah

Where are we going?

His arms tighten around me, and he smiles, exhaling and then drawing a deep breath of my scent, all without moving his nose away from the hotspot at the base of my throat. From anyone else, it would have me ready to throw a punch, but not from him.

Wherever you want. He says, and his voice is buttery soft where it brushes against the inside of my head. I think about it for a second and then nod, pressing a kiss to the corner of his mouth and then running for our bedroom without saying a word.

"If I check the tag in that sweatshirt, is it going to say 'Shawn' in little black letters?" he asks. I don't have to look at his face, let alone his eyes, to know why his voice has darkened. I don't need help knowing why his heart is beating hard against his chest, and the scent of him is pressing on me, even from a few meters away.

"If it isn't, we need to discuss who you're letting get undressed in our bedroom," I say, smiling. "I'm all for exploring your sexuality and all that, but I *was* under the impression that we were exclusive, so maybe we should have a talk."

He's laughing and I'm smiling and it's easy to fall into his arms and hold up the book I've brought with me. I feel my smile soften into the one he likes the most, and he sees the change immediately. His face softens and brightens all at once, and I know that he'll say yes to whatever I ask him. So, I keep it simple.

"Come outside and read to me."

"I would love to," he says, shoving the last of the fruit on his plate into his mouth. It only takes a second before the plate is in the sink and he's tossing me over his shoulder like I don't weigh a full two hundred pounds. He's wearing the sweats he slept in and a short-sleeved t-shirt, so I don't feel like I can be blamed for putting both hands on his butt cheeks so I can feel them flexing while he walks.

Any girl brought nearly face-to-face with an ass like that would want to touch it and I stand by that. I'm in the midst of that train of thought when he pinches my exposed butt cheek and the book falls from where I have it pinned between my chin and his back.

"Turnabout is fair play," he says, giving my ass a playful smack and turning around to squat down and retrieve the fallen book. While he's squatting, he puts me gently back on my feet. The air is chilly, and there are goosebumps on both of us, but I can already feel my skin heating to compensate for it. All I have to do is wait, and my body will make sure I'm comfortable.

In the meantime, I have to figure out why the sight of

Shawn staring down at me, his eyes full of light and love, makes me feel like I want to fall over.

"Where do you want to read?" I lead him to my favorite tree, and he picks me up to hoist me into the branches, saying something about me being a lady, I mostly ignore it as I climb into the higher branches, the bark stinging against the cold soles of my bare feet. He waits a few branches below until I'm settled and then climbs up to sit behind me, his warm chest against my back and one leg wrapped around mine to hold us in place.

"Am I allowed to know why you want me to read to you?" he asks, kissing the top of my shoulder and then my neck. I laugh and tears well up in my eyes, unwelcome and immediately frustrating.

"My mom loved to read," I tell him, twisting a little so I can see his face and trusting him to keep me on the branch as I do. "My dad does too, but he really only reads medical journals and legal proceedings and stuff. That's just the kind of thing he finds interesting. But every Saturday for my entire childhood, Aviva and I would come outside and find them curled up in the same place. They'd sit at the base of this old maple tree and he would read to her for hours. He never complained about it or looked unhappy. He'd just take whatever trashy romance novel or crazy-thick sci-fi book she was reading at the time and read it to her. Always. They didn't miss one Saturday my whole life."

"Funny, isn't it? What a man will do for his mate?" he says, opening the book and kissing the side of my head. He flips until he finds the page where I left off and begins to read, not bothering to ask me what line I was on. I settle back against his chest and let him for a few long hours before I have the courage to do what comes next.

"Shawn?" I'm staring at the number at the bottom of the page, nervous.

"Hm?"

"Ask me," I tell him. I reach for the branch above us and use it to pull myself up and twist myself all the way around so we've face-to-face on the thick branch we've chosen. "Ask me to marry you."

To his great credit, he doesn't sputter or hesitate. He just smiles and closes the book around his finger.

"I ask you every night when you fall asleep, Aliyah," he says. And even though I know, it feels good to hear.

"But ask me now, while I can answer you," I say, feeling the hysterical joy or the idea bubbling up inside of me. It spreads across my face as a grin that probably looks like it's painful, but I don't care.

"Snowball, will you marry me?"

"Page three hundred and eight," I tell him, nodding to the book in his hand. He turns obediently to the page and there, just as it has been for months, lives a little purple sticky note that simply says 'yes' with a little heart next to it. Three hundred and eight, for the day in the snow where I realized it was always going to be him and me.

A yes, for the first time he asked me, when I wasn't actually asleep.

Sometimes, while dead asleep or in the shower, things occur to me. Usually, these are things that I should have known all along, things I should have seen from the very beginning and somehow still managed to miss. Things that change everything in a matter of seconds, for the worse or for the better.

I had one of those moments today, and it still doesn't feel real, even hours later.

I don't know how I didn't see it.

Let's back up, though, because this morning was fine. I was in my office working at my desk until around lunchtime, when I realized my entire body was stiff and decided I needed to take a break. I walked a few laps around my office and then lay down on the floor to stretch my back and hips. I was in the middle of a deep stretch of my lower back and cursing myself for sitting still too long, when something shifted in my brain and the pieces of a puzzle I didn't know I was trying to solve clicked into place.

I'd been contemplating a run, even though I knew it might mean I didn't come back to my office to continue my work, and that option went straight out the window when I remembered the sex talk my mom gave Aviva and me as little girls. I remembered what she taught us and then what I went on to teach others as a Healer, about consent and the magic that protects female royals.

The magic that protects Aviva.

I was off the floor and out of my office before the thought had completely finished forming in my head. I took the stairs two at a time and threw open her door without knocking. She was in her bedroom, wrapped in nothing but a pale pink towel and wringing water from her long curls with a t-shirt.

The scent of her was thick in the heavy, damp air, and the entire room smelled of blackberries and irises. The steam clung to everything in the room, including me, and smothered me in the very real, very pregnant scent of her.

If I were less angry and more aware of my surroundings, I would have startled myself with the sound of the door slamming into the wall and bouncing back toward me, but I barely notice it. It clicks closed behind me, and she turns her head toward me, looking only mildly surprised to see me standing in her bedroom. Like she knew this moment would come and had been waiting for it, however impatiently, just so it would be over.

I grab her by the back of her neck, and she drops the t-shirt. When I shove her toward the wall beside her dresser, I make sure she'll hit it square and on her back, because I would never forgive myself for hurting her or the baby, not ever. She, to her credit or as proof of her guilt, does not fight back as I pin her to the wall with one firm arm across her chest and press in close enough that her towel is held up by my body.

"You did it on purpose," I spit the words at her, searching her face for anything that could prove me wrong. I see something flicker in her eyes, and I can't decide if it's guilt or confusion. Her brush falls to the floor, knocked off her dresser by a stray elbow that could easily belong to either of us. She grabs my arm with both hands and tries to pull it away, down, or off, so she can breathe more easily. It doesn't budge.

"What are you talking about?" she gasps, her words small. She's still pulling at my arm, playing up the amount of force I'm applying like she thinks it'll make me let go. It won't, and some part of her knows it. The same something flickers in her eyes again, and this time, I see it clearly enough to know that I am right. I drop my arm and turn away so she can't see the colors I know are flashing through my irises in rapid succession.

She stands in silence, holding her towel in place with one hand so it covers most of her bits, and waits for me to speak. She doesn't try to lie or talk her way out of it, and that almost makes it worse. Because my sister has never been accused of anything she didn't try to fight, right, wrong, or otherwise.

"I'm sorry," she says, and I can hear the tears in her voice. I feel the air move and know that she's reaching for me, but I step out of the way and leave her hand hanging in the empty air. I don't have it in me to comfort her, not in this. "I'm so, so sorry."

"You got the same talk from Mom that I did. You knew how it worked, and you did it anyway. You did this to Greyson, to us, on purpose," I tell her, turning back to see the words land. My fingers jerk violently as I pull them through the strands of my curls, and the pain feels like a cool breeze, clearing away the cobwebs of ignorance and shaking off the haze of my anger. When I meet her eyes, she looks like she wants to disappear, like she could sink into the floor and cease to exist. What really steals the anger out of me is the way she has her arms curled around her stomach, like she's shielding the baby. Shielding the baby from me.

As though I'd ever lay a hand on something that was so fundamentally, irrevocably *mine.*

I don't care if it's instinct or manipulation, because it works, and the last embers of my anger die out, turning to a heavy, wet feeling of disappointment.

"I thought I was going to be Alpha," she says, as though that makes any of it better. If she'd been Alpha, the baby would be the Heir, and Greyson would be the King, and the Elder Council might, maybe, could possibly look the other way in the face of her blatant disregard for their rules. Or my father could challenge for custody, since the baby was conceived while she was Aiyanik. Or Anya could have Greyson married off to her daughter in spite of everything, and she could be alone, with a bastard instead of an Heir and no partner to help her.

"He deserved to consent, Viv. You should never have taken that choice away from him," I tell her. I know I'm right, I do, but I also know her intention wasn't to hurt him. To hurt us. It doesn't matter, because that's what she did the second she let the contraceptive magic fall. She stole something from him, and there's no trace of remorse in her.

"I know."

"Until I come back for you, you will remain in this room," I tell her, turning to walk toward the door. I stop with my hand on the knob and look back at her over my shoulder. "And Viv? The only person that crosses this threshold in the meantime is me, are we clear?"

I see the weight of the command settle over her shoulders, and she nods.

"Yes, Alpha," she says, and there is not a single ounce of fight in her voice, no fire in her eyes, no indignation. She simply submits to my orders and lets me leave. I don't slam the door on my way out, but I do stand right outside her bedroom with my hands on the railing and try to catch my breath for a full minute. When I speak, I raise my voice only enough for it to carry through the space below, to the gaming room that Kelly's voice is drifting out of.

"Kelly Rosendes, get up here please," I say, my knuckles white where my fists curl around the railing. I hate myself a little for what I'm about to do, but I know it has to be done.

I know Aviva. I know Greyson. I know that if I don't force them to obey my order, they'll find every reason they can to ignore it. So, I summon Kelly, who hears my voice over the headphones he has on and comes running, his game still making noise as he follows my voice and climbs the stairs.

"Hey Al. Thought you were going to be in your office all day?" says a voice from my right. I'm so busy watching Kelly approach that I don't notice him until he's right beside me. Greyson. Smiling like it's any other day and carrying a shopping bag. I hold up a hand, and he stops walking, frozen in place like he thinks he's done something wrong. And he hasn't, not really. He has done nothing but love every selfish part of my sister from the very beginning, and that makes what comes next even harder.

"Yes, ma'am?" Kelly says, clearing the steps and planting himself in front of me, hands clasped, and chin raised. He's the picture of respect, and I love him for it, because it reminds me that what I'm about to do is part of my role as Alpha and not anything else. I'm not doing it as her friend, or her sister. Not doing it out of anger or jealousy. It's just duty.

"I need you to second my override," I tell him, turning toward the small keypad and scanner beside Aviva's door. There's one by every door, just in case, but I've never used it before. I've never needed a lock to keep me in when I'm told to stay, or to keep anyone out. I wasn't the wild child; that was always her.

I place my hand on the scanner, and the surface is smooth and cold under my palm. I type my code into the keypad, each button silent, and step away as the light for secondary approval lights up. It's a safety measure, to make sure Alphas don't take advantage of their power, and right now, it's putting Kelly in a difficult position. I wish I could make it easier, but I can't, so I just stand between Greyson and the door, and wait for Kelly to swallow and place his hand on the scanner. The lock on her door slides home, and the scanner light turns red. *Locked,* it says, and I almost want to sigh in relief.

The silence after the locking stretches beyond my dismissal of Kelly and beyond my small nod to a crestfallen Greyson. It haunts me all the way back to my office, heavy and cold, and stays with me long after I've returned to my desk chair.

I don't begin working, though. I can't bring myself to do anything.

Worse than the silence still ringing in my head is the feeling deep in my toes, spreading little by little up my legs and into my hips. I drop my head into my hands and check the calendar. I should have three more days before my next injection. Funny, how cancer doesn't care about your plans.

I open the bottom drawer of my desk and withdraw the case full of syringes, each clear and tinged pink by the venom—Aviva's venom—contained within.

Three units later, the dull ache at the base of my skull has faded and the creeping cold has retreated too, only lingering in the very tips of my toes. I kick the drawer closed and throw the empty syringe at the wall across the room, where it hits with a metallic noise and falls to the ground on the thick rug.

None of this is new to me. I know what the creeping cold means. Know how to fix it. Know what happens if I don't. I know that after the cold spreads through my body, I begin to shiver, and that my bones will start to ache as the tumor grows, rapidly digging itself into the tissue of my brain so that it can never be removed.

I've only ever let it get that bad one time, and it was the first time, before we knew what was making me sick and weak and tired. Before we knew why I was so volatile. And now, with the help of Aviva's venom—and an incredibly lucky experiment conducted by Theodora—I can live a normal life.

Until the day when I can't anymore.

But that's a whole different conversation that I'm not ready to have yet.

Because 'what if' is my enemy, and I don't have time for her.

"Ali!"

"We're wolves, please don't yell at me unless you're dying, it hurts my ears," I say blandly, glancing up for a brief second as Elijah jogs through my open door and flops sideways into my chair. It's graceful, but also makes him look like a ragdoll, and I can't help but smile.

"You got a second?" he asks, holding up a notebook like he has prepared for this encounter. When I nod, he sits up straight and looks down at it before he meets my eyes, mouthing something to himself. "I wanted to talk to you about the school thing."

"Of course you do," I say, as though I don't have Georgetown's webpage open on my own screen. I fold my hands and turn my full attention to him. "Let me hear it."

"It's... I wrote myself some notes so that I wouldn't have to remember what everyone had decided on, and I wanted to share them with you," he says, turning the notebook around so I can see it. The more I read, the more impressed I am with the amount of work they appear to have put into the research process.

"So, Rose, Kelly, and you have decided on NYU. That's in New York City, I think?" He nods.

"It's a massive city, and we thought it would be a good opportunity to practice blending in while being in a place where no one pays any attention to anyone else. Rose wants to study psychology and dance, which they have. Kelly wants to do Music and thinks he might decide to go to law school. And I want to study engineering and statistics. They have those programs, and we looked at the admissions requirements; there's no reason we shouldn't get in." I smile at his confidence and wonder if they've looked over the SAT information like I have. It's supposed to be a big, scary exam, and I thought I was silly when I didn't feel nervous before or after my practice one. I contemplated forging their exam results, but I may not have to if they're willing to sit for it for real.

"I saw a few others on there too, show me again?" he holds the notebook up. "Shawn and I talked about how he wanted to study addiction. We picked UC together because it's a good school. Greyson picked Michigan, that's another Northern state. That says graphic and video game design, is that what he decided on?"

"I think so. I was just talking to him about it. He says he doesn't need help knowing how to do physical art, but that he wants to find a way to transfer those skills into tech. And then Rachelle picked a school in New York, too, but a smaller one. She wants to study mathematics." He tosses his notebook into the empty chair beside him and leans forward. "They're not the only ones who want to participate. They're just the ones who have already found where they want to go. Marcus mentioned maybe going, so did Saoirse and Tatiana. Some of them asked for time to think about it. And all the young ones wanted the opportunity to try school except Leighann, who was shit scared of being outside the wards."

"I can't really blame her for that," I say, standing and walking over to the whiteboard on the wall. I start a list for myself.

Shawn – Addiction Counseling, University of Cincinnati

Elijah – Electrical Engineering & Statistics, NYU

Kelly – Music Performance, NYU

Greyson – Graphic & Game Design, University of Michigan

Rose – Psychology & Dance, NYU

Rachelle – Mathematics, Rochester Institute

Marcus, Saoirse, and Tatiana are all listed as "maybe."

I draw a line and start a new list next to the first one, this time, of everyone under eighteen who would need to be enrolled in school. I decided to humor myself and start my list by writing the youngest members of our pack, yet unnamed. It ends up being more than a single list, because by the time I'm done, I have three columns and everyone is listed.

"This is what we're talking about right now?" I ask him, and he nods.

"Have you talked to the others?" There are only a few not represented on the lists. I feel a faint pang at the thought of Katerina—left behind, still safely tucked away in Playa Del Rose with her new baby. I don't even remember seeing a birth announcement.

"Briefly, they wanted time to research and consider. I kind of think they want to see how it goes before they commit, honestly," he says. He scans the list twice and scrunches up his face. "Why didn't you put yourself on there?"

"I don't know what I'm going to do yet," I tell him, glancing at my computer and thinking about how many hours I've already put into researching. He rolls his eyes.

"You know you're going to go. If not to be an example for everyone, then because you love to learn. Don't play with me," he gets up and walks over to me, taking the marker out of my hand and printing my name at the top of the list. "So where are you going to go?"

I stare at the list for a moment and fold my arms protectively over my chest. I hate that he's right. I hate that he knows me so well. And yet, I also don't.

"Georgetown," I tell him, aiming for confident instead of scared. "I'm going to study pre-med at Georgetown."

6
Aliyah

When the world lights up gold, I am alone.

There is no Banshee scream or pull in my gut—no threat in the cool night air around me. No evidence that I should be concerned, save the shimmering night air and the way little flecks of glitter seem to fall through the air like snowflakes. Everything is so, so still.

It's ten minutes past three, and I'm sitting in the back of my Bronco with the hatch open and a heavy blanket draped over my lap so I can look out at the gently rolling waves without feeling the bitter cold. I hate being cold.

One minute, there is nothing but me and the lake, and then there's a girl standing on the surface of the water, her bare feet leaving no marks as she walks toward me—her steps long and graceful.

The walking on water part is creepy enough, but

then she gets close enough, and I can see her more clearly. Everything about her puts me on edge. She's a head taller than me—nearly six feet, by my guess. Her hair is long, bleached to a near-white in the moonlight and twisted back away from her face to fall down her back.

There's crackling golden energy in the air that surrounds her, dissipating slowly as she approaches and tickling softly as it falls harmlessly to the lake's surface. With her scent comes something dark—wispy bonfire smoke and night air—but there's nothing about her to suggest she's ever been near something so dirty.

Everything about her is pristine, cast in shades of white and gold like something off a biblical page.

"Your Keeper told me where I could find you," she says when she's close enough that I can see her face. Her storm-colored eyes come to rest on my face, and I can see that her irises are too big—too wide in her delicate face. My heart stutters and skips—Cici.

"You were at Noonchester Falls?" I demand, leaning forward and putting my weight on my knees in case I need to move quickly or run. I reach for Noonchester Falls, and I feel nothing out of place. Even at a distance, the land seems to pulse its comfort. It's satisfaction.

"Yes, it's a beautiful reservation," she says, dipping just slightly at the waist as she stops walking, a sign of respect. I note in the back of my mind that while she does not bow deeply enough, she does so with a significance that feels adequate. Something only those with practice seem to achieve. "My name is Wanderer, and I need your help."

I watch her carefully for a moment, eyes dragging over her and searching for any sign of danger. I see the way her clothes hang on her muscled body, the softness around her middle and on her thighs so like my own. I smell her in the air, under the smoky scent of the fire, and I see her watching me back, like a snake in a wolf's body.

Like something—older.

"Are you asking me for help personally?"

"Yes," she says, clasping her hands behind her back. "But right now, all I'm asking is that you listen. You and your Betas can make the final decision together after I've gone, and whatever you decide, I'll respect it."

Her body is relaxed, and my instincts tell me that I should be too. Nothing about her feels like a threat, but every line of her looks like one. From the slope of her shoulders to the way she holds herself balanced before me—every part of her is a weapon. It just isn't aimed at me.

Her target is far more distant—like a storm on the horizon. I can practically see it gathering behind her.

"Speak, Wanderer."

I can feel the tension still coiling in my muscles, and I know that she can too. My hackles are raised, and my teeth are sharp enough to draw blood where they press against my lips. She shows no fear as she raises her hands and conjures an image in the cool night air between us.

"This is Abbigail," she says. The image between her hands solidifies, then shifts, like a trading card. Back and forth, the face of a girl turns to the face of a wolf, and then comes back. "She's very like you and very like me, but also very unlike anyone else I have ever known. She's my entire world and my heart outside my body, and she's in danger."

The strange sharpness of her magic in the air strikes me like lightning, raising the hair on my arms and making my teeth itch. She lets the image dissipate and lets her hands fall loosely to her sides.

"What is it that you want from us?" I ask her. She has me

and she knows it. Every fragment of my attention is tuned to her, and I can't see anything but the way the world around her seems to bend and shiver. Her heart beats slowly—steady as a drum. And a second beat at her throat—rhythmic and even.

"There will come a time," she says, "likely in the near future, where I won't be able to protect her anymore. When that time comes, I would like your permission to send Abbigail through a portal to you. Once she's safely inside the wards of Noonchester Falls, I'll be able to do what I need to do and know that she is safe, removed by a world from everything that could hurt her."

"And the price?"

"In exchange for your agreement, I will owe you a debt greater than my own life. A debt I will pay over and over again if it means her heart continues to beat," I can hear the honesty of it in her voice, and something tells me that she's the kind of person I should want to have on my side.

"What can you offer us, exactly?" I ask her, hoping that she can't read the eagerness and excitement I feel on my face. She might be able to smell it in the air, if she can smell anything over the smoky scent of fire and rich wine that radiates from her. The air over the water crackles like there's a storm rolling in, and a chill rolls over my skin.

"Whatever your heart desires, little wolf," she purrs, her voice nearly a song. "I could give Tatiana back Katerina, let her meet her niece. Elijah could have the girl. I could protect Greyson and Aviva. Leighann and Maeve. You. I could help you survive without the Elder Council, if that's what you want. I can give Cristianna the chance to say goodbye."

There's a heavy moment of silence, and the air seems to still.

"I could give you the chance to say goodbye," she says, and then, just like with Abbigail, she conjures a shining image of my mother between her sorcerer's hands. Her bright smile is like the sun, her freckled cheeks sun-darkened to the beautiful gold I always envied in her and Aviva. Wanderer may still be talking as I stare at the image, but there is no sound I can hear. There is nothing but the radiant smile and the slight turn of her head, playing over and over and over again while I stare like a little girl in awe.

"Why?" My voice cracks, and I have to try again to get my words out. "Why would you do any of those things for us?"

"That's exactly what I want to know," Kelly says, his shimmering, projected form appearing to my left as Shawn's appears to my right. I wonder for a second if Cici sent them, but realize just as quickly that she's the only one who could have, and roll my eyes at myself.

"The world is about to be cruel to you," she says softly, reaching up to touch the heavy necklace that rests at the base of her throat. The stone looks old and shines slightly in the moonlight. I can feel the pulse of energy the touch releases even at a distance and I catch myself wanting to stare at it. *Into it.* "And I can help you."

Kelly and Shawn both move in close, watching me watch her and scanning the horizon at regular intervals.

"To protect the thing that matters most to me, I'll protect the things that matter most to you. An even trade. Them," she gestures with one long, delicate hand at Kelly and Shawn, "for her."

The image of the girl appears again, the blue-eyed girl and the brown wolf, shifting gracefully back and forth as she raises her chin to let out a silent howl I can almost feel.

"Why can't you protect her yourself?" Shawn asks, eyes sharply focused on her face. Somewhere in the distance, a clock chimes. Wanderer swears colorfully, her words turning from English to a language I don't understand.

"Let me make my offer abundantly clear," she says, taking two long steps forward to bring herself nose to nose with me under the hatch of my truck. I swallow against the terror called up by her proximity and force myself to meet her stormy, midnight gray eyes.

She takes a deep breath.

"If you do this—when you do this—I will give you whatever you demand of me. Each of you can ask for something if that's what it comes to," she's right in my face, looking only at me, but she makes no move to touch me and gives no indication that she plans to harm me. "Whatever it takes. Whatever price."

She curses again at something I can't see or hear, and her face softens, her eyes filling with tears like quicksilver in the moonlight.

"My kind do not often write blank checks, Aliyah Trevonaire, and I am offering you a book of them. As many as you can cash. I need to know that she will be safe. Please," her voice breaks on the plea, and I want to say yes, but I can't.

"I'll take some time to talk it through with my Betas. If we can help you, we will, but I can't make this decision without their input," I tell her, very aware of the impulse to give her whatever she needs in exchange for the image of my mother. She reaches into the pocket of her strange robes and withdraws a crystal, almost the same as the one hanging from a leather cord around her throat. She offers it to me, and when I take it, it pulses painfully in my palm.

"Break this when you have decided," she says, stepping back all at once and turning with a flourish toward the center of the lake. "I'll talk to you soon."

She takes off running, first in her human form, and then on the four legs of a wolf, large and the same white-blonde color as her hair. A rift opens in the air in front of her, and when she reaches the center of the lake, she disappears into it. It closes as soon as her tail is through and leaves only the most delicate shimmer of gold behind to prove it was ever there at all.

Kelly and Shawn both turn to look at me at the exact same time, and we all say, at the exact same time:

"What the fuck?"

The package from Wanderer is probably on my desk before I get home, but I am still absently rolling the icy crystal between my fingers when I finally see it hours later. The parcel is plain enough to be innocuous, wrapped in brown paper and tied with a purple strand of jute twine that looks like it's hand-spun and hand-dyed. I can smell the fibers from across the room, even before I pull the ends to free the small card from the knot. When it falls to my desk, all I can smell is the same bonfire scent and cedar-smoked vanilla that I smelled when she got close to me at the lake.

The card reads:

I'm a woman of my word. To protect her, I'll pay any price. But before you decide, you should read this. The second letter is for your eyes only.

I set the second sealed letter aside and pop the seal on the first one. The paper is thick, rich under my fingers, and heavier than anything I've ever felt before. The letter itself is written with a flourish, like calligraphy but softer, and sealed with an inverted lotus flower in rich gold wax.

I like to consider myself a pretty intelligent person, even if I'm not always smart, but the more I read, the less I feel like I know.

I have studied hard my entire life and done my best to absorb everything that every teacher has put in front of me.

I didn't become the youngest Medic and then the youngest Healer in my territory by being lazy, and I definitely didn't manage to be chosen as Alpha without someone deciding I had a firm enough grasp on the world to pull it off. And yet, reading what Wanderer has written makes me feel like I have spent the last decade and a half of my life with my head under a rock.

If what she writes is true—and I have every reason to believe that it is—the council has been lying to us since we were children. Lying to us, misleading us, and manipulating us. All for their own gain, to protect their power.

In school, whether we were in the Elderlands or the res schools, we were taught mathematics, literature, history, and world culture. We learned that before reservation laws were established, packs killed each other over land and resources every day, and we learned that before the Wolflands, the humans killed us just for sport.

They taught us that the Elder Council was established to represent the interests of the realm and to keep the peace between the packs while maintaining balance between the territories. They taught us that the humans are dangerous to us, not to be trusted, not to be loved, and not to be brought home—under any circumstances. Even the ones that masquerade as our friends, they said, would hunt us for our pelts at the first chance they got.

They taught us that by befriending humans, we would be putting the vampires, the witches, the warlocks, and the rest of the creatures that make up the Night World in danger. The humans, they said, were as much or more our enemies than the vampires would ever be.

They were wrong.

Or, well, they could have just been misinformed. That could be a kinder, less accusative way to explain it.

Either way, today has been a lot, and I feel like I need a

drink.

Wanderer's version of history says that there were originally hundreds of independent packs, and most were smaller than a hundred members at any given time. The wolves she speaks of were warriors, every single one of them, and they lived off the land while they practiced their gifts and did what they could to live by the laws of nature. They lived in the human world before the Wolflands, and when they moved, they shared the space—often even their packs—with the persecuted. They lived with vampires and with fae, with the little people, and with witches, and all manner of creatures in need of sanctuary from the humans and the human world were welcome. They fought, but no more often or more intensely than the humans or the vampire covens ever did. No more than any species did.

She says that the Wolflands don't exist naturally, that the entire realm was made as a rift between worlds and gifted to us as a sanctuary where wolves could run and hide during a time when the humans were hunting us for pelt and bone. She says that her mother—Aiyanik—was the witch who forged the realm, and that as she died, she sealed the magic to her young daughter. That she was killed to make sure there would never be a time when the sanctuary she made wavered or fell.

Her version of history says that the Wolflands were peaceful for centuries.

Until Anya Kivleneiks.

Until one woman started hunting and collecting wolves with gifts, with the intent of turning them into soldiers. She stole many straight out of the camps their packs made and disappeared without a trace, leaving a trail of bodies behind if anyone tried to protect them. She even offered rewards for those willing to provide her information that led to a new acquisition.

To this day, no one knows how she managed it or how she concealed herself from the hunting parties that chased after her.

That's when the Elder Council formed—when history's rewrite began.

The packs saw that they had an internal threat to deal with and the opportunists—many of whom had long craved a central structure—encouraged the Alphas to band together so that they could protect their people. Preying on fear was easy and effective. Anya drew attention from the humans with her hunting patterns and went to every part of the realm and the human world looking for trophies to add to her collection. She sent our kind running scared, back to their safe places, and then she followed them there. The humans got caught in the crossfire, and from that conflict rose a new generation of wolf hunters, more vicious than their predecessors and infinitely more effective.

This new breed of hunter didn't hunt for sport. No, their motivation was worse. They hunted for survival and claimed our markings to prove that they got their revenge.

Our people turned to someone they could trust, in the face of the chaos. Someone whom they knew the humans would never break and the pack leaders would never be able to find. Someone who could complete the masterpiece of a realm we had already been given. They hired a warlock to protect their home, to ensure that they would never have to stare down the barrel of a hunter's rifle on their own turf or have to worry about their children being stolen from their beds in the dead of night.

And she gave it to them.

She. Wanderer.

She built them reservations and put up wards around them. She taught them about the magic that binds us all to our land and created the Guardians to protect the Elderlands. And then, as a failsafe, she created the Keepers and gave them the magic they needed to anchor the wards. With her magic imbued in the land and the Keepers to keep it alive, the packs could thrive. She even changed the way that the lands in the realm gave out gifts, unifying packs under universal kinds of magic and leaving the nomads to claim whatever they were offered.

With the establishment of reservations and the incentivization of membership, hundreds of packs became dozens, and then dozens became three. The Aiyanik people had been settled on their land for a few hundred years by then, but the Blackwoods were more of a loose collection of packs with similar mindsets until their unification. The Kivleneiks were then—and are still—a mystery, and extraordinarily little is known about their overall structure. Anya seized the power that was available to her and held onto it even when the Elder Council challenged her.

And then, when she was satisfied with the rest of the work she had done, Wanderer helped establish the Neutral Lands. A safe place for those who didn't want to be bound by pack rules—where Nomads could be protected without giving up their independence.

The peace, though, only lasted for a hundred years before three packs became four, and then five. And then, with us, six.

As the packs divided, she says, the children stopped attending school in the Neutral Lands, where they were taught the same histories and the same skills. It was the first sign of the packs operating like independent states instead of a network of connected people. It's when they stopped all non-essential communication, too.

There's something validating about knowing that there's a reason beyond privilege for the disparities in the education I got and the one that Shawn, or Sutton, or Kelly had access to. I notice it often when we're all together, and it breaks my heart every time.

The people we trusted altered the history they taught us, changing things as they felt like it so that they never looked like villains, and we grew up believing what they told us. Because they didn't give us a reason not to.

By the time I've finished the first letter—all seventeen pages of it—my head is throbbing, and my eyes hurt, and I'm angry.

I grew up believing that humans were dangerous, that they were the reason that many supernatural species were dying out, but none of that is true. Not only are the other night and day creatures not on the verge of extinction because of their interactions with humans, they're thriving.

I even learned that Vampires make excellent musicians, which is a theory I tested by opening up a browser and playing music by some of the people she named. I think it was my way of proving to myself that at least some of what she said was true.

By five minutes after six, all I have left to read is the second letter, written on the same heavy parchment as the first. It's folded precisely and sealed with the same wax and seal, which pops easily when I run my finger under the edge of the parchment. The smell of her hits me as I unfold the letter, different than the scent clinging to the twine, but similar. This time, it's like ocean salt and vanilla. There's a wildness to the scent, like flying or falling, something I can't place. I pick up the first letter and smell it, going back and forth between the two until I can detect the similarities.

Until I can tell that there are two scents on the second sheet of parchment and that one of them is the same as what's under the rich smokiness I keep smelling.

On the page, I see my name in the same flourished writing, and then everything else is written with precision, a different Alphabet and a different utensil. The Hebrew words spill across the page, and my eyes take a second to adjust, scanning over the careful strokes until I remind myself to read it in the order it's meant to be read. I have the same problem with books, so it is far from the first time I've had to give myself that reminder.

I picked up my pen intending to tell you what I found in the crisp, well-formed letters and perfectly straight lines of text, but I might just have to read it again first. Maybe twice.

Definitely more.

Ms. Aliyah Jade Trevonaire,

I trust now that you understand both the seriousness of my offer and the gravity of my situation. Abbigail is everything to me, and I will do everything in my power to keep her safe. I regret deeply that I can't tell you what's threatening her, but I also promise that I can keep it from coming near you as a result of your aide.

What I said when I saw you, about giving you all the opportunity to say your goodbyes to the loved ones you have lost, was true, and so was my offer of giving you the freedom to live your lives as you see fit. Everyone deserves to live, love, and die on their own terms, and I can give that to you and your people. I want to give you the chance to see your mother one last time, so that you can say goodbye properly, and I know that she would want that too. I knew her, you see, and I always envied her. She had this confidence that I've only ever been able to fake, and she had this way of making me feel like she saw me for more than who I've spent my entire life pretending to be. Her death was a tragedy, and the world is a worse place without her. I hope that her memory is a blessing to you, as it is to me.

I'm not writing this because I want to go over everything I offered you tonight. After all, I know you remember each part of our conversation as well as I do. What I write to discuss is much more personal, something I want to give you out of pure selfishness and self-indulgence, if you let me.

The greatest gift I can offer you and your family is security, and while some of that will come from the wards I rebuild for you; the rest has to come from you. My family is like yours, fundamentally, and we have trained for years to ensure that we are the fastest, smartest, strongest opponents any of our enemies ever face. If you let me, I want to help your family learn the same things. Wolves used to be warriors, and it kept them safe. If you're going to survive what's coming, I fear that you may need to reach for that warrior's spirit and prepare to fight back.

Come see us, let us help you, and while we can't teach you everything before the world descends into chaos, Abbigail can teach you the rest while she is with you. I can promise you that you won't regret it.

Behind this, you should have a spare sheet of parchment. Record your list of demands on it, along with any questions you may have for me in the meantime. I will respond before the moon is full. And when you're ready, come to the coordinates at the bottom of the page. We'll know you're coming, and we'll be ready.

Don't forget to break the temper stone I gave you when you're ready to see me again.

I need to thank you now; in case my time runs out before I find another chance. I see the love you have for your people, and I respect you for it. Know, though that I also see the love you have for the boy with the quiet soul and remember that your love for him has a value greater than you can possibly hope to know right now. The love you have for them will keep you going, push you forward even when your body aches desperately for rest and peace. It's your love for him that will burn bright enough to bring you the light that will guide you back from the darkest parts of your soul.

When you find your crucible, take his heart with you, and it will bring you back to him.

You're doing all the right things, and you should be proud.

Wanderer

P.S. Tell your sister that she may find being in her wolf form more comfortable, the babies will be less restless and she'll have a chance to get some sleep.

I put the letter down on my desk next to the piece of blank parchment and stared at it for a long time, searching the page for mistakes to make myself believe that 'babies' is one. There isn't a single stroke out of place on the entire page, every word is precise, and every line is perfect. There is no trace of even a single hesitation.

Babies.

Fuck.

7
Aliyah

I've barely lain down in bed when Shawn knocks and throws the door open. I look at the clock and groan. It's nearly eight in the morning, and by every measure, I should be getting ready to go down for breakfast, but I have absolutely no energy to even consider getting dressed.

The letter and the blank piece of parchment are both sitting on the small desk across the room, and the parchment is mostly empty, despite the hours I've spent staring at it. The emptiness haunts me, stark and cruel, even at a distance.

"You don't have to knock, you know," I say. I knew it was him before he actually knocked on the door, because I could feel his presence in my mind, close and warm and comforting. He closes the door behind himself and comes to the side of the bed, where he picks me up so he can lie down under me and be my pillow. He buries his face in my hair, and I can feel his chest and stomach expand as he breathes in my scent, like he's starving for it.

"I know."

"You feel tense," I tell him, and I mean it. His arms around me are rigid, tight like he thinks I could vanish at any moment.

"Do I?" he says, aiming for playful and missing by a mile. He forces a smile against my head and traces shapes across the bare skin of my back, right where my shirt is riding up and my sweats are riding down.

"Don't lie to me, please," I plead, and something about it takes all the tension out of him.

"I'm sorry," he says. I put my hands on his chest and my chin atop them so I can look at him without hurting him. "It just feels surreal that we could lose all of this over something Aviva did, I guess. And then there are these threats from other reservations and the random Warlock that showed up and could have killed you."

His hands flatten at the small of my back, and he lets out a long, slow breath, like the truth of the words and the weight of what he's saying are settling back over him and he's not sure he can take it. I reach for his presence in my mind and the rush of fear is immediately suffocating. I can feel that he's drowning, and I'm afraid that if I don't do something, I could lose him in the uncertainty curling around us.

"I trust Wanderer. I don't know why, but I do," I say, and then it hits me. "You know about what Aviva did?"

"I didn't fail sex ed, Ali. And I definitely didn't avoid getting the talk three separate times because my brother kept getting caught with his pants down. I knew the second you said she was pregnant, and I would bet Greyson did too," he says, and it's the first time I've considered the possibility that Greyson has known all along about the entrapment. Greyson is a smart man, royalty just like us, and it's entirely likely he got the same education in sex magic that we did. He knew and he stood by her anyway.

"I have to believe that all of this is going to work itself out," I say, kissing his chest and resting my forehead on my hands so that I can breathe in the musky scent of his skin. "I need you to believe that too if we're going to get through it."

"Why are you so sure?" he asks me, stroking my hair and taking low, steady breaths. "Why aren't you scared out of your mind?"

I think about it before I answer, and I realize that I feel no fear. Plenty of anger and other things, but no fear. I raise my head and look at the marking on my arm, the lines deep and dark against my skin. It gives me my answer.

"Because I can't be," I tell him. I sit up and straddle his hips, tracing the mark with my fingers. "Fear could paralyze me, and I can't afford that. Everything I feel, everything I'm doing, I'm doing for all of you. There is only one possible outcome I can allow, and that is the one where we are all here, together and safe. Nothing else is acceptable."

His eyes are heavy on my skin, following the curve of my neck down to the swell of my breasts, then tracing over the softest parts of my stomach on his way to the point where our bodies meet. When his eyes come back up to me, they're dark, and his heart is racing.

"When you talk like that, it makes it really hard to be afraid, you know," he says, his big hands coming to rest on my hips. His thumbs find bare skin and stroke, slow and soft as he watches me.

"Good, you shouldn't be afraid. Not for a second, not while I'm standing between you and the bad things," he pulls gently on my hips and I fall forward, catching myself with both hands on either side of his head.

"Who protects you while you protect us?" he asks, looking at my mouth.

"You do. Your existence, all of you, is all the protection I need," the world shatters around us as he kisses me, our bodies colliding until there's no space between us, no room for anything but the heat flaring through us. He breathes my name like it's a prayer he's dying to say, and I roll my hips, following the rapid flush of blood across his jaw and down his throat with my teeth and tongue.

"Ali," he says again. And then, for a long time, neither of us says anything at all, because our bodies are talking for us. His hands are on my skin, his nails leaving red lines behind as they bite into my flesh. I taste his blood in my mouth when I bite his bottom lip and chase his moan with my mouth.

Our clothes fall to the floor or get lost in the sheets, and there is nothing but he and I as we come together, the hard length of him pressing into me as he pins me to the bed. I could break his hold, and he'd let me, but I don't.

For those long, blissful moments, I am full and free and his. Not an Alpha, not a leader, just his mate. Mate. *Fuck.*

We made our list of demands today.

Our first request, unanimously, is to meet Abbigail before we invite her onto our land and into our home.

Our second request, also unanimously agreed to, is to say our final goodbyes to the people we've lost. For some of us, it means people who are alive and out of reach. For others, like me, it means bringing life back to the dead.

Third, we asked her to make good on her offer of training. She says she can teach us how to protect each other and ourselves, and that's all any of us has ever wanted. Wolves used to be warriors, and we want to know what that feels like.

Fourth on our list, we asked for our freedom. We want to be set free from the Elder Council, given the ability to negotiate with them as an independent entity. And with that come wards, strong ones, the strongest we can give ourselves. It might be pushing it to ask her to put so much strain on herself, but part of me doesn't care. She said anything, and I'm counting on her being a woman of her word.

And for our final demand, we asked her for an alliance that would extend beyond the short term. Beyond whatever is happening now and into the future. Something permanent, so that we know we always have an ally when we need one. A powerful one.

And that's it. That's all we asked her for. We talked for hours about how much more we could demand and decided that it wasn't us, wasn't in our nature to try and exploit a desperate person, no matter what it might mean for us.

Really, we don't need anything else. We all agreed that we would have considered granting the girl sanctuary without the book of checks we were offered. We would have done it because we've seen enough hatred in our lives and we would never leave someone to face hell alone, not as long as there was something we could do about it.

We wrote out list and, as promised, she responded before the full moon, agreeing to everything we asked of her. We're supposed to meet her and her family on a farm in Mississippi tomorrow, at the coordinates at the bottom of the letter, and she's supposed to get us there somehow. It'll be the first or second time ever leaving the realm they built for us for some of them, and that brings its own combinations of fear and anxiety. There's excitement too, though. I can smell it on them, see it in their eyes.

They want this. Possibly more than they've ever wanted anything. And they're hungry for what's being offered.

The only thing I can't help but wonder as I lay here and stare at the ceiling, is what we're going to find when we step out onto that field tomorrow.

What does Wanderer's family look like?

The gateway that opens to take us to the human world opens in the middle of the sidewalk outside the front door, only a few feet from where we have gathered to wait for it. It shimmers with the same brilliant gold light that clung to Wanderer when she appeared in the middle of the lake, but the center is solid, swirling, and shining. When I look closely, I can see them staring back at me, clustered together like we are, and watching us through the gateway.

"You can come through whenever you're ready," says a voice that is familiar and also not. My ears twitch and strain trying to place it, and then I hear her in my head, her voice whisper close.

In this life, my name is Anastasiya. I look into the gateway again and then I see her, standing at the front of the gathered group with her long hair braided down her back. I look at Shawn, then at Kelly, then at each of the faces behind them, trying to decide if they've heard her too.

They have.

"All at once, or one at a time?" I ask her through the shimmering surface. She laughs and the sound carries, echoing off the house behind us.

"Either is fine. The portal is stable enough for all of you."

Portal, she called it. *Interesting.* I stare at the portal for another few seconds and then decide that I might as well take the risk. I step forward, bringing myself face-to-face with the molten center of it, and then I step through.

The portal grazes my skin like feathers and diamonds,

both sharp and gentle. The air on the other side of it is stifling, hot and thick, and sticky in the worst way.

"Hello Aliyah," Wanderer says, smiling at me. I'm standing a dozen feet in front of her, staring at her family as mine follows me, one by one, through the portal. While I wait for them, I stare at her, too distracted to pay attention to anyone else.

Control your face, Alpha. Her voice is whisper close again, but there's a tone of warning in it that echoes in her eyes. I tell my face to relax and continue to stare. She's shorter than the first time we met, barely five feet, and her eyes are vivid purple, her irises too big for her face. She's still built like me, a little, her thighs and stomach soft, and her hair is mostly the same, the slight texture of it is hidden by the twisting of the strands into the braid that reaches her ass.

"Is that all of you?" The girl beside her asks. Her voice is warm, and immediately my eyes snap to her face—the same face that I saw in the images Wanderer showed me. I look over my shoulder and do a quick headcount, then nod.

"I believe so," I tell the girl, who smiles and looks at Wanderer—Anastasiya, I remind myself. The portal closes behind us with a gentle tinkling and a soft whoosh of air, leaving behind only the faintest trace of gold. I'd been expecting a lot of things when I stepped through the portal, but the little white farmhouse and big red barn weren't even on my list of possibilities. I never imagined there would be so many of them, either.

"Welcome," Abbigail says, taking Anastasiya's hand and squeezing her fingers. "We're glad you're here."

There's a soft hint of an English accent to Abbigail's voice, and it's pleasant to listen to. Anastasiya reaches up and brushes a curl away from the girl's face, and I hear her say something in a language I don't know.

"There's no word for that in English," Noah says, looking a little startled to have said it out loud, but mostly too curious to care. I look from him to Kelly and realize they both have the same look on their faces, their magic bubbling just under the surface of their skin.

"It was Russian," Abbigail says, smiling fondly at Anastasiya and turning her head to kiss her hand. I feel Tatiana and Noah both open their mouths to speak, but they beat me to it.

"Most of it was, but the term of endearment at the end wasn't." Wanderer's eyes snap to my face and flare gray for a split second, like she's afraid. "It's a little bit of a lot of things, but something like 'the one I love with all I am, more than I love my own life.' What language is that? I don't recognize it."

"What do you mean? I told you already--"

Drop it. Be careful what you say. I warn, letting them all hear it. Obedient silence answers, and Anastasiya regains control, giving out instructions with a cool calm that reminds me a little of my mother. I almost laugh when I remember what she said, about knowing her and envying her for that very thing.

We spend the day sparring, running, and shifting, and it's easily the hardest workout I've ever been through. We climb trees and wield long staffs, then we stop for lunch and have wolfsbane tea in the afternoon sun.

"How do you feel?" Abbigail asks, folding herself gracefully to the ground beside me and stretching her long legs out in the grass as she pops the last piece of her dessert in her mouth. Her mouth, I realize, looks soft as it spreads into a pretty smile. She doesn't look or seem sore or tired at all, even though she's been right there with us all day, hitting the ground just as hard and pushing her body just as far as we are.

"I feel like my muscles are made of jelly and I'm pretty

sure I'm going to have bruises on my hips, shoulders, and ass for weeks," I tell her, finishing my tea and setting the cup in the cool grass beside me, grateful for the small bit of shade I've been able to steal for myself. "I've never felt so strong in my entire life."

"Feels good, right?" She says, bumping our shoulders together and smiling.

"How about you?" I ask, still convinced she's some kind of superhuman. She laughs, and the sunlight turns her blue eyes to a sparkling glimpse of the sea.

"Well," she says, pulling her shirt up to show me her back. "I already had bruises, so most of my pain isn't workout related. I feel pretty good, but we've all been through this before."

"Those look like rope marks," I say, because I apparently have the tact of a starfish.

"They are. Or, well, some of them are," she pulls her shirt back down and twists to show me the matching marks on her thighs. "Some of them are bite marks and stuff, too."

"I'm sorry, I shouldn't have said that," I say, changing positions just to have something to do. "I wasn't trying to pry or be rude."

"Why would you be sorry? We're all friends here. If you want, I can take you on a tour of the dungeon before you go home. Ana has a really beautiful walnut St. Andrew's cross, and there are tons of cool things in there."

The word clangs through me like the ringing of a bell, and I feel my mouth drop open without my permission. She's talking about it like it's a casual part of her life, and I don't know what I'm missing.

"Sex," she says suddenly, dissolving into pure, joyous peals of laughter. "It's a dungeon for BDSM and sex, not the scary kind you're thinking of."

"A dungeon for sex," I repeat, feeling very out of my depth. She nods.

"Try not to scare our guests, my love," Anastasiya says as she approaches. I don't notice her until she's in my line of sight, and I start to scold myself before I realize that she makes virtually no sound when she moves.

"She asked!" Abbigail squeaks, laughing again and leaning into Anastasiya's side to demand a kiss be placed against her temple.

"We're about ready to get started again. Do you feel okay enough for that?" It's Russian that coats Anastasiya's voice, but I can tell that there's more beneath it, like Wanderer's voice is trying to come through, and she's barely keeping it down.

"Everybody feeling like they can keep going?" I ask, my voice conversational. I can see them all, split off into groups and conversing with their new friends in the patches of shade they have found. Some of them have chosen to embrace the sun, even stretching out like cats and soaking in the warmth. The different variations of yes come at me from all angles in the form of head nods and thumbs up, and softly spoken replies. I nod to Anastasiya.

"Alright then. Can you find Aleksandr and get everybody lined up?" She asks Abbigail, tugging gently on the shimmering golden collar circling her throat. Abbigail makes a soft noise of appreciation and gets up, bouncing off toward the barn without saying another word.

"So, this is your family?" I ask Anastasiya, shifting closer to her so that we can drop our voices low.

"Aren't they incredible?" She asks, and I don't have to think about my answer.

"They're more than that."

8
Aviva

"You know, you don't have to push your little feet into my ribs, little one," I say. I've been trying to keep my voice soft and sweet. I don't want them to know me any other way. Not until they have to. But if they don't get their little tiny feet out of my ribs and stop punching me in the bladder, I might have to get a little unkind.

I've been talking to them all morning. We've walked the length of the room a thousand times, and they've listened to my description of the nursery I'm going to build. We had to negotiate on a few details. For example, they've decided that they don't like blue or green, so we're settled on yellow.

They weren't fond of an animal theme, so we settled on gingham and celestial imagery.

They also don't like it when Greyson isn't around, which feels both relatable and insulting.

"Vivi?" Ali says from the door. I'm so focused on talking to the curve of my belly that I don't even notice her until she says my name. I nearly jump out of my skin.

"Hey, come in," I tell her. I'm supposed to be pretending to hate her, but I can't do that right now. Not while there's no one around to see it. Not when I want her to love them as much as I already do, and definitely not when she's the one who's going to have their lives in her hands. Mine too, probably.

"I didn't mean to scare you," she says, and she actually looks sorry. I kind of think I might have been too convincing. Too bitchy and too hostile. She looks like even she might believe it.

"You didn't. We've been negotiating," I tell her. My hand is resting on my belly in the spot where the gentle kicks are coming from, and when I reach for her, she comes. I place her hand there and hold it. "Can you say hi? This is your Alpha, and she's going to be the one that helps me bring you into the world."

The answering kick is so fierce that I nearly pee myself and also lose all the air in my lungs.

"Hello to you, too, little wolf," Ali says. She moves out of my way to let me run to the bathroom, like she knows, and I think she probably does. I won't be the first person she's helped through labor, and I won't be the last. I shouldn't feel a pang of sadness at that. At the idea that it won't be special for her the way it will be for me.

"I need to decide whether I want to know the sex," I say. I've been playing with the decision for weeks now, never any surer than I am now, no matter how long I think about it. I'm peeing in the dark with the door open, but it isn't the first time I've talked to her like this, and it won't be the last.

"What does Greyson think? Have you talked about it?" She asks. And we haven't. Because we never talk about anything.

“No, haven’t had the chance,” I tell her, my mood souring a little. I can hear her moving around as I wash my hands, but I can’t tell what she’s doing.

“That makes sense. It’s a decision you two have to make together, and talking to him might help you decide what you want,” she says.

“What are you...?” I ask as I get out of the bathroom. She’s the first thing I see, sitting with her legs crossed on the corner of the bed. The bed that she has made.

“I don’t want to know what goes on in those sheets, and I definitely don’t want it on me,” she says, and we both laugh. It’s the belly-deep, whole-body laugh that only she seems to bring out in me, and it feels good. It’s like my body needed it and I had no idea.

“I did just change them,” I tell her when our laughter dies down. She makes a face at me and I start laughing all over again.

“Alright, alright, you win. Oh my,” I say, wiping the tears from my face with one hand and pressing into my ribs with the other, hoping to soothe the cramp the laughing caused. “Did you need something when you came over here, or were you just passing by?”

“Neither,” she says, twisting a long curl around her finger and then tucking it behind her ear to stop herself from continuing. Our mother spent years trying to break her of the habit, and I think of her every time I see Ali struggle with it. “I was thinking about you, so I came to check on you.”

“You were... thinking about me?”

“Is that so hard to believe?” She asks, and there’s no sign of a lie anywhere on her face or in her eyes. The longer I look at her, the more I realize that the answer is no. No, it isn’t hard to believe. It's actually really easy to believe, because that's the kind of person she is. The kind of person she has always been.

"No. No, you've just been busy, so I was surprised you were thinking about much of anything when you didn't have to be," I say. I sound insecure, and I hate it. Hate the soft quiver in my voice and the way that even my baby knows I'm feeling sorry for myself.

"You're still my sister, you know," she says, and I don't look up from where my hand is resting on my belly. "When everyone else is focused on the baby, when I'm angry with you, and when you do stupid things. You're still my sister. I still love you, and I still want your happiness as much as I want my own. You know that, right?"

No, I want to say. No, I don't. Because I don't deserve that kindness. That infinite, patient kindness that she seems to have for me. I don't deserve her warmth or her understanding any more than I deserve for her to worry about me. Because I don't treat her well enough to be worthy of any of those things, let alone all of them.

But I want it. Want to be worthy so badly I can taste the metal of it on the back of my tongue.

I don't say anything to answer her question, and when she asks me if she should leave, I don't say no. I let her go and close the door behind her before she can turn around and say anything else.

When the door swings closed and locks, I don't feel anything but relief.

9
Aliyah

The letter is on my bedside table when I open my eyes, and I hate the idea of reaching for it so much that I don't for a long time. We spent three days with Wanderer and her family, starting at eight each morning and ending near midnight, and now that it's over my bruises have bruises. My body is healing, trying its best to recover from what I've put it through, but it's taking time and I'm miserable while it's happening. I know they all are too.

I take a deep breath, check to make sure Shawn is still sleeping soundly, and force myself to sit up. The letter is written on the same rich parchment as all the others and when I pop the seal, I see that it's written in the same elegant, flourishing script. This time, she has written in English.

I begin to read.

Aliyah,

I hope that it's alright that I call you that, I feel that after this weekend, we are friends enough to be on a first name basis, but if I'm wrong, you should tell me. I wanted to write and thank you for spending your weekend with us. We never have visitors, and it was incredible to get to see our families mingling like old friends. I don't know about yours, but mine loves the opportunities they get to make friends.

We spent years learning what we've only had a short time to try and teach all of you, but I hope that you will continue to work hard like you did yesterday. If you do, I think you will find the movements come more easily each day and feel more natural. You have an incredible family, and they are capable of incredible things. I know you know that, but I thought you deserved to hear it. I consider it a gift to have been able to spend time with all of you, and I am grateful that you took me up on my offer.

I'm writing to ask a small favor. If you don't mind, I'd like to send some things to you, so that they'll be there when Abbigail arrives and she will have reminders of home while it's far out of reach. I've also arranged gifts for each member of your pack, as a token of friendship, I will send them along with my brother tomorrow when he comes to you. If you show him where Abbigail will be staying, I'll be able to deposit her things directly into the room so that you don't have to deal with any of it.

I don't know if she told you while you were here, but she likes you. She wasn't sure what to expect when I told her you were coming, and neither was he, but they were both pleasantly surprised. I think he might have found a friend in your Greyson, and I hope I am right. He sorely needs friends, and watching them was the most relaxed I've seen him with a stranger in a long, long time.

You are all welcome on our land, in our home, any time you wish, and we would be more than willing to continue working with you. Our families are evenly matched in many ways, and that isn't something I often find.

I've included a few spare pieces of parchment this time, so that you may reach me if you need to, and I've sent you a package. It should be on your desk, just like the last one. It's large and heavy, so I apologize for that in advance. It contains a collection of leatherbound journals. The blue ones are for Abbigail, please give them to her when she arrives. The gray one is for you. It functions similarly to the parchments and will allow you to write to me even after I've run out of time. I can't promise that I'll write back at first, but I would be grateful if you would write anyway, just so I know that all of you are alright.

I can feel the time ticking away, and I worry that there's nothing I can do to prepare for what comes next. I know I can't slow it down and it haunts me each second, like the reaper is coming for me.

Here's to hoping I'll see you on the other side. Until then, keep fighting.

Best,

Wanderer

It's signed with the same inverted lotus symbol, the one that she seals her letters with, and the one I'm starting to think was once how she wrote her name. I drag myself out of bed and walk to the window, careful not to wake Shawn as I disentangle myself from the twisted sheets.

Beyond the bulletproof glass of the full-length windows, the water clinging to the trees seems to sparkle in the light, and I can't decide if the trees are really greener or if I'm just seeing them clearly for the first time.

Aleksandr might be the most beautiful male creature I have ever seen. When he steps through his portal and into the middle of my office, he leaves a shimmering trail of her golden magic behind. Where it touches him, it sparks and turns black, like little shards of onyx.

"Good morning, Mr. Volkov," I say, smiling at him from behind my desk. The parcel full of books is still wrapped and is sitting on the floor beside me. His eyes go straight to it, and when they find me, they're endlessly black in a way that feels like they eat up the light in the room. A shiver runs down my spine, and instead of thinking about his full lips or inky hair, I'm thinking about how easily he looks like he could kill me.

"Lexie," he says, swallowing and straightening his immaculate suit. It's all black, made of beautiful fabric, and tailored perfectly to the shape of his strong arms and lean waist. "We're friends."

"Right, Lexie. It's nice to see you again," I tell him, though I feel like I might be lying. I'm not entirely sure. "How do you want to do this?"

"I'm here, and the door is closed. I can start with you, if you want."

I swallow, hard.

"Okay, we can do that," I say, and I feel no fear. No fear of him, no fear of seeing her, nothing but pure excitement. He smiles at me, a broad, beautiful, terrifying smile, and steps back until he's against the wall.

His magic is black when it pours out of him. Inky and silken as it spreads through the room and fills the air with his rich, musky scent. There's an emptiness to the feeling that it brings, completely the opposite of the way it feels to be in the presence of Wanderer's magic, and the air grows steadily colder as the black tendrils fill the room.

"Call for whoever you want to see," he says, his voice distant and deep. Through the cloud of magic that has consumed my office, I can see his handsome face, and his irises have spread their inky blackness to his entire eye. He looks like hell and still I feel no fear.

"Natalia Renee Nathair," I say, my eyes filling with tears at just the mention of her name.

"Natalia," he echoes, his voice filling the room and ringing painfully in my ears like the beating of a heavy drum. My name is the next thing I hear, and it's her voice speaking from within the depths of the darkness. She takes shape slowly, each new piece of her forming out of the sharp end of a tendril until she's smiling at me, her hand raised to her mouth and her eyes shining with bright, crystalline tears.

"Mom," I feel myself say, and then I'm falling into her arms and she's catching me, keeping my knees from hitting the floor. Once I'm in the center of his gathered magic, it feels like cool water, licking at my skin and sending little goosebumps over my flesh. It's strange, but not entirely unpleasant.

The problem with seeing someone you've lost is that it doesn't matter how much time you spend thinking of things you want to say or preparing yourself for the sight of them. You're never ready. Never really prepared to see them, hear them, *smell them* again.

And I am definitely not ready. I spend the entire hour I have with her mentally recording every detail of her beautiful face, even though I see so much of it in myself and Aviva every day. I want to tell her about the pregnancy, but that feels like it's Aviva's to share, so I settle for telling her about Shawn and the Elder Council and Anya Kivleneiks.

And she tells me that she knows I'll find the answers to all of it. This tells me that the Elders made the right choice and that she knows I will do what's right, no matter the cost. She tells me that I deserve to be happy and that no matter how long it takes, I should never stop fighting for it.

She tells me she has no idea who killed her or how she died, and it breaks my heart, because some part of me was hoping she would have answers for me.

I feel my connection to her weakening after a while, and when I look at Aleksandr, the Necromancer is grimacing in pain, his face slick with a thin layer of sweat. I know I have to say goodbye, even though I don't want to, and I think she knows it too. She kisses my face and strokes my hair while she tells me she loves me, and then she's gone.

More quickly than she came, she vanished into the smoky tendrils, the scent of her lingering where she stood. It's kinder, probably, than watching her disappear a piece at a time, but it still hurts. I breathe in as much of her scent as I can steal from the air and wipe the tears from my face with both hands.

"You can stop," I tell Aleksandr, who's shaking from the exertion. His magic snaps back to him in a rush, and the vacuum it leaves nearly knocks me over. His hands spark for a few seconds after the last black tendril is gone, and I'm reminded again of little shards of onyx, razor sharp and deadly.

"Did you get what you needed?" he asks me, wiping his face with a red handkerchief he produces from a pocket in his coat.

"Yes. And thank you. I could tell it was hard for you," he laughs and shakes his head. "It's supposed to be hard. If it wasn't, we'd be tempted to do very, very stupid things without power. It's all about balance."

"It's kind of beautiful, your magic," he laughs again. "You look like a dancer when you... Do whatever that was. It's interesting to watch."

"I think my sister is ready to join us," he says, glancing at his watch and nodding to the spot where little sparks of golden light are beginning to gather. We back away and let the portal rip open the air in the middle of the room, its swirling surface solidifying just before she steps through and vanishing as soon as she's fully in the room with us.

"It smells like magic in here. Did you get to see your mother?" She asks me, shaking the sparks of magic off and shifting rapidly to her taller, more intimidating height. Her eyes are gray when they meet mine, and her hair is loose around her shoulders. This time, without the strange robes, I can see delicate golden lines twisting over her skin like liquid lace.

"What are those markings?" They're beautiful, curling around her ear and down her neck. She's wearing a tank top and black jeans that hug her thighs, so I can only see the marks on her upper body, but I would put money on them wrapping around her legs and feet too.

"Warlocks' marks. They'll fade in a second," Aleksandr steps forward and kisses her on each cheek as a greeting.

"You must have a different name too," I say, looking at him. "Not just Aleksandr?"

"My name is Warrior," he says, eyes flashing that full blackness again. Harsh black lines appear along his neck and the back of his hands, more coarse looking than hers. "And I have those marks too."

"We should get started on the wards," Wanderer says, her markings gradually fading to unmarred skin. "It's going to take some time. Do you care if he uses your office for the rest of the day?"

"No, of course not. I think they worked out a schedule for who goes next already, so I have all day to help you however you need me to." I grab my sweater off the back of my chair and shrug it on.

"Wonderful. Come on."

I follow her out of my office and through the residence, wondering all the while how she knows where to go. She heads for the nearest stretch of the wards and plants both hands against the surface, which lets out a happy ripple, like it's welcoming an old friend. I suppose it kind of is.

"I'm going to build a permanent portal here, so you can come and go by car or on foot. It's going to take some time. You may want to try and find your Keeper. I'll need her help," she says. Her magic is gathering in her hands and spinning around her like a rainstorm, golden and molten and warm. The wards are drinking it up like they're starving for it, and I can't help but stare at her.

Cici, can you come here, please? We're in the driveway.

I remember the sound of my mother's voice, and I can't help but wish I'd thought of asking her about Wanderer while she was here. Some part of me already knows what she would say.

I'm getting out of the shower, give me five minutes.

"Cici will be here in a few minutes," I tell Wanderer, and she nods without turning her attention away from the wards. Whatever she's doing is beautiful, and after a few more minutes, she starts to back away from the wards, her magic still pouring out of her in steady waves and soaking into the surface of the mostly transparent wards.

"Did you get what you needed from Natalia?" She asks, lowering herself to the ground in the small patch of grass that takes up the center of the circular driveway. She leans back against the post that holds the key box and takes the heavy stone necklace off, dropping it into her lap.

Some part of my brain notes the way she says my mother's name—the familiarity there.

Her magic rears like a horse and charges forward, like it has been set free. The sight is unlike anything I have ever imagined, and I can't look away. There's a rope of magic running between her and the wards, thick as an ancient spruce and radiating the scent of cedar and vanilla. And she shows no sign of fatigue, basking in the sun and asking me about my mother.

There's no polite way to ask how powerful she is, so I don't, but I know in my soul that there's no unit of measurement for power like that.

"Hey, sorry, I'm here," Cici says as she approaches, and before I can answer, a tendril of Wanderer's magic snaps out to grab each of us, raising our feet off the ground and wrapping us in a shimmering layer of gold.

I have no words, so I say nothing as I hover there, the rush of her power singing in my blood and sinking into my bones.

I think about the shimmering gold of the collar around Abbigail's throat and wonder if they're the same, the collar and Wanderer's magic. They must be.

I wonder briefly how that works, and then I don't think about anything at all, because her magic is in my eyes, in my mouth, and in my brain. There is no beginning and no end, nothing but the magic and the wolf inside of me, rolling over to show its belly.

When I'm next able to move my limbs and open my eyes, I'm on the ground on my back with Shawn and Aviva both looming over me, talking too fast for me to follow. I blink until my eyes focus and then look for Cici, who I find half-sitting beside me with Sutton and Tatiana practically holding her up. Beyond Shawn's shoulders, half obscured, Wanderer is being held at knife point. The wicked blade is firmly grasped in Rose's hand, pressed against the column of Wanderer's throat, and neither of them is moving.

Everyone is staring at me except for Warrior, who emerges from the residence calling his sister's name and lets himself be brought to his knees as soon as he's close enough to see that she's alright. Brandon's hand rests on his shoulder like a warning.

The foggy, blissful haze in my mind is clearing, but slowly, and the idea of sitting up makes me kind of sad. I flick my eyes to Wanderer, who smiles discreetly and twitches her long, graceful fingers. The haze collapses on itself and retreats, leaving my mind perfectly sharp and clear.

"Would you all please put your weapons away?" My voice cracks, but I push myself into a sitting position, easing Shawn and Aviva back enough so that I can see Rose and Wanderer. The blade gleams menacingly in the fading light of the day, black and bright.

"Are you hurt?" Rose demands, her fingers biting hard into Wanderer's arm and her knuckles tight around the handle of the knife. It was a gift from me, that knife, and it matches the ones clutched in Elijah and Brandon's hands, where they linger beside each of the warlock siblings.

"I'm not hurt," I tell her, meeting her dark eyes and then looking from Shawn, to Kelly, to Greyson. I turn to Cici and take her hand, squeezing her fingers. "Are you hurt?"

"I would not have come here just to hurt you," Wanderer says. She's careful not to move too much, but the tip of the blade still pierces her skin, a drop of shimmering blood running down the column of her throat and toward her white shirt.

Rose's blade pulses, alive.

"If she wanted to hurt or kill me, she had plenty of time

to do it when we met. Lower your weapons, I won't ask you again," Rose's dark eyes search my face, and no one moves until she does, loosening her grip on Wanderer's arm and lowering the vicious blade to her side. "Brandon, let him up."

"What was that?" Shawn demands then, touching my face and pressing a kiss to my forehead before he turns to look at Wanderer, eyes blazing.

"Magic," she says simply. "Ward magic. I was doing as you asked."

"Can you teach us how it works?" Standing is easier than I expect it to be, and as soon as I'm on my feet, I extend my hand to Cici and pull her to hers. "I think that would help them feel better, to know what you did and why."

There are murmurs of agreement and head nods all around, but no one moves except for Warrior. He takes slow steps toward his sister, slipping between bodies until he's at her side and can take her hand. When they touch, their magic shimmers, and I swear there are swords strapped over their backs. The image is gone too quickly for me to be sure, but my curiosity lingers long after she begins to talk, walking us through the way that wards are made and the weaknesses that they have. We listen, each of us hanging on her every word, until she asks if it would help to see an example of what they can do.

"That would be great, actually. What do we have to do?" The wards look the same as they always do, nearly invisible except for the soft iridescent shimmer they give off in the light, but the longer I look at them, the more aware I am of the crackling golden magic within them. The heavier and more reactive they feel.

"I need a volunteer with a high pain tolerance," she says, and her smile is a little unsettling. Warrior looks faintly amused standing at her side, like he knows what's about to happen.

"I'll do it," Elijah says, raising his hand as he sheathes the long blade he wields at the small of his back.

"Is he healthy, Healer?" she asks me, and I nod, growing wearier by the second.

"Yes, he is. Perfectly."

"Pass through the wards and wait on the other side," Wanderer tells him, pulling away from the group to stand beside the shimmering wall. As her presence draws nearer, the magic pools, crackling bolts of gold snapping around her. "This portion here is a portal, it can take you anywhere you need to go, but practice using it when it's dark at your destination so that you aren't noticed."

"And the rest?" Elijah asks, gesturing broadly at the expanse of the wards not centered on our driveway.

"The rest is... like a bulletproof blanket," she says, stepping back until her heavy boots meet the grass and watching Elijah follow. "They're not unbreakable, but breaking them will take more than your worst enemies will want to spare in lives and magic. That's not what makes them interesting, though."

She motions for Elijah to step through, and he does, shivering as the thin layer of magic passes over him. He turns and faces us from the other side, his features just barely distorted by the magic racing between him and the rest of us.

"Aliyah, tell the wards that he's an enemy. You can say it out loud or with the magic in your blood," my first instinct is to tell her I have no idea what she's talking about, but those long fingers twitch again and I feel it, the sparking, electric shimmer of her magic under my skin. I don't mean to gasp, but I do, and it takes me a few seconds to blind away my amazement well enough to follow her instructions.

"Done," I tell her, and I know that it worked, because there's a soft sheen of red in the magic in front of Elijah.

"Try to pass through the wards and come back inside," she tells him, suddenly wearing the same mildly amused expression as Warrior. I want to tell him no. To yell that it isn't worth whatever is about to happen, but I don't know why, so I don't let myself say anything.

Elijah takes a breath and a step, and the howl of pain he lets out when he touches the wards shoots right through all of us, even before we register the angry, bloody red pulse of light that they emit. Elijah shoves at the wards, trying desperately to step back, but he can't.

"Say his name," Wanderer says calmly, like we can't all feel his heart stuttering in his chest.

"Elijah Rockwell," I say, sounding as frantic as I feel. As soon as it's out of my mouth, he stumbles forward through the wards, falls to his knees in the grass, and vomits violently. I'm at his side in a moment and she helps me pull him to his feet, holding half his weight so he's balanced between us.

"I'm going to take the pain away, okay?" she tells him, and he nods miserably until her magic snaps out over him. His heart steadies and his breathing comes more easily, then the color returns to his face and his legs steady.

"What the fuck was that?" He demands as soon as he finds his voice, and the laugh that comes out of me is nearly hysterical.

And the more she tells us, the less I want to know. I listen anyway.

10
Aliyah

"Hey, can I talk to you?" I ask, jogging to catch up with Wanderer as she continues her casual stroll along the wards, her magic singing in the air and sinking into their surface. There's still a small stream of blood dried on her neck, and she still isn't wearing the necklace with the stone on it. I saw her give it to Warrior and didn't miss the concerned look or exchange of sharp words that followed.

She turns to look at me and slows her pace until we're shoulder to shoulder, walking through the trees.

"Hello," she says with a smile. "Thank you for not letting your Delta slice my throat."

"They're protective," I tell her, laughing. "But, I think you would like Rose. She's one of the good ones."

"Those blades they carry, you had them made, didn't you?" I nod and step over a root that nearly snags my foot.

"The stones in the handle are harvested from the mines in the mountains. I can smell it."

"You're familiar with the kinds of creatures we share our reservations with, I assume?" She nods and smiles.

"I have long had close friendships with the little people. I find their kind fascinating and have a sincere appreciation for their simple way of life," summoned, a small female steps out from behind a tree and offers her a diamond the size of her palm. It's uncut and dull, but heavy as Wanderer takes it and smiles at the girl. She's gone as quickly as she appears, and she does little more than wave and curtsey at me as she goes.

The little people like her. *Interesting*. She's turning the stone over in her palm when I look at her again, and I can see the wonder sparkling in her big eyes. I smile.

"They help us with things we don't have enough people to do ourselves, for the time being, but as our numbers grow, they'll focus more on the harvesting of our natural resources for use and export," I can hear the falls in the distance, but we continue to follow the curve of the wards, the night gradually taking over and chasing away the remaining light. Wanderer offers me the diamond she's holding, and when she pulls her hand back, the shimmer of her magic lingers, setting the newly cut stone shining in my open hand.

"For now, it's cooking, gardening, cleaning, and repairs, I imagine. But you didn't chase me down to talk about the little people you share your land with, I'm sure," I feel my cheeks heat, and I hate they she's right. I hate that I've come to her to ask about her letter in the first place.

"You said babies," I say, deciding it's best to get it over with instead of letting myself avoid it. "In your letter, when you were telling me how to help Aviva sleep, you said babies, not baby."

Wanderer laughs at me. Not cruelly, but still. And I want

to shove the question back into my mouth, turn around, and forget what I asked.

"If you thought I was mistaken, you'd have done an ultrasound or counted their heartbeats," she says, and she's right. "You're asking because you're scared, and you want me to tell you that it was an accident so you can breathe a little easier.

"I knew as soon as I read your letter, probably even before that. I know how the magic works, how dangerous pregnancies are, and how our bodies try to avoid multiple pregnancies if they can. I knew that the likelihood of her having multiples—or of me eventually having them—was high, especially because we're multiples, but I was hoping," I cut myself off and sigh, my head throbbing painfully at the base of my skull.

"One baby is an easier problem to solve than three," she says, and I do actually trip over a root. The only thing that keeps me from falling face-first into the decaying carcass of a fallen tree is her grip on my arm. She waits until I've found my footing and gotten my balance before she lets go, and then she looks at her hand like she's been burned.

"Is everything okay?" I ask, watching her stare at her palm. Something cold and uneasy forms in my belly, and I don't know what it is.

"No, yes, everything is fine," she says. It's the first time I've ever felt like she's lying to me.

We've decided to have a meeting. All of us. And it starts in ten minutes.

I've spent every moment of my free time over the last forty-eight hours writing draft after draft of the severance letter I'll ultimately send the Council of Elders, and I'm no closer to knowing what the final version if going to look like than I was when I started. I have no idea how to simultaneously thank them for all that they've done for us and tell them that we want nothing to do with them without sounding harsh or impolite. And trust me, I've tried a few hundred different ways.

I am, unfortunately, very aware of the clock that's hanging over my head, and I spend an unreasonable amount of time thinking about how little time I have left before Aviva's ready to deliver. I have never been a last-minute person, and I feel more anxious about what I have to do every day that I fail to do it.

That's actually how we came to have this meeting in the first place. I was in my office on draft eight or draft eighty, when I realized that we have never taken the time to establish pack rules. It's something we can manage without for now, but that becomes more important the second we officially declare ourselves independent. I had planned on writing them during week one, because it seemed important, but then things got complicated, and I never came back around to it because nothing happened that made it feel urgent.

And that is how I came to be standing in the sublevels of the residence, waiting for everyone to arrive so our meeting can begin. I'm expecting the meeting to take a long time, because these kinds always do, and I'm expecting to walk out of the meeting with a loose set of rules that we can all agree to as a foundation.

Instead, when I walk out three hours later, I'm in awe of what we've accomplished. I'd expected a loose collection of rules and guidelines, but I'd ended up holding a book of rules nearly as dense as what we followed in Tamarak.

I walked out of the room fifteen minutes after they had all departed, holding two lists. One is a list of expectations for pack leadership, and one is a list of reservation rules stricter than I would have written on my own. They voted unanimously to accept both in the end, and I still haven't gotten over the surprise and awe of it.

I feel better about the letter-writing process knowing that we have our first official document in place, even though it barely scratches the surface of everything we will have to do in the coming months.

If I can finish the letter, I'll feel even better.

At the rate I'm going, Aviva and her babies will be teenagers before I'm through, and that is a very, very bad thing.

From the desk of Aliyah Trevonaire – Alpha

Wolflands Council of Elders:

It is my sincerest wish to begin this letter by thanking each and every one of you for the opportunity to lead the incredible group of young people that represent this year's expansion project into Noonchester Falls. Being considered for the role of Alpha would have been compliment enough, but being chosen over the others considered is the honor of a lifetime, an honor I will not soon forget the value of. I have spent every moment thus far grateful for the opportunity to serve, and I intend to spend the rest of my life just the same. In servitude, in whatever way my people need.

I sincerely wish that the entire purpose of this letter was to share my gratitude, but it isn't, and I need you to know that the decision I am about to share with you is not one made lightly or quickly. This letter alone has been drafted and redrafted so many times that I cannot count the versions anymore, nor remember what any version before this said.

I learned something during the last rewrite, about myself and about why I was struggling so hard to find the words I needed. What I learned was that in trying to be diplomatic, I was forgetting to be myself, and that made every word feel false. When the foundation is unsteady, the house will fall. In the spirit of being the most honest version of myself, I have decided to tell you in plain terms of our decision.

It is my honor, privilege, and duty to inform you—as Alpha of the Trevonaire—that we have chosen to step away from your counsel and all of the benefits that would come with remaining. We do not wish to be a part of your trade alliances, we do not wish to benefit from your infrastructure, and we will not be bound by your rules.

We, the Trevonaire, have made this decision together and agreed to it unanimously, as evidenced by the signatures you will find at the bottom of this page. We all wish to thank you for the opportunities you have given us, but politely decline to grant you our continued subordination.

This letter should serve as our official notice that we will be keeping our Keeper, Cristiana Noonchester, as well as our land at Noonchester Falls. Attempts to reclaim either will be considered acts of aggression, and repeated acts of aggression will be considered a declaration of war.

Further, we remind you that you and all guests to our reservation will be expected from this moment on to follow posted policies and procedures. No unauthorized personnel will be admitted to our reservation without permission and anyone who attempts to enter uninvited will be considered an aggressor and handled accordingly.

It is the declared intention of Trevonaire to pursue individual alliances with those who are willing to accept our independence unconditionally and to serve as a safe haven for those who find themselves in need of one.

We are, as mentioned, united in these decisions and expect that they will be respected the same as they would be coming from any other Alpha.

We will no longer allow ourselves to be bound by rules and regulations we did not have a say in creating, but we want you to know that we have no intention of creating enemies or tension by publicizing our decision. If you have any questions, comments, or other concerns regarding the contents of this letter, feel free to take advantage of the sanctuary at Noonchester Falls or send your response via courier. I will respond to all questions as best I can.

Thank you, sincerely, for your time and understanding.

Aliyah Trevonaire, Alpha

11
Aliyah

I finished the letter.

I delivered it to the council myself last night since their office is on neutral ground.

I didn't have it in me to stay while they read it.

Ali,

I wanted to be the first to write you in response to the letter that we received last evening, and I hope that I will be. I owe you that much. I hope you don't mind my informality, and if you do, I hope you will tell me so I can make an effort to change it. My wish is not to offend you. In fact, it's the opposite. I want nothing more than to support you.

I want to start off by saying that I am proud of you. Not only for the way that you have handled yourself in this situation, but for the way that you have behaved from the moment you were chosen as Alpha. I may not have shown it well in those early moments, but I assure you I was proud of you from the very start, and I am so incredibly sorry for letting you think that I wasn't.

Next, I would like to say, in the plainest terms possible, that your decision changes nothing in the eyes of the Aiyanik people. You have always and will always be a welcome guest here, and you may come and go as you please, even now. While I would ask that you make the difference in social and diplomatic visits clear, I want you to feel welcome to return at your leisure, a right you will maintain for at least as long as I am Alpha.

I respect and support your choice to declare independence, and I know in my soul that your mother would have too.

We, the Aiyanik people, feel confident in declaring that —without need for negotiation—we are the proud allies of the Trevonaire in every way. We will trade with you, support you, defend you, and honor you as allies should from now until the very end. I've included a draft of a trade agreement and a treaty in the letter, both of which I believe you will find written in your favor. If you do feel the need to make revisions, feel free, and we will be happy to meet with you to discuss them.

Finally, before I let you go, I'd like to formally offer you my ear, any time you need it, and in any capacity you might find useful.

Best of luck and all my love,

Demetria Marshall, Alpha

P.S. I love you to the moon and back again. I'm so proud to have the opportunity to sit front row as you become the woman I have always known you could be.

I'm lying in my bed rereading a few of the letters I've received and planning out my responses when Cici appears in the doorway looking very nervous.

"Cici? What is it?"

"We've been summoned," she says, wringing her hands and shifting her weight back and forth. "By the Council of Elders. We have an hour."

I don't bother restraining myself when I groan in frustration, but I do drag myself out of bed and shove my feet into my leggings, still in a ball on the floor. Being summoned isn't suspicious on its own, especially not when it comes on the tail end of a letter like the one I sent them, but being summoned in the middle of the night with only an hour to prepare definitely is. It takes a minimum of forty-five minutes to make that run in perfect conditions. In the pitch dark, we'd be lucky to make it if we left right now.

I finish dressing slowly, shedding the oversized t-shirt of Shawns and pulling on a bra. I'm shoving my hands into a sweater I bought myself when I look up and find that I've been thinking so loudly I've summoned all three of my Betas. They're all standing behind Cici, crowded into the door like they might force their way past her to get to me.

I pull my sweater on and push past them, shoes in my hand. I don't have it in me to explain myself more than once, so I decide that I won't and I stick to it.

"Everyone up. Get dressed and be outside the bay door in two minutes," I speak the words aloud, and through the bond we share, and I feel them all snap to attention. I shove one foot into one shoe and nearly fall putting on the other, but Shawn catches me, steadying me with both hands. I head for the bay door immediately, watching those who were lounging in the common space scramble to get to their rooms and listening to those in their rooms scramble to get out. I can hear the abandoned video game sounds coming from the game room, even, but they barely register. Something doesn't feel right.

The night air is cool against my skin when I step out into the darkness through the ever-open pay door. The ward magic over it is mild, only designed to keep the outside air and creatures from coming in and pups from wandering out. It's the same as the magic on all the other doors and windows, but it feels more intense when I step through it. Instead of calming me, the night air raises my hackles even further.

"What are you thinking?" Shawn asks. Greyson and Kelly are behind him, all trailing after me as I pace along the side of the residence. The first group of pack members steps through the bay door and into the night air as I answer, so I don't speak.

Do you ever get the feeling that someone is laying a trap, just waiting for you to walk into it and thinking you're too stupid to notice? I ask them. They look concerned, intrigued, and angry all at once, which feels like an appropriate assortment of emotions. Cici hovers just out of my sightline, dressed in the same gray jeans and black shirt she often wears, but there's something in her face that tells me she feels the same unease I do.

"We told them we were keeping Cici and our land. I'm guessing whatever is about to happen is their way of challenging that," I say. Most everyone has trickled out into the night air, including a very sleepy Leighann, and the last stragglers are close enough that I can hear them.

"What's the plan?" Kelly asks, looking very alarmed.

"They don't know about our gift," I say to everyone. Cici catches on before the rest of them, by a full three seconds. "If this is their play to take back Noonchester Falls, we let them think it's working."

I explain my plan as quickly as I can, keeping an eye on my watch as I do. I know from our experimentation that Aviva can only push away from her body for ninety minutes without it wearing her down and posing a risk to the babies, so I set my watch's times and watch our bodies drop to the ground in little clusters, obscured by the residence and away from the wards. Only Cici and Leighann remain upright. It takes a few minutes for our magic to gather enough that we look solid and real—something we've only been able to manage in the Wolflands. I ask Leighann to remain behind and watch from the top of the residence while we're gone. She's small enough to be nearly invisible, and it'll let me know what's happening while I'm away. Cici's job is to stay as far away from the wards as possible and out of sight.

"The Elders can't know that they're looking at a lie, and they can't know that we're suspicious of them. If you have anything to say or anything to share, say it in here," I touch the side of my head and glance down at my watch. "By leaving our bodies behind, they can't hurt us, and we don't have to try and run back if I'm right about what's about to happen."

"What happens if you're right?" Sutton asks. She's in the middle of the pack, barely visible behind Rachelle's shoulders.

"Let's hope I'm not. I need you all to trust me for a little while. Can you do that? I promise I'm not going to let anything happen to any of you," they don't hesitate to agree, their nods and yips and howls like music to my sensitive ears. Behind it, I can hear something moving in the brush, and the feeling of unease in my belly turns to anger.

We run the whole way in our human forms, passing through the trees instead of moving around them and flying freely over the three lakes that lie between us at the Council chambers. I check as we approach that Aviva's belly is concealed, and then begin to intentionally move like a human, my footsteps loud on the cobblestones outside the Chamber doors.

We have two minutes to spare when I throw the door open and lead them inside.

Time to see if I'm right. Keep your eyes open.

The Elders look at us when we enter the room, may in disgust at my lack of respect for tradition. I don't care that I didn't wait to be announced, and I don't care if barging in is rude. It's the middle of the night, and with every passing moment, I become more convinced that an attack is imminent.

When the last person is through the door, it slams shut and the lock is thrown. The feeling in my belly grows and a growl threatens to slip free of my mouth. I barely force it down.

The Elders are all present, the entire council gathered and the chambers full. They're wearing the same intricate robes they always wear, each colored based on the pack they represent. I stop myself and scan the room again.

The number is right, but the faces are wrong. Some of the representatives have been swapped out, twenty of them, by my count. The entire Aiyanik delegation and half the Blackwood group have been changed. Beside me, Kelly's dragging critical eyes over the Rosendes Elders.

What do you see, K? I ask him, careful to keep my face blank. He's biting his tongue, and his ears are twitching, the distinctly canine gesture almost charming,

Magdalena's heart is racing, and she's sweating bullets. There's bruising on both of her wrists—handprints. I follow his eyes to the old woman, and when the Elder beside her—a stranger to me—sees us looking, he pulls her robes down to cover her hands. She flinches like she's been hit. Sitting where Cyan Vianbry should be and wearing the mantle of Chief Elder is Hadrian Rosendes, his lined face drawn in contempt, completely unhidden.

"You called us and we came," I say. Hadrian stands and his robes billow around his as he moves. He looks like a bat stretching its wings. I flash him my sweetest smile and pretend I don't see the gun he's wearing under his robes.

In my head, I feel Leighann tense, her eyes tracking the shadows around the wards. She's crouched low on the roof, a wraith moving across the metal surface searching for a threat with every one of her senses. Heer eyes are the sharpest in the pack and when she begins counting the seconds between glimpses of a shadow in the trees, I have no doubt that what she sees is a threat. I have even less doubt that I would have missed it, if I had been the one looking. Hadrian opens his mouth and starts to speak just as I feel a flicker along the wards, like someone is running their finger over the surface.

"Why do you assume we want something from you?" he asks me, and I don't laugh. It's an act of sheer willpower. "We were hoping to discuss your letter."

I don't need Leighann's magic to tell me it wasn't true because the lie feels like acid under my skin. I also don't need help noticing the suspiciously low number of Elder Guards and Guardians.

Find Cici and hide. I tell Leighann, and she drops from the roof into the center of our discarded bodies, grabs Cici by the hand, and drags her into the woods. The few Elder Guards in the room begin to move, slowly closing around us and resting their hands on their weapons. I don't see who gives the order, but I give one of my own.

Stand down. Do not engage. Let them believe the lie.

Every instinct in me tells me to fight. To howl my defiance and tear into everyone who dares think they can hurt my family. But I don't. I do what I've been taught to do my whole life. I keep my eyes open, smile, and play the game.

"Elder Rosendes, I find your charade of diplomacy revolting," I tell him, my voice sweet and mild, just like I've practiced. I don't grant him the respect of calling him Chief, because it's a title he's stolen, even if only for a moment. The air in the room shifts and chills, and I know without a shadow of doubt that my instincts were right.

"I'm sorry to hear that, Ms. Nathair," he says. The room crackles with pheromones and soft rumbles. "Because you see, Cristianna Noonchester and Noonchester Falls both belong to us."

The guards lunge for my Betas, and I laugh, watching with glee as their projections vanish, leaving the guards to spin around, stupidly looking for their marks. The guys reappear behind the guards that were meant to grab them and disarm them, the moves honed from the intense practice I've seen them do in the time since our weekend with Wanderer's family. The guards' knees crack as they hit the ground, and they don't care to fight back, the claws at their throats razor sharp and ready. I force the proud smile off my face.

"Cristiana Noonchester is no one's property, and you cannot have my land," I say simply. "This meeting is over, and it's time for us to leave. Thank you so much for making it very clear who my allies and my friends are."

We turn and leave, shoving the remaining guards aside on our way out. When I'm clear of the Elder Guards, my Betas release the guards they're holding with fierce shoves that land them on their stomachs. I'm nearly into the square when a Guardian attempts to grab me. It's a misguided attempt to stop us from leaving, ordered with a shout by Hadrian, but it's the last thing he does before Rose whips her blade across his throat and leaves his head on the cobblestones.

"That's my Alpha," she growls at the others approaching us. They freeze, hands raised, and stare at her, watching the blood drip from the blade at her side.

Inside my head, Leighann's presence sharpens, and a growl builds. The wards are shaking, filling the air with a low hum as something gathers beyond them. She drags Cici farther into the trees and shoves her deep into a cave I've never seen before. I only notice the cayenne pepper she's been scattering because it makes her sneeze. I can feel her steady heartbeat, and I know that I don't have to ask her if she's okay.

Don't let them see you snap back, I remind everyone. They're clustered together and heading for the dark shadows behind the Elder's chambers, but they're too slow. The Guardians are closing in around us and as I turn to tell them to hurry, one lands a blow along my jaw. Rose is there a second later, Elijah by her side, and the guard doesn't move again.

As I rub my jaw, I see the Elders through the still-open chamber door and realize that they're watching us. I can feel every pair of eyes, but only some of them are cold. Those who are standing and radiating anger, barely containing it enough to keep themselves from joining the fight. Those who remain seated—the original Elders—look desperate to help, desperate to do something to change what's unfolding around them.

Interesting.

The others clear the side of the building and dive into the shadows, moving fast. They're gone in an instant, and I'm the only one left in the plaza. Hadrian still stands in front of Cyan's chair.

"Trying to take what is mine, will be considered an act of war, Hadrian. Remember that," I tell him, and then I run for the trees, daring the Guardians to follow just so that I can embarrass them one last time. As soon as I'm deep enough into the shadows, I snap back to my body where it rests in the damp grass of Noonchester Falls.

Waking up hurts, because the pain in my jaw is very real and the ground is very hard. There are hands on either side of my face, but I don't know who they belong to. They're warm and the voices around me are panicked. My watch begins to go off.

The timer I set.

I open my eyes and gasp, sucking down air into lungs that burn for it, and I drag myself to my feet. There's no one left in the clearing behind the residence except for the person who had been knelt beside me in the dewy grass. I expect it to be Shawn, or Greyson, or literally anyone other than Abbigail Barlow, who is naked as hell and staring at me in confusion. There are still sparks of gold in her hair.

Her blue eyes are full of tears when she stands up.

"Why am I here?"

12
Aliyah

Abbigail is wearing Shawn's button-down by the time we get to the driveway. He didn't even hesitate when he saw her, pale skin marred by endless goosebumps as she attempted to adjust to the cool night air surrounding us. She buttons just enough of the buttons to be decent and looks around, eyes searching the wards and the faces around her.

"So we can protect you," I tell her finally, her question still hanging unanswered between us. Greyson is taking Aviva to the sublevels, Rose is glued to my side, and Elijah is waiting for me a few feet ahead, with Kelly by his side.

"It seems like you're the ones that need protecting," she says, those depthless eyes still flicking back and forth along the wards, like she sees shadows moving. It's the same thing Leighann was doing, and it feels ominous in the same way, too.

"Where did you come from?" Kelly asks, looking both confused and intrigued. His eyes slide over her body in a slow drag, lingering for a moment on the swell of her breasts and the softness of her thighs before they come back to rest on her pretty, freckled face.

"I'm not sure. I was sleeping next to Annie one second and then falling from a questionable height onto my ass behind your house the next. Ali's body was on the ground, and she wasn't moving, so I panicked, and now I'm here. None of that matters now—how can I help?" She's putting on a brave face, but there are tears shining in her eyes, and I can tell she's shaking. I reach my hand out toward her, and she shakes her head.

"I'm not asking for your sympathy," she says, gritting her teeth and raising her chin. Those eyes snap to the wards, and I turn to follow her gaze, but I don't see anything for a long moment. "You have unwelcome guests and they're closing fast."

The delicate collar around her throat pulses in warning, and barely a heartbeat later, the wards flare, the night lighting up in brilliant gold and then falling idle again.

"They've breached the outer perimeter along the Northern Border, but only the spies they sent ahead have come near the wards. They seem to be dancing along the edges, trying to figure out why they feel different." Sutton and Rachelle are both out of breath, naked, and talking fast. "The battalion is coming straight for us, but they're sending soldiers out to surround us too."

Leighann, leave Cici there and come back to me. I'm sending Sutton to guard her. Sutton throws herself into the air and lands on all fours before I've finished giving my instructions, and Leighann's acknowledgement comes in the form of a mental head nod. She pokes her little head out of the cave they're in and whistles to alert Sutton to their location, careful not to breathe in the pepper she's dropped all over the ground.

"Everyone spread out and tell me what you hear. Abby, Shawn, Kelly, you're with me. Rose and Elijah too," I watch as they disperse, slinking through the night like predators and more than happy to hunt the prey that's closing in. The door to the residence opens and closes, revealing Greyson's familiar shape. He walks straight toward us and holds out a pair of sweatpants for Abbigail.

"Aviva wanted me to give you these," he says. "It's too cold for you to be out here without clothes."

He turns and heads back to the house. He only makes it a few steps before he turns back and points at me, looking at Abbigail and my Deltas.

"Keep her alive," he says firmly. "And preferably, unhurt."

Abbigail steps into the sweatpants she's been given, and when she's done, she nods at me. We run as a group to the Northern border, silence following us and practice concealing every step through the underbrush.

Leighann falls into step beside us about halfway and says nothing, her little legs working doubly hard to keep up until Elijah scoops her up and puts her on his back.

Stop, we're almost to the boundary. Spread out and tell me what you see."

What *I* see when I focus my eyes through the heavy darkness is a battalion of Kivleneiks soldiers, flanked on either side by units of Guardians. Standing proudly at the front of the legion are Anya and Elisabeth Kivleneiks, a short girl with black hair and red eyes between them. Her sharp gaze searches through the darkness, and when they meet Leighann's, both girls gasp.

"Mini," Leighann breathes, her head even with my hip. She reaches forward, but Abbigail hushes her, holding her still with gentle hands and sparkling blue light.

"We know that you're there, Aliyah Nathair," Anya says. My stomach churns at the grating sound of her voice, and I step forward until we're equidistant from the wards, on opposite sides of the boundary line. Abbigail raises her hand and tosses a small ball of light into the air above us. It sets the shadows dancing and casts everything in a silvery light, including the trees.

"I didn't invite you here," I tell Anya. Her husband is nowhere to be seen, which is unusual. Her face twists into a mockery of a smile, and she laughs.

"And yet, I am here. What are you going to do about it? You're just kids and you're all alone," she says, looking around at the small army she has brought to our front door. I scan the rows of soldiers intently, looking for anything I can use, and what I find is Saya. She's on her knees amongst the soldiers, with blood on her face and caked into her hair. Her wrists and ankles are bound, and her clothes are covered in fresh dirt.

I'm so focused on her and what her presence could mean that I don't hear their approach through the trees. They aren't even trying to be quiet.

My father is the first one to break through, Demetria at his side—radiant as always.

"You're half right, Anya," Demetria says, chin raised in defiance and eyes hard. "They are just children."

Demetria Marshall looks like she has been dragged out of bed, shrugged on a cloak, and come to our defense. My father beside her looks just as disheveled. He's wearing his usual khakis and sweater, but he has no shoes, and his socks have been shoved into his pockets. The rest of the Aiyanik that they have brought with them, soldiers and civilians alike, appear to have been equally rushed. They still look ready to bleed and die for us.

Mikael Blackwood arrives next, looking the epitome of poise and composure as he steps through the trees.

Andromeda Ravenswell leads her battalion of soldiers into the bubble of light a second later, stepping out from between the trees on silent feet with her long dress tied in a knot at her hip. I can hear their hearts beating steadily against their ribs, and I can smell each soldier, their scents saturating the air.

I'm still processing what I'm seeing when the Alphas and Betas peel away from their people and kneel in the underbrush in front of me, inches from the wards and as close to me as they can get.

"Aliyah Trevonaire," my father says, eyes fixed on my face. "If you'll have us, we'd like to formally declare ourselves your allies. Now, and tomorrow, and every day after that."

Andromeda is smiling at me, her striking face sharp in the silvery light, and so is Demetria. Mikael isn't smiling, but he also isn't glaring, so I consider that a good sign. I nod my head without permission, and the relief that washes through me is so thick it makes me shake.

"We'd be honored to have you," I tell them sincerely. One after the next, they raise their left hands and reach through the wards, their faces contorting in pain as a delicate band of color wraps around their wrists. Allegiance bands form, and they do not shy from the pain. They do not look away from me, not even to admire the rippling of the wards. When they stand, they turn and part, placing themselves between me and Anya without obscuring her from my sight.

"Anya, these children have asked nothing of us that should warrant this," Andromeda says, her voice silky and seductive. Anya's eyes soften for a moment and then turn back to ice. She opens her mouth to speak, but she doesn't get the chance because we all become very aware of the rustling trees and racing heartbeats approaching through the dense forest.

Lucien Ravenswell steps into the minuscule clearing and smiles the charming politician's smile he is known for—the one he has passed on to Kelly.

"When you fuck off back to where you came from," he says, flicking his fingers to call forward twenty soldiers, each dragging a bound and gagged Elder along with them. They're each dropped unceremoniously onto their knees and abandoned in the damp leaves. Every single one of them was present at the ambush, and none of them had been chosen by the packs they claimed to represent. Now, instead of being full of condescension and self-righteousness, they all look terrified. "Take these folks with you. There's no room in the Elder Council for traitors."

Incoming. Shawn says, ears twitching. I glance at Leighann, and her eyes are still fixed on the little girl. Abbigail's are snapping back and forth between the trees, searching for something. *They're a hundred meters out.*

I draw my shoulders back and take a deep breath.

Everyone close on my position. They move.

"Anya, this is your doing. Why don't you and your guests come forward and speak?" my father says, a sweeping gesture and a charismatic smile hiding his disdain. I can hear it. I've never met Anya Kivleneiks in person, but she looks so much like her daughter that I feel as though I have. She stiffens, her body going rigid. Her spine is already ramrod straight, but her shoulder pulls back, and I watch her barely restrain the urge to bare her teeth at the sound of her name.

"I take it that you," she says, spitting the last word at Shawn and me and dragging the little, red-eyed girl with her as she moves forward through the throng of bodies. Her eyes remain fixed on my face as she closes the distance between us. "Are Mr. and Mrs. Shawn Marksberry? Pleasure to officially make your acquaintance."

I feel my stomach drop and my ears ring as the Guardians slow and stop just out of sight. I can see their golden eyes in the darkness, but no one else does.

"They're glamoured, you can only see them because they want you to," Abbigail whispers, her voice incredibly soft. Beside me, I feel Shawn raise his chin and smile. There are flames in the eyes that look out at us from within the trees.

"That's Healer and Mr. Aliyah Trevonaire, actually," he says, and my stomach twists, flops, and drops to my feet at the sound of those words in his warm voice. His smile turns cold. "And I assure you, the pleasure is all yours."

I don't laugh, but only because I'm too busy counting the golden eyes among the trees and trying to be discreet. The little girl in me loves the way the words sound, and the Alpha in me sees them for what they are, a line drawn in the sand and a dare for her to cross them. He's giving her the chance to hang herself, and I hope she takes it. It'll make all the rest of this easier.

As they approach, each member of my pack clocks the guardians and contains their surprise, trying their best to follow my lead through their unease.

"I see," Anya says, clicking her tongue and eyeing us. "Well then, Healer Trevonaire, it's a pleasure to make your official acquaintance."

There's a smug look on her face, and she's radiating a level of confidence that feels out of place in the circumstances. The little girl at her side is watching us with keen eyes—her dress grasped in Anya's fist and her face bruised.

"Mrs. Kivleneiks, I have to ask," the rest of my pack falls into line behind me just as I take a step forward, passing through the wards and exposing myself to everyone on the other side. Shawn curses, and my Delta's tense, immediately demanding that I step back—their voices are harsh against the inside of my head. I turn the volume down on them and plaster a diplomatic smile on my face. "What, exactly, do you stand to gain from all of this?"

She grins, her sharp canines on full display, and I can't help but think she looks very, very foolish.

"Today I've gained new pack members, I'm regaining something that I thought was lost, and I am learning a great deal about my adversary," she says. I take a step to the side and block Leighann from her view. Her cold eyes snap to mine, and I realize she has no idea that she has already lost. Behind her soldiers, the Guardians return to their human forms and step out of the tree line to stand like murderous sentries behind each of the Kivleneiks soldiers. A Guardian slips around to stand behind Elisabeth and extends her claws to silently press one razor sharp edge against her carotid artery. Her body goes rigid, and she gasps, careful not to move.

"Mum," she says, eyes dropping to follow the long, tanned arm to the face of the Guardian holding her. The girl bares her teeth and Elisabeth looks away.

"Not now, Lissy," Anya says, waving a hand. Elisabeth shudders and closes her eyes tightly.

"Mum," she says again. And Anya turns her whole body, hand raised like she plans to strike her. She freezes when she sees the Guardian, then pales one shade at a time as she takes in the sight of the others, each one holding at least one of her soldiers with claws, blades, or guns.

"Mini," Leighann whispers from behind me, taking advantage of Anya's distraction to wave her sister over. The little girl looks up at her captor for a brief second and holds up a finger.

I can feel the message she doesn't speak. *Not yet.*

Everything that happens after that happens in fast forward. Anya spins in a slow circle, dragging the little girl so aggressively that she falls and has to scramble back to her feet. When she falls again, she slips free of her dress and stumbles forward toward the wards.

Anya reaches for the sword at her hip, throwing the girl's dress aside and reaching to grab her. Before I can reach for the girl, the Guardian pushes Elisabeth to her knees and kicks out, sending Anya's blade flying through the air. On the other side of the wards, Abbigail's collar flares, and my Deltas fight my orders, desperate to follow me through the wards and into the action. The little girl, Maeve, runs flat out toward the wards and hits them with a high-pitched scream.

"Her name," Abbigail yells, turning to Leighann. "What's her name?"

"Maeve! Maeve Verdigris! Ali!" she screams. She runs toward the wards and reaches through to hold on to her sister. I dodge Anya as she reaches for me and turn to face the wards, leaving the Guardian to protect my back.

"Maeve Verdigris," I whisper to the wards, and they shimmer, letting the girl tumble through. She lands in the dirt. I'm oddly grateful that she was wearing a layer under her dress, so she doesn't tear her skin on impact.

"The rest of them, too," Abbigail says, and I spin back to the rapidly increasing violence. The Kivleneiks soldiers are fighting back against the Guardians, lashing out at everyone they can reach, and now that they know the wards are solid, they're knocking our allies into them and taking advantage of the debilitating pain. There's a dead Guardian on the ground behind Anya, and there's blood on her hands. Her soldiers are falling or surrendering left and right, but the violence is still spreading. "Aliyah!"

A feeling like ice water crashes over me, and I turn my

attention to Abbigail, suddenly very aware that I'm standing perfectly still amongst the chaos. To my left, Andromeda hits the wards and screams. The Kivleneiks' soldier that's stalking toward her has blood dripping from his mouth and is prepared to gouge her with his claws. I force myself to focus through the overwhelming feeling of being out of my depth, and I tell the wards that she's a friend. She falls through and lands in a crouch, immediately charging her opponent and taking him to the ground. Her dress is torn and bloodstained, but I know that it isn't hers.

I spin around in a slow circle, touching the wards with the tips of my fingers as I tell them who to let through. On my own wrist, bands of color declare my allies—I don't have a clue if I even felt them form. When I come full circle and am facing my own pack again, I see Leighann and Maeve standing with their hands clasped together, their magic burning in their eyes.

There's something both very intimidating and very creepy about the way the air around them crackles, burning and building and collapsing in on itself as they cling to one another. Their eyes remain fixed on Anya, like they have no grasp on the chaos at all.

"Surrender," they say, and Anya whirls around to look at them.

"Don't you dare," she growls, holding up one long, bloodied finger as though she can't feel the magic already building in the air around us. As if she thinks she can stop what they've started. I know it won't hurt me as surely as I know that I'm not prepared for what's about to happen. It feels like butterfly wings and static electricity all around me, on my skin and in my hair, in my mouth and in my lungs.

"Surrender," they say again. Their magic builds, and the chaos slows around me as it does. One by one, the Kivleneiks soldiers raise their hands and fall to their knees, eyes glassy and distant, like they're seeing something very far away. They could be, for all I know. I've never been on the wrong end of this kind of magic.

Anya staggers, and Elisabeth looks a little bit smug about it, raising her hands of her own volition like she wants us all to know she isn't a threat. I look at the girls and almost gasp. There's verdigris on their faces, their hands, and poking out from under their clothes in patches. Their magic seems unbothered by it, but it's strange to me all the same. I remember what Saya said about their mother and her theory that it's protective. I wonder if they'll let me take samples.

Saya—her name lights up in my mind, and I realize for the first time what about her makes me so uncomfortable. The scars she bears—they're surgical. Precise.

Like some kind of experiment.

"Surrender," they say again, and Anya Kivleneiks falls to her knees in the dirt. My mouth drops open.

"Surrender," they say, one final time, and Anya raises her hands, blood running down her chin as she says the words they want to hear.

"I surrender."

"I can't be here," Abbigail says, her back to the Guardians who are gathered and turning over the captured Kivleneiks' soldiers. We're standing outside of Medical, where I've spent the last two hours tending to the allies who were injured. The dead have been lined up beyond the wards for collection by their packs, and even looking at their bodies makes me feel like there is ice in my spine, fragile and cold. It isn't even the death that's the problem; I've seen more of that than I care to recount. It's the fact that they died for or because of me. That's the part that sucks the air out of my lungs. That's the new part.

"What do you mean?" She's stiff and still dressed in

borrowed clothes.

"They all smell like her. Like Anastasiya," she says. She's tracing the delicate line of her collar with one finger and looks like she might cry at any second. I take a deep breath, and I can taste the Guardians on the breeze. The scent of them wraps around me, and I realize that she's only half right. I doubt I should tell her that, though. Not if she doesn't know about Wanderer.

"Of course. Go. Find Aviva, and she'll help you get cleaned up. I'll come find you when I'm done here. She leaves without looking back and my heart breaks for her.

I knew this was coming, but she didn't, and she has to be confused and scared.

"Andromeda," I say with a smile, picking up on the sound of her footsteps as she approaches and turning to look at her. I've stitched up the deepest of the wounds on her shoulders and cheek, but her lip is split and swollen, and she's covered in dirt.

"We're going to head for home," she says, leaning against Medical and looking at the Guardians. "Do you know where they came from?"

I laugh without meaning to, the sound a little hysterical even to my own ears, and then immediately apologize.

"They're called the Guardians," I tell her. "They're the human world's equivalent of the Elder Council, I think. Their Alpha is called Wanderer, but I don't think I've seen her among them."

I don't mention the fire that seems to cling to them—the way that it flickers and burns even in the darkest shadows. I don't call them Hellhounds aloud. Hellhounds don't exist.

"What kind of name is Wanderer?"

"Your name is Andromeda," I point out. She raises her

hands in surrender and laughs, then whimpers and touches her split lip with gentle fingers. "I really can heal that for you, I don't mind."

"I'll be fine, Ali. I promise. I appreciate it, but it isn't the first or last split lip of my life." She looks down at her dress and frowns, but doesn't say anything. I can tell she wants to, but she doesn't.

"Do you know what happened to the nomad girl? The one that Anya had bound?" Andromeda looks at me like I've lost my mind.

"I didn't see any nomad girl. Or anyone bound. And I haven't seen anyone since we arrested them. If she were here, she's long gone now."

13
Aliyah

I find Abbigail after the last of our allies have dragged away the last of their prisoners, and she's a mess. There are tear tracks on her face, and she's sitting at the kitchen island eating ice cream right out of the container, like I do when I'm having a bad day. She's clean through, freshly showered, and wearing clothes that look like they fit her decently well. I walk to the freezer, get myself a pint of ice cream, and climb onto the stool beside her with my spoon in my hand.

"I'm sorry that you had to witness all of that," I say first, because I am. She has no idea what she's wrapped up in and neither do I, but whatever it is, I know it's serious and I know she didn't need to deal with our shit the second she fell through that portal. I don't feel bad for her, because I know how bad it feels to be pitied, but I definitely don't envy her at the moment either. I wouldn't want to be in her shoes in a million years, and I'm more than impressed that she's taking it with such grace.

"Why am I here, Ali?" she asks, stabbing at her ice cream with her spoon and wiping away a fresh wave of tears.

"I don't know," I tell her, hating that it's the truth. She laughs bitterly and turns to face me, her cheeks red and eyes glassy.

"Don't lie to me. For fuck's sake, we both know I don't deserve that," she says, and I want to tell her the truth so badly it hurts, but I don't have any truth to tell. Instead, I settle for telling her what I do know.

"She didn't tell me. When she came to ask us to provide you sanctuary, she didn't say why," I don't say her name because I don't know how much she knows about Wanderer and I don't know enough to answer the questions that it would bring. "You have some kind of memory magic, don't you?"

She nods and laughs, crying a fresh wave of tears.

"It sucks right now, honestly, because I never forget anything and all I keep doing is looking for what I missed. What I did wrong," her words turn the entire situation upside down and I realize that she isn't seeing the same picture as I am. I grab her hand and my ice cream before I drag her off the stool and toward the room we've set aside for her.

"There are some things you desperately need to see."

My love,

I feel something akin to comfort knowing that I am sending you—my most prized possession and the thing I love most in this whole world—to a place I know you will be safe and to people I know will be able to help you as much as you will be able to help them.

I simultaneously feel something not unlike fear laced with devastation knowing that our last night together was fueled by anger and betrayal. I should have known I was out of time. I knew I was close, but I should have paid more attention. Either way, I should have apologized more quickly for what I put you through and apologizing now, while you can't see me on my knees, begging for your forgiveness, feels like too little and far too late.

I need you to know that I made more than one mistake in all of this and even now, sitting in a room you have never seen, surrounded by pieces of a life that feels like it belongs to a stranger, I can smell you on my skin. I am not this person anymore and that is entirely because of you. I have on your sweater and your Converse sneakers, but what's making me feel like I can't breathe is the scent of strawberry shampoo and peanut butter candy and old books that radiates off of them. Everything here, in this ridiculously beautiful place with its equally beautiful view, feels utterly hollow without you to here to share it with me.

I know that I deserve every heartbreaking second of every miserable minute of this for the way I've hurt you.

You may not believe this right now, and it may feel like a lie when I say it, but Noonchester Falls is the safest place for you right now. I promise you that it's temporary, and I wish I could tell you what temporary is going to mean, but I can't.

For now, I'm going to be selfish and ask you to promise me something. I know the first thought you had reading that was 'anything', but I'm not sure you'll feel that way when you hear what I'm going to say next. I need you to promise, Abbigail Barlow, that you won't come to look for me. You can't go anywhere we used to go, and you can't talk to anyone we used to know, unless they come to you first. More than that, you can't run my photo through facial recognition. I've already told Janie not to allow it, but I'm telling you not to try because I know you will.

You've always been obedient, and that has always been a point of pride for me, because your simultaneous ability to listen when necessary and challenge when appropriate made you a brilliant submissive. Bluebird, I need you to be a good girl and listen to me now, because both our lives and the lives of everyone we love hang in the balance. I know you. I know you love me and that you believe in me. I know you trust me. And so, for those reasons, I know that you'll listen to this, my final request.

However unfair, I know that you'll obey.

You are the only thing that is going to get me through what happens next, and I can't find my way home to you if you let yourself get caught. Promise me that you will keep yourself and Aliyah's people safe while I can't.

I pause to wipe my eyes and laugh softly at the teardrops on the page, evidence that Abbigail didn't bother to do the same. She's sitting across from me on the floor, watching me read, and our pain is creating a feedback loop in the room. The air is heavy, and we're both a mess. She smiles sadly and gestures for me to keep reading, her wedding bands sparkling happily in the dimly lit room. My heart tells me I can't take any more, but I know that I must, so I do.

I'm running out of time—no, I'm out of time. I wish it weren't true, but it is. I hope you'll forgive me for saying all this less elegantly than I wanted to, but I can feel the darkness creeping up on me. As soon as the spell is complete, I'll be gone, and all that remains of me will be what you carry in your heart and in that brilliant, wicked mind.

There's a package in Aliyah's office. Inside, there are four journals. One of them is for her, and the other three are for you. In hers, I've done my best to record everything I think she needs to know to get through the coming months. In yours, I've done much of the same. You'll find letters, assignments, memories, photos, and other things I hope will make all this a little less painful for you. Each journal works exactly as your old one did, and the paper is spelled the same way. When you write on those pages, the text will show up in my journal, and when I am able, I'll read every word like a woman starved. I want you to write every day, and I want you to fill as many pages as you need to. Drown me in your words if that's what it takes. Never stop writing to me until it's enough to bring you home.

In addition to the journals, I've sent everything I think you will need to be comfortable at Noonchester Falls. Your clothes, the blankets from my bed, your favorite books, and everything else I could think of are there, hastily thrown into boxes and sent through a portal to you before they found me.

I've also sent you Janie. Or, well, a version of her.

In our final months at Home Base, I asked Minuet to replicate her for you, and when last I was in the Residence at Noonchester Falls, Lexie and I installed her. I hope that she is as helpful to all of you as she was to us. She has a message for you, and it will play when you power her up, but there are also others, recorded and set to become available on certain days. I hope that they will bring light to your eyes, even if only for a moment.

I had more to say, but they're finishing the spell. I'm out of time—this time for real.

Please remember that I love you more than my own life.

One day, you'll know how powerful that statement really is.

I love you and I am so, so sorry.

A

There's blood on the parchment that has barely dried.

I have so many questions, but every single one of them dies on my lips when I look up at the girl sitting on the floor across from me. She has her knees drawn up as far as she can get them, and she's crying openly, one hand clamped over her mouth to stifle the sounds she can't hold in.

When Wanderer came for the first time, we'd decided on the empty room at the end of the hallway on the second floor for Abbigail. It's one of the largest and arguably one of the best in the entire residence. It's in the corner, and two walls are glass, just like in my room. The room was empty then, but it's full to the brim now. There's a king-size bed against the wall, perfectly made with a soft, tufted headboard and piled high with pillows. The wall of bookshelves is packed with books of every shape and size, and there's a thick, plush rug on the floor under us. Nearly every inch of the space is full of boxes of clothes and decorations, books, and collectibles. The closer I look, the more I can see the urgency. The more I can picture Wanderer throwing things violently through the portal as she raced against whatever was coming for her. Whatever clock she could hear counting down.

Abbigail can see it too.

"You knew, didn't you?" She asks me softly, swallowing her tears. Her voice is wrecked and rough, but her eyes are sharp when they meet mine, penetrating, like she can already see my answer. "When you came to us and we trained alongside you, you knew she was leaving."

"That's why we were there," I tell her honestly. I can't bring myself to pretend, not after all that I've seen today. After all that I've read. I hand her back the letter, and she folds it carefully before she tucks it away in a book. "And you knew that, or you wouldn't have asked."

"Show me," she says. Not a question. She looks like she might start crying again, her eyes wide and shining. The whole room smells like the ocean, and I know that it has to be coming from her, from the magic popping and crackling around her. She holds out both of her delicate hands and waits for me to offer up one of mine. When I do, she holds tight and closes her eyes.

The feeling is unlike anything I can remember feeling before. She's there, like a wisp, inside my head. She must have some way of knowing where to go, because she finds the memory she is looking for almost immediately, and then we're both there on that lake shore when Wanderer appears and turns the world gold. When she's seen what she needs to see, she drops my hand and stands.

What happens next feels like something out of a sci-fi novel, and I'm pretty sure it's the coolest thing I've ever seen.

"Janie, power up," she says. I look around for a second, and then I can feel the 'are you crazy?' look settle over my face. I'm about half a second from asking her who she's talking to when my ears start to buzz. The sound is soft, completely beyond the human range, and it makes my ears twitch as it builds and shifts. It goes gone a few seconds after it starts, and then there are a series of other noises, buzzing, clicking, whirring sounds that are almost painful. The wall next to the door to her room turns into some kind of screen and lights up. I don't understand what the words on the screen say. She laughs and wipes her face, looking to me like I'm going to get the joke and then nodding.

"It says 'forsaken, only by the damned.'" She tells me. "It was a sort of inside joke. I've never seen the boot up screen, so I didn't know it was there."

I drag myself off of the floor and try not to groan in pain as I do. We stand side by side and watch the screen as Janie powers up and opens some kind of homepage. Down the left side of the screen, the names of every member of the Trevonaire pack are listed. Abbigail's name is both listed and highlighted. On the right side, there are icons that I don't understand. And behind all of that, there's a photo of Anastasiya and Abbigail, presumably on their wedding day. They're both beaming and they look so incredibly happy that my eyes sting with tears again. Abbigail doesn't try to stop the ones that run down her face.

"Janie, can you hear me?" she says, and I still don't understand who she's talking to. Even if the computer is voice activated, there's no way she's expecting it to talk back to her. I no more than finish the thought when a scarily realistic female voice fills the room, coming from speakers I can't see.

"Of course I can hear you. What can I do for you, Archivist?" the voice—Janie—says. The only change on the screen while she speaks is the audio line at the bottom, which rises and falls with every word.

"Do you know who this is?" She asks the computer. Janie. She gestures at me, and I stop myself from thinking that there's no way she possibly could when I remember that my name is on the screen just like theirs. The bar highlighting Abbigail's name shifts and rises to mine, then darkens. My face fills the screen.

"Aliyah Jade Nathair-Trevonaire, Alpha, Noonchester Falls," Janie says. Abbigail waves her hand, and the homepage comes back up.

"Can you play me the last message Anastasiya recorded, Janie?" she asks. The computer whirrs for a second, but nothing opens.

"No, I cannot. The final recording is scheduled to become available on your birthday," Abbigail rolls her eyes and folds her arms over her chest. She mumbles something to herself and takes a deep breath.

"Janie, please play whatever video Anastasiya wanted me to see today," she says politely. I can tell she's bracing for whatever comes next, so I try to do the same. The computer clicks once and whirrs softly, then a video window opens, and the entire screen is full of Wanderer's face. Wanderer's, not Anastasiya's. Abbigail's breathing falters, and she hesitates for a second before she waves her hand, pushing the recording into motion.

"Hello, beautiful," Wanderer says, and I nearly jump out of my skin at how close her voice feels. If Janie's was scary-realistic, Wanderer's is worse. It's like she's there. Like I could close my eyes and convince myself she's in the room, talking to us from a few feet away. "If you're watching this before the first snow has fallen in Noonchester Falls, I have run out of time more quickly than I ever could have imagined."

Wanderer shifts in the frame so that we can see the room around her, and Abbigail gasps. Among the tangled mess of blankets visible over her shoulder, Abbigail is sleeping on the bed, her bare legs exposed, and her curls braided back from her face. The video quality is good enough that I can tell there are bruises on her exposed ass cheek.

"I was there for this," Abbigail breathes. The video continues.

"I'm sure you can tell that I'm sitting in my bedroom, but if you look closely enough, you'll see that you're sleeping right back there behind me. You've been out cold for a couple of hours and I'm hoping I can climb back into bed next to you when I'm done so that you'll have no idea I've gotten up at all. We'll see how that goes. We both know what happens if I wake you, so I don't know how hard I'll try," Abbigail's cheeks burn, and she shifts her weight. I start to wonder why and then I realize, she's talking about sex. About how they'll have sex if she wakes her. I try not to let my imagination run wild and force myself to focus on what Wanderer is actually saying. "I'm recording this video for you because I know it will make you feel better to see me when I tell you that everything is going to be okay. There are some things that I have to tell you that you aren't going to like and I couldn't bring myself to tell you in a letter, like I plan to do for so many other things."

Abbigail raises her hand and the video stops.

"I don't know how much more of this I can take tonight," she tells me, and I feel for her, because my heart has broken and been jammed back together more times than I can count too. I take her hand and squeeze.

"We stop when you say so and if that means we come back to it tomorrow, we do it. We're going to get through this. You and me, together," she gives me a grateful smile and closes her eyes, holding on to my hand like it's a lifeline.

"Janie, play."

Wanderer opens her mouth to say something and there's a sound that gets her attention, coming from just off the screen. She turns to look at it, twisting nearly one hundred and eighty degrees in her chair, and Abbigail gasps, yanking her hand free to cover her mouth. She stops the video and walks forward, touching the back of Wanderer's shoulder with her fingers.

"Abby? What's wrong? What do you see?"

"The lash marks," she says, sounding like the air has been punched out of her lungs. On the screen, under her blue-tipped fingers, I see the marks she's talking about. Deep, angry marks from a whip, visible where the loose sweater that Wanderer is wearing has fallen off her shoulder. "She recorded this a few hours ago."

"What do you mean?"

"Look," she says. She turns and pulls down her borrowed pants to show me the bruises on her ass and thighs. When she zooms in on herself in the background, I know they're an exact match. "She recorded this right before she sent me through that portal."

"Are you ready to see what happened, or do we need to take a break?" I ask her, forcing her to turn and look at me by putting my hands gently on her shoulders. She meets my eyes and then looks at the screen.

"I have to see it. Will you stay?" I offer her my hand and she takes it.

"Janie, show us what happened next," I tell the

computer. The video zooms back out and begins playing. I realize when I see the shadow that the noise we heard was a person. Wanderer waves whoever it is away and looks back at the screen.

"Sorry," she says. "Gia has officially lost her mind, but that's no surprise to you or anyone else."

She settles back in her chair and winces, immediately sitting forward again. She mumbles something that sounds a little bit like 'crazy girl' and then 'shadows don't run' before she refocuses, pulling her knees up to her chest and her sleeves down over her hands.

"She's nervous," Abbigail breathes, watching the recording with frightening intensity. There's a look in her eyes that I know immediately I never want to turn on me.

"I think I should just start from the beginning. That's usually the easiest, right? Okay, so... Hello, my name is Wanderer," she says, smiling a kind of crooked, nervous smile. "I was born a long time ago, and my mother's name was Aiyanik. She died when I was young, and I had no siblings until I found my... wait, shadows..."

Whatever she's about to say is cut off by the sound of the door flying open and she's up, out of her chair, and on her feet so fast that it's just a blur of color on the screen. I barely see her start moving before she's across the room, whisper-yelling at the intruder. When he gestures to the door, he turns his face just enough that I can see him. Warrior, not Aleksandr.

Whatever language they're speaking, Abbigail must know I don't understand it, because she starts translating for me.

"It's time to go," she says. It's Warrior speaking, his face half-cast in shadow.

"It's too soon, you know we can't leave now. I'm not

done. We're not done," that's Wanderer.

"We knew it would come. We knew..." his voice drops to low for her to hear him.

"Wanderer, they're here. Whether you like it or not, we are out of time," on the screen, he looks at Abbigail, still asleep on the bed but stirring. "They're out of time. It's over. We have to go up now if we want to live."

Wanderer turns and looks at Abbigail, her wounds on full display for the camera. When she looks back at Warrior, her face is set.

"Let me save her, and then I'll go with you," she tells him.

"You are being foolish. If they find out that we've done this, we will be executed," Warrior says. He steps farther into the room, and I realize that there's a heavy sword strapped over his back. The same sword he wore hidden under a glamour that day when he came to visit us.

"Fuck the contract, Warrior. I can live with every awful thing I have ever done in my life, but I won't let her pay the price for a mistake we made. I won't lose them for any amount of money, and if you didn't agree, you'd already be up there." Something that sounds like a scream splits the air, and they both curse colorfully. It doesn't need translating.

"Together," Warrior says, handing over a sword that must belong to her and helping her clip it to her back over her lash marks. "We will save her together."

Wanderer turns and takes his hands in hers, their magic whipping through the room and solidifying into a portal made of liquid gold and flickering black flames. Abbigail's body floats up and disentangles from the blankets first, and I expect the video to end after she's gone through the portal, but it doesn't. In a maelstrom of fire and sparks, the contents of the room and of another room I can't see fly through the air. They stand fast through it all, never wavering as more and more flows through the portal in the middle of the room. Another scream.

"We have to go now," he says, and this time, Wanderer nods. The portal flickers and closes, and they stand in the darkness just staring at each other.

"What have we done?" He asks, looking around the room. He drags on hand through his inky curls and squeezes his eyes shut like he has a headache.

"We've saved them," Wanderer tells him. "We just had to kill them to do it."

The silence that follows is both long and heavy. When they move, they move together, turning in lockstep toward the door. Before they reach it, Wanderer hesitates.

"I love you," she tells Abbigail through the screen, and then a bolt of golden light flashes through the air, coming right for us as we watch. The video ends.

Abbigail is crying openly beside me, her fingers tangled up in mine, and our joined hands held against her chest. I don't know what to think, and I don't think she does either.

"Janie, can you bring up any of the cameras from within the base?" she asks, her voice full of desperation, and I can hear her heart breaking all over again.

"I am no longer connected to home base, but I can show you an aerial image," Janie says. Abbigail nods, the screen shifts. Over the video, an image appears. It's the same farm we traveled to when we went to train with them, and it looked almost completely untouched. Abbigail closes her eyes and focuses hard on something I can't see until a shimmer of blue spreads over her skin. I follow her eyes back to the screen and the image Janie is showing us has changed.

"Better than I expected, but worse than I hoped," she

says. The previously pristine land is dotted with black scorch marks and soaked with blood. There are drag marks leading toward the center of the empty field from both the barn and the farmhouse, and the grass has been pressed flat by the blades of a helicopter a short distance from the still-burning pyre. Abbigail closes her eyes again and undoes whatever she did. I blink and the image on the screen is back to flawless, perfectly unmarred grass.

"Do you think you could give me the journals she left for me? I have to write to process all of this and she would prefer I did it there," she says. A gentle wash of cool water slides over my face and hers, erasing the tear tracks and cooling the redness.

"Of course. Will you be okay for a minute?"

She nods, and I narrow my eyes at her, searching her face until I'm sure that she's being honest. I practically ran to my office, jumping over the railing to avoid the stairs and then vaulting over it on my way back.

When I hand her the three heavy books, she breathes them in and sighs, smiling a little.

"They smell like her," she says, and carries them to her desk to put them down.

"I'm at the other end of the hall if you need me tonight, okay? I will wake up every hour to let you cry if I have to," I tell her, and she laughs. It isn't a joyful laugh, but it's enough. She wraps her long arms around me and pulls me into a tight hug that reminds me how much taller she is, and she doesn't let go until our hearts are beating at the same rate.

"Goodnight, my friend," she says, and I see it for the dismissal it is. I close the door behind me on my way out and head straight for my bedroom, where Shawn is sitting up and waiting for me.

"Finally. Are you okay?" he asks as soon as he sees me. He must not have heard me run through the house, because he's looking at me like he's been worried I might have died.

I let him gather me into his arms and kick the door closed before I start crying, and I don't stop until the sun starts to heat up the room. At some point, he helps me out of my dirty clothes and carries me to the shower, where he washes the dirt and blood from my skin. He washes my hair, massaging my scalp and rubbing down my neck, over my shoulders, and down my back with his soapy hands before he rinses. He even takes the tiny scrubber to my nails to make sure there are no traces of the day left behind.

When he turns off the water, he has already wrapped me in a fluffy towel—one of the big ones that actually goes all the way around me—and twists my hair up into a plop on the top of my head without being asked.

"Do you want to talk about it, or do you want to try and sleep?" He asks me as he sits me on the edge of our bed. He kisses my forehead and steps away from me just long enough to grab my favorite sleep shirt and a soft pair of underwear.

"What would I even say?" I ask him, staring somewhere in the middle distance without focusing on anything. He kneels down in front of me, smiles, and takes my hands.

"You can say anything you need to or you can say nothing at all," he promises, kissing each of my hands. "As long as you're okay and I don't need to be worried I could lose you, I can wait until you're ready to tell me what's going on in there."

14
Aliyah

The journal from Wanderer is way nicer than I originally gave it credit for. I should have known, probably, when I picked up Abbigail's, but I was so out of it that I hardly noticed the heavy leather and the hand-stitched binding.

The cover is decorated, burned to show an angel staring at her own reflection, surrounded by ice in the world and fire in the reflection. Like a title, the words 'The Righteous and the Fallen' are burned above the image. It pulls at something deep inside me, and it takes me a second to figure out that it's the story of Lucifer I'm thinking of. I don't know much about that part of human mythology, but I remember enough to know that's what I'm seeing.

The artwork is beautiful, and in the dim light of my desk lamp in my otherwise dark office, the gray-stained leather looks almost black, the marks like cuts on flesh.

The book makes a pleasant cracking noise when I open

it, and I can smell her on the heavy, rich parchment. It's like vanilla and white citrus, more Wanderer than Anastasiya.

On the first page, there are only a few lines of text, all written in her familiar flourishing script.

The information on these pages is intended specifically for Ms. Aliyah Trevonaire.

To be granted access to the information within, swear by blood you will not share anything you learn.

Proceed with caution.

I turn the page and find it blank. The next one is, too, and the one after that. Every page in the entire book is blank. I go back to the first page and find a new line of text below the rest.

Swear by blood.

The words feel ominous, and I almost close the cover. I stare at the page for a full three minutes before I finally tell myself not to be such a baby and drag a claw over my forearm. A small pool of blood forms, and I watch until it's big enough that I'll be able to drop it onto the page.

"Alright, Wanderer, show me what you've got," I say to the empty room. I turn my arm and let the little pool of blood drop. The parchment soaks it up so fast I almost question if it was there at all, and the original text fades away, replaced by something new. The cut has already healed when I finish wiping the blood from my skin.

I look down at the book, and the first page is covered in words, I sigh, force my eyes to focus through the astonishingly little sleep I've gotten, and begin to read.

Pleasure to meet you, Aliyah,

By the time you're reading this, we will likely have had the chance to meet, but since we haven't at the time I'm writing it, I'll start with an introduction. My name, or the English equivalent of it anyway, is Wanderer. You can call me that, if you like, but you don't have to. Most people in my life call me Evelin and most people in the life I lived with Abbigail call me Anastasiya. I answer to almost anything, so whatever you like will work just fine.

I have a lot of things that I want and need to tell you, because there is much that you need to know to understand what you have landed in the middle of. I'm going to do my best to tell you everything in a straight line, but I can't promise that's going to happen, so I'm counting on you to keep up.

You and I met tonight for the first time, and I think I scared you. I wish I could tell you that it doesn't happen often, but it does. I hadn't intended to seek you out in such an isolated place, because I didn't want you to feel threatened, but I'm not entirely sure how long I have before they realize the spell has fractured. They may not notice, but even if they don't, we're close to completing our contract, and they'll pull us out once we do.

If you don't mind, I'm going to skip some of the boring parts of my life, like where I tell you I was born in a little town by the water on an island that doesn't exist anymore, to a woman who fell in love and a man that wasn't allowed to stay. You may know my mother's name by now, and you may even have figured out that she's your pack's namesake, but if you don't and haven't, surprise. Your people are named after my mother, who was one of the most powerful beings of her time and would likely have continued to grow stronger if she'd been allowed to live.

That doesn't matter, though. Nothing matters for the sake of this conversation except for what happened after I met my brother. You may know his name as Aleksandr, but I call him Warrior, and the people in this life with us call him Elijah. Abby calls him Lexie.

If you can bear with me, I'll tell you everything you need to know to trust me and, hopefully, if I have time, everything you need to know to bring Abbigail home to me.

Are you ready?

Good, me neither.

I turn the page.

It's probably worth mentioning before we start that I'm currently under the effects of a spell that is intended to completely separate me from my previous life and memories for the sake of making me into a whole new person. It's also worth mentioning that until a few days ago, it was working perfectly. If that sounds half as terrifying to you as it feels to me, you'll have a slight idea how it felt to watch the girl I thought was my twin sister burn in a funeral pyre.

We'll come back to that, I hope, but for now, let's talk about Warrior. His name was Johnathan when I met him, but I won't make you remember every name we've ever had. I'll call him Warrior instead.

Warrior was living in Louisiana, right around New Orleans, and he was the apprentice to an old piano maker. He spent every day in the old man's shop and every night dancing with every beautiful person he could get his hands on. He was cocky and charming and sharp as a tack. At the time, his eyes were still hazel, but he had the same inky black curls you know him for.

He was beautiful in those days, young and unburdened by the things he's seen now, I miss them sometimes. But I wouldn't go back. When you met him, he was my quiet, mostly distant baby brother, and that version of him is similar to the kind of person he was when we met. For all his charisma and the vivacious energy, he always had, he was never present. Always kept everyone at arm's length. I didn't learn why until much, much later. Once he figured out that it was okay to be gay, I got to know the real him.

My Warrior, the real, unguarded version of him, has a rebel soul and a big heart and a laugh that bounces around a room and makes everyone smile, even on the worst days of their lives.

The day I met him; I stumbled across him by accident.

The piano maker he worked for was the youngest son of an Italian immigrant and his wife was an old gypsy woman native to New Orleans. His wife has long blonde hair that she always kept braided and a love for long skirts in bright colors. She's from an old line of witches, gifted with telemetry magic, and has a wild heart capable of more love than you can even imagine. Her name is Jessabelle, and you should remember it because she's important.

I was looking for her when I walked into the piano shop that day.

When I had been in New Orleans the year before, I let myself be caught out in the bayou after dark, alone and unarmed. I had my magic, but it and I weren't on the greatest of terms. I'd learned English by then, but I was struggling with the way they used it that far South. Nothing followed the rules, and everything sounded so strange that it took me forever to decipher anything.

That hesitation is what landed me with a serrated blade between my ribs and my hands bound behind my back. The young man who stabbed me hadn't even taken the money I was carrying before he left me there. When the man had bound me, he wrapped my hands in some kind of cotton, soaked in water from the bayou. Without them, I couldn't pull the knife out, and with it in, I couldn't heal. Now I would be able to solve that problem on my own, but then? Absolutely not.

The gypsy woman came through a few hours later and found me, my magic trying its best to keep me alive and only barely succeeding. She must have recognized the predicament I was in because she pulled the knife out and used it to free my hands. She didn't take off the thick gloves she was wearing, even after they got wet, and I was polite enough not to ask why she had them on in ninety-five-degree weather. She helped me sit up and stayed with me while my magic repaired the worst of the damage. As soon as I'd healed enough that I could, I ran.

I'd gone back to New Orleans to thank her for saving my life.

When I walked into her husband's shop, I was enveloped in the scent of sage and wood oil, and there was a boy playing at an old baby grand piano in the corner. He had his back to the door, and I'd been careful coming in, so the bell above it hadn't made a sound. I didn't know the song, but the bow was playing with such joy and singing at the top of his voice, and I loved everything about it. I stood just inside the shop and watched him play for a long time before the old man came out of the back to ask him something, and saw me there.

He threw the rag he was holding at the boy and asked him why he was ignoring the beautiful girl who was "obviously taken with him," and Warrior's face flamed with embarrassment as he looked at me over his shoulder. He stopped playing, but kept singing, and spun around to face me as he rose from the bench and came toward me. I could feel the magic in him, but there was something else, something I couldn't place.

Until he took my hand and his hazel eyes flared with hellfire. I knew in an instant that he was like me. He hadn't meant to show me, I'm sure, but he was young and surprised, and he only barely managed to keep singing when it happened.

I didn't know just how like me he was until a few weeks later when Jessabelle collapsed at dinner. I'd been casting all day, working with the witches in the quarter, and I was tired. I was so tired, but she'd saved my life, so I knew I had to save hers. Without thinking, I reached out and grabbed hold of his wrist for stability, and I knew as soon as my magic touched his what he was. Who he was. To me.

Meeting him changed me. It broke open a part of me that I'd kept hidden for hundreds of years. I see Warrior in Aleksandr sometimes, and I wonder if the spell is fracturing for him, too. Like right now, I'm writing this and he's down the hall playing the piano and singing that same old song. If I asked him to name it or asked him where he learned it, he wouldn't have a clue. He sings it just as well as he always has, and he hasn't missed a note.

Now, you should probably take a break here, but I have a feeling you won't. You and Abbigail are alike in that way, so I won't push it. I'll stop this entry here just in case you decide to be responsible and end by telling you that if you have any questions, anything you need to say, or anything you're confused about, you can record it on the back of this page. If all goes to plan, Jessabelle will write back to you within forty-eight hours.

Remember the promise you made when you opened this book. No one can know about the things I share with you, and Jessabelle can't know who or where you are. It's the only way you, I, my brother, and Abbigail make it out of this alive.

Good luck,

Wanderer

I stop reading and close the cover, hating myself a little for not being able to keep going. I'm so tired that my bones hurt, and I know that if I tried to sleep, I would just end up staring at the ceiling. It's been this way for days, and the only sign that it's getting better is the reduction of the persistent ache in my head. I know it's trauma and that I have to let my body process it, but that doesn't mean I like it.

The urge to shove it all into a box and put it on a shelf is strong, but I know better.

I refuse to make it any more likely that I end up with PTSD.

15
Aliyah

On the whiteboard in my office, next to Marcus' name, I write "Computer Science, University of Cincinnati." Next to Saoirse, "Mathematics & Economics, Ohio State University." And then, finally, next to Tatiana, "Agriculture & Horticulture, Ohio State University."

I close the marker and put it down just as Cici knocks on the door. I turn and smile, welcoming her in with a wave of my hand.

"What do you think of this whole college thing?" I ask her, curious. She smiles and glances at the board. There's something wistful in her eyes, and it doesn't disappear when she looks at me again.

"I love it," she says, taking me by surprise. "I would have loved for my boys to have had the kinds of opportunities that you're giving these kids."

Her words go through me like lightning, and I feel my mouth trying to drop open, but I stop it before it can.

"Cici, did you have children?" I ask her. She nods and pulls her necklace out of her shirt. Inside, there's a small picture of her family. Three sons and two parents. The man in the photo is looking at her like she hung the moon.

"Tyler, Christian, and Jeremy," she says, looking at the picture herself before she closes the locket and tucks it away. "They died six months before I was chosen as your Keeper."

Six months.

"That's why you wanted to die," I say without thinking, and she nods, looking down in shame.

"I didn't want the land to save me. I never wanted to be a Keeper. I just didn't want to be remembered as weak."

Her words strike a chord deep inside of me, and the note is still humming when I notice she's holding something in her hand.

"What did you bring?" I ask her, holding my hand out for the piece of parchment. It feels cheap in my hand compared to what Wanderer uses, and I don't remember ever thinking that way before. My name is written on the front of the folded letter, and below it, reads 'ATTN: Trevonaire Pack.'

"They arrested thirty-eight people complicit in what happened the other night in the Elder Council's Chambers. They've received testimony from Cyan, Magdelena, and several others to back up what you all reported, and their trials have been scheduled for next month," she says. I turn the letter over and open it up. The broken seal is gray, the wax luminescent, and is stamped with the scales of justice. The seal of the Council of Elders.

I scan the words quickly and look up, relief washing over me. I see it echoing back at me from across my desk, and I let myself smile.

"They believed us. They proved that we were telling the truth and they're going to do something about it," I tell her, and she nods, my smile bringing one to her face.

"They believed you."

"What about the soldiers? And the Elder Guard? Have they said anything about them?" I scan the letter again and find nothing.

"Not that I've seen. They may not tell us what happens, especially if they find that everyone was just following orders. And they won't tell us how they handle Anya, because she's an Alpha and they won't humiliate her like that. Even they don't want her as an enemy," she says. I kind of understand that, because if I hadn't been forced into it, it's likely something I would have avoided too.

I'm about to say as much when the light over the Sanctuary door in my office turns blue. I look at Cici like she's going to have answers, but she shrugs at me.

"Want me to come with you? Or I can call for one of the Betas?" she asks, standing and glancing over her shoulder at the open door to my office. Beyond it, I can hear voices and laughter echoing through the room, a far cry from the way it has been the last few days.

"All of them, if you don't mind," I tell her. She turns immediately and walks out into the room. I hear her say their names one at a time, and then a few seconds pass, and I hear her whistle at Kelly so he'll hear her over his headphones. One of the girls complains about the sound, but all my Betas come running, sliding through my office door like chickens on skates and then lining up in front of me like I didn't just see it happen. Shawn is last, and I don't find it surprising. Cici had to say his name three times to get his attention.

"What do you need?" Elijah asks, hands clasped behind his back. They're all dressed for the day except Kelly, who is wearing sweats and a matching sweatshirt. I decide it's good enough almost as soon as I ask myself whether I should make him change.

"We have a visitor," I say, nodding toward the light that's still shining bright blue. Their heads all turn as they follow my gaze—their reactions range from dread to excitement.

"Do you know who it is?" That's Shawn. He takes a deep breath in through his nose, and his eyes widen.

"Who do you smell?" I ask them, breathing in and searching the air for a scent I know. I can't smell anything but them, and the air is so saturated with their scent that it won't matter how hard I sniff, I won't pick up anything without getting closer.

"Cyan," Shawn says, looking nervous. "Chief Elder Cyan Vianbry. And it smells like she's alone."

No Elder Guard, for the Chief Elder? The real one? I decide not to dwell on how wrong that feels and lead them into the Sanctuary in a line, like ducklings. Inside, waiting with her legs folded elegantly in front of her, is Cyan Vianbry, completely and utterly alone. She rises when I enter, and it feels surreal when she bends at the waist to greet me.

"Aliyah, it's good to see you again," she says, smiling with her entire face. Her eyes crinkle and shine with the light of her genuine joy, and it spreads over me like a beam of sunlight.

"It's always wonderful to see you," I gesture for her to sit and she does. I sit down opposite her and my Betas line up behind me. It feels like overkill, but given the circumstances, I think it's the best option. Besides, this way, I don't have to tell them about the meeting when it's over. "You usually come with guards, though. Is everything okay?"

I don't speak any of the awful scenarios I'm thinking about into existence, because none of us deserve the worst-case scenario. Across from me, Cyan laughs, and the sound is equal parts bitterness and hysteria.

"The entire Elder Guard is being questioned sharply, so we're all down to our one personal guard for a while. I didn't think I needed to bring Leilani with me here and I thought her presence could be... difficult, for you. So I told her I was planning to stay in for the afternoon and slipped out when she wasn't looking," her description of her behavior sounds so much like something I would do and so much like my own thought process around everything, that I almost want to hug her. I feel that way about her regularly though, so I don't give in to the urge.

"I'm grateful for your thoughtfulness. I'm glad you didn't have to see the aftermath of what happened here the other night. It has rained for two days and it feels like the land is trying to cleanse itself," I tell her. She shifts, her heavy robes moving with her and sending up a cloud of her scent. Rosemary and oud, rich and warm like her smile.

"I've seen plenty in my day, but I was fortunate not to have to witness that kind of bloodshed so young. I know young people are resilient, but it doesn't seem fair to me. I wish I had been able to stop it," she says, looking down at the parchment in her hands. It looks to me like she's staring at her hands themselves, studying the lines and spots on her skin. Her perfectly manicured nails. The delicate tattoo on the inside of her wrist that I never noticed.

"Why couldn't you?" Kelly asks, brash as always, and I'm relieved to see that she doesn't look angered by it. She just looks really, really sad. Almost devastated. I don't blame her.

"They came to our Chambers in the middle of the day

and told us of their plans. They demanded we swear fealty, and many of us refused. We were arrested by our own guards and taken to the cells below. When the others saw us beaten and removed, many of them chose not to fight back, and I don't hold that against them," she says. Her jaw flexes like she might be lying, but I think she's allowed to feel whatever she's feeling. "Magdalena rushed to us as soon as she could and released us. We were able to summon the rest of the Elder Guard and send word to the other packs in time to get you help. I was afraid it wouldn't be enough."

"It was," I assure her, wanting badly to take her hand and say it until she believes it. "Andromeda and Mikael made it in time. My father and Demetria came too. And Lucien rounded up as many of the traitors as he could before he came our way."

"What you did bought us the time we needed to fight back," Shawn tells her, hands resting on the chair behind my head. "If you hadn't sent them, we'd be burying our own people, or worse. We owe you a debt."

"No," she says, smiling at him and then at me. There are tears in her eyes. "You have never owed me anything, and even if you did, what you're doing with what we gave you more than repays it. That's why I'm here, actually."

She wipes her face with the edge of her wide sleeve and looks down at the parchment she's holding. It's sealed like the one Cici brought me, the scales of Justice cast in shadow by the angle. They look harsher than normal and it feels right after all that has happened. It feels like justice should be harsher now. Like the people who ultimately cost others their lives deserve to have to pay for it. Maybe not with theirs, like the old law might have demanded, but somehow. If there is no punishment, there's nothing stopping them from doing it again, like a really fucked up feedback loop from hell. Cyan takes a deep breath and holds out the parchment to me.

"I know you've expressed your interest in breaking contact with the Elder Council and I respect that decision, if that's what you want to do. I want you to know that it isn't your only option. We want you to know that you don't have to do this alone," she says. I pop the seal and unfold the parchment. My first instinct is to skim the words, but I force myself to read carefully, holding it where everyone behind me can see.

Aliyah Trevonaire –

We write you today in the wake of something tragic, and we want you to know that what we are about to say has not been influenced by the actions of the Kivleneiks. The first draft of this letter, in fact, was started the night we received yours, and we regret that we could not finish it in time to prove to you that our support of your endeavors does not come with strings. There are no conditions that we feel the need to put forth in regards to the support we intend to pledge to you and your people.

The opposite, in fact. We come to you humbly, and we hope that you will see our desperation in every word, because we do not want you to leave. We are not blind to our own shortcomings and we are not too proud to admit when we are out of our depth. We are far beyond our depth now and we know it. We're aging, you see, and with that comes a great deal of wisdom. Each of us comes to the table with our own story to tell, our own background, and our own perspective. What we lack, though, is your story. Your background. Your perspective. We cannot hope to speak for the generations of young people that have risen to power in the years we have remained in the Elderlands, and even if we could, we have no intention of pretending that we have that right.

The Council of Elders was formed to serve and guide, to keep peace and bring prosperity. It cannot do that by refusing to adapt to the changes happening in our reservations and in our people. We say all of this because we need your help, and in exchange, we will meet your demands.

Keep Cristiana Noonchester. Keep Noonchester Falls. Protect your people however you see fit.

And in doing so, teach us how to do the same.

This letter was drafted by only a select committee at first, but we figured out quickly that we were dealing with something worthy of the complete Council of Elders, so we summoned everyone back to our Chambers and started again. The Council is united in our decision to offer you and your Betas their rightful places as the representatives of Noonchester Falls. We know that you will not be able to be present each day, and we have no intention of holding your prior commitment to your people against you, no matter what the by-laws say. There are two meetings a year that we require everyone to be a part of and if you can commit to that, it's enough.

If you want to negotiate your own trade alliances, you are more than welcome to do so, and if you decide that you meant what you said about our infrastructure, we will respect that. We won't even demand that you be bound by our rules.

Instead, we hope you will help us write new ones. Better ones. So that we can continue to serve our people with their interests in our hearts. Many of us have lost sight of that purpose over the years, and we are grateful to you for bringing it back to us.

We hope that you will at least consider our offer and if you choose to decline, know that we will not hold it against you.

Thank you,

Council of Elders, Elderlands

At the bottom of the page, there are signatures in every shade of ink, some pristine and some sloppy. I tried twice to count them and failed. I see names I recognize and names I don't, but it's the names of people I know well that bring tears to my eyes. Names of people like Theodora.

"There's no way I read that right," Kelly says when he's finished. I know he must have read it twice, because I did, and when I look back at him, he looks like he's in complete disbelief.

"You did," Cyan says, smiling softly and folding her hands in her lap. "We don't need an answer now, but I wanted to deliver the letter myself. I didn't think a courier would do justice to the magnitude of what we're offering."

At the edge of my vision, a shimmer of gold flashes where Cyan's hands are folded in her lap.

Abbigail's bedroom door is open when I approach, and she's sitting on the floor writing in one of the heavy journals that Wanderer sent her. There's a cushion beside her, and her knees are red, but that isn't what gets my attention. What makes me smile is the way she's singing to herself, rocking back and forth as she writes. I find myself watching her for a long moment, and I nearly jump out of my skin when she speaks.

"You can come in," she says without looking up. Her pen is still moving across the page, but she has stopped singing. I approach the door and try not to let my embarrassment show.

"I wasn't trying to be weird. You just looked... happier. I was afraid to disturb you," the threshold of the door is digging into my collarbone the way I'm leaning against it, but I don't care. She puts her pen down and closes her journal, tossing it over her head and onto her bed.

"I said you could come in," she says with a laugh, looking at me with her eyebrows scrunched together and her nose wrinkled up. I let myself laugh.

"That's a horrible face," I tell her, pushing off the door frame and walking into the room. I sit down on the floor beside her and she's still laughing when my ass hits the ground.

"I know. I make a lot of awful faces. They used to make Lexie laugh," she tells me. There's still a note of sadness in her voice, but it isn't as intense, and it doesn't look like it overwhelms her as much. I still don't envy her position, but I'm grateful to be able to give her a safe place to feel all the things she feels.

"I only met him twice, but I don't think I ever heard his laugh. Maybe at a distance while he was talking to Greyson, but definitely nothing more than that," I replay our days training rapidly behind my eyes, convinced that I'll find something if I look hard enough, but I don't. In every memory I have of Aleksandr, he's stone-faced, except for when he looks at Abbigail or Anastasiya. Even his so-called wife doesn't elicit more than a polite smile from him. The only person who got him to relax the entire time we were there was Greyson.

"He has a nice laugh, but it's definitely rare. He's a little bit difficult to get to know," she tells me. She's twisting her rings around her finger and staring off into the distance.

"Why do you wear them on your right hand?" I ask. She looks down at them and watches the stones twinkle in the midday sun for a moment before she answers me.

"They were Russian. Lexie and Nastya—Anastasiya. They were born in Russia, and I was raised there. It just seemed like the obvious choice when the time came," She leans back against the bed and sighs. "It was the night they lost their sister that everything changed. We built Valyria's funeral pyre, and it was like flipping a switch. As soon as we lit it, something broke inside both of them."

"She mentioned something about that, I think," I say, mirroring the way Abbigail is sitting. When I stretch my legs out, they're substantially shorter than hers.

"What did you need? When you came over here?" She

asks after the silence has stretched between us for a long moment. I have to think about my answer for a second, because there are a lot of things I think she should know.

"The Chief Elder came to see us this afternoon. They've offered us positions in the Council of Elders, and they... they want our help." I should have brought the parchment with me, but I didn't, so instead, I offer her my hand. She looks down at it and then takes it in both of hers, holding tight as she steps into my memories and watches the meetings with Cici and Cyan. When she drops my hand, she looks impressed.

"That's a very generous offer," she says, turning toward me and resting her head on the mattress as she watches me. "Are you going to accept it?"

"I think I should."

"I have a stupid question," she says, laughing at herself and tucking a curl behind her ear.

"I find that hard to believe. What're you thinking?" She closes her eyes and shakes her head, licking her lips as she weighs the best way to phrase it.

"What the hell is a Council of Elders?" she sounds so exasperated.

"They're sort of the same and sort of different from what you said about the Guardians, I tell her, turning and resting my head so that we're looking at each other. The thought of the Hellhounds makes me nauseous, even though I still haven't convinced myself that they're real. "The Council of Elders is the big fancy, official name for the entire Council, but the entire Council is only together a few times a year. When it's a partial Council, it's the Elder Council. They're... I don't know what to compare them to in the human world. They're our governing body—or as close to one as we have. They have a specific tract of land in the Neutral Lands that belongs to them, and the building that houses their residences and their meeting chambers is called the Elder House. It's really beautiful."

"And these Elders, they're asking for your help because they're old and don't know how to lead people five generations younger than them?" I nod.

"Sounds silly when you say it like that," she snorts.

"It sounds like they should teach human governments a thing or two."

I rub my wrist, thinking again of Elder Vianbry's tattoo. The burning must be psychosomatic. I almost ask Abbigail if she recognizes it, but something stops me. I'm pretty sure there's some growing in the greenhouse—pretty sure I saw it tucked into a corner separate from everything else.

16
Aliyah

The floor of my office is made of beautiful hardwood that hurts my ass if I sit on it for too long. It's the entire reason that one of the first things I bought for myself was a thick rug, and that rug is the only reason that I can sit on the floor for more than five minutes at a time.

I'm sitting on the floor, numb from the waist down, when the quietest of knocks comes from my door. It's closed, but unlocked, and the girls have been standing outside for five minutes. I figured they were waiting for one of them to have the nerve to knock, but I didn't want to rush them, so I waited. I put down the letter that I'm reading and look up as they open the door.

Leighann is the first one I see.

"Ali?" she says, her voice small and soft. "Can we come in?"

They're hovering just inside the door, and they're clinging to one another like they're afraid I might send them away. Maeve's eye is still bruised faintly, but her hair has been brushed and braided, and she's wearing clothes that fit her. It's uncanny, how perfectly identical and completely opposite they are.

"Of course you can. Both of you are welcome in here anytime," I tell them. Maeve trails close behind Leighann until they're standing in front of me. She sticks her little hand out to me, and when I take it she curtsies, like something out of an etiquette lesson.

"I am Maeve Verdigris," she says softly. It doesn't seem like she's whispering; it just seems like maybe her voice is that soft all by itself. "It's my pleasure to finally make your formal acquaintance."

She squeezes my hand gently and then lets go, backing up to stand beside her sister. She sounds so like Leighann that it's almost unreal, but also so different that it's like they were born a hundred years apart. The sound of her voice, her formal words, and the careful way she strings them together have me wondering what Anya Kivleneiks put her through in the years she had them under her thumb. I can't even say definitively how long of a time we're talking about, so I have no idea what kinds of trauma she's been through. I smile at her and make sure it's genuine.

"Hello, Maeve. I promise you that the pleasure is all mine," I tell her. She cocks her head in the same way that Leighann does while using her magic and I wonder if she's searching my words for a lie. She probably is, and that's okay; it's what I would do too. "You can call me Ali. I don't bite."

Her eyes snap to mine, and she raises an eyebrow, her magic burning behind the vivid red of her irises.

"You do bite," she says, and I have the distinct

impression of being watched by a snake as her eyes hold mine. Leighann stifles a giggle and says something in a language I don't understand as she pulls her sister back and away.

"Apologize," she tells Maeve, and the girl barely contains herself as she turns her attention back to me.

"I am sorry," she says. "But I am not wrong. I will work on being careful about what I point out."

I'm confused for about half a second longer, and then I realize that she's calling me out on the lie. I don't bite in the metaphorical sense, which was what I meant, but I do bite in the literal sense. I bite Shawn. When we...

"Did you girls need something?"

"Oh, kind of? I wanted you to meet my sister officially, but I also wanted to see if you'd be up for... for taking us shopping?" Of all the things she could have said, that was the last thing I was expecting.

"What do you need to go shopping for?" I ask, curious more than anything else.

"I have plenty of clothes, so it doesn't have to be right now or anything, I was just thinking and... and I thought that it would be nice if she could have some things of her own, you know?" I look more closely at Maeve, and that's all it takes for me to see that she's wearing Leighann's clothes, has her hair braided with Leighann's little hair ties, and has Leighann's shoes on her feet. They both look like they're bracing for the impact of being told no, and I decide right then that there's nothing I need to do more than I need to take them shopping.

"Of course, I'll take you shopping. We can even go upstairs together and make a list of what you need for your room, so we don't forget anything important. How does that sound?" Maeve looks from Leighann to me twice, then nods enthusiastically and smiles the most brilliant little smile I have ever seen. She's missing one of her canines, and the little gap in her teeth makes the grin all the more charming.

"Can I go ask Greyson if he wants to go? He loves shopping and it'll be fun," she's bouncing on her toes before I even nod, and she takes off running as soon as she has my blessing, dragging her sister with her.

A few heartbeats later, Maeve comes walking back into the room. She crosses my office, gets down on the floor beside me, and wraps her little arms around me so tight I wouldn't be surprised to find little bruises in the shapes of her fingers.

"Thank you for taking care of her," she says, pulling back to look at me. She's all but sitting in my lap, and her eyes are rimmed with tears.

"Don't thank me, sweet girl. She's family, and now so are you. We take care of family here," I say. She kisses my cheek and smiles at me one last time before she walks out of my office again.

"Hey Snowball," Shawn says, looking up at me from our bed and resting his book on his stomach. My eyes drag over his bare shoulders and chest, then snap back to his face.

"Hey," I say, remembering the ridiculous collection of bags I'm carrying and becoming very aware of all the places that the plastic is biting into my skin. I kick the door closed as I come through and drop the bags onto the couch before I climb into the bed and rest my head on his stomach. He sinks his fingers into my curls and scratches gently at my scalp, easing some of my tension with his touch while he waits for me to tell him about my day.

"Did you buy anything special?"

"I didn't buy a single thing for anyone but myself," I tell him proudly, looking at the pile of bags over my shoulder and trying not to let myself feel any amount of remorse. When I look back at him, he's smiling.

"That's what I like to hear. You wanna show me what you got?"

"Yes, actually. But first, I want a kiss." I have to adjust to be able to reach his mouth, but I don't mind because the kiss is worth it. Lush and soft, like he missed me as much as I missed him. I hope he did—I know he did. I believe that with my entire body and soul.

"What's going on in there?" he asks, touching my temple and dragging his fingers down the side of my face. He presses his thumb into my bottom lip, and it takes every ounce of my self-control not to bite it.

You do bite, Maeve had said, and she had been right.

"How did we get here?" I ask Shawn. He cocks his head and sits up a little, like he can't answer me and be comfortable at the same time.

"You and I? Or...?"

"Yes? No? Kind of? All of us. How did we manage to cause so much trouble? Aviva is an unmated, unmarried twenty-year-old girl in violation of pack law. We have declared ourselves independent. We've befriended a warlock and are playing host to her wife. And if that wasn't enough, we acquired a little girl and have started some kind of war with a mad woman. We haven't been at this long enough to have this much going on," I close my eyes and take a deep breath to keep my frustration from taking over. I feel like an utter failure, and I don't know where it's coming from.

"Let's try listing them the other way. Okay? We didn't cause trouble, we spoke up. Aviva is pregnant with our first pack babies, and we have defended our beliefs to the Elder Council. We have made a powerful ally and done the right thing by her and her wife. We rescued a kidnapped girl. We fell in love," he turns my words back at me so easily and with such grace that I almost forget to argue. Almost.

"It's not funny. I'm completely serious. We've done nothing but create chaos at every turn, and I just don't understand how that came to be our reality." I roll so that I'm lying beside him, and I've barely stopped moving when he catches my hand, tangling our fingers together.

"We're special. And you can't honestly tell me you'd change any of it," I close my mouth before I say anything I don't mean, and really consider his words for a minute. Would I change any of it? Probably not, because change would mean sacrifice, and that's what I've been avoiding at every turn. Even if I change his question and ask myself whether I regret any of it, the answer is still no. Do I wish Aviva hadn't been so confident? Of course, I do. Do I wish she'd been the one to tell me? Obviously. But the rest of it? Every decision I made was to protect them. Aviva and the babies, sure, but also the rest of my pack. My family. My people.

I broke us from the Elder Council to protect them. I took Wanderer's offer for them. I'm considering the Council of Elders' offer for them. I saved Maeve for Leighann and for myself, so I can live with my reflection. The only thing about it that I regret, I regret on principle, and that is the possibility of war.

If there had been any other option that would have protected them, I would have taken it in a heartbeat. But there wasn't. Was is the option I was given, and if that's the price of admission, then I'll pay it a thousand times over to protect them.

"It just seems like there's no end to this," I say finally, staring at the wooden ceiling and holding onto his hand like the anchor it is. It's the only thing that keeps me tethered to the world some days. Today didn't feel like it was going to be one of those days until it was. Until I was back home and the contagious joy of our shopping trip had faded down the hall.

"There is, we just can't see it yet. He tells me. He squeezes my fingers once, then twice, and then a third time. "Just remember, you aren't carrying the weight of it alone."

From the desk of Aliyah Trevonaire – Alpha

Good morning,

My hope is that this letter will find you well, recovered from our previous encounter, and in pleasant spirits. I also hope that you will forgive me for taking a few days time to write and send this, as I was trying to give both myself and you time to heal and recover. Now that we have both done those things, I am reaching out to you and to each of your counterparts to share my deepest gratitude for your support and my most sincere condolences for the losses each of you sustained as a result of that support.

You were under no obligation to back us up, and you did it anyway. That choice will not soon be forgotten, and though I can never express to you how much we appreciate your support, I can tell you that even the thought of the alternative makes me shudder. I feel confident in saying that I would have buried more than one of my people if we'd entered that fight alone, and I am not to proud to admit that they would have been just as likely to end up burying me.

Since you have each declared yourselves my allies—and shown proof of your dedication to that role—I feel that it is time for me to officially do the same. Know that with all that we are, we, the Trevonaire of Noonchester Falls, will support you and defend you in the face of all threats, both internal and external.

We are proud to make this declaration and will honor is to its fullest extent.

With thanks and appreciation,

Aliyah Trevonaire, Alpha

I'm reading Wanderer's next letter when I hear them, and it takes all the self-control I have not to immediately follow the sound through the house.

It's quiet at first, like hearing music play from someone else's headphones, and then it changes. The longer I focus on the sound, the clearer it becomes. I strain my ears for a full minute before I give in and let myself open my bedroom door. The sound comes from Abbigail's room, floating through the cracked door and filling the space beyond with warmth and life. I let myself walk down the hall, but stop just outside her door, peering through the gap at the room and people taking up space within it.

Abbigail is the one singing, and she's doing it with her whole voice this time, instead of hiding it under her breath. She isn't alone, though. Leighann and Maeve are both balanced on the sill of the open windows, one leg inside and one in the cool night air. Piper is lying on her back on the bed, and her long red hair touches the floor where it hangs over the side. Sarah is the only other person I hear or smell, so I know the bare feet twisting the desk chair back and forth have to be hers.

They're all humming along as she sings, like they know the tune even though they aren't sure of the words. I don't mean to sing along, but I start to a few seconds before I knock and push the door open. Every single face turns toward me, and they all look surprised. But not Abbigail. Abbigail just looks impressed. She's holding a tiny string instrument in her hands, and it's covered in hand-painted turtles. It looks completely absurd.

"You sing?" Piper asks, rolling over so I'm not upside down, and accidentally ending up with her hair stuck to her face.

"Singing lessons twice a month since I was four," I tell her. Abbigail motions for me to sit, so I do. The plush rug is buttery soft under my hands and feet, and the room smells like sea salt.

"Was that standard where you're from? Teaching people to sing?" Piper asks. Her hair is mostly out of her face, but she's still fighting with the fine strands. I've spent plenty of time at Archimedes Landing over the years, but I've never had much reason to spend time in their Academy. I never thought to consider the things they teach there, especially not the things beyond the 'standard' curriculum. I rarely leave the medical building at all while I'm there, and it shows. I feel like I'm being set up to say something stupid, even though I know that isn't her intention.

"More so for Aviva and me, because of who we are. Everyone studies some kind of art in school in Tamarak Valley, though. Aviva and I had voice lessons and piano lessons on opposite Mondays. I danced two days a week, studied Hebrew and Latin every morning, and took self-defense on Tuesday and Friday. I devoted every other free minute of time I had to studying medicine and tried to travel to other reservations at least once a week," I tell them, feeling like I'm saying too much. Like I'm waving my privilege in their faces. "I wanted to make sure I did good for more than just my people."

Abbigail looks at me like she wants to say something, but she doesn't.

"You had time for all of that?" Sarah asks, still absently spinning the chair with her feet. I nod.

"I also play the violin," I add. I look at the horrible little instrument in Abbigail's hands, and I have to ask her about it before my curiosity kills me. "What the hell is that thing?"

"It's my ukulele," she says, holding it up proudly and spinning it around so I can see even more of the awful paint job. It's an aggressive shade of teal under the turtles, and it kind of hurts my eyes. "A very nice man in a souvenir shop gave it to me on my wedding day."

We laugh and sing and tell stories in Abbigail's bedroom until the sun comes up and no one leaves. If there were any doubts lingering in my mind about whether or not I made the right choice with Wanderer, they'd be long gone now.

"Politeness is stifling to curiosity," I say, my stomach growling angrily as I turn and look at her. "Ask whatever you've been trying not to ask since last night."

I was in the kitchen making myself coffee and waffles when she came out of the sublevels, and we'd done the small talk thing for a few seconds before falling into a companionable silence. But now, sitting with my plate in front of me, I can feel her eyes on me, and it's driving me insane.

"That's actually pretty similar to a book quote I really like," she says, smiling and smearing peanut butter on a bagel in a thick layer. She closes the jar and brings her plate around to sit beside me on a stool. "I was going to ask why you chose medicine."

"Oh, that's all?" I lick syrup off the back of my hand and wipe my mouth before I answer her. "When I was little, my mother encouraged Aviva and me to explore. She wanted us to try everything we were interested in and keep searching until we found what fit. I was already curious about medicine, and it's what I wanted to do from the start. Call it a natural predisposition or blame it on my gift, but neither of those is the real reason.

I humored my mother and father by studying diplomacy and medicine for a while, because I didn't want to disappoint them or feel like I was taking the easy way out. That's what medicine felt like, the easy path. It was as easy for me as breathing. Natural. Like I was born to do it. I tried for their sake, but it didn't matter what else I looked into; I always came back to medicine. In the end, there was no competition. Nothing beats it."

I cut another bite and am in the process of shoving it into my mouth when I glance over and see Abbigail staring at me, searching my face for more information. I keep eating, and at about the halfway point, she realizes that I'm not going to tell her anything else if she doesn't come up with a question to ask. She puts her bagel down on her napkin and turns her stool toward me.

"Who is it?" she asks, and she must see the confusion on my face, because she amends her question immediately. "The person you love that's sick. Who is it?"

The silence that stretches between us is long and heavy.

"Me."

Her mouth falls open, and she stares at me like I've just birthed a goose, pupils dilated and breathing shallow. I should probably be offended by the warring pity, confusion, and concern in her eyes, but I'm not. My ability to feel anything in the face of pity is long gone, wasted on my father and the other Healers over the years. I feel nothing other than mild sadness as I motion for her to follow me and carry my plate of waffles to my office. She closes the door behind us, and I jump up onto the edge of my desk so that I'm facing the blank spot on the wall where Wanderer set up Janie.

"Janie, can you hear me?" I've been practicing which commands she responds to and mimicking Abbigail when I'm not sure how to make her do what I want. She whirrs and clicks, then we're staring at the home screen.

"I can hear you."

"Can you open my medical file, please?" Abbigail sits

down on the floor and leans against my desk, just far enough away that I won't accidentally kick her.

"Authorization code, please," Janie says. A red laser shines on me, and I press my fingers into the grid under the skin of my chest. When it lights up, she scans it, and the file opens on the screen. Abbigail is staring at me when I pull the collar of my shirt back into place.

"Nathair tech," I tell her, wishing I weren't so self-conscious about it. "We use them for medical identification. They're completely self-sufficient, and they keep track of vitals. It syncs with the computer system in Medical every time you enter, and keeps all my medical data so that I can be treated in the field."

"Everyone has these?" She asks. I shake my head.

"Royalty mostly. The Alphas, Betas, Deltas, Heirs, Keeper, Healers, and Elders," the list seems longer when I say it out loud. "One push on the sensor shows an identification pattern used for confirming identities, two consecutive gives you access to medical records. Three sends out a location ping."

"So you can treat anyone and not have to worry about mismatching blood or missing some crucial preexisting condition," she says, looking thoroughly impressed.

"Cuts down on the need for keys, too, when everyone has an unchangeable, unhackable, unstealable identity marker that can be read by the scanners on all the important doors," I pull my legs up and fold them under me, completely unconcerned for the papers I'm squishing as I do, "I should probably start at the beginning."

So I do. I tell her about the scanners in Medical and about learning to read the results when I was nine. I tell her about Theodora and how she thought it would be a good idea for me to practice on myself instead of using the equipment on other patients. I tell her how fun she made it sound and how excited she was to show me how to do it.

And then I tell her about the results. About how Theadora was the second person to realize what they said.

About how I beat her to the diagnosis by thirteen seconds.

"She was so scared," I say after a moment of silence. Theodora's face is displayed on the screen, and I'm choosing not to think about how Janie got it. "It wasn't even her tumor, but she looked like she was going to collapse onto the floor. I'll never forget the sight of those tears in her eyes. It was the first time I ever saw her cry."

I slide off my desk and minimize the photo of Theodora in favor of pulling up the scans in my file. They use Aviva's brain as the comparison, and even someone with no medical knowledge can see the difference when they're side-by-side. I blow the image up as big as I can and zoom in on Aviva's brain, its core structures cast in shades of black and gray. I feel like I'm teaching a class, a little, but I don't mind.

"This is the primary Thelluxian structure. The one in your brain looks just like this. It's named after Trinity Thellux, the first Healer to map the wolfen brain in the sixties. The technology was new and finicky, and she still managed to beat her competitors to readable images by two years. This is the part of our brains that keeps us in control of the change, lets us come back to our human bodies when we want to, and keeps our wolves within reach when we need them. It's part of the reason for the high mortality rate among the bitten. Without this structure, their brains often struggle to adapt, and they lose half of themselves. Insanity is the only outcome, and nearly seventy percent of those who find themselves facing life without being whole commit suicide." I spin the image around and focus in on the area above Aviva's brainstem, where there is a smaller structure made of the same dense gray material.

"This is the secondary Thelluxian structure. It's what makes it possible for us to receive the gifts that the land gives us, something that the bitten are never able to do. You can see here that the area between the two structures is supposed to be a light gray color. That's your regular, run-of-the-mill brain matter. But mine..." I zoom out and switch to my own scans. When the same area is in focus on the screen, I feel something cold settle into my stomach. "Looks like this. This pretty, lacey monstrosity is cancer. It's unique to a small number of species in the supernatural world and often behaves erratically. Usually, it's a sign that there's too much magic in a person's body. Mine is inoperable, because it's wound so tightly around the essential structures in my brain that any attempt to remove it would kill me or leave me without access to my wolfen form."

"Which is basically the same thing as killing you," Abbigail says, standing up and approaching the screen to look closely at the delicate tendrils of my tumor.

"I've never lost a patient," I tell her, calmly. "Except for myself, inevitably."

"Never?"

"Let me borrow your arm," I say, holding out my hand. She offers it to me without hesitating, but she's still looking at the screen. "I need you to watch this. It's going to hurt for a second."

"Go ahead," she says, blue eyes finding mine. I extend one claw and drag it over the delicate skin of her forearm, just deep enough that a healthy line of blood forms. She lets out a sound between a gasp and a moan, and I ignore it. "I can heal almost anything, either with my skill or with my venom. As long as the heart still beats, I have a chance."

I lean down and bite into her wrist. As soon as my canines pierce her delicate skin, I can taste her, the wildness of her wolf, and the rich saltiness of her essence, all wrapped up in the drop of blood that touches my tongue. Beyond the way she tastes, I can feel her injury in my bones. I close my eyes and let the venom sink into her, wondering in the back of my mind if this is what it feels like to her when she uses her own gift.

It only takes a small amount—a drop or two—to heal a superficial wound, so I release her arm a few seconds later and let her watch my venom work on both the cut and the bite. She watches the wound close like it's the most incredible thing she has ever seen, and I can relate to her awe.

"It doesn't seem very fair that you can heal everything but yourself," she says when the last traces of the wounds have gone. I don't mean to laugh, really, but it comes out anyway.

"First time dealing with twin magic?" I ask her. She shakes her head.

"Anastasiya and Valyria were twins," she says, and then, like she has answered her own question, her eyes widen.

"Aviva and I are twins in the traditional way. Not just multiples, but actual genetic twins. I can heal everything but myself, so she can only heal me. Her venom is the only thing that has kept me alive this long."

I tell her about the vials in my desk drawer, even going so far as to pull the box out and show them to her, and we stand in silence in my office for a long time while she absorbs everything. It's all I can do not to stare at the scan of my brain still displayed on the wall.

Her eyes don't leave the vial of pinkish venom until I close the box. When they meet mine again, there are tears there.

Like, even she can see how cruel it is. I wonder if I could push her to tell me more about Anastasiya and her sister, and decide it's safer to wait. She looks haunted now—more so than before—and I feel a twinge of regret knowing that it's my fault.

17
Aliyah

"Ali?" Greyson says, somehow managing to linger in the doorway and peer around the corner to look for me at the same time. Sometimes I forget how much smaller I am than everyone else, and I wonder if that's why I find it so impressive. Trying to do both things would have me flat on my face, and I know it.

"You need me?" I ask, poking my head out of the sanctuary, where I've been cleaning unnecessarily, just to make myself feel better. I asked the little people to bring fresh flowers, and they did. There are hot-house peonies in a jar in the middle of the table now, and the scent of them is potent in the small room. I never really liked the smell of flowers, which is probably a me thing. Greyson sniffs and gives an appreciative nod.

"I was hoping we could talk, but if you're busy, it can wait," he says. I roll my eyes and put down the bottle of cleaner

I'm holding.

"I'm not busy. Close the door and tell me what's on your mind," I tell him. I dip into the bathroom to wash the cleaner off my hands, then put on lotion as I sit down. That's how long it takes him to commit to putting his own ass in a chair. He doesn't look like he knows what to do next though, so we sit in silence for a long time before he finally sucks down a breath and starts talking.

It takes me a full two minutes to understand what he's talking about, but that's because the first thing that comes out of his mouth is an apology.

"Greyson, what? I need you to start… somewhere near the beginning, maybe?" I say, playing his words over in my mind and still struggling to understand what he was getting at.

"I need to ask Aviva to marry me," he says. And of all the things I was expecting to hear, that isn't even in the top ten. "You're her closest relative, and I wanted to ask you first. The traditions of marriage matter to me."

Elisabeth's face flashes in my mind.

I wonder if he's using the word marriage purposefully, or if he means something else—something more. I don't voice my curiosity, and I don't express my concerns, because I can tell he isn't here for that.

"I would never deny you my blessing. I think Aviva would be lucky to have you, and I would consider it a blessing to call you my brother," I tell him honestly. The image of him holding Elisabeth flashes behind my eyes, and I wonder if he's thinking of her now, too, as he wrings his fingers. "I have one question, first."

"Of course," he says, sitting forward.

"Is this what you want?" I don't know what I'm going

to see when I ask, but the uncertainty is written all over his face, and there's heavy sadness in his eyes. I know in the span of a few heartbeats that it isn't, and I realize that this is the actualization of his plan. He's doing his duty by Aviva, whether his own emotions line up with the expectations he has for himself or not.

It breaks my heart a little.

"It's what I have to do," he says, and whatever doubt I still had is gone when I look past the magic to the deep well of complicated feelings that hide in his eyes and come out on the canvases that he can't seem to keep enough of.

"I want you to be happy," I tell him, because it's true. It's so true that it hurts, and it isn't just about him. Aviva's life hangs in the balance here, and so does Elisabeth's. I have my suspicions about his relationship with both of them, but they deserve happiness and consideration, too. Things I can't give them, because I'm not him. And Aviva has spent her whole life imagining her perfect mate and the ceremony they would have with their friends.

This isn't that. I know it isn't.

"I want that too," he says sadly. I can't tell him to fight for it, but I want to.

"Have you picked out a ring yet?"

"No, but I'm hoping I can show it to you and see what you think before I give it to her. Is that okay?" he asks.

"Of course it is. I would love to be a part of this special moment," I say, and I know Aviva would hear the false sincerity, but he doesn't.

"I'm more nervous about being a father than I am about the rest of it, and I feel like I shouldn't be. I mean, I already have Leighann, so I should be ready. Is it crazy that I'm not?"

"Absolutely not. Everything about this is different.

You took Leighann because she needed you. You were ready because you had to be. You should be nervous. And there are going to be so many differences between her and your infants that it'll barely feel like it's the same thing at all," I tell him. I think back to all the babies I helped Theodora deliver and realize that Aviva's will be the first I do alone. I shut down the slash of anxiety that goes through me and do my best to stay present. My skills have gotten me through things far harder than childbirth, and I have to believe that they'll be enough when the time comes.

He tells me about not getting to hold his baby sister when she was born and about never having held anything that small or delicate. I tell him that everyone feels that fear, especially fathers, and that he'll only ever have the relationship he wants to have with them. My heart squeezes in my chest when he tells me that he wants to be the dad they show in movies, with the smiles and the father/daughter dances and the bedtime stories.

I think he's more capable of that than most men I know, and I tell him so.

"My mother didn't tell my father that Gabby was a girl until the day she was born. Did I ever tell you that?" he says. He's staring at a photo I printed of Aviva and me when we turned sixteen. It's in a frame she bought and left for me with a bland note and instructions to pick a good picture.

"No. I don't think I know much of anything at all about your sister, actually."

"My mother hid her sex until she gave birth. My father assumed she was a boy, and my mother let him. When the Healer handed her to him, he was so angry that he handed her right back. She stayed with my mother in the maternity wing for a few weeks, and then he arranged for her to be sent to live with my grandmother. I didn't meet her until she was four years old and my grandmother died," he says. And I wonder if there will ever be an end to the heinous things he tells me.

"I'm sure that was hard on you and your mother. I'm sorry that your father put you through any of that; you didn't deserve it."

There's a long silence, not uncomfortable, but heavy. He's trying to figure something out, and I leave him as much space as I can to do that without feeling like I'm breathing down his neck.

"What does this mean for Elisabeth?" he asks me, and her name chases every thought out of my head.

"I guess that depends on what you want it to mean," I say, the most non-specific answer I can give. I want his next steps to be his to choose.

"I need to see her before I can do this. I need to tell her myself. She deserves that."

"If that's what you need," I say. But I can tell it isn't. I wonder if he's even aware of the way his eyes change when he says her name, or the softness that comes to his face when he thinks of her.

I think back to the sight of them on the floor of my office, both sobbing desperately, and wonder who I would react that way to. Aviva, for sure. Shawn, probably. But I can't think of anyone else. Maybe my mother, but I can't be sure of that.

And he didn't hesitate to catch her. To hold her—watchers be damned.

There's something powerful in that kind of instinct.

PART THREE

1
Aliyah

I'm reading another one of the entries from Wanderer, and I feel like the more words I read, the less I understand—a feeling I'm starting to get used to. I started in the common room with the leatherbound book in my lap, but the weight of their curious eyes got to be too much, and I had to leave. I locked both doors to my rooms and have been sitting in the corner at my little desk since, grateful for the heavy soundproofing.

There's a photo tucked between the pages I'm on now. The delicate script on the back isn't Wanderer's, but it identifies the people in the photo as her, Warrior, and Serafina. She tells me, about halfway down the page, that Serafina is the girl she loved before Abbigail, the one that she spent the first portion of her very, very long life with.

I see the appeal. Serafina is stunning. In the photo, she looks more like Warrior's sister than Wanderer does. She has the same high-contrast coloring, even. Where the deep black curls are pleasant on him, they're stark on her, draining her delicate face of all color and highlighting the brightness of her red mouth and eyes.

When I met Warrior, his eyes were hazel, serious, and flecked with gold. In this photo, they're entirely black, like acid and ichor. Wanderer describes Serafina's eyes like rubies, but that doesn't feel right to me. They're too hard and too cold and too bright for that. They don't sparkle in the light, they emit it. Like there's fire in the flecks of deepest red.

Serafina's beauty is the opposite of Abbigail's, I think. Where one is all sharp lines and angles, the other is warm curves and soft edges.

When I turn the page, I find other photos.

On the back of a family photo, she lists Abbigail's mother, Elizabeth, her own mother and father, her brother, and a sister I didn't know existed. I assume it's the sister Abbigail mentioned, because the resemblance is uncanny.

There's another of Abbigail, Wanderer, and that same girl in the snow—this time, Abbigail's mother has her arms draped over their shoulders like a blanket. Closer to the camera, I can see that the girl's eyes are milky and unfocused—blind.

The last photograph is just Abbigail, standing on a rocky beach with sunburn on her cheeks. On the back, in her unique script, she's written "Home."

This time, I'm going to write a response to Jessabelle, like she said I should. I don't know what I'm going to say or if I really believe I'll get an answer, but I have to try.

I pick up my pen and nearly touch it to the paper three times before I finally start to write.

Jessabelle,

I know that you don't know me, and I have no way of even guessing how this message will appear to you, so I don't know how to make it make sense. I hope you'll know what to do either way. My name is Ali, and I don't know if Wanderer told you before everything fell apart, but I am a friend of hers and I've been given the task of protecting something for her until she can come back for it.

I guess I'm asking what you can tell me about her? The version of her you know, I mean. I am trying to understand, and I think you might be able to help.

I hope we talk soon,

Ali

I put my pen down, close the journal, and change into running clothes, long overdue for a break.

Aliyah,

I had been planning on using this entry to tell you about my life in New York and about how going back as a werewolf is going to complicate it. I wanted to tell you about the Guardians and what they mean to our worlds, because something tells me that you've never been taught about them.

But now? Now I have better things to say. For the last two days I have been in Scotland. Abbigail stayed back at Home Base with the others, and now I have a potent desire to tell you more about her. After all, you deserve to know who's sleeping down the hall, don't you?

For clarity, when I say "I" here, I mean Anastasiya, the girl I was when Abbigail loved me. The girl she actually knew.

Let's start with the basics.

Abbigail was born on the first day of February in 1943.

I'm almost exactly a year and a month older than her. She is an only child, and her mother, Elizabeth fled London with her the day after she was born. She used the sanctuary network to evade her husband and made her way to Russia, where my mother was waiting. Elizabeth lived with us until the day she died, and Abbigail stayed after that. We lived in that same little house together until the day that Ascendio Vendicta came for us.

Elizabeth Barlow was my mother's best friend and a wonderful cook. If not for her talent with balaclava, I doubt my father would have let her stay. Elizabeth returned to London regularly over the years, but Abbigail always stayed behind. Always stayed hidden away where she would be safe.

We were young when Elizabeth died. He poisoned her during her last trip to London, when he realized what she'd done, and he thought that she would give up Abbigail for the antidote. She didn't. She never would have.

By the time she returned to us, the clock was already ticking. My mother searched for answers in every tome and called on every friend she had to try and find an answer, but she found nothing. When Elizabeth collapsed in the snow outside our house, we knew she was dead before she even hit the ground.

Abbigail hadn't even known her mother was sick until she saw her fall.

Only my mother knew Elizabeth was a wolf, and when she died, telling Abbigail became her responsibility.

Aleksandr and Abbigail were best friends from an early age and Abbigail and I... well, I think we always knew where we would end up. I wonder often if our mothers might have known too.

She and Lexie used to sit at the piano in our living room together for hours, trading off on who would sing and who would play. Sometimes I still find them that way. Even now, after all these years, they still sit like that. Now, he plays for her, and she sings for him, like he's forgotten his own voice. Other times, he draws while she writes. My favorite are the nights when they smoke together and eat everything they can find. They'll sprawl out on the floor and talk for hours about absolutely nothing, and I love it.

All the time, they're the center of my whole world. He's himself when he's with her, and she is utterly safe with him. I wouldn't trade their moments together for anything in the world. I'm myself with her, too. She has that effect on people, I've noticed. Hopefully you'll agree.

Now, we can start talking about the fun stuff. Everyone likes a good love story, right?

Mine and Abbigail's starts on a beautiful winter day, not long before we lost Elizabeth. Abby was sitting on the counter in the kitchen with my mother, telling her about a new spell she'd mastered, and I was in the back room sparring with Aleksandr. I got so distracted watching her that he stopped trying to get my attention altogether. She wasn't even doing anything interesting. But I couldn't stop looking at her.

I think I still struggle to look at anything but her, and I think I'm okay with that. Have you seen her?

I look at her, and this primal voice inside of me roars that she's mine.

I think some part of me knew I loved her, even then. We were young, and girls weren't allowed to love girls. That wasn't an option, because it meant you wouldn't have any babies. I never wanted babies anyway, and I would have given anything in the world to be able to take her hand and never let go. I knew Russia wouldn't have me. Wouldn't have us, and I was okay with that price. I would have given up anything for her. I still feel that way.

I didn't think she would ever be able to love me the way I loved her. Not until a few years later, anyway.

There's a picture among the pages of the four of us in the snow. That photo is from the day I finally realized she'd loved me all along. We were trying to teach Aleksandr to fire a bow, something Abbigail has always been good at. He'd been struggling with it for weeks, and asking her for help outright would have been too much for his pride, so he just kept trying to figure it out himself.

I was sitting in a tree, well out of his sightline—and his firing line—writing in my journal, when I took a crossbow bolt to the shoulder. I was removed quite ungracefully from my place in the tree and placed in a heap on the ground.

Aleksandr was so afraid that he had seriously hurt me or that I would yell at him, that he froze and didn't move. He just stood there and looked stupidly at his bow like it was to blame for the problem he'd created.

Abbigail was running before I hit the ground, though. Straight to me. She was by my side so fast that it felt like she flew, and when she reached me, she was so afraid that it startled me. I think it startled her, too.

We were eleven then.

When she turned sixteen, I kissed her for the first time. We were alone in the house because my parents had taken Valyria to see a special doctor in Germany. Aleksandr had insisted on going with her, and it had made me feel better to know that she wouldn't be alone.

She tasted like peanut butter candy, and she smiled at me like I'd done something wonderful. It might have been her birthday, but it felt like mine.

I gave her a case of peanut butter as a present that year, and I've done it every year since. You can't buy peanut butter in Russia.

We fought for the first time a few months after that, and it hurt me more than anything else could. I felt like my heart had been pulled out of my chest and dropped to the ground at my feet. It was my fault and I knew that, but it felt like the end of the war. You remember what it's like at seventeen, I'm sure. The fight only lasted a few hours, and when it was over, we fell asleep clinging to one another.

Ascendio Vendicta came for us in April of that same year. We were sixteen and we could feel something coming, but we didn't know what it was.

The night before they came, my father found my mother trying to leave him, and he beat her. When he stepped in, he turned his attention to me, which gave her just enough time to grab her bag and leave us all behind. The armed guards and team of soldiers arrived the next morning to pick us up, and my father, well... Honestly, it doesn't even matter what he did, because I killed him with his own gun before he could plead, and then we went with them willingly.

We had no other path forward, and we knew it.

They sedated us heavily, and I surfaced a few times. We travel first by car, then by plane, and then by car again. It took us days of travelling to get to where we were going, and when we arrived, we were barely able to stand. The place was massive and very, very white. I hesitate to tell you this next bit, because it really isn't my story to share, but I'm going to tell you anyway. We affectionately refer to the place they took us as "the lab" even now. The quarters we were given were several stories underground, and when we were deposited there, they stripped us of all of our belongings. It was nothing but white tables, white chairs, a white kitchen, and forty white doors that led to forty white bedrooms. Inside, there were white beds, white walls, and white sheets.

The only color anywhere came from us, and it was disgusting.

I'm not ashamed to tell you that the next person who came through the door took the full force of my dissatisfaction. I was as polite as I could be, and I informed her that there were some things we were going to need if she wanted us to continue being on our best behavior.

Remember, at this point, Abbigail is only sixteen. That's important.

The woman obliged, out of fear for her life, and brought us back the things that had been confiscated. She promised that we would get the rest of the things we demanded and turned to leave. As she did, she bumped very intentionally into Abbigail.

I grabbed her by her arm, pushed her into the wall, and told her that she had no right to treat us like second-class citizens. She called for the guards, and a fight broke out.

I'm sure you can see where this is going.

My mother left before she told Abbigail anything, and I didn't know either. She didn't know to be careful when she was fighting back against the guards. In the human world, you activate the werewolf gene in one of two ways. You either turn eighteen or you kill someone. Without a reservation or the magic of the Wolflands, our wolves often go their whole lives as humans.

When the fight was over and the guard on the floor didn't move, I realized that the popping sound in the air was coming from her.

All I could do was clear the room and stay with her through it.

She didn't bite me that day. That came much later, but she had the opportunity to. I gave her every chance to bite me or even kill me, and she didn't.

The actual bite was as much an accident as her killing the guard had been, though. I was coming in from an assignment, and I had to pass through the training facility to get back to the residential unit. I was badly beaten because I had a different handler than I normally did, and he thought it was okay to hit me every time I told him that he was wrong. He hid me again every time I turned out to be right.

So, picture me, beaten and bloody, with one eye swollen

shut and a split lip. I even had handprint bruises around my throat. I was still handcuffed when she saw me, even though Admiral Scott—my usual handler—would have taken them off upon our arrival, and my replacement handler was dragging me along behind him by the chain between my wrists.

I didn't even realize she was in the room until she called out my name. I looked up at her and, as they say, that's all she wrote.

She was on the guard in a second, and when he threw me to the ground to try and subdue her, she changed. Admiral Scott was the first responding guard and directed the others to stand down. Instead of trying to intervene on his own, he approached with his hands up and knelt beside me to uncuff me before retreating.

He was the only one who had really paid attention to us. He knew the guards would hurt her and that if they did, I would hurt them. All hopes of keeping us compliant hinged on him keeping the guards from getting too close, and he knew it. So he did what he had to do.

She bit me as she was coming down, more out of reflex than anything else. She bit me because she was in pain and didn't realize her canines hadn't retracted until it was too late. After that, all we could do was wait to see if I would live through it. You know the odds as well as I do, and they did too. Everyone thought I was a dead girl walking, but Abbigail never believed it. Never doubted me for a second.

She forgave herself for it eventually, but she still wonders sometimes if I would go back and change it. I don't think I would. You could put me there a thousand times, and I would never pull away from her. There's nothing in the world that would make me want to give this up. I'm sure you can relate to that too.

She's beautiful as a wolf. I know you'll agree.

Take care of her for me.

Until next time,

Wanderer

2
Aliyah

Before every full moon, there is a hunt.

When we hunt, we hunt in packs, and we always look for the freshest, most desirable prey. We don't want deer or rabbits, not for a full moon. That's everyday eating. No, for a full moon, we want the predators. The big cats, the predator birds, the biggest, baddest beasts in the forest.

So that's what we search for.

We're on the trail of something particularly delicious when Abbigail comes to a screeching stop and howls. There's pain in that sound. Pain and fear. I bring the entire party to a halt and whirl on her, in my human form, so fast that I stumble a little.

"Abby? Abbigail, what is it?" I ask. She's on her knees, vomiting into the underbrush so violently that I can see the muscles in her back flexing.

"Gia," she breathes, clearing her throat and wiping her mouth with the back of her hand. "The scent we're following. It's Gia. She's... She was one of our human companions."

"That scent isn't human," I tell her, because it isn't. I take a deep breath just to be sure, and in the early spring air I can taste her.

"Let me show you," she says. She holds her hand up, and I squat to be within reach. The image comes as soon as her hand touches my face, like it was in a hurry. The girl she shows me is pretty, with long dark curls and a strong nose. Brown eyes, freckles, and thick eyelashes. The scent hits me a second later, and it's purely human at first, rich and meaty the way all humans smell. Then she shows me a series of other images, violent and bloody.

A baby.

A new scent floods my senses, this time more primal. More full and rich. It tugs at my instincts, screams *hunt* in the back of my mind.

She shows me the girl's face again. Giovanna.

"The baby made her smell that way?" I ask Abbigail. She looks less pale now, but not particularly well.

"The man who... The baby is part fury. They're a predator species. She never smelled the same after she gave birth. And this... She smells hurt. Badly, horribly hurt. Only a massive amount of blood loss would smell like this," she says. I breathe in through my nose and search for the scent she showed me amongst the bloody, primal scent. It takes me less time than I expect for the scent to register. Under the fear, the tears, and the overall desperation, there's Gia.

"Gia was human?" I ask. Abbigail nods.

"Was human. Is human. Could still be human, I don't know. Her father was CIA, I... Anastasiya saved her, and she stayed with us after that. Her father knew she was with us, and it meant he didn't have to worry about her being a target," she says. It takes me a little time to push my instincts aside and remember what I know about human government and intelligence.

The CIA is the United States' foreign intelligence agency. They're spies.

"What do you need us to do?" I ask her.

"I don't know."

"Abby, I need you to think. What do you need us to do? If you say we go after her, we go after her. If you say we put her down, we put her down. If you say we hunt, we hunt. This is your call because she's your person," I tell her. The others are waiting patiently, watching us and scanning the forest to make sure nothing comes to investigate our voices. We're far outside the reservation borders, and there are more than just nomads to be found here.

Plenty more.

"I have to help her," she says finally, dragging herself off the ground. There's mud clinging to her knee and hands, but her color has returned.

"Today was always meant to be a day spent hunting for sport," I tell her. She laughs without humor, "You take the lead."

We run full out for twenty-one minutes before we skid to a collective stop. Abbigail sniffs cautiously at the ground and moves forward a single step at a time until she stops altogether and shakes her head.

"The ground is doused in essential oils; your nose will burn for days if you get too close," says a voice from beyond the line in the dirt where the oils have been spilled.

The air around the girl smells like sage and marijuana,

the scent of her thick beneath the cloud of smoke she brings. She has black hair and yellow eyes. There's a scarf covering her face from the nose down, and her skin is almost completely obscured by her long dress and gloves. Her feet are bare, though, and she's digging her toes into the mud as she watches us.

She appears unharmed, but she's scanning the forest like she knows there is something out there.

"I was supposed to draw them a boundary. Make sure that nothing finds them. But I didn't sign up for this," she says. A twig snaps, and she jumps. Rose has been staring in that direction for a full minute, but hasn't alerted to anything, so I'm not worried yet.

In the distance, I hear the Banshee scream.

"What did you see?" I ask the girl, shifting and trusting the others to have my back.

"They're going to kill her," she says. "They've been killing her for days. Her father won't budge, no matter how hard she begs."

"Gia," I say. "The girl they have, her name is Gia."

"Yes. They don't know you know her. They're trying to find out who built your wards. They think her father knows," she says. Abbigail whimpers quietly and drops her head.

"Why do they want to know that?" I ask the witch. I can feel the clock ticking, see it reflecting back at me from the depths of her strange eyes.

Something is coming. The scream feels closer—like I could see her face if I turned my head. Any louder and I know my ears will bleed.

"Can't break them if you don't know who built them," she says.

The gunshot comes before she finishes talking, and the sound of a rifle in the distance is right there with it. Rose is on me in a second, pressing me into the underbrush as the bullet flies through the air and strikes the young witch between the eyes.

"They killed her," Abbigail says, in her human form again, and digging her fingers into the ground as Kelly holds her down. Rose and Elijah are both scanning the trees, looking for any sign that there are more bullets to be fired. They find nothing, and they're confident enough that they let me up off the ground.

Time of death, 2:04 PM. If we don't bury her, she'll rot here, but we can't take the time.

I need a perimeter sweep, I say, reaching for Rachelle and Greyson. I feel my words reach them. Feel them tense and begin moving. Neither of them says anything, but I feel the alarm go through each person they pass as they run for the bay door. They take Marcus and Saoirse, taking off in all different directions and running hard.

"Something isn't right," Rose says. "There should be something else out here. Someone else. They wouldn't just leave this place unguarded.

"Unless they had nothing to lose," Abbigail says, pushing Kelley off and getting to her feet. Her entire body is muddy. "Unless they're already at Noonchester Falls and they've decided that they're going to attack whether they get the information or not."

"Are you sure Gia is dead?" I ask her. She nods.

"Did any of you see anything out of the ordinary on our way here?" I ask. Kelly, Rose, and Elijah all shake their heads in turn.

Take Aviva and anyone underage to the sublevels. Go

now, I tell Shawn. His panicked response is cut off by Aviva's immediate movement—compliant for once in her life. I hope that they'll all make it in time.

I can still feel the clock ticking from behind the dead witch's eyes.

"Home. We're going home. Run as hard as you can, and if that means we split up, do it," I tell them all. They each nod and I look at Rose.

I'm not leaving you. Don't you dare tell me I have to, she says. She doesn't leave room for argument, just falls into place beside me and waits. I shift, and when I do, I bump her with my head.

Together, I tell her.

And we run.

We run hard.

It takes us almost an hour to get back to Noonchester Falls. Rose stays right with me the entire time, barely straining to keep pace with me. Abbigail and Kelly break off and approach from the north. Elijah separates from us just enough to make it look like he's alone, and Rose and I run up to the wards where they exist nearest to the falls.

As soon as we get within eyesight of the barrier, I see them. They're spread through the forest and wearing scent-concealing clothing, but I clock them and so does Rose. We both identify the same hole in their perimeter at the same time, and we run through it so close together that we might as well be one person.

They react too late, firing their arrows and calling out after us as we streak past them.

We're inside the barrier a moment later, and as soon as we are, I can smell the blood.

Aviva? I call out, still running, this time toward the residence. Abbigail and Kelly are fighting somewhere just to my left, but I can't stop to think about their violent snarls. When I see Elijah, there's blood on his maw and confidence in his stride.

Are you hurt? I ask him. He chuffs.

Not a damn scratch.

I laugh internally and slide through the bay doors, looking for any sign that there are still people above ground that shouldn't be. I find nothing.

I can smell her blood. Can you tell where it's coming from? I ask Rose. She shakes her head, sniffing at the air. She jerks her chin and starts to run, so I follow.

We have visitors. North of the residence, just beyond the barrier. Kelly says. I can still hear him snarling. *The diplomatic kind, this time. Closing fast.*

Greyson, can you hear me? I say, swinging in a wide arc to head toward the sound of Abbigail and Kelly still killing Kivleneiks soldiers. Greyson doesn't respond.

Shawn, find Greyson and Aviva. Take someone with you. Aviva is hurt.

He's already moving, using that extra keen sense of smell he has and following the scent of Aviva. The midmorning sun on top of the hard running has us all baking and tired. We don't slow down.

We're coming up behind you, Saoirse says. I don't have time to look at who she has with her, but they fall into line behind Rose and me as we slow to a stop near Kelly and Abbigail.

In her human form, Abbigail drags Kelly through the wards by the scruff of his neck, and if I were less concerned about my sister, I would probably laugh.

"They stopped fighting. Let them surrender you complete dunce," she says. The way she lets him go makes him stumble and feels insulting, but even he seems to think he deserves it.

A golden shimmer shows me the word *brittunculi* in my mind.

"Do you hear that?" Abbigail asks, ears twitching toward something none of us can see. I hear it, though. I nod, and she goes, slinking into the trees to follow the sound. Kelly joins us, falling in line to my right and looking very unbothered by the state of his fur.

Snowball, how fast can you get back to me? Shawn asks, his voice calm in the way it always is to prevent me from knowing he's about to lose his shit. I feel myself still.

Did you find Aviva?

I did. He says, And then a scream of pain rips through the world, tearing a hole so deep in my heart that I nearly stumble. I would know her voice anywhere. I look around, so unsure of myself that I feel like I'm drowning. Kelly nods.

Go. Take Rose. We'll be fine. They'll wait for you, you know they will. He says. And he's right.

Rose and I peel off as Rachelle and Marcus rejoin the group. They, like Saoirse, seem confident that there is no imminent threat. But I still haven't seen Greyson.

I need you to tell me what's going on. I tell Shawn. At the edge of my hearing, I can tell he's talking calmly to Aviva, trying to keep her relaxed.

Babies. Many babies. And I have never helped anyone have a baby before, he says. I almost laugh, both at the timing and at the idea of him trying to help anyone give birth. Only heaven will save him if we ever have children. There will most certainly be a broken hand or two in the story of his life.

The scent of Aviva's blood grows stronger by the second.

What's her heart rate at? I ask him as we approach. I shift mid-stride, but Rose doesn't; she knows how vulnerable I'll be and she isn't taking any chances. Her magic can't buy her time if she can't sustain it—mine can't either.

"Too fucking high," Shawn answers, out loud this time. He's holding on to one of her hands and pressing his t-shirt into a nasty gash on her head. He's telling her that she can't push yet and she's telling him that she can beat his ass, which is a good sign, believe it or not.

"Vivi," I say as I drop to my knees beside her. "Viv, honey, what happened?"

"Someone got inside," she says, pointing over her shoulder to where there's a body on the floor of the barn. I can smell the vomit that followed the kill on her breath, and I know that there will be no recovering from what happened today. What is still happening today. Not for any of us, not for a long time.

"Where's Greyson?" I ask her, pushing up her skirt and trying to work while I listen. The body on the floor is human—I can smell it from here—which means that the wards haven't fallen.

"What do you mean? I thought he was with you. He went out on a perimeter check, and I haven't seen him since," she says. Her eyes are wide with fear, but only some of it has to do with the fact that she's in active labor.

"Were you unconscious?" I ask her. I wave my hand, and Shawn removes the shirt from her forehead. The gash is deep and bleeding in the way that only a head wound can, but she isn't disoriented, and I can't see bone.

"Yes. I don't know how long. Are they okay?" she asks. She's talking fast—panicking—and her hands haven't left her stomach, like she's not sure she can trust her body anymore.

"How badly do you feel like you need to push?" I ask her. She winces and tries to force a smile.

"I can wait as long as you need me to," she says. It's a lie. I would know it even if I weren't between her thighs, looking at her daughter's head. I look at Shawn, then at Rose, then at Aviva again.

"Baby girl one is ready to meet you, and I don't think we have time to make it to Medical. Can you do this here?" I already have her blood on my hands, and I have no way to attempt to sanitize anything, but I don't have a choice. This baby is coming whether we're ready for her or not.

"Without Greyson?" she asks, frantically shaking her head. The curls not glued to her forehead by the sheen of sweat I'm just noticing bounce around her face and hit Shawn, who sputters.

"Yes, without Greyson. You don't need him—you've got me. You can do this. I'm going to get you through this," I tell her. She searches my face for any hint that I could be lying, then settles back and plants her feet.

"Tell me what to do," she says. And the answer is easy.

"Listen to your body, Vivi. When you need to push, push."

The oldest daughter of Aviva Nathair and Greyson Marquis is called Samantha, and she greets me with a scream the moment I bring her into the world. Her birth certificate will list her birth date as April 7th—5:16 PM.

Shawn leaves us and comes back with my emergency maternity kit, so I cut and clamp her cord before I hand her to her mother, who lets out a well-deserved sob at the sight of her sweet face.

Still no sign of Greyson, Shawn tells me, wiping Aviva's face and handing me my portable ultrasound machine so I can get a look at the others. They seem content to stay where they are for a little while longer.

Do you hear that? I ask Rose. I know better than to ask Shawn, because I know he can't hear anything.

It sounds like the ocean. Like waves, crashing hard.

Abbigail, we both say at the same time.

"Viv, honey, do you need to push again, or do you feel okay right now?" I ask her. She's holding Samantha against her chest and holding on to Shawn's hand, but she seems stable. Her vitals are.

"I think I'm okay right now. Is something wrong?"

"No, everything is fine. But I think I can get you moved to Medical before you're ready to deliver two and three. Do you think you can let Shawn carry you?" she nods, looking at Shawn and smiling. Nothing about it threatens me, and that surprises me. I'm grateful to have had the forethought to take my ring off before the hunt, because if I hadn't, it would be forever tinged by the scent of her.

"We're going to Medical?" Shawn asks me. I shake my head discreetly.

Something's wrong. I need you to take her to Medical, and then I need you to tell me the minute she starts feeling like she needs to push. You don't have to do anything but monitor her vitals and tell me what you see. He looks very uncomfortable, but he nods.

"I have to touch you to pick you up. Is that okay?" he asks her. She nods and bends her knees. The hand that was holding his comes up to rest on her belly, and he takes her weight easily, standing without a grunt or a grimace.

"I'll be there as soon as you need me, okay?" I tell her,

stroking her hair and touching Samantha's face. "You and me, remember?"

"Whatever's out there," she says, looking out into the trees. "Don't let it hurt him. He deserves to meet his daughters."

"I promise," I tell her. I hope I can keep it.

I turn to Rose, and we take off running in the direction of the sound, growing louder by the second. When we find Abbigail, she's crouched on the ground in the middle of a small clearing with one hand on the ground and the other sparking wildly at her side. In a tree behind her, an archer is poised to fire, and in a shallow arc in front of her, there are five Kivleneiks soldiers. I can tell two things by the way they're staring at her. First, they can't find an opening to strike, and second, they haven't heard our approach over the sound of the ocean in the air. One look at Abbigail herself tells me that it's as intentional as it is effective.

She's covered in blood, but none of it's hers. I know, because the magic in her collar has healed every injury and lingers in the faint scars, still working.

The air around us is alive with Abbigail's power, the roiling, twisting tendrils of water like snakes, ready to strike as soon as someone makes the mistake of moving.

I don't see the girls behind her until Rose nudges me and jerks her chin.

Fuck.

Drenched in blood and hiding behind separate trees beyond the clearing are Leighann and Maeve Verdigris. Abbigail is protecting them so thoroughly that there are individual tendrils of magic curled around the trees they're clinging to, ready in case anyone approaches from behind.

Once I see them, I know that the fight is inevitable.

Rose and I look at one another, nod, and launch ourselves at the Kivleneiks soldiers, who notice we're coming in the exact moment that we make contact with them. Abbigail throws a snare of magic out to keep Rose from being triple-teamed, and the attacking wolf whimpers as she falls to the ground in a heap of tawny fur and blood.

"Get them inside," Abbigail roars, still human as she gets her hands around another soldier's throat and squeezes.

I look up, and Rose doesn't have time to warn me before there are claws in the softest part of my side, ripping violently at my fur and turning the white strands a violent shade of red.

Rose is on him in a second, and there's something intensely personal in the way she rips his throat out and tosses it at the only surviving soldier. The man has the good sense to tuck his tail and run back in the direction of whoever he reports to. I change and run to Maeve. Abbigail grabs Leighann and slides her onto her back so she can help me walk.

Rose remains at my side, her large form marred by so much blood and emitting such a thick scent that I almost gag. She's more alert than I've ever seen her, but every few seconds, she looks at the wound in my side, and I feel her mood darken further.

Vitals are stable, no desire to push, Shawn says, and I sigh in relief. We've only been out here for fifteen minutes, but labor can progress erratically, and the last thing Aviva needs is to be alone and have something go wrong.

"Your timing is impeccable," Abbigail says as we cross back through the wards and into the safety of Noonchester Falls' primary reservation.

"You looked like you were holding your own," I say. My voice is weak, and I can hear myself struggling to breathe. They can tell too.

"They were all going to attack at once. I lose concentration at three," Abbigail says. She puts Leighann down and says something to her that I'm too dizzy to hear. Leighann and Maeve start running before I can protest, and the ground pitches up at me violently. The only thing that keeps me from landing on my face is the arm that Abbigail slides around my waist.

I don't know what happens after that, because the last thing I see is Rose backing toward me, closing Abbigail and me in where the barn meets the firewood storage shelves.

Then, everything goes black.

I have no way of knowing how long it will take before I'm on my feet again, but what I do know is that I fight my way to consciousness for one reason and one reason only.

Because my sister needs me, and so do her daughters. I reach for my magic and grasp it with everything I have. Around me, time grinds to a halt. I force myself upright.

For them, I stagger into Medical.

For them, I stay on my feet.

For them, I find a way.

Macie and Alis Marquis are born on either side of midnight. The grip I have on my magic is like a vice, and I can feel the sweat pouring down my back. It takes every ounce of venom I have to keep Aviva's heart beating.

Macie is so silent that I'm sure I've lost her. I check for a heartbeat three times before I convince myself that it's real—that she's alright.

Alis screams loud enough for both of them.

I don't know what happens after that.

3
Shawn

Walking into Medical is always interesting because I'm never sure what I should expect. This time is no exception. The garage doors are closed, so I round the building and use the normal door instead. It's definitely the first time I've ever been inside Medical here and probably the first time I've entered any medical building on my own feet through a normal-sized door without some kind of awful injury. I'm enjoying the absurdity of that thought when the harsh, clean smell hits me. It's not bleach or anything nearly that overwhelming, but it's sharp and noticeable. Instead of hurting me, the complete lack of anything in the air that has me straining, searching for some hint of what has happened here.

I find nothing.

I smell absolutely nothing until I'm at the door to the room Aviva is in—it's cracked a few inches and leaking warm, heavily scented air into the sterile hallway. Greyson is the person I see first, one of their girls resting on the bare expanse of his chest. She's so small that he looks like a giant, and her little hand is fisted tightly around his smallest finger like a claim.

My Father, it seems to scream. I wonder if he can hear it in his sleep. She's called Alis, I think. After the girls' grandmother. She and Greyson are both asleep so deeply that they don't stir.

Aviva is awake, though, and she's sitting up in bed with one of the girls between her legs on a changing pad. The baby is in only her diaper, and Aviva is holding up two onesies, asking which she'd rather wear. The way her voice softens when she talks to them is cute, and her face is incandescent in the painfully white light. Even with half the room turned off, the light is draining the color from her golden skin. The green eyes are the first thing I notice. They're all Natalia, shining up at Aviva from Samantha's face.

Greyson is pale in the strange light, except for the parts of him lit by the window. The third baby is in a bassinet made of clear plastic beside the bed, and I don't even think Aviva knows she's awake.

She's still, her wide green eyes fixed on my face through the thick plastic. I don't know enough about babies to know if she can see me, but it feels like she can. She has Aviva's golden skin and a head full of fine dark curls, and those eyes look like they never end and they're looking through me, into my soul. They're all Greyson—a family heirloom that has been passed down for so many generations that no one would ever question where she comes from.

Macie, she says in that whisper-close way that defines the pack bond. Her voice is clear and soft. For a brief second, my own face flashes in my mind. I see myself watching her, head cocked and face blurry through the window. There's recognition in her big brown eyes—like she knows me somehow.

Over there, she seems to say—eyes flicking over my shoulder. *Help her.*

Ali's face flashes in my mind then—perfect and warm. There's something sweet in the way the little girl thinks of her. Some connection thrumming between them that I can't begin to understand. I hold her stare for a long time before I have the strength to walk away. I wave at her as I go, and I carry the weight of her gaze with me as I follow her instructions and continue down the hall looking for Ali.

Ali, who I don't see anywhere.

Ali who I don't hear, or smell, or taste in the air.

Ali who, when I knock on her office door and push it open, is still wearing her bloody scrubs and is sitting on the floor with her knees pulled up to her chest and big, painful tears pouring down her reddened cheeks. The clock on the wall ticks forward and backward one second at a time—frozen in the middle as she clings to her magic.

"Ali," I breathe, barely with it enough to shove the door closed before I'm on the floor beside her, her hands in mine. She's holding on with everything she has, and I can feel it breaking something inside of her. Something is splintering deep inside of her—inside of both of us.

I say her name again, and her breathing hitches. A third time and her blue eyes move to my face, so slowly that it looks like she's struggling to move at all.

"Shawn?" I hate that I can hear the question mark at the end of it. Hate that she sounds surprised to see me there, on the floor in front of her.

I hate the look in those eyes of hers most of all. Broken and desperate and alone. It's our mating bond—the splintering feeling is the bond breaking.

I doubt she even realizes she's pulling strength from it.

"I'm here," I tell her, wishing I had been the whole time. Wishing I knew when this started. "I'm here and you're okay. I promise you're going to be okay."

There's blood in her hair, caked into the strands where she pushed them away from her face with bloody hands. There's more on her cheek, just out of range of the tear tracks. Her scrubs are covered in it, drenched and dried. But what really gets me is the flaking blood on her fingers, thick around her nails, and packed under them.

Some of it is Greyson's, but most of it belongs to Aviva. Aviva, who is a mother now. Aviva, who almost died under Ali's hands as they fought to bring those girls into the world.

Aviva, who lives because Ali refused to accept any other outcome.

Ali's blood is there too, in the mess of it, and I know her bandages are saturated. The bandages she had to talk Rose through putting on her because she couldn't do it herself.

"I'm going to pick you up," I tell her, and then I do it before she can stop me, one hand under her knees and the other around her back. She's heavy, but I don't let myself make a sound as I pull her weight to me and stand. I never make a sound. The hours I've spent in the weight room are the only reason that Aviva and I made it to Medical, but they started out of a desire to carry Ali.

Predictably, she doesn't make a sound as the movement sends pain flaring through her entire body. I can see it in her eyes, though it never makes it to me down the splintering mating bond. I'm as careful as I can be as I straighten up, doing my best to be aware of her injuries.

"You aren't going to like this, but I have to do it," I tell her, carrying her to the bathroom connected to her office. It'll be better than the decontamination shower by a mile, but it isn't going to be pleasant. I sit her down on the shower floor and stand so that my body is shielding hers before I turn the water on.

The initial blast is like ice, and it soaks me through in a second. Below me, Ali is barely touched at all by the spray, the few stray drops that got past me speckling the cuffs of her pants. I grit my teeth and wait.

Once the water is warm, I take a deep breath and kneel in front of her, clearing the way to the water to hit her instead of me. She gasps and smacks at my hands as I catch hers, but calms when I begin scrubbing the dried blood from her fingers with the little brush she keeps on the shelf. She has one in our bathroom too, and I've watched her use it.

Watched her scrub until her skin was red just to make sure that she wasn't carrying any trace of it under her nails.

She's not crying anymore, but she's breathing hard, eyes closed against the onslaught of water and scrubs tinting the water red on its way to the drain. I strain my ears trying to decide if the clock has resumed ticking, but I can't hear anything over the roar of the shower.

"How did you know where to find me?" She asks as I switch hands, pulling the clean one down on a clean patch of her thigh. I shake my head and shove my hair out of my eyes, content to let the water hit me in the back of the head if that's what it takes, and still irritated by my hair being shoved forward.

"I figured you'd be out here, but I had no idea I'd find you like this, or I would have come sooner," I tell her. This hand is easier to scrub clean because there's less blood caked into the lines of her knuckles. I put it down when it's clean and sit. With my back to the opposite wall and our legs slotted together, we take up the entire floor of the shower. She's safely tucked under the wash of hot water, but now that I'm not, I can feel myself trying to shiver.

"You came. That's all that matters," she tells me, and there's something vulnerable in her face that makes me want to shield her with my body and fight the demons she can't run from. Instead, I drop my head back against the wall and let out a soft laugh.

"You are ridiculous," I tell her. The ceiling is boring, so I look back at her again. "I would fight any demon, any creature, and living thing to be by your side through the worst moments of your life. If I could not run to you or fight my way to you, I would crawl on my knees. I would drag myself across the ground with my fingertips until they were caked in mud, cracked, and bleeding. All for you. Only for you."

"But?"

"But nothing. Barr nothing. You are my mate, Aliyah. And for as long as that is true? Until the day you light my funeral pyre? I will continue to fight to be by your side. I don't even need you to let me because I'm going to find a way, whether you like it or not. Her cheeks darken, and the combination of the blush and the redness from crying looks like it hurts. "You don't have to do any of this alone."

"Did you see them? When you came in?"

"I did. And you know why I got to see them?" She shakes her head. "Because you saved them."

"Of course, I saved them. They needed me to save them, so I did. I don't understand your point." Of course not. Of course, she doesn't understand. I lean forward and take her hands, a single stream of water hitting me on the top of the head. Something warm flares down the mating bond.

"Ali, baby, Greyson and Aviva have three beautiful daughters, because of you. As we speak, he is asleep with one of them on his chest because of what you did. Aviva is asking the oldest one which onesie she wants to wear, because of what you did," I tell her, hoping she understands. "We aren't building three funeral pyres because of what you did. Because you didn't hesitate. Because you saved them. Because you are that incredible. Those girls have two parents because of you."

"They almost didn't, Shawn. I almost lost her. I almost lost two of the three of them. Greyson almost had to bury two of his daughters and the woman he loves. I almost had to bury my baby sister," she says, sounding more hysterical by the second.

Make her see. Says the same soft voice. Though the pack bond, she feeds me something warm, and I don't hesitate to push it down the bond toward Ali with everything I have. I hold her as tightly as I can and repeat myself until her breathing slows down.

"You did everything right, my love. You did everything right."

Slowly—one at a time—other voices join me until we're all there. All speaking down the bond to her.

Blue eyes find mine, and I can see the strength building within her. With each new round of reassurance, the connection between us stitches itself back together.

She stitches herself back together.

No one celebrates the full moon. The fire remains dark, and the reservation is silent. No one dares make a sound.

It takes days before I hear anyone speak above a whisper, and while I'm all for recovery, I have a deadline. The twins' birthday is coming and I have work to do.

Before I slip out of the bedroom, I leave a note on the

table beside Ali. I wish my handwriting were better, but it'll have to do.

When she opens it, she'll see the truth:

Here goes nothing.

I took a trip to the humans' territory today. You know I never do that unless I have to. It was the second trip I've made in the last month or so, and both times I've told you I was going for supplies. Both times, the supplies were secondary to the real reason that I went.

Remember the day that Wanderer and her brother were here? We all got a turn with him, but I haven't ever lost anyone. I hadn't, but you had. And you had lost someone that I needed something from. I used my turn with him to talk to your mother, just like you did.

I'd been thinking about it for a long time. About what Wanderer and Warrior could offer us that we didn't already have, and I realized that all I needed was you. And that to have you, really have you, I needed your mother's blessing. It's tradition, and even though you aren't big on all of them, I know that one's important.

Your mother was thrilled to give it. So was Theodora when I snuck away and asked her. I didn't bother to ask your father because I knew his opinion didn't matter. But I even asked Aviva.

That one was a wild conversation, but she ultimately gave it.

Whether it seems like it or not, I genuinely think she wants you to be happy.

So, now I have everything I need, even the ring. That's what I went to town for the last time. Your mother told me that the last time she took you there, you stopped in front of an antiques shop to stare at a case of jewelry. There was a ring there with a diamond shaped like a tear and a curve of pearls beneath it. She said you fell in love with it and begged for the ring and the necklace that matched it. She couldn't buy it for you, but she wanted to.

So she told me about it. Told me that the ring was the only condition. If I could find it for you, I could marry you.

So I found it. I've been looking for it since the day I realized I was going to marry you, and I finally found it.

I've fallen more in love with you every day since the first one, and now you are the first thing I think of every morning and the last thing I think of when I go to bed at night. You're the thing that makes each day interesting. You're what I crave when I'm alone and what I need when I'm struggling. You're my strength and my salvation, my light and my stars. And now, I want you to be my wife. My Mate.

I know that you're afraid. I know that you grew up in the same world that I did. But I am not the kind of man who would ever want to take away your power or your autonomy. I will rule beside you or beneath you, in whatever way you see fit, for as long as you'll have me, and I will never diminish you the way another man might.

They'll call me King, but you'll always be Alpha.

My Alpha. My Mate. My Wife.

Mine.

4
Shawn

Turning twenty-one is a big deal for humans, but it's an even bigger deal for wolves, because it's when we get our voting rights. Everyone becomes an adult at twenty-one, no matter how fast they age or how mature they are. Even the royals don't get to vote until they're twenty-one.

Ali and Aviva were born twenty-one years ago today, and we've been planning the celebration for weeks. Obviously, now that Aviva can drink again, the party can be a little more traditional.

"Come on, why are you so slow?" Rose asks, she's waiting in the grass beyond the bay door, and there are more bags in her arms than I know what to do with.

"Because if I go fast, I wake her up and we ruin the whole thing?" I tell her. I don't flip her off, but I might as well have, because she glares at me and sticks out her tongue as I take an armful of the bags from her.

"Are Marcus and Rachelle already out here?"

"Yeah. Kelly is up too. And Greyson is keeping Aviva in their room so that she won't see anything," she tells me. When we round the house, Marcus and Kelly carry massive logs for the bonfire while Rachelle sets up tables and drags around kegs of wine.

"What are they going to do with the babies during the celebration?" Rachelle asks, looking up from where she's using rocks to level one of the kegs. I didn't even realize we were close enough that she could hear us, but it's a good question.

"I called Gabrielle," Kelly says, grunting as he stands up a log and bends to level it before Marcus brings over the next one.

"Who the hell is Gabrielle?"

"Greyson's sister," he says, ducking out of the way just in time to avoid being hit with the log on its way into place. He punches Marcus in the arm for almost decapitating him, and then gets out of the way. "The girls don't have anyone that can be invited here to watch them, and they're going to want all of us to participate. Greyson suggested Gabby. Aviva has met her, and he said she would be okay with it."

"I literally didn't know Greyson had a sister," Rose says, looking to Rachelle, who also looks surprised.

"Mikael sent her away a few days after she was born. She spent the first four years of her life with her grandmother. She only came home because her grandmother died and she's been at the school in the neutral lands since, pretty much," Kelly explains. He sounds like he's telling the truth, but I'm still a little confused. Most royal babies are announced and spend their lives as public figures. I've never even heard of this girl.

"She has Delilah's maiden name. We met her a few years ago," Marcus says, backing away from the fire frame before he stands up, so he doesn't smack his head.

It's then that I realize my arms are asleep. The bags have choked off blood flow, and my hands are turning blue. I set them down on the ground and help Rose put hers down too.

"What are you talking about?" I ask my brother, racking my brain for any memory of someone that could be Greyson's sister, and coming up empty.

"What did you bring?" Kelly asks Rose. She lights up and kneels to dig into the bags.

"They're lights. You push them into the ground, and they can be walked on and everything. I thought it would be cool, especially with the lights we're putting up," she explains. They've already got the four-by-fours that are going to support the lights and the wire that will hold them laid out in the grass. I can tell that putting them up is going to be a pain in the neck.

"Do you remember the girl with the butterflies down her spine? Hair dyed black? Green eyes?" Marcus says. I can see him trying to pick out details that will help me, but when I realize who he's talking about, all I can think about is what made her important to him.

"You mean the girl you got caught sleeping with during solstice? The one that laughed at you when Rishe slapped you across the face?" I ask him. He immediately looks like he regrets everything about the conversation.

"You slept with Greyson's baby sister?" Rachelle asks, coming to stand with the group.

"*That's* why Rishe slapped you?" Rose says at almost the exact same time.

Kelly and I both just laugh, because there's nothing else we can do. I don't know how Rachelle didn't know, given how close they are, but I also don't know if I want to ask for any more information. If I ask, they might tell me, and that seems like a bad idea.

"Why else would Rishe have slapped me?" Marcus asks Rose, who looks like she might want to smack him. I can think of plenty of reasons why any woman would decide that slapping my brother might be in her best interest.

"I figured she found out you were sleeping with Rachelle, honestly," she says, and apparently Rachelle isn't the only one who missed something, because what?

"We're never going to get this done on time," Kelly says, pinching the bridge of his nose and closing his eyes.

At the edge of the clearing, a young woman appears. Her hair reaches her waist, and she's barefoot. I feel her presence, but she doesn't make a sound.

"Gabrielle?" Marcus says, turning toward her. She steps forward into the clearing and smiles—she has the same green eyes as Greyson, but there's something feral in the way she stands.

She nods.

"I'll be silent," she says softly, striding through the clearing toward the Residence without another word.

Welcome to Noonchester Falls, I tell her—reaching for the fragile thread of connection I feel between us. As she steps through the bay door, she turns her head back toward us and holds out her arm.

Her marking looks just like ours.

Welcome home, you mean? She says softly. The connection between us vibrates and strengthens. If I weren't so focused on the task before me, I'd have so many questions.

"Shawn?"

"I'm here, hold on," I call to her. I'm coming down

the stairs and trying my best not to fall on my face. I can't see anything around the pile of presents I'm carrying, and I don't want to fall down the stairs. That's a bad way to start a birthday.

"What is all that?" She asks. She's holding the note I left in her hand, but it doesn't look like she's opened it yet.

"Your presents, obviously," I say, sitting them on the floor by her desk and coming to kneel in front of her. She's sitting up, her legs thrown over the side of the bed, and her hair sticking out in all sorts of directions.

The clock on her desk says it's 11:45. I have fifteen minutes.

"You didn't have to get me anything."

"I know," I say. I kiss her just because I can, and grab her comb off the dresser without moving away from her. "How about I braid your hair while you read?"

She nods and yawns. I know she knows what time it is, too. The Nathair twins have woken up at midnight to celebrate their birthday since they were born. It was their mother's idea, she told me once. She wanted their birthdays to be special, so she would wake them up and they'd go sit by a bonfire and make marshmallows and dance.

I slowly detangle her curls as she reads through my note, and the small box tucked into my pocket feels like it weighs a thousand pounds. I know how fast she reads, so I expect that she'll finish more quickly than she does. I don't notice that she's rereading each line two or three times until I've almost finished her second braid.

"My Alpha. My Mate. My Wife," she says softly. She doesn't reread those words.

"Mine," I whisper in her ear. The little box is in my hand then, and my arms are around her middle. When I open it, she gasps.

"How did you?"

"Say yes," I tell her, brushing the sensitive spot behind her ear with the tip of my nose.

The clock says 11:58.

"Yes," she breathes. She turns around so fast that she knocks me onto my back. Her mouth is on mine, and her thighs are on either side of my hips, and the ring fits perfectly when I slide it onto her finger.

"Mine," I say, and then, with a smile. "Are you ready to celebrate your birthday now, Snowball?"

April 16th begins with a kiss.

When the music starts, I'm on my knees between her thighs, and she's chasing the taste of herself on my tongue. I don't want to move, but we have to. We have somewhere to be.

I take her hand and lead her out into the warm night air. It's all magic—Blackwood magic—and it's decadent. The night is warm, and the wide-open sky is clear—not a cloud in sight to block the stars. I can tell as soon as Marcus takes control of the music, because he cranks the volume until the bass is rattling the windows.

"What did you do?" She asks me, looking up at me with wide, impossibly blue eyes as we walk.

"Let's call it... keeping with tradition," I tell her. I bend down to press a soft kiss to her mouth, and then we turn the corner, and she gasps.

It's perfect. Every detail is exactly right. Rose has strung lights up around the fire and woven the strands together beautifully, so the whole area is bathed in soft light. She was right about the ground lights, too. the little specs tucked amongst the blades of grass are glittery and shining under the layer of dew they've collected.

"Fire!" Marcus roars, and he throws a match the length of my forearm deep into the heart of the structure he's built. The full moon's unused fire might have been the foundation, but his version is a monstrosity. It's taller, easily wider than he is, and it roars to life with such force that he jumps back. The initial burst of flames flickers and flashes with shades of pink and green as the sachets of herbs begin to catch—Rose had Theodora make them, and they're beautiful. I turn my head and see Aviva and Greyson, frozen like we are, at the opposite corner of the house.

"Oh my G-d," Ali breathes, and I see Aviva say it at the same time. Neither of them looks away from the dancing fire.

"You know you have to dance with me, right?" I ask her. She laughs and shakes her head.

"I'm a horrible dancer; we talked about this."

"No, she's not, she's just scared," Aviva yells. I don't hear the words, but I read them on her mouth. Greyson laughs and Ali blushes.

"Come on, I say, taking her by the hand and kissing her ring as I lead her toward the warmth and light of the fire. Rose finds us just as we reach the edge of the pool of light.

"You look so good," she says. She holds both of Ali's hands when she steps back to look at the outfit I picked out for her, but she doesn't seem to notice the ring. I'm surprised, honestly. Rose notices everything.

"Doesn't she?" I ask. I've done my fair share of staring since I helped her get dressed. Every inch of skin I covered, I kissed, promising to do the same when the celebration is over and it's time to take the jean shorts and silky top back off.

I can still taste her and it's making it hard to focus on

anything but the way the fire's heat is saturating the air with her scent.

"You did this?" Rose asks me, looking Ali over with heavy eyes and then raising an eyebrow as she flicks those same eyes to me. I nod.

"Picked it out myself," I say, letting myself be a little proud.

"And you did this?" She adds, pulling Ali's hand up so that the ring flashes in the firelight—that's more like it. When Ali looks up at me, the look on her face makes me feel like I could jump into the sky and take flight. Her eyes are wide, and her cheeks are red, and she looks so incredibly, effervescently happy that I don't even hesitate. I slip an arm around her waist, kiss her, and smile at Rose.

"Checkmate."

"You bastard," she says, fond as ever. She wraps Ali up in a tight hug and says something I can't hear over the music. Ali laughs and nods, looking down at her ring and then back at Rose again.

If I had to lose to anyone, I'd want it to be her. She's the only person in the world I can imagine trusting with Ali's heart—the only person fundamentally worth something so valuable.

Then Rose's dark eyes are back on me, and she's pulling me in for a tight hug. She smells like cocoa butter and lychee, just potent enough to cover the real scent of her. I like it.

"You better take care of her; do you hear me?" She says. Her mouth is near my ear, but she's still half-shouting over the music. "Know that the minute you stop deserving her, I'll be there to snatch her from you—and I will never give her back."

"Rose!" Ali protests. Rose flips her off, and she giggles, talking to someone I can't see as Rose continues to hold on to me. Her voice is far colder when she speaks again.

"If you hurt a hair on her perfect head, I will come for you in the night. Do you hear me? You be the best mate she could have dreamed of, or I will be," she says. I know she's laughing, and I know it's a joke, but I feel the need to defend myself anyway. To scream from the hilltops that I will be exactly that, every day of my life.

One look at Ali and Kelly tells me I don't need to. She's showing off her ring, and her smile has her eyes shining in the light, and she looks so happy. My heart swells in my chest at the knowledge that I did that. I get to keep doing it for the rest of my life.

My mate.

"Come on, it's time to dance," Rose says as she pulls away from me. She grabs Ali by the hand and drags her away from Kelly with an undignified squeak that I almost miss. I'm left alone and I don't mind it, because the music is loud and the fire smells good, and I can watch all the conversations happening around me without having to participate in them.

I kind of love it.

What I love most is the bitterness on Aviva's face every time someone asks about Ali's ring. The way Greyson keeps looking back at the residence, like he would rather be there with his daughters than celebrating with his girlfriend. The way Ali is trying—and failing—to convince Rose that she doesn't need to dance.

I see Aviva approaching before they do and watch her mouth.

"What the hell are you doing?" she asks Ali. If I couldn't see the light in her eyes, I would think she's being mean.

"She won't dance with me," Rose yells. I can almost hear the words, but not quite. She looks a little sad and is clinging to

Ali's hand like she knows she'll run away the second she's given the chance.

She would. Right back to me.

"You're doing it wrong," Aviva counters, and it only takes a second for her to step between them and press her ass against Ali's hips. "She won't dance unless she knows you're going to dance with her."

And then Aviva begins to move, and Ali laughs. It takes three heartbeats—three painfully, agonizingly slow heartbeats—for Ali to start moving too. And Greyson and I? If it were possible to drop dead from arousal, I'm relatively sure we both would. We share a pained, desperate look.

Because the twins? The twins can dance. And they know it.

There's a familiarity that comes from spending your whole life with someone who's exactly the same as you. I know because Marcus and I see the benefits in combat practice and in other areas of our lives—but this is something else entirely.

That familiarity combines with the music and the wine that Rachelle brings around to have the girls laughing and grinding, and clinging to one another.

If I didn't know they were sisters, I would think they were together, it's that seamless.

When Ali moves, Aviva answers, and when the music changes, it only takes a step for them to fall into a new rhythm. They go from dirty dancing to ballroom dancing and back again. Eventually, they settle on something that's a little bit of both, colored with laughter and light, and skin shining with sweat.

I lock eyes with Rose, and her cheeks are red. She fans herself playfully and winks at me.

I can't even be mad at her for looking, because everyone

is. It takes everything in me not to fall to my knees before her and howl.

Every pair of eyes keeps coming back to them, and I can't help but feel like that's the way it was always meant to be. The Nathair girls—the Trevonaire girls—are the center of the universe while everyone else looks on in amazement.

BONUS CHAPTER

The reservation at Noonchester Falls is massive.

The sprawling spread of land is contained within the boundaries of the primary and secondary reservations, like a bullseye. The outer ring of the reservation consists of ancient Rowan trees, wild elderberry plants, old growth ginger, and a myriad of other untamed greenery. But the inner reservation? The primary? That land is nearly clear, rolling gently under a medical building, a collection of residential buildings, a school, a barn, a greenhouse, and a garden spread larger than three human football fields. Tucked out of sight at the highest point within the wards in the nearby mountains is the reservation's namesake–Noonchester Falls.

Like Sutherland Falls, found in the human world's "New Zealand," Noonchester Falls consists of a series of individual falls, cascading over obsidian and shale. Half the width and twice the height of their closest visual twin, the falls originate and terminate with silken black water, too deep in both the river above and the pool below to view the bottom.

The pack residence looks like a human boarding school and has been constructed to provide a permanent home for both the thirty young wolves considered the founding members of the yet to be named pack—and the children they are all expected to have in the coming years—the home boasts a heavy front door made of native Rowan wood, polished and glossy around the stained glass of the door. The glass itself is both handmade and rumored to be bulletproof. The common area is consumed by a large kitchen, fireplace, seating area, and dining room, though the style combines the vaulted ceilings of the Marquis Manor and the earthy warmth of Elder House in the Neutralands. The styles have been managed well and complement the more rustic exterior and the generally wild territory beyond, by all available accounts.

Designer Lillian Teskallia herself has been quoted as saying that the moon is visible through each skylight when full and has hinted at other similarly thoughtful design choices, though much of the reservation continues to remain a mystery to those outside the Elder Council and those overseeing its development. We know from sketches released last May that the living quarters for founding members are contained along the rear of the primary residence, stacked three stories high and twelve across like books on a shelf. Each room awaits not only the selection of a roster–set to be released next month–but also the selection of an Alpha, who will mark each door with a name in a bid to welcome new pack members to their new home.

It is that decision that has held the Council of Elders in its grasp for longer than any other. Because the worst thing you can do is choose wrong, where choosing an Alpha is concerned.

And so, they continue their debates, asking for more and more evidence from each of the candidates in hopes that they'll find their answers somewhere in our words. Some complain. Some outright refuse to continue submitting their materials. But I'll give them whatever they ask for if it means making sure they make the right decision for all the young people they're sending to the new reservation.

It's quite literally the least I can do.

The woman reading falls silent, the composition book held firmly in both hands as she surveys the room before her, daring them to speak before she has said her piece. A woman in her seventeenth decade of life, Cyan Vianbry holds her shoulders square and demands respect from those before her, even when sitting. She closes the worn composition book, places it on the table before her, and folds her long fingers over the speckled surface in silence. When she inhales, she raises her eyes to look around the room at the other Elders, sitting quietly in the rotunda of their chambers.

"This choice cannot continue to debilitate us," she says, leaning forward onto her elbows. "Never have we had anyone show dedication like this, seen hope like this. The pack that will occupy Noonchester Falls will face nothing but challenge in its formative years, and our children–those that we have chosen to carry this burden–deserve a leader who will be the brightest star in their endless constellation. You have asked me to break tradition by casting a vote between the Nathair sisters, and I have done so."

Elder Vianbry stands, taking the worn book with her as she retrieves her cane from the back of her chair. Across the room, a dark-haired woman stands too, hands flat on the table before her.

"You must tell us, Cyan," she says, and a hush falls over the room, the other elders in various positions between sitting and standing, frozen in time as they wait for the Chief Elder to speak. Waiting for her to dole out the punishment they expect is coming. Elder Vianbry squares her shoulders even as she supports her weight on the table before her, and the woman who spoke shrinks in on herself as the realization of her disrespect sinks in. She does not back down.

"If I am to change these girls' lives, Rhiannon, I should like to tell them first," Cyan says, her voice cold and level. Cyan Vianbry is neither accustomed to nor inviting of challenge. When she scolds the woman—Rhiannon Markell—the woman sinks back down into her chair as though she might disappear.

The room is still cloaked in a veil of awkward silence, a few seconds later, when a cough sounds from the door of the chamber, and all heads turn sharply in the direction of the sound. In a room full of wolves—even elder ones—it's rare that anyone has the capacity to sneak up.

"My deepest apologies, Elder Vianbry, but I have something I think I should share with you. I think it might prevent you from having to make this decision alone," a voice says. The woman moves to stand in the light of the room, head bowed just slightly in submission.

"Welcome, Viviana. Please, come in," Cyan turns to face the other Elders, gesturing politely to their guest. "Viviana Errapel, Chief Healer of Archimedes Landing."

A protest forms and falls from the lips of several Elders in the room, but fades when Cyan sits back down and yields the floor, silently demanding their submission.

The woman takes the stairs to the small stage one at a time, her tenth decade of life wearing on her knees and hips, and she turns to face them with a serene look.

"I know most of you," she says, "but I'll introduce myself anyway. I'm Viviana Errapel, and I've been a Healer for almost ninety years. I have seen a lot of things in that time."

The woman pauses and takes a deep breath before she begins to speak again.

"The bad things–the really bad ones–they stay with you. They haunt your dreams, they sneak up on you in the dark, and they never get any easier to carry," she says, "but the good things–the really good ones–they stick with you too. More than every baby you deliver and every child you make smile, there are moments that define you, refuel the fire that made you want to do this work in the first place, and give you a little hope that the world is more than injuries, death, and dying. For me, there is even a single moment that defines my entire career."

"What's your point?" a voice asks. No one reacts. They remain silent, facing the woman as she runs her hand over the length of her long braid. She pulls a silver strand free of the end and watches the speaker with intention as she drops it to the concrete floor. There is nothing but defiance in her tired eyes.

"My point," she says, with a harsh look across the room, "is simple. A few years ago, just as I began planning for a retirement that would never come, there was a hunting party that went out into the mountains to search for a small family of missing nomads. A mother, father, and two little girls had been separated from their troop while traveling through a snowstorm, and even though they had spent nearly a month searching, they hadn't been able to find them.

They came to us because we were the closest, and they begged for help. The girls, they said, were only five years old, and the mother was recovering from a miscarriage when the storm separated them." She stopped, like what she was about to say caused her pain.

"The hunting party found one of the girls chained to a table in a cabin in the mountains. Her parents were in the other room, and they had all been doused with kerosene before their captors left them. The parents burned alive, and the little girl might have too if the hunting party had arrived a moment later."

"Leighann Mizrahi," Cyan says softly, rifling through the files before her to hold up a picture of the young girl. The Healer nodded and smiled fondly at the lavender-eyed little girl on the information card.

"You all know this part of the story. About how Greyson Marquis ran into the flames to save the girl and got them both out before the fire could do any more damage. You also probably know that he was gravely injured, and that the girl was burned over a significant portion of her body, badly enough that even her healing couldn't touch most of it.

What you probably don't know–what I know you don't know–is that we had a guest in Medical that day at Archimedes. Aliyah Nathair was months from her graduation, still a junior Healer, but she was there working with us, refilling our Apothecary, and practicing a new method of suturing. She was the first one they met when they came into Medical, Greyson with a dislocated shoulder on top of his severely burned hands and arms, and Leighann with... well, a lot going on. She was unconscious, barely breathing, burning up, and hypoxic. Greyson was holding the little girl to his chest like she was something precious, and he begged us to help. He begged us to save her.

And Zachariah Blackwood—my nephew—told him no."

A small gasp spread through the room, and Viviana shifted to sit on the edge of the stool in the center of the small stage.

"Zachariah took one look at that girl and came to the same conclusion I might have, if it had been me.

She was dying, already so close to it that he insisted we should try to make her comfortable and wait it out.

But Aliyah? Aliyah saw her. Saw past the damage and saw the little girl clinging to the last threads of life she could grasp. Saw her lavender eyes and her small hands and the dress that was fused to her skin in so many places, and... And she fought back. She climbed off the floor, shoved Zachariah out of her way, and took the girl from Greyson, who she firmly told to sit down and not move until she could check him out.

If any of you have met Greyson Blackwood, you know that on its own is something of a feat.

Zachariah tried to pull her back repeatedly. He fought with her for a full minute before she called out for security and asked to have him restrained. She had no real authority to do it, and they had no real reason to listen to her, but they did. They were coming toward him when he raised a hand to strike her.

The blow, in my medical opinion, would have caused a concussion and rendered Aliyah unconscious. It would have been assault, and assault on a Royal at that, but it never came, because she spun around, knocked the man flat out, and turned back to her patient before he had fallen into security's arms.

She worked on Leighann Mizrahi for sixteen hours that day. She stopped for two minutes to help me push Greyson's shoulder back into place, but she didn't stop working for anything else, no matter how weak the girl's pulse remained."

The woman stopped to laugh softly. "She was helping me with Greyson's shoulder when Zachariah regained consciousness. He started yelling at her immediately, and she was so annoyed that she forgot to warn the poor young man before addressing his shoulder luxation. Security sedated him that time, and he didn't come back around until Leighann was stable, clean, and resting.

She walked over to him just after he became lucid, squatted down in front of him, and told him that just because he wasn't worth saving, it didn't mean he could condemn another person to die."

"If you are to vote for which one of these girls will lead, I think you should vote knowing that I didn't retire that year and haven't retired yet. I have welcomed Aliyah Nathair into my reservation regularly, and I would put my own life in her hands again, and again. She's the reason that Zachariah Blackwood no longer practices medicine, and Archimedes Landing is better for that."

GLOSSARY

Aiyanik – The oldest and most traditional werewolf pack in the Wolflands, known for its strict succession laws and political influence. Their magic is a closely guarded secret.

Alpha – The leader of a pack, chosen either by succession or selection. Responsible for maintaining order, representing the pack politically, and forging magical and territorial bonds.

Alpha Apparent – A formal title for an Alpha who has been selected but has not yet claimed territory or completed their bonding with a Keeper.

Apothecary – A medical and magical workspace where healing tonics, remedies, and wards are prepared. Run like stores for reservation inhabitants.

Archimedes Landing – The ancestral lands of the Blackwood pack. The second largest reservation by area, primarily composed of flat, open land.

Blackwood – A werewolf pack in the Wolflands, known for their powerful weather-based magic.

Bondfire (Bonfire) – A traditional social gathering, often celebrating birthdays, betrothals, or rites of passage. Packs use bonfires to reinforce bonds, offer stories, or cast public spells.

Elder Council – The ruling political body overseeing major decisions for the Wolflands. Responsible for selecting Alphas, Keepers, and laws.

Delta – A rank in pack hierarchy, typically responsible for protection, enforcement, and acting as elite guards. They are often assigned to high-value individuals, such as heirs.

Elderlands – The territory where the Elder Council is based and where major political ceremonies take place. It is considered neutral and sacred ground. Governed by the Chief Elder.

Elizabethian Mountains – The ancestral lands of the Kivleneiks pack and the smallest of the reservations in the Wolflands. Completely isolated by the Alpha and segregated from the other packs by Neutral Lands.

Greenbriar Landing – The ancestral home of the Ravenswell pack. The second smallest reservation by size, and largely composed of plains and rolling hills.

Heir – In traditional pack structures, the firstborn is the Heir—designated future Alpha.

Healer – A werewolf trained in magical and medicinal arts. The role holds status and power within a pack dynamic.

Keeper – A supernatural role selected by the land itself to balance an Alpha. The Keeper's life is often bound to the magic of a pack's territory through a traumatic, ritualized process. Their bond protects the territory and amplifies the Alpha's connection to it.

Kivleneiks – A werewolf pack in the Wolflands known for their political leanings and largely isolated from all others. Largely considered an unknown by the rest of the Wolflands.

Little People – Magical entities found in pack territories, often tied to ancestral lands. Rarely seen but often glimpsed.

Mate – Bonded partner, chosen through instinct or declared through ceremony. Mate bonds can be romantic, political, or spiritual, depending on pack custom.

Neutral Lands – Territories not claimed by any one pack – used for trade, travel, or rituals requiring neutrality.

Noonchester Falls – The newest reservation in the Wolflands – the home of the Trevonaire pack.

Playa Del Rose – The ancestral land of the Rosendes pack, primarily composed of tropical, ocean-front land and rain forest. Separated from other reservations by a buffer of neutral land.

Ravenswell – A werewolf pack in the Wolflands known for their eidetic memories and archives collection.

Reaping – A magical ritual in which the land tests Keeper candidates. Those who are rejected die; the one who is chosen returns to life transformed and magically bound to the land.

Reservation – A designated, warded territory where a pack lives. Each reservation is protected by magical borders and governed by its own internal rules.

Rosendes – A werewolf pack in the Wolflands, gifted with linguistic mastery and known for their translation skills. Politically close to the Ravenswell pack.

Selection – The formal process by which the Elder Council interviews and evaluates Alpha candidates.

Spare – The second child in a traditional pack structure, held in reserve in the case of the Heir's death or failure.

Souls – Spirits that live on ancestral lands and are tied to the

Earth magic within them. Docile, peaceful remnants of those who have died.

Tamarak Valley – The ancestral land of the Aiyanik people and the largest reservation in the Wolflands. Situated in a valley between large mountains and bisected by a large river.

Wards – Magical barriers used to protect pack lands and individuals. Built by Warlocks and other magic wielders, they are linked to the life of a Keeper and respond to the instructions of an Alpha. warlocks.

Wolflands – The broader world inhabited by werewolves, encompassing all the known pack territories and neutral zones.

Wraiths – Spiritual entities that appear during major magical events or death rituals. Their presence often signals change, death, or rebirth.

ABOUT THE AUTHOR

A twenty-something inhabitant of the Pacific Northwest, Rowan believes in the power of stories and the significance of the role they play in people's lives. Their time is spent between writing and teaching and they share their home with their spouse, two dogs, and two crested geckos.

Rowan is a lifelong scholar and spends their free time working on projects related to representation, accessibility, and equality. As a disabled person and a member of the LGBTQ + community, representation, equality, and accessibility are things that they look to foster in all aspects of their life. They also enjoy spending time exploring their beautiful surroundings with their spouse and fur babies.

THANKS

I want to start this by thanking my spouse, who absolutely does not understand what it's like to be a writer and does their best to be supportive anyway. I know that the world appears to you in notes on a staff and theory so above my head that I will never understand. Much the same, it appears to me in words on a page, and I don't expect you to try and keep up with all the pages I put out into the world. I can't stop writing any more than you can stop obsessing over what notes you hear in the dinging of the car door.

This is a thank you for all the time that you have spent putting up with the manic nights and endless hours in front of the computer. Thank you for putting up with the unreasonable number of Uncrustables wrappers that this book brought into the world and all the hours you have spent reading. And thank you, most of all, for trying.

People like me aren't built for the faint of heart. We aren't always easy, and it would have been so easy for you to give up on trying to understand. I keep waiting for it, and somehow, you continue to amaze me.

The next round of thanks goes to people that I haven't seen in years, but think about often. Jen, Kristin, Kelly, Stacie, I'm talking to you. If any of you are reading this, I hope you know that it wouldn't exist without you. Each of you had a hand in shaping this or in shaping me, and without the kindness and inspiration you brought into my life, this book wouldn't be the only thing that didn't exist. None of you will ever know how important you are to me or how much of a difference you made by being exactly who you are and encouraging me to do the same.

I love each of you.

More than that, though, I respect and admire each of you.

Catch me telling stories and speaking your praise into the world for another lifetime. It will never be enough. I'm not in your debt, but I am at your service, now and always.

Next, in rapid succession, I want to thank the following people for their contributions to this work, large and small:

My father, who gave me my bipolar disorder and then never let me see it as anything other than the gift I still believe it is. He taught me what it was, helped me understand it, and never let me forget that it could be as much a blessing as it is a curse. I wouldn't be here without it or him. He did a lot of stupid things in his life, but I have to believe that he made up for it by teaching me that it was okay to love my fucked-up brain as much as he did.

The Amandas, who have a place in my creative process,

even while they're halfway across the world. Who remind me to be kind to myself and to keep writing when it's hard, because the only way that I can fix it is if it exists first. Who know that, in the end, I'll figure it out. Even when I don't.

My best friend, who should be here with me for this and can't be.

My mother and sister, who aren't in my life right now but should be. For all the variations on my life that I have imagined, this one never even crossed my mind. I shouldn't be celebrating this accomplishment without them, but I am, because the hatred and division that has taken over the world has made keeping them close impossible. Maybe the next time I write an acknowledgements section; they'll be in it for a different reason. But right now, they are here for the nights of tears and the months of deterioration that went into the decision to walk away. There is no place in my world for the ideologies that have taken over their lives, and I can't bring myself to compromise my standards in the name of keeping them close. If either of you are reading this, I hope you know that it never had anything to do with love.

I love you both with everything I am. But you can't love someone like me and believe the things that you do. The two are now and will always be mutually exclusive.

And finally, thanks to two people I will never meet, but will live the rest of my life grateful for. First, Dr. Jay Dolmage, who currently chairs the English Department at Waterloo. Thank you for your research, the work you have done and will still do in the field of disability studies, and the ways you have challenged my normative thinking.

Last, but never least, a triumphant scream and a teary-eyed thank you for Dr. Kay Redfield Jamison. Thank you for your words and your context. Thank you for the comfort that you have given me and the understanding that your story has brought to my life.

In An Unquiet Mind, you discuss the reality of a life with bipolar disorder and how it comes with storms, dry seasons, and killing seasons. You go on to say that it is these seasons, these moments of "restlessness, of bleakness, of strong persuasions and maddened enthusiasms" that bring color. And for the first time in my life, seeing what yours looks like, I found something I never had. Seeing what you have accomplished and who you have become gave me back hope. I will never be able to thank you for that.

I hope, from the bottom of my heart and the depths of my soul, that each of you finds the happiness and inspiration that you deserve. May your coffee (or tea) always be hot, your shoes always be comfortable, and your endeavors always be successful. I consider you each a blessing in my life, and one day, I hope that I can be to someone else as you have been to me.

If I can, then not only will I have succeeded in my own goals, but I will have been a part of ensuring your legacy lives on. It should.

Made in United States
Troutdale, OR
06/16/2025